GIRL LOST

THE KING LEGACY #1

GIRL LOST

KATE ANGELO

Revell

a division of Baker Publishing Group
Grand Rapids, Michigan

© 2025 by Kate Angelo

Published by Revell
a division of Baker Publishing Group
Grand Rapids, Michigan
RevellBooks.com

Printed in the United States of America

All rights reserved. No part of this publication may be reproduced, stored in a retrieval system, or transmitted in any form or by any means—for example, electronic, photocopy, recording—without the prior written permission of the publisher. The only exception is brief quotations in printed reviews.

Library of Congress Cataloging-in-Publication Data
Names: Angelo, Kate (Romance fiction writer) author
Title: Girl lost / Kate Angelo.
Description: Grand Rapids, Michigan : Revell, a division of Baker Publishing Group, 2025. | Series: The King legacy ; 1
Identifiers: LCCN 2025001466 | ISBN 9780800746636 paperback | ISBN 9780800747367 | ISBN 9781493451371 ebook
Subjects: LCGFT: Thrillers (Fiction) | Romance fiction | Christian fiction | Novels
Classification: LCC PS3601.N554426 G57 2025 | DDC 813/.6—dc23/
eng/20250314
LC record available at https://lccn.loc.gov/2025001466

This book is a work of fiction. Names, characters, places, and incidents are the product of the author's imagination or are used fictitiously. Any resemblance to actual events, locales, or persons, living or dead, is coincidental.

Baker Publishing Group publications use paper produced from sustainable forestry practices and postconsumer waste whenever possible.

25 26 27 28 29 30 31   7 6 5 4 3 2 1

For God,
who fills me daily with
unimaginable peace and joy.

For Jerry,
my prayer warrior, trusted adviser,
biggest supporter, and best friend.

And for the lost sheep.
I rejoice that you will be found
and carried back into the fold,
just as I have.

Then Jesus told them this parable: "Suppose one of you has a hundred sheep and loses one of them. Doesn't he leave the ninety-nine in the open country and go after the lost sheep until he finds it? And when he finds it, he joyfully puts it on his shoulders and goes home. Then he calls his friends and neighbors together and says, 'Rejoice with me; I have found my lost sheep.' I tell you that in the same way there will be more rejoicing in heaven over one sinner who repents than over ninety-nine righteous persons who do not need to repent."

Luke 15:3–7

1

LUNA ROSATI COULD DISAPPEAR into any crowd, any city, any life. Except this one. This life. It had a way of pulling her back. Like a riptide dragging her under.

10:42 a.m. and the man who held the key to the life she'd left behind was twelve minutes late. She'd convinced herself she was ready for this moment. Now that it hovered before her, Luna wasn't so sure. Not about finding her daughter—that was nonnegotiable—but about facing everything she'd left behind.

She stared out the diner's picture window, her gaze fixed on the empty street, bracing for the moment her carefully constructed life would change.

The morning sun glinted off a passing car, and an elderly couple strolled by. Both moved without any hustle or bustle. Millie Beach was mostly locals. No surprise there. It wasn't exactly a popular vacation destination. The small beach town had all the crime of Miami and none of the beauty.

Eighteen years ago, she'd walked away from this place and vowed never to return. But vows made in storms weren't always kept in the calm. Which was why she was sitting in the back corner of the same rundown diner from her childhood, watching the street through the glassy expanse up front.

The dumpy place hadn't changed a bit. Same faded tan linoleum. Same yellowed Formica tabletops. Same cracked red vinyl chairs. Everywhere she looked, same, same, same. Except the deepened lines etched into the faces of the waitstaff.

Age and a two-pack-a-day habit had not been kind to Marge. The owner frowned from her perch in the kitchen. She'd never liked newcomers. Preferred to keep it to the regulars.

A younger version of Marge appeared at Luna's table. "What'll you have?" The square name tag on her grease-stained shirt said her name was Angie.

Wow, this was Marge's daughter? The woman had aged double time. Strands of gray laced her dark curls. Dark-brown sunspots speckled her weathered face. Indelible kisses from the unrelenting sun reflecting off the ocean in a town where sunblock was for tourists.

Luna picked up her plastic-covered menu, feigned a glance, and dropped it. "Lemonade for now. I'm waiting for a friend."

Angie narrowed her eyes. "You waitin' on Stryker?"

"You know him?"

"'Bout the only one who comes in this time a day. Tourists don't come in for a while yet, and you don't look like a tourist. I get a feelin' I seen you somewhere before."

Luna caught the lie before it slipped out. Years of deception and faking her identity were more natural than truth. But she didn't need a cover here. Not in the town where she grew up. Here she could be herself. Here she could be Luna Rosati. "Yeah, I'm waiting for—"

The bell over the entrance tinkled when a man pushed the glass door open.

Luna looked up, and something inside her fractured. She could hear it. The sound like stepping on a glass pane. A resounding crack that broke open everything she'd worked so hard to keep bottled up all these years.

"Spoke too soon about the tourists." Angie knocked her swollen knuckles on the table. "Be right back with that lemonade."

Angie's words drifted over her unabsorbed. She couldn't take her eyes off the guy she used to know, now standing there all grown up. Hair shaved into a classic crew cut. A far cry from the boy with the unruly mop of sandy blond hair she'd remembered. The khaki-colored linen suit hung on his broad shoulders with a confidence that shouted law enforcement.

Funny, the last time she'd seen him in a suit was at his father's murder trial.

Corbin King removed his sunglasses and scanned the room with intense brown eyes. His Adam's apple rolled when his eyes met hers.

She didn't dare move.

With nonchalance, he strolled over and snagged the vacant seat opposite her. His elbows found a comfortable spot on the table, fingers intertwining while still cradling his sunglasses.

Her tongue skimmed her dry lips, primed to seize the conversation first if anything came to mind. There was nothing to say. But also, everything.

His dark eyes penetrated her. "What are you doing here?"

A dozen cutting remarks tumbled through her mind ranging from "How dare you?" to "Please go away so I never have to see you again." The reflexive restraint honed during her tenure at the CIA barred any of those from slipping past her lips.

Instead, she said, "I'm meeting Stryker."

Corbin looked over his shoulder at the empty restaurant. "Here?"

She didn't respond.

Angie set a glass of lemonade on the table with a clink and smiled at Corbin. "Get you anything, doll?"

She hadn't called Luna a doll.

Corbin dropped his sunglasses on the table and leaned back to look at Angie. "Coffee. And a few moments of your time, if you don't mind." He reached into his breast pocket and withdrew a black wallet. A deft flip revealed his credentials. Florida Department of Law Enforcement. "I have a few questions for you."

Impressive. Corbin had done well to work his way into Florida's version of the FBI.

Angie flicked her eyes between Luna and Corbin, and she coughed a phlegmy laugh. "Am I in trouble, Officer?"

"No, ma'am. Just have a few questions about a missing person. Can we chat in private when I'm done with my friend here?"

"Sure. I guess I ain't goin' nowhere." She sauntered back to the kitchen, shoulders squared and a touch of extra height in her stance.

"What are you doing here, Luna?" The honeyed tone he'd used on the waitress morphed to granite.

"Since when does the FDLE investigate missing persons?"

"Since when do you talk to Stryker? Or any of us, for that matter?"

"Why do you keep answering questions with another question?" Although she knew good and well she'd started it.

The squiggle of a blue vein bulged at Corbin's temple, and she kind of enjoyed it. "Since we gave our baby up for adoption. Since you cut me out of your life." His finger stabbed the table to punctuate each sentence. "Since you left town without a word and never looked back."

Another crack formed. His words knifed her heart. Images of a teen beggar girl on the streets of Pakistan played through her mind. The one with dark hair and eyes that mirrored her own. The girl's striking resemblance to herself had brought Luna back to the time when she held a tiny life in her arms. The baby girl she'd given up—not because she wanted to, but because she refused to let her child suffer the life she'd had.

The daughter she'd brought into being was somewhere out there in the world, and she needed Stryker to tell her where.

The pang cut deep, but Luna gathered her composure and locked her emotional armor down tight. She wasn't the only one who'd walked away. "You broke up with me, Corbin. You told me you didn't want to be a father. You made that choice. I just made sure our daughter had a future."

The skin around his collar flushed crimson. She could see his neck straining. "I can't believe you—"

A sharp glint of light flashed through the storefront windows. Whatever Corbin was saying faded into nothingness. She watched Stryker emerge from his rusty old Jeep parked across the street. His hair, a blend of salt and pepper, hung in a knot at the nape of his neck. Aside from the silver strands, he looked like the same athletic man she'd known when she was a teenager.

Years melted away. She saw the man who'd seen the good in her, even when she was a mess of anger and bad choices. The man who'd taken a lost and confused girl and forged her into something stronger, something more. He'd pulled her back from the edge, shown her a different path. And somehow, against all odds, the rebellious girl who'd once cursed every cop in sight had become a government agent.

He'd challenged her, pushed her, never let her give up on herself. And she hadn't. Would he still recognize that girl in the woman she'd become?

A black SUV slammed to a halt outside. Doors flew open. Three dark figures jumped out, faces swallowed by masks, bodies muted by black tactical gear.

Guns. They had guns.

Luna was on her feet before she knew what was happening. Her brain put it together on the fly. *Outside. Help Stryker.*

Corbin's chair scraped back. Clattered over. He was on her heels.

Stryker wouldn't go down without a fight. With his reflexes, he could disarm a shooter and break a few bones faster than she could blink. His resistance would buy them the priceless seconds they needed to get outside.

One man pointed a Taser at Stryker and squeezed the trigger. Two barbed probes shot through the air and embedded into the back of Stryker's neck, sending fifty thousand volts of electricity screaming through his body. The other two men caught him under the arms before he hit the sidewalk and hauled his limp body into the back seat.

Luna and Corbin burst outside. Shouts. A woman screamed. But Luna's eyes were laser focused on the dark vehicle. The doors slammed shut.

Corbin had his gun out. "Police! Stop or I'll shoot!"

The SUV's engine roared. The vehicle lurched forward, tires shrieking, grabbing traction. It fishtailed, sideswiping two parked cars. Then it swerved back on course, speeding down the street. It blew through a stop sign and disappeared around the corner.

Bits of red and yellow confetti littered the street and sidewalk. Luna crouched and used her fingernail to scrape up a few of the tiny round dots.

Corbin sprinted half a block chasing after the vehicle before he stopped. Feet set shoulder width apart. Knees flexed. Arms extended and ready to fire.

She marched over and slapped her palm on the muzzle of his gun to shove the barrel down. "Put that away. You can't shoot into a busy street at a fleeing vehicle."

He was breathing hard. "No plates. They wore masks. Should be able to get surveillance footage and interview witnesses." Like her, Corbin was already thinking of the next steps.

She had her phone out, thumb hovering over the screen. The secret code used to send secure cables to the Agency wouldn't work on this plain smartphone. The only person whose number was stored in this one had just been kidnapped.

Corbin muttered something Luna couldn't hear. He had a hand on his waist. The tail of his blazer was pushed back, showing the gun in its holster on his hip. He rattled his name, badge number, and their location into his phone. "I'm reporting a confirmed kidnapping in progress. Requesting immediate backup and notify detectives."

With Stryker gone, she had no reason to stay. Time to start searching for him. She did an about-face and went back inside.

Angie was on the phone in hysterics. It'd be a wonder if the dispatcher could make sense of the gibberish behind her sobs. Luna marched to the table and picked up her purse. Paused long enough to drain her lemonade and toss a twenty on the table before heading back outside.

Corbin fell into step beside her, phone still pressed to his ear. "Where are you going?"

She kept walking.

"Hey, you can't leave a crime scene." He grabbed her shoulder and spun her around.

She caught his hand in a wrist lock and rotated his forearm until his knees buckled. "You've gotten slow in your old age." She flashed a thin smile and shoved him, releasing her hold.

Corbin stumbled a few steps. The look on his face was almost worth the agony of seeing him again. She turned and headed for her car.

The last person she'd ever wanted to see was Corbin King. Not here. Not now. Not ever.

"Luna! You can't just walk away. Luna!"

Stryker was not only her mentor but a father figure. She wouldn't stand by and let someone hurt him. Besides, he was the one who'd arranged the adoption. Handled everything himself, outside the system when she was too young and emotionally wrecked to question the details. Back then, she hadn't wanted to know. Convinced it was better that way. But that had changed.

Now, without Stryker, she had no way to find the only blood relative she had left. And after everything she'd lost in Pakistan, she could not afford to lose anything else.

The weight of it all didn't matter.

She would save Stryker.

She would find her daughter.

And she would do it without Corbin King.

2

THAT STUBBORN, stubborn woman. Obstinate as ever after all these years.

A light breeze caught Luna's dark hair, and the long strands fanned out like an ebony banner as she marched away. The tendons in Corbin's neck vibrated. Why couldn't she stay and talk to him for once?

He shook his head. That woman had serious walls up.

No, not just walls—she was fortified better than Fort Knox. He shouldn't be surprised. Rather than face pain and work through the messy stuff, Luna always cut and ran. They'd done everything wrong, and they'd paid for it.

Apparently, he was still paying for it.

Back then, he'd thought their bond was elastic enough to always bring her back. But now it was painfully clear she would always run.

Even from him.

The wail of distant sirens snapped him back to the present. Backup was approaching fast, and if he wanted to maintain his involvement in the case, he had to insert himself as the first responder.

Using his phone, he photographed the scene in wide shots first to document the layout. The street. The diner. The few cars lining the street. Next, details. Stryker's Jeep. The skid marks where the SUV had peeled away. The gash in the side of the cars.

His eyes fell on the sidewalk, where paper dots lay scattered. Those telltale markers from a Taser could be critical evidence linking the kidnapping to the suspects. He crouched and snapped photos, ensuring he captured the placement of each.

With no witnesses and the evidence secured as best as he could manage alone, he turned and stepped inside the diner. The air around him seemed to shift, just for a heartbeat. This was Stryker's place, but Corbin avoided coming here. Every corner, every worn booth, reminded him of Luna—of how empty it felt when she'd left.

He pushed past the feeling and crossed the worn linoleum in a few long strides and found Marge cradling a bawling Angie in her arms.

"They shot Stryker! Right in the street! They just . . . shot him!" The waitress had her head buried in Marge's shoulder, muffling her words.

Crying women. He'd never been great with them. Whatever came out of his mouth always made things worse. "Look, they didn't shoot him. Not with a gun, okay?" He tried to soften his tone. "Taser. It was a Taser. He'll be fine."

At least he should be until the kidnappers got Stryker to wherever they were taking him. Then . . . well, he didn't want to chase that rabbit trail. One problem at a time.

Angie lifted her head and shuddered a breath. Dark trails of mascara cut through the tears on her face. "What'd they want with him?"

"I don't know." But he'd find out. "Listen, I need to ask you a few quick questions. Anything you can remember could be vital."

Angie's hand trembled as she wiped her nose with a palm. "It . . . it all happened so . . . so fast. I . . . I don't know if I seen anything good or not."

"That's normal to feel that way. You might remember more once the adrenaline wears off."

She sniffed. "Yeah, maybe."

Marge held her daughter with one arm. Decades of cigarette smoking showed in her sagging skin and nicotine-stained teeth.

The boys in the neighborhood used to steal smokes from her unattended pack on the counter. He'd tried one once. A feeble attempt to impress Luna. To prove he was one of the cool guys. The smoke had caught in his lungs and sent him into a coughing fit. When the tears cleared from his eyes, he'd found Stryker hovering over him, arms folded, shaking his head. That little stunt had earned him a ten-mile beach run with Stryker by his side, lecturing him all the way.

He looked again at the women sitting at a table, hands clasped together, clinging to each other for support. The incident had hit them hard. Not because they'd witnessed the crime. They'd seen their fair share of violence living in Millie Beach. But they knew Stryker. Everyone did. These women loved him because he made the world a better place. A safer place. And now, maybe the world wasn't so safe after all.

"Either of you notice any unusual people hanging around or strange vehicles parked nearby?"

"I was back in the kitchen." Marge sounded like she gargled with gravel every morning. "Didn't see nothing but the backs of yer heads runnin' out the door. Thought you'd outgrown them dine and dash days, though."

"Wait." Angie straightened. Her puffy eyes widened, and she pulsed a finger in his direction. "I remember you. Yeah. You and . . . and that girl who was in here. Luna and Corbin. You're them Warrior kids, right?"

Small towns. You either loved them or hated them, and right now he was leaning heavily toward the latter. In this town, everyone knew everyone else's business. Or thought they did. It came in handy during investigations. Not so much when your own life was on display for the busybody gossips.

He didn't want to talk about Luna. Wasn't sure he *could* talk about her without betraying the storm of emotions that raged inside. Every question they might ask would be one he'd tortured himself with over the years.

Like why the very thought of her name still sent a jolt through his system.

Forget it. Get the conversation back on track.

"That's right. I'm Special Agent Corbin King. Police are on the way to take your official statements about the kidnapping. In the meantime, do you have security cameras? Any surveillance I can take a look at?"

"That one there." Marge nodded toward a dome camera perched above the register. "Plus, we got one out back to keep an eye on deliveries."

"Nothing out front?"

"Nope." Marge pulled a napkin out of the dispenser and dabbed at a dark streak on Angie's cheek. "We ain't that tech savvy."

Of course not. That would be too easy. They'd have to check the other businesses lining the street. Find witnesses. "The register camera. Does it cover the dining area?"

"Lil bit." Marge shrugged. "Not out to the street, though."

"Okay, I'll still need access to it."

Angie leaned to her left, craning to see around him. Through the massive plate glass windows dominating the front of the diner, he saw the police cruisers. A green and white Silverado with the Broward County Sherrif's logo on the side pulled up, and the driver's door swung open. Detective Blade St. James unfolded himself from the vehicle.

"Hang tight. I'll be right back," he said, heading up front.

Blade towered over the uniformed officers gathered around him. He motioned up and down the street, issuing rapid-fire commands. No doubt ordering them to secure the area, pull video, and interview witnesses.

The door chimed, and Blade filled the doorway.

"Well, if it isn't the world's tallest garden gnome." Corbin had used that insult before, but Blade still grinned at him.

"And hello to you, Mr. Discount Miami Vice Wannabe." Blade met him with a handshake.

Blade was nothing like his hard-edged name suggested. As a kid, he'd been bullied for his tenderheartedness and doughy physique. But time in Stryker's court-ordered Warrior program at the Kingdom MMA Gym had transformed him. Transformed them both, really. Blade had shot up like a weed, stretching his brawny frame to six-foot-four. The program had given him the confidence to own his size. Corbin . . . well, Corbin was still figuring that part out.

"You just wish you could look this good in a suit. But hey, thanks for coming." His caseload had kept him buried, leaving little time for anything—or anyone—else lately.

"Soon as I heard Stryker's name on the box, I hauled it over here." Blade's massive hand found Corbin's shoulder and gave it a firm squeeze. "How you holdin' up, brother?"

"I'm hanging in there." Something loosened in his chest at the sight of Blade, the only person who truly got it. The only one who'd walked through the same fire and come out the other side. No one else understood what they'd survived together.

Juvie had been inevitable. Corbin, for a string of stupid mistakes fueled by anger and resentment. Blade, for the noble act of defending a stranger with a knife. But Stryker had intervened. He'd rescued them from the system, offered them a home at the Kingdom MMA Gym, and given them something no one else had. Hope.

Stryker had seen something worth saving where everyone else saw trouble. For Corbin, whose only experience with family had been the sting of his father's fists and a mother too lost in her bottles of cheap vodka to notice the bruises, the Warrior program had been his salvation. Years of sweat, sacrifice, and shared pain on those mats had forged a connection deeper than any blood tie. They'd bled together, learned to trust each other, and become the family Corbin never knew he craved. So yeah, they were brothers. Not by blood or court documents, but in every way that mattered.

"Except all this." He circled a finger. "They took Stryker. In broad daylight."

"You saw it?"

"Right through that window. A dark SUV—black, maybe blue—pulled up. Three masked dudes dressed in black hopped out, tased Stryker, dragged him in the back, then hauled off. Happened in a matter of seconds. I'd dropped in to interview the staff about Carlie Tinch."

"The commissioner's daughter? That's your missing person case?"

"Runaway, most likely. She's got a history of it. Not to mention shoplifting, drugs, you know." Corbin scratched the stubble on his jaw. "But bad things happen to runaways, especially young girls. I wanted to take another shot at interviews. See if any new leads materialized."

"How long has she been missing?"

"Six weeks. The commissioner's breathing down my neck. Wants me to find her and convince her to join Stryker's Warrior program."

"That's actually a great idea. Could really help her."

"Come on, man. I'm not a babysitter. Tracking a runaway feels like a punishment, not an assignment."

"Hey, remember where we came from? This girl needs help, just like we did."

Blade was right, but it didn't make the assignment any less frustrating. "I just don't see why he stuck me in charge when the local PD can handle it. I'm overloaded as it is. *Was* overloaded. This morning, Tinch pulled me off every other case and said this was priority."

"Maybe he wants the best." Blade jingled the coins in his pocket. "Think about it. You find Carlie, get her into the program . . . you could change her life. Just like Stryker changed ours. Who's going to be better than you?"

"You."

"True." Blade flattened his lips and nodded. "I am a better detective." Then he smiled. "But he didn't ask me. He asked you. He's got his reasons."

"Well, I'm worried. Six weeks and not a trace."

"You think she's . . ."

"I don't know. I just know I have to find this kid. Alive." To tell the head of the FDLE that the top law enforcement agency couldn't find his daughter was one thing. To tell a father his child was hurt or dead . . . the thought stuck in his throat. "Anyway, I'm working on it. My guess is she's holed up with a friend, avoiding the cops. I'm on it, but we have an active crime scene here. We need to find out who took Stryker and why."

"Got it. Let's keep the lunch crowd out." Blade stuck his head outside and ordered an officer to guard the door. He flipped the sign over to closed and gestured. "Lead the way."

As they made their way to Marge and Angie, Corbin righted the chair he'd knocked over and pocketed the sunglasses he'd left on the table. Angie's tears had dried up, and she scrubbed at the mascara trail with a napkin.

"I believe you ladies know Detective St. James."

"Yeah," Marge said. "You're 'nother one of them Warrior kids, ain't you?"

"Oh, right." Angie pointed the wadded napkin at Blade. "Now I remember. Y'all were Stryker's first students in the, uh, what's it called? Intervention program. Six of you, right?"

There used to be six. Then things with Luna exploded. And she'd left. Because of him.

Corbin deflected the question and told Blade, "There's a camera over the register and another out back. Nothing that can see the street."

"That's a good start." Blade withdrew his notebook and scratched a few words. Old school. Always with the notebook and pencil. He claimed the act of writing helped him think. "You two able to come down to the station and look at a few photos? See if you recognize anyone who's been hanging around here lately?" He spoke in that deep, smooth way that reminded Corbin of a radio psychologist.

"I tol' Agent King here, I was in the kitchen. Didn't see nothin'." Marge squeezed Angie's shoulders. "But sure, darlin'. Ang and I'll give a look."

"Thank you, ma'am." Blade flashed a high-wattage smile. "That'd be helpful."

Angie's seat creaked. She flashed a look at Marge. "I don't know if I wanna go down and waste hours lookin' at books. Them guys had masks. And besides, the two of them saw more than me." Angie flicked her hand in Corbin's direction. "They ran out in the street and everything. Maybe they ought to be the ones going."

Blade's eyebrows shot up. The pencil pointed at Corbin. "You ... and ... ?"

"Luna. Luna was here."

"Luna? Like, Luna-Luna? Our Luna?"

"Yes." Why did he have to keep saying her name? "Said she was waiting to talk to Stryker."

"'Scuse us a moment, ladies." Blade caught Corbin by the elbow and steered him to a table by the front door. "You're saying Luna Rosati was here. Today. In this diner?"

"For the last time, yes."

Blade tucked his pencil and notebook into his breast pocket. "Did you know—"

"I had no idea."

"Wow, I can't believe Stryker didn't say anything. I haven't seen her in forever." Blade cut his eyes to Corbin's. "I know you've missed her, but so have we."

"I know. Stryker should've told us." At least him. But no. He had to stumble into this ... this hornet's nest of his past by accident.

"So ..." Blade folded his arms over his chest. "How'd she look?"

An image of Luna flashed unbidden in his mind. The first time he saw her at the Kingdom Gym, small and fierce, knuckles raw from hitting the heavy bag and eyes mirroring the same defiance he felt inside. A lost girl finding her fight. The woman he saw today had grown. Changed. But the same fire still flickered in her depths. He could see it smoldering beneath a polished surface. All her teenage sharpness was gone, replaced by soft curves and full lips. Lips he used to savor. He felt a smile creep up. "Amazing," was all he could manage.

"Where is she now?"

"No idea. After they took Stryker, she left so fast there was practically a Luna-shaped hole in the door." It certainly wasn't how he'd wanted their reunion to go. Not that he thought they'd ever have one after all this time.

Blade tucked his hands into his pockets. The change rattled around. "I can't believe she'd just show up and not tell us."

"Yeah, tell me about it. I tried to detain her for questioning, but . . . well, I couldn't force her." His wrist still throbbed from her grip. And she'd called him old.

"So Luna shows up after I don't know how many years, and that's the day a bunch of thugs kidnapped Stryker." Blade shook his head. "You know I don't like coincidences."

"You think it's connected?"

Blade pulled his hands from his pockets. "I don't know, but I'll find out. I won't stop until we find Stryker."

"And neither will I, but you take over here. I have to find Luna. Talk to her." He turned to leave.

Blade caught him by the bicep. "Hold up. You came here to do a job." He jutted his chin at Marge and Angie.

Corbin pulled his arm back. "Look. The only woman I've ever truly loved showed up today. I pushed her away once, and it broke me. I'm not letting her go again. Not this time."

"I get it, but Stryker needs you." Blade's expression softened. "Carlie needs you more."

Carlie had vanished seemingly into thin air. Every day that passed was a day her parents went out of their minds with worry, torturing themselves with the what-ifs.

Boy, did he know that feeling. The gut-wrenching angst of not knowing what'd happened to Luna all these years. And he'd searched too. Used all his authority. But after she joined the Marines, it was as if she ceased to exist.

Blade left him standing there but stopped halfway and turned. "Hey, God brought her back for a purpose..."

He didn't finish the sentence. Didn't have to. Stryker had etched those words into his heart over a lifetime. Stryker always said God revealed his purpose in his own timing. It was up to each person to remain obedient, so he was standing right where he was supposed to be when God's timing lined up.

Blade took the seat across the table from the women. Their worried faces brightened into small, tentative smiles. Blade was doing his thing. Working his magic. Setting them at ease with that tender heart of his.

One thing was certain, time was running out. For Carlie, for Stryker, and maybe even for his chance to make things right with Luna.

But, yeah. Okay. He'd do what he came here to do. He'd find the answers.

Even if it meant Luna might slip out of his life and disappear again forever.

3

THE MIDDAY SUN SLANTED through the window, painting a swath of light across the worn oak floorboards of Stryker's bungalow. Luna perched on the edge of a worn leather desk chair in front of Stryker's computer. The scent of coconut wafted in on a breeze that ruffled the edges of the gauzy white curtains. It should have been peaceful here. Should have been a place for her to unpack the emotional baggage she'd hauled from Pakistan. But all she felt was a sharp jab of worry.

It had been eighteen years since Luna had last seen Corbin King. Eighteen years since she'd given him her heart on a silver platter only to have him hand it back broken into a million pieces. And yet, there he was. Standing there, all six-foot-two inches of him, in a finely tailored suit and mirrored sunglasses.

What was she thinking? Of course he'd changed. She'd changed too. People changed. They grew up. They moved on. So why, after all these years, did the mere sight of him punch her lungs and stop her heart in the same instant?

Shake it off. There isn't time for this. "I should've just stayed in Peshawar," she said with a sigh.

Stryker and his promise to help her find her daughter pulled her back.

And now he'd been kidnapped. But why?

He'd made enemies. Drug dealers, gang leaders—they didn't appreciate his efforts to pull kids away from their influence. She knew he couldn't save every kid. Some were too far gone, lost in the darkness. But Stryker dedicated himself to helping any within his reach. Even the ones who were still fighting their own demons, searching for a way out.

She'd been through enough training to recognize that struggle herself. It was how she chose her assets. It was in the eyes. The ones hungry for something more. The ones desperate for a different path.

None of it added up. Why would Stryker's enemies kidnap him in broad daylight? They could have just shot him. The small-town street was quiet but not *that* quiet. They had to know there'd be witnesses. Most likely the kidnappers wanted something. Information or something Stryker possessed.

Whatever it was, Luna needed to find it, and she bet clues were in his computer.

The monitor had gone dark, but she nudged the mouse. A photo of the ocean filled the screen, a sky ablaze with fiery hues of orange and crimson. A classic Florida sunset.

And a blinking cursor waiting for the password.

Trying to guess was useless, but if he was like most adults of his generation, he probably had a list of passwords tucked away somewhere.

She scanned the top of the desk. No stray notepads. She pulled the top drawer open. Pens. Pencils. Paper clips. She tried the next one. More of the same. She slammed it shut. *Okay, where would he keep his—*

Her gaze landed on a framed photo on the corner of the desk. A much-younger Stryker grinned back at her. He had his arm slung around a group of teenagers, all of them flashing peace signs and goofy smiles. She was in the photo, sandwiched between Corbin and Blade.

Luna picked up the frame and wiped the thin layer of dust off the faces. They'd all been so young then. So full of hope. Except for Harlee. She'd scowled at the camera with her arms crossed over her chest, looking every bit the hardened gang member Stryker had rescued from a life of crime.

She put the frame back where she found it. Wow, she'd missed them. All these years, she'd been so busy outrunning her pain, she'd boxed up the memories of that time. Refused to look at them. She'd forgotten about her friends. Forgotten what they all went through. Forgotten what Stryker had done for them. How he'd rescued them from their aimless, lonely lives. He'd offered them a place to call home, welcomed them into a found family, and helped them find their purpose.

And she'd walked away without a goodbye.

Stryker's dog-eared Bible with a worn leather cover lay on the corner of the desk. She flipped it open. His handwritten notes filled the margins. Highlights and underlines punctuated verses throughout. A thicker piece of paper, white and folded, peeked out.

Ah-ha. The passwords. She slid the sheet out and unfolded it. It wasn't a list of passwords. It was a single line of type: *They're watching. Don't trust anyone.*

What had Stryker gotten into?

Gravel crunched outside. No time to ponder. She snapped a picture of the note with her phone, tucked it back into the Bible, and stood.

Police cruisers pulled into the driveway. Time to go. She headed for the back door, grabbing her purse from the sofa on her way. She had every right to be here. Stryker had practically begged her to come. But explaining to the cops why she was snooping around while he was missing . . . That was a conversation she wanted to avoid.

Luna stepped outside just as heavy fists pounded the front door.

Stryker's boardwalk began where the grass met sand. She followed the narrow wooden slats that snaked through tall sea oats and spiky sea grapes. A flock of seagulls scavenged for scraps near the trash cans by the boardwalk entrance.

The beach, deserted except for a lone jogger and her dog in the distance. Good. At least something was going her way.

She slogged through the soft sand down to the water's edge and started jogging. The public beach access where she'd parked her rental car out of sight was a good mile down the coast, but she needed the time to shake loose the thoughts in her head.

By the time she reached her car, her chest ached. Years of living in an arid climate had taken a toll. The humidity was like breathing through a wet wool blanket. She hit the unlock button on the key fob, yanked open the door, and practically dove inside, where a blast of heat hit her. The Florida sun had turned the car's interior into a sauna. She cranked the engine, set the AC on high, and settled back to wait for the arctic air to reach her.

Okay, so she'd struck out at Stryker's. She hadn't been able to get into his computer, and she was no closer to understanding who took him or why. A daylight kidnapping. Witnesses. It was brazen, almost theatrical. They were sending a message. But what message? Was it connected to her past with the CIA, or something else entirely?

She glanced at the clock on the dash. 12:15 p.m. She should head back to the diner. Talk to Corbin. Demand a role in the investigation.

But how could she explain her sudden return? Her involvement in all of this?

No. She couldn't go back there. Not yet. Not until she had a better understanding of what was going on.

The confetti from the Taser . . . that was a start.

The anti-felon identification dots scattered out by the dozens every time a Taser cartridge deployed. Under a magnifying glass, the dots revealed a serial number that pointed to the cartridge's origin. From there, she could trace the name of the purchaser—and maybe even their location.

Problem was, she couldn't exactly walk into the Millie Beach Police Department with evidence taken from a crime scene and ask for a favor. And right now, she was just a civilian with no badge, no gun, and no authority. The cops would trace the AFIDs, eventually. But "eventually" might be too late for Stryker.

And there was the risk of another accidental reunion with Corbin.

Langston could help. But he wasn't happy with her. Not after she'd turned in her resignation. She pulled out her phone and typed the number from memory. Her thumb hovered over the call button. Should she do this?

With a deep breath, she pressed the screen. The phone rang once. Twice. Three times.

Each ring brought a fresh wave of dread. What was she going to say?

"Dough Bro's Pizza, this is Sandy. Will this be pickup or delivery?"

"Delivery."

"Got it," Sandy said. "Address?"

"444 Fox Lake Drive, Clinton, North Carolina."

"Very good. Can you verify the last four digits of your credit card number?"

Luna gave her the numbers.

"Perfect. Now, what can we get for you?"

"One large supreme with extra olives." Her stomach growled at the thought of food.

"Okay, let me put you on hold for one moment."

The line clicked several times while the Agency verified her identity.

"Langston." Deputy Chief Harris Langston. Ten years of working together, and he still hadn't lost that hard edge.

"It's me, sir." She squinted one eye, waiting for the quiet disapproval that was somehow worse than yelling.

He harrumphed. "Thought you were off finding yourself."

Finding herself. Right. After ten years at the CIA, she'd buried herself under a layer of fiction so deep she wasn't sure she could ever dig the real her back out.

"There's been a wrinkle."

Silence. Then, "A wrinkle?" He didn't sound surprised. Annoyed, maybe. "You quit the Agency and you've been stateside less than thirty days and there's already a wrinkle?"

"You could say that." She glanced at the windshield. The AC was finally winning the battle against the heat.

"Spit it out."

"It's my mentor." She avoided using real-world identities.

"Your mentor? What about him?"

"Someone kidnapped him this morning."

The silence stretched, punctuated only by the faint hum of the air conditioner. She could practically hear the gears turning in Langston's head. Calculating. Assessing.

"Sounds like a job for the locals."

"They're on it." Luna turned the AC down, and the fan quieted. "But it's personal. This isn't some random act of violence. They took him for a reason."

"I understand. The thing with your daughter . . ."

"It's more than that." She couldn't tell him everything. Not over the phone. Not when she wasn't sure who might be listening. "They targeted him. Maybe because of me. They might kill him if I don't find him first."

Another long silence. Then, "What do you need?"

"For starters, I need in his computer."

"I know a guy." Langston didn't hesitate. "Brilliant mind. Egghead type. Does some consulting work for us. Mostly helps us with the really big, really bad cyber stuff. Trust me, if anyone can get you what you need, it's this guy. And I think you know him."

Her heart stuttered. Jett Nu? No. It couldn't be. "Is this your 'top gun' contact?"

"Yeah, I'll get you his number. Encrypted, of course."

Of all the people, in all the world, Jett would be the one she'd call. Jett, ever the bookworm, spouting facts from a medical textbook, telling her all about what to expect when she was expecting. Jett, his eyes filled with compassion, assuring her that she would get through it. That she would be okay.

"Thanks," she said. "You're a lifesaver."

"Just returning the favor." Langston paused, and she could almost hear the wheels turning in his head again. "About your resignation..."

"Listen, I don't want to—"

"Just hear me out. I know you've made up your mind. And I respect that. But you're a good agent. One of the best I've ever seen. We've invested a lot in you. And I'd hate to lose you. Not like this."

"I... I appreciate that." What else could she say?

"Just... think about it, okay? For all of us."

"I will." She wouldn't, though.

"Good. Now go find your mentor."

The line went dead before she could ask about the AFIDs.

She stared at her reflection in the phone screen. Langston was right. She was a good agent. A great one. She'd given the Agency ten years of her life. Sacrificed everything.

Was she willing to throw it all away now? To walk away from her career? And for what? To chase after ghosts? To try and reclaim a past that was gone forever?

She should just walk away. Leave Millie Beach and never look back. She'd lived the last eighteen years just fine. More than fine. She'd thrived. Built a good life for herself. A life of purpose.

But what about her purpose? The one God had mapped out for her life?

That thought stopped her cold.

Stryker had shown her kindness when no one else had bothered. Back when she was just a skinny kid with too-big eyes and fierce self-reliance that refused all help. He'd taken her in without question. Welcomed her into his world of structure and kindness. He'd become the only father she'd ever known. The only one who'd stuck around long enough to earn the title.

And her daughter. The baby she'd given up all those years ago. The tiny face that haunted her every moment since. The little girl who carried half her DNA but whom she'd never heard call her "Mama." Not once.

Maybe that was purpose enough.

But knowing her purpose and fulfilling it were two different things. And one thing stood clear. She couldn't tackle this alone. She needed help. Drawing in a breath, she made her decision.

She dialed the number.

4

THE DINER'S SURVEILLANCE CAMERA hadn't caught the kidnappers. Just Luna. Sitting there, waiting.

Luna. The sight of her, even after all these years, had sent a shock wave through him.

Corbin watched Blade lead Angie to a quiet corner of the diner for questioning. He glanced at Marge. If he wrapped this up quickly, he could try to find Luna. He *needed* to talk to her. Needed to understand why she'd come back. Why now? Why here?

A tsunami of questions threatened to drown everything, but he couldn't dwell on Luna now. He needed answers about Carlie, and Marge might have some.

The older woman stood with her arms folded across her chest, her weathered face set in a scowl. Smells of burned coffee and grease hung in the air. He could use coffee right about now, but Marge wasn't offering.

"The real reason I came in here today was to ask you a few questions about Carlie Tinch," he said. "Mind if we sit?"

Marge's scowl deepened. "Ain't got time to sit. Got a business to run, you know."

Corbin glanced around the empty diner. "I saw the video, Marge. It looked pretty quiet in here all morning."

Marge huffed.

He had at least one thing in common with Marge. He didn't want to be a part of this interview right now any more than she did. "Listen, I have a missing kid, and it's my job to find her before trouble does. You'd be doing me a huge favor if I can have a few more minutes of your time."

"Fine. But make it quick." She jerked her chin toward a nearby booth. "Sit."

They settled into the cracked vinyl seats. "I'm investigating Carlie Tinch's disappearance." He placed his phone on the table with the screen showing a picture of Carlie. "This is her. She's been missing for a while now, and we're trying to retrace her steps. I recently learned she was a regular here. Anything you remember about the last time you saw her, even if it seems trivial, could be really important."

Marge squinted at the photo, then peered over her bifocals at Corbin. "Carlie. Sweet girl, but trouble. Always trouble." She tapped a long, nicotine-stained fingernail on the table. "Let's see, now. Last time I saw her . . . yeah, she was here. With another girl. Ashley, I think."

"Ashley Phillips?" Corbin pulled up another photo on his phone and showed Marge.

"That's her." Marge coughed into her fist. The phlegmy rattle didn't sound good. "Those two. Thick as thieves."

Ashley. Carlie's "bestie" as the girl had put it during their first interview. "Do you remember anything about that morning?"

"They sat right there." Marge pointed to a table in the far corner. "It was busy, I remember that much. Angie called in sick, so I was filling in. Don't do much waitressing these days. Not as strong as I used to be."

Corbin nodded. "Did you overhear any of their conversation?"

Marge chuckled, a dry, rasping sound. "Overhear? Honey, in

this place, I hear everything. Those two girls? They were gabbing away like magpies. Mostly about their parents. Typical teenage stuff. The world's against them. Nobody understands them, blah, blah, blah. Ashley complaining about her twin brother, like always."

"How do you know they're twins?" He'd somehow missed that detail.

"They come in sometimes as a family on Sunday after church. Locals. Been coming since they were little squirmers who couldn't hardly sit still."

Corbin nodded, making a note to interview both Ashley and Andre again. "Was Ashley doing most of the talking, or was Carlie equally involved in the conversation?"

"Ashley was telling Carlie that her parents never pay attention to her. Too busy with work, gone all day. Then when they get home, they work even more. Said they hole up in their office, don't even bother making dinner anymore."

"Did Carlie respond to that?"

"Hold your horses," Marge grumbled. "I'm getting there. Ashley complained that the only time she sees her parents is when they're fussin' with Andre. Didn't hear why Andre was always in trouble, though. Had to get food to the customers while it's hot, you know."

As if on cue, Marge launched into a complaint about how hard it was to keep the diner going. "Hard times, economy. People get mad when I raise the prices. And now, with that cop blocking the entrance and the closed sign up, I'll be losing a whole day of wages."

This place had been here forever. A staple of their small town. One he didn't visit. There were too many memories for him here, and the thought of Marge struggling and closing down, it didn't sit right. "I hear you, Marge. We'll figure something out for the diner later. Let's keep going."

Marge took a deep breath. "Well, I was serving a customer. You know how it is. Missed bits and pieces. But I did hear Carlie tryin' to be supportive. Said she could relate because her parents were real pieces of work."

The commissioner had pulled Corbin for this case to keep the details of his personal life private. Hadn't wanted anyone to know about his wife's struggles with mental health issues. The commissioner knew the dirty details of Corbin's past and decided he could be trusted with his own.

Marge said, "And Carlie's pretty sure her dad just plain hates her, wishes she'd been a boy so he could have a son to follow in his footsteps."

Another thing Commissioner Tinch wouldn't want the whole town hearing. Though he doubted it was true. According to her father, Carlie was smart and driven. A bit rebellious, maybe. Angry that her father wouldn't let her get away with sneaking out or stealing her mother's medications. "Did you believe Carlie?"

"Well now, I do hear a lot of how people talk around here." Marge scratched her neck, then studied the underside of her fingernails. "I know that them teens have all their emotions runnin' wild. Every little thing that don't go their way, seems to them like they're being tortured worse than them folks in Japanese POW camps. They have problems, but not real ones." She paused, giving Corbin a knowing look. "Not like you and Luna."

Corbin's heart skipped a beat at the mention of Luna's name. They'd had problems, all right.

He remembered them sitting at their corner table, the same one where they'd shared their first milkshake, two straws, one glass, a nervous laugh bubbling up between them . . .

Luna's fingers shredded a napkin into long strips that she wrapped around her finger. "I missed my period. I took a test." Her eyes, fixed on the tabletop, refused to meet his. "I'm pregnant."

Pregnant. The word splintered his focus. Everything else drowning beneath the blooming terror. His father's face flashed before him, contorted in anger. Too many times he'd seen that same expression in himself. The hot rush of rage when some punk looked at Luna the wrong way.

The tightness in his chest, the clenched fists, the struggle to keep it all in check...

"What are we going to do, Corbin?"

Everything was slipping away. College plans, career dreams, his entire future—all of it shredding like the napkin in Luna's hands.

Eighteen. He was eighteen, and Luna sixteen. Too young to be parents. They didn't even have jobs. To others, he'd be just another statistic. Another deadbeat teen dad. Another failure.

The clatter of dishes from the kitchen pierced through his spiraling thoughts. Marge talked on, her words barely registering. He had to push away the past and deal with the present.

But Luna's words lingered. *"What are we going to do?"*

"You listening, boy?" Marge's sharp tap on the table snapped him back to the present.

The seat creaked as he shifted. "Sorry, Marge. What did you say?"

Marge rolled her eyes. "I asked if I could smoke."

"Here? You know about the no smoking laws, right?"

"You think I don't know that?" Marge snapped. "I mean out back."

"Oh, sure," Corbin agreed, relieved to have a moment to collect his thoughts. He followed Marge out the back door into a small concrete area littered with cigarette butts. The heat hit him like a wall, and he tugged at his collar as Marge lit up.

He waited while she took her first long drag before he prompted, "You were talking about Carlie's and Ashley's problems with their parents."

Marge blew out a stream of smoke. "Right. Well, like I said, I missed bits of it. But I remember Carlie saying something about how if she disappeared, her father would never even notice until he got a text that her grades had slipped."

"And Ashley's response?"

"Ashley said her parents wouldn't notice either. But she got all morbid about it. Said if she slit her wrists, her parents would only complain about the bloody mess she'd made."

Corbin winced. There was teenage drama and then there was a crisis. A cry for help. "Pretty dramatic stuff."

Marge sucked smoke into her lungs. She blew it out as she said, "Yeah. I had to seat some customers."

The smoke stung his eyes, and he shifted, trying to put space between them without taking a rude step away.

"When I came back to refill the girls' drinks, they seemed all serious. So, I'm not ashamed to say that I eavesdropped. Didn't like no suicidal teens making plans in my diner. Wanted to see if they really meant it."

She flicked the ash off her cigarette. "I was busing the table beside them and heard Carlie saying they should just run away together. Said she had enough money for both to get to New York. They could get jobs, be roommates, and their parents would have to spend the rest of their lives wondering what happened to them."

This was new information. No one had mentioned this before. Not even Ashley. "Did they make any concrete plans?"

"Not that I heard." Marge breathed out a long stream of smoke. "But Carlie gave something to Ashley."

"What was it?"

"I didn't see. Just heard her say, 'Here, this will get you through the weekend.' Then Ashley paid for their food and they left." Marge dropped her cigarette and stubbed it out with her toe. "On the way out, they made plans to sneak out and go to some party."

Corbin's mind put it together. Carlie giving Ashley something to "get her through the weekend" could mean a lot of things, but given Carlie's history, drugs seemed like a strong possibility. "Either of them mention a boyfriend?"

"If they did, I didn't hear it."

No surprise. Adults seemed to be the last ones to know when a teenager was in a relationship. He sure hadn't told Stryker when he'd started falling for Luna.

But Ashley would know if Carlie had a boyfriend. She hadn't mentioned it during their first interview, but her parents had been there. Now her best friend had been missing for weeks. Maybe she would be more forthcoming.

"Is there anything else you remember, Marge? Anything at all?"

She shook her head. "That's all I got. Now, if there's nothing else, I got to get my restaurant back in order."

"Thank you, Marge. You've been very helpful." The new details filled in a few more gaps.

As Marge headed back inside, he lingered. The Florida sun had turned the alley into an oven. He yanked at his tie.

Carlie Tinch, the commissioner's daughter, wasn't just a rebellious teen. She was dealing with serious family issues, that much he'd known. But possibly sharing drugs with her friends and making plans to run away? That was new. It sounded like more than just typical teenage drama.

He thought about his own teenage years, about the pain and confusion he'd felt when Luna told him she was pregnant. How scared and overwhelmed they'd both been. How badly they'd handled it all.

And Luna? She'd vanished. Disappeared from his life without a trace. Just like Carlie.

5

THE DRIVE FROM STRYKER'S HOUSE to the Kingdom MMA Gym took fifteen minutes, but Luna needed another fifteen to work herself up to go inside. Which was stupid. She'd walked into the apartment of a Pakistani arms dealer without backup—she could go into the gym and face her friends.

She could do this.

Some of her best memories were at this gym. Luna smiled to herself. She'd had fun in the ring with the others. The way Corbin used to wrap her hands before sparring, his touch gentle, his gaze warm. How he'd stood up for her against some tweakers who'd tried to steal her backpack, his fists clenched, his jaw tight. She'd felt safe with him, a feeling she'd craved after years of chaos and uncertainty.

They'd whispered secrets in the halls, shared dreams under the watchful eyes of Stryker.

Her smile faltered. She'd loved him. Thought he loved her too. They'd planned their future. A small house with a porch swing. A dog. A life far away from Millie Beach. A family. They were supposed to raise their daughter together. Be the kind of parents they'd never known.

A childish dream. A dream shattered when Corbin decided he didn't want to be a father. Those were the kinds of thoughts that had kept her awake most of last night.

It didn't matter. She'd moved on. Corbin didn't want to be a father? Fine. Then he didn't need to know that Stryker had promised to help her find their daughter.

That had been the other thing keeping her from sleep. Good thing she didn't need much.

Luna flinched at the sharp tap of knuckles on her window, then smiled. A lot could change about a person from age thirteen to thirty-six, but she'd know that brilliant smile lighting up those dark, almond-shaped eyes anywhere.

Victoria Crew.

Except, no one dared call her Victoria unless they wanted a hard jab to the nose.

Tori whistled as Luna climbed out of her car. "Oooh whee! Look at you, girl!" Tori's arms went out for a hug. "You're lookin' fiiiiine, Mommie."

Tori was a beautiful blend of Greek and Korean, but any time she set foot near the gym, her accent turned Puerto Rican. A token of her childhood upbringing in a foster home located in the Miami neighborhood known as Little San Juan.

Much like herself, Tori had always been a chameleon. Hard-nosed and professional when the situation called for it, but she could turn on the charm in a blink. It was how she was in the ring too. Coming at you hard and fast one minute, then loose and playful the next. It threw her opponents off trying to keep up.

Luna grinned and hugged her friend for the first time in forever. She stepped back and made a show of looking Tori up and down. "Whoa. Girl, you're lookin' pretty hot yourself."

Tori flicked the ends of her hair. "Different, huh?" She'd added chestnut highlights and cut it shoulder-length with chunky layers, giving her a trendy, tousled look. "First time I've cut it in . . . well, ever. You remember the waist-length black curtain, right? This is new, like, a few weeks new."

"Beautimus." Funny, she'd always envied Tori's long black hair, but this new look? It had attitude. Just like Tori.

Tori's wide smile lost some of the brightness. She clasped Luna's hand and squeezed it. "I can't believe you're really here."

Luna didn't like the knot that formed in her stomach. She owed her friends an explanation, but now wasn't the time. "I talked to Jett. Stryker was kidnapped and he said—"

"I know. Jett called right after he talked to you. Blade caught the case. Harlee and I already started investigating. Unofficially, of course."

Tori started walking and Luna followed, heading for the entrance. Tori kept talking. "Jett can't make it. He's in some sort of sensitive intelligence-sharing discussion."

Luna's heart sank a little. Hearing Jett over the phone had her longing to see him.

Tori said, "Harlee's using Jett's software to sift through the data he's sent. We're waiting for something to pop." She talked like Luna hadn't been gone for years.

"And Stryker's computer?"

"That was easy. His password is literally 'password' with the 'at' symbol for the *a*." Tori rolled her eyes skyward. "Ay bendito. The man hasn't logged in to that machine in weeks." She pulled open the door and held it for Luna.

Inside, the familiar thuds of gloved fists striking heavy bags and the sharp aroma of sweat and musk brought memories crashing back. Nostalgia hit hard. Things were the same, but different. She glanced around the room, half expecting to see Stryker on the mat with his training pads up, taking punches.

"Bigger, right? A few years ago, Stryker did a massive remodel. We have triple the square footage. Finally added both training rings." Tori gestured to the square boxing ring and a hexagon cage with steel panels and vinyl-coated chain-link fencing for mixed martial arts fighting.

Wide-open ceilings exposed steel beams painted black to match the walls. On the second floor, a horizontal mirrored window looked out over the gym. Stryker's corner office was gone, replaced by heavy bags of all shapes and sizes suspended from a rack made from steel beams. Treadmills, cardio, and weight-lifting equipment lined the wall on her right.

"Stryker turn this place into a fitness club?"

"Are you kidding? This is the place where fighters become warriors!" Tori flexed her bicep. Luna didn't miss the baseball-sized knot that bulged out. "The men and women here are either in the Warrior program or they have a badge. Same as always."

Stryker started the Warrior program as a mission to get delinquent kids off the streets and into the gym. Luna remembered how he'd marched into courtrooms, convincing judges that these troubled teens didn't need juvenile detention, they needed structure. They needed purpose.

And so the program was born. Instead of sending kids like her to juvie, the courts began placing them with Stryker. His approach was simple yet effective. Martial arts training alongside law enforcement officers. Breaking down barriers one sparring match at a time.

Luna could still picture the separate dormitories he'd set up—boys on one side of the building, girls on the other. Those plain rooms had been the first stable home many of them had ever known. Including her. The rules had been clear. Finish high school, attend church services, and put in cleaning hours at the gym. No exceptions, no excuses.

But Stryker had given back more than he'd demanded. Food when they were hungry. Clothes when theirs had worn thin. A place to sleep when home wasn't safe. For Luna, it had been the first time an adult had ever followed through on their promises. The first time someone had expected something from her and believed she could deliver.

They passed two sweaty men grunting and grappling on the floor mat and paused to watch. "That's Chief Inspector Wilkins and Agent Jones," Tori said.

"Wilkins has nice moves."

"Another day I'd have you teach him a thing or two." Tori elbowed her.

A few rounds of throwing a guy around could help clear her head, but she wasn't here to relive her glory days. She'd come to do what CIA operatives did best. Recruit assets and collect intelligence. Even if that wasn't her job anymore.

She jogged up the gunmetal gray stairs behind Tori. Their shoes clattered on each grated stair. They headed down a short hallway and hooked a right.

"This is the new office. It's shared with all the trainers."

The darkened office wasn't what Luna had expected. It looked more like the analyst room at Langley. Each of the four desks had multiple monitors with some running video footage of the gym. The hexagonal ring had cameras from every angle, and Luna imagined the trainers reviewed the fights for improvements. The room was empty except for a woman sitting behind an ultrawide curved display.

"Brought you something." Tori hoisted herself up onto the small conference table and sat with her legs pretzeled.

Harlee Bay swiveled in her chair and pinned Luna with a look somewhere north of the Arctic. Aside from the sleeves of tattoos high on both arms, a scar cutting through her eyebrow, and a general air of menace, Harlee hadn't changed much. The Kingdom MMA Gym logo, a roaring lion wearing a gold crown, emblazoned the front of her tank top.

Luna wiggled her fingers in a wave. "Hey, Harlee." Well, that was pathetic.

"Hey." Harlee was on her feet, crossing the room. "Missed you round here."

They hugged, stilted and awkward. Harlee avoided eye contact, glancing at Tori, her computer, the floor. Everywhere but directly at Luna. Frosty reception aside, it was good to see her friend. *Were they friends?*

Harlee wore her blond hair pulled into a chignon with stray tendrils falling around her heart-shaped face. She'd grown to somewhere around five-ten, and her athletic frame was firm and toned as ever. Tori and Luna used to envy Harlee's six-pack abs.

Harlee swiveled her seat to face the screens and began clicking the mouse. The monitor had several windows covering every inch of the screen. A terminal window ran lines of code while another window flashed through photos one after the other. Harlee had paused a video at the moment the Taser hit Stryker.

She peered over Harlee's shoulder. "What's all this?"

Harlee didn't look at Luna. "While you were away, our boy Jett developed this software."

"Facial recognition?" She wasn't sure how that would help since the men wore masks.

"It goes beyond that. Pulls video from any camera connected to Wi-Fi for biometric surveillance. It's military grade. Used by the NSA. It sees everything."

Luna's heart did a little stutter. "Jett created this for the National Security Agency?"

"He created it for his tech company and licenses it to the NSA and pretty much every other American intelligence agency."

Oh, she knew about the software. It analyzed body shape, gait patterns, heartbeats, the cadence of a voice, even the pattern of an individual's iris. The kind of tech that made privacy a myth.

Had Jett or Harlee tried the algorithm on her? Had they seen her working with bomb brokers and arms dealers all over Asia?

Possible, but not likely. The CIA specialized in countermeasures, one of which included hacking into systems to delete the agent's biometric data linked to an alias.

Tori asked, "Anything on Stryker's home computer?"

"Pretty sure he hasn't touched it—except to check the weather—since I set it up for him."

"Were you able to access his deleted browser history?" Luna asked. "Sometimes what's been erased tells you more than what's still there."

Harlee's shoulders stiffened. "I'm not some amateur." She didn't even dignify Luna with a glance.

Luna bit her tongue, recognizing the verbal slap for what it was. Apparently, her habit of questioning everything had only worsened the already frosty reception. Before she'd called Stryker, she'd done a bit of recon. Pulled files. Tracked career movements. Checked relationship statuses. Not because she intended to rekindle anything with Harlee or the others but because walking in blind wasn't in her nature.

"So, you're with the ATF?" An olive branch disguised as small talk.

Harlee offered something like a grunt in response.

Luna looked to Tori for help, but she only shrugged.

It seemed clear Harlee wanted Luna to pay for leaving without saying goodbye. Luna couldn't blame her. Corbin had done the same thing by shutting her out after the breakup, and look what it had done to her heart. Those sleepless nights included mourning their friendship even more than their romance.

Luna grabbed a chair from the desk behind Harlee and rolled it to sit beside her. She wasn't sure if she'd ever return to the CIA, but her job as a covert agent was all about changing adversaries into friends. And she was good at her job.

Very good.

She studied Harlee. Her deep blue eyes scanned the computer screen behind thick, dark lashes. The monitor cast a soft blue hue over her skin.

"Harlee, I'm sorry. I know I hurt you when I left. Hurt you more by not checking in." Harlee looked up, and Luna summoned a small smile. "I want to . . . to fix it. Make it up . . . whatever. There will be time, I promise, but right now... could we work together? Can we do this for Stryker? All of us?"

Harlee leaned back in her chair and crossed her arms. "All of us?"

She didn't have to say it, but Luna knew she meant Corbin. Clever woman. Harlee was trying to get her to agree to set aside everything to work with Corbin too. If it meant getting Stryker back safe and sound, she'd do it.

If there was one thing Luna could do, it was fake it for the greater good. "Yeah. All of us. For Stryker."

A slow smile appeared on her face. "Good, because look who's here."

Luna followed her finger to the security camera feed on the monitor. Blade and Corbin were inside the gym, about to head up the stairs.

Harlee anticipated a reaction, but Luna had years of experience concealing her emotions and controlling her reflexes.

"Perfect timing. It should only take a few minutes to trace this, then we'll have some intel to share when they get here." She held out four pieces of confetti in her palm for Harlee to see.

Tori hopped off the table and leaned in for a closer look. Her eyes flicked up to Luna's. "AFID dots?"

"Found them on the sidewalk. I'm sure the crime scene crew retrieved a few by now, but at least we'll have a head start."

Harlee picked up her phone and dialed. She smiled at Luna. "Nice."

The best way to eliminate your enemy was to make them your friend. All she did was approach from a place of humility. Found a common interest, then offered up a favor. "No big deal."

Tori patted Luna's shoulder. "Good call." Luna wasn't sure if she meant the Taser dots, or how she'd handled Harlee, but she expected it was both.

Harlee was on hold when Corbin and Blade came in.

A huge grin broke out on Blade's face when he saw Luna. "C'mere and let me get a look at you." Blade was a big guy with a broad chest and delicate blue eyes. Dark brown hair fell across his forehead in an unintentional style statement. Part professional, part just-rolled-out-of-bed.

He cupped his massive hands around hers. "It's so, *so* good to see you."

She pulled her hands free and slid her arms around his middle and hugged him.

A hot tear formed in the corner of her eye. She'd missed this. Missed the human connection. The familiar touch of people she could trust.

When Luna released her hold on Blade, he ran his hand over her hair. "Don't worry. We'll make sure you get your reunion with Stryker too."

Corbin stared at her as if he was waiting for her to say something.

"The company came back with a name." Harlee scribbled on a notepad. "The Taser cartridge was purchased by Charles Abercorn. He bought three. I've got the address. It's on the corner of Prosperity and Fifteenth."

Blade had his phone out. "I'm getting a warrant. It's almost one o'clock. The DA should be back from lunch by now."

"Ah, there you are." Harlee clicked a button and enlarged a mug shot of Abercorn.

He was a gaunt man, his face hollowed and shadowed, his skin stretched tight over prominent cheekbones. Heavy-lidded eyes stared back at her from the photo. A Santa Muerte tattoo stretched across his neck, from shoulder to ear. The Saint of Death. She suppressed a shudder. How could anyone worship death when life itself was a miracle, a gift?

"Did they say how he paid? Credit card?" Corbin had moved to stand closer to Blade, and Luna's traitorous heart fluttered when his shoulder brushed past hers.

Harlee clicked around the computer. "Used a prepaid gift card. Untraceable. But here." She tapped the monitor. "This is the place."

A street view image showed a dingy white bungalow with a

jungle of a yard. The native plants had run wild and started crowding the house. From the blurry photo, Luna could see the sagging chain-link fence surrounding the property. One section of the four-foot fence looked like it had been peeled back, pulling the rusted support pole to a forty-five-degree angle. "Place looks abandoned."

"I guess we'll find out when we get there." Corbin used his phone to snap a photo of the address and headed for the door.

Blade held up a hand. "Whoa. Broward County has this case—"

Corbin shook his head. "This is Stryker we're talking about. He could be in that house."

"This isn't the case you're on, my friend." Blade wasn't backing down, but his tone had Luna thinking there was something in the undercurrent.

"FDLE can take jurisdiction anytime," Corbin said.

"State boys can't come in and take over. They have to be invited."

"So do it." Corbin's neck flushed red.

Blade's eyes flashed. "Fine, but I'm driving." He rested a hand on Tori's shoulder. "You guys hang tight here. Text me if you get anything."

Harlee nodded, and Tori said, "Be safe."

Luna followed Blade. She wasn't about to sit this one out.

"Wait, where are you going?" Corbin lifted his hand like he'd planned to grab her shoulder, then thought better of it.

"With you." She didn't really want to, but she'd come this far.

"No. Not a chance." The muscles of Corbin's jaw tensed, probably biting back a few choice words.

All eyes were on her.

"Look, I know you don't want me involved, but this is personal for me too. I promise I'll follow your lead and stay out of the way. I just need to be there."

"Sorry," Blade said. "No civilian ride alongs today."

Luna always avoided outright lying, but withholding information was a necessity as a CIA operative. Not only for her own safety, but for others. She'd gotten pretty good at the wordplay involved and found it always better to offer something that had a shred of truth attached. Truth had a way of cementing a bond between two humans.

She glanced around the room, knowing that they deserved an explanation for her years of absence but also that she couldn't give them the full one until she'd been officially released from the Agency.

So, she told them the only story she'd been cleared to give. "I'm not a civilian. I'm an undercover federal agent."

6

HE'D COME TO EXPECT SURPRISES with this job, but the last thing Corbin imagined was running an operation with the woman who broke his heart. What was she doing here? Why had she come back after all these years?

He leaned his shoulder against the side of Abercorn's dilapidated house. Sweat glued his shirt to his back beneath his tactical vest.

The broken miniblind offered a sliver of view into the silent interior. No movement. No sound. Too quiet.

Officer Salas had arrived ahead of them, warrant in hand, and waited at the foot of the steps. Officer Gordon covered the back door. Luna stood to Corbin's right with Blade between them. They'd found an extra vest for her, but it was too big and gaped around the armholes and neck. She wore black jeans and a dress shirt with the sleeves cuffed to her forearms. Hair pulled into a low ponytail. A hand on the gun in a paddle holster at her hip.

She looked the part, he had to admit. But her presence here . . . it unsettled him. How she had inserted herself into this operation, he still didn't understand. He'd spent years imagining their reunion, replaying it over and over in his mind. But every scenario he'd imagined ended with her in his arms. Not with her standing beside him in a tactical vest, as if the past had never happened.

On the ride over, he'd pressed her for details about her undercover work, but she'd said it was classified. That'd been her answer to all his questions.

Classified.

She was shutting him out, just like always.

Probably this was a bad idea, but it was clear she wasn't going to back down, and he didn't have time to argue. If they didn't let her come, she'd likely find another way to interfere. At least this way she might stick around long enough to talk. As long as she followed his lead, this might work out.

The rotted wood creaked and groaned beneath their feet. One wrong step and one of them would fall right through the ramshackle porch.

Blade slammed his fist on the front door. Three loud bangs rattled the windows. "Police! Search warrant! Open up!"

Corbin held his breath and listened for movement inside. Nothing.

"Police! We have a search warrant!" Blade banged again. "You have ten seconds to open the door or we're coming in!" Blade nodded at the door as he drew his weapon. "Ready?"

Corbin had his gun out. Luna took her position. When she was ready, Corbin leaned in and tried the knob.

Locked.

Of course, it couldn't be that easy. He gripped his weapon and brought it up to sight. The adrenaline surged, and he took a deep breath before nodding to Blade.

Officer Salas stomped up the steps. He rammed the sledge into the door and ducked back. The wood splintered with a crack and burst open an inch, stopped by a brass security chain.

Corbin put his shoulder to it. The metal plate tore from the jamb, freeing the door.

Following the barrel of his pistol, he slipped inside and stood with his back to the wall. "Police! If anyone's in here, come out with your hands in the air!"

His vision sharpened, scanning the small kitchen and sparsely furnished living room for immediate threats.

Nothing.

In two heartbeats, Blade, Luna, and Salas crossed the threshold and walked inside the darkened house.

The floor plan was simple. Living room on the right. Small dining area followed by a kitchen on the left. A long, dark hall straight ahead divided the house down the middle. Four closed doors likely concealing three bedrooms and a bathroom.

Corbin covered the front while the other three disappeared down the hall to clear the bathroom and bedrooms. He stepped into the kitchen.

The sink had a hand towel draped over the top, probably hiding a stack of dirty dishes. Two of the four kitchen chairs sat cockeyed as if the last people sitting there didn't bother pushing them back under the table.

A quick sweep of the kitchen revealed no place to hide. No basement door. No trapdoor. Just a grimy linoleum floor and peeling wallpaper. A doorway beyond the kitchen led to a cramped mudroom. Old avocado-green washer and dryer units stood side by side against one wall. He checked the washer. Empty. The dryer too.

The shelves above the laundry units were lined with cleaning supplies. He spotted a can of charcoal lighter fluid on a shelf above the washer, tipped on its side. Reckless. A fire waiting to happen.

An ice chest held a few empty two-liter soda bottles. He nudged the overflowing laundry basket with his foot. Nothing.

The back door had a small window covered with faded floral curtains. He peered out at the overgrown yard. A chain-link fence sagged in the distance, choked by weeds. Officer Gordon picked his way around the rusty lawn chairs.

Shouts of "Clear!" rang through the house, extinguishing any hope that Stryker was here.

He turned from the mudroom and moved back through the kitchen, stepping into the living room just as Blade stalked over and holstered his weapon. "It's empty. No signs of Stryker or anyone else."

Corbin clicked his own gun away. "I guess Abercorn would be stupid to use his own name and address when he purchased the Taser cartridges."

"If it weren't for stupid criminals, I might be out of a job," Blade said.

"Hold on a sec!" Salas called out. "Y'all better come see this."

He followed Blade down the hall as Luna emerged from the back bedroom. They crowded the hallway near the small bathroom.

The light was off. In fact, all the lights in the house were off, and the windowless room made it darker. He made out the shapes of bottles of cleaning solution, a small can of paint thinner, and several two-liter bottles standing upright in the bathtub.

A meth lab.

That explained the lighter fluid and plastic bottles in the mudroom. Abercorn was cooking meth, not kidnapping old men.

They needed to get out. Now.

"I can't see a thing." Blade reached for the wall switch.

"Wait! Don't touch—"

Too late. A single yellow spark spat from the empty socket above, igniting a line of fire that streaked across the ceiling.

Booby trap.

"Out! Out! Everyone out!" Blade yelled, shoving Luna toward Corbin.

Luna stumbled into the hall and stood there. Wide-eyed. Unmoving. Mesmerized by the blue-white glow zipping along the lines of fuel. It hit the wall beside her in a burst of orange.

"Luna! Let's go!" Corbin snapped his fingers in her face. She blinked and jerked to attention. For some reason she still wasn't moving. Something about the fire had her rattled.

He grabbed her arm, tugging her toward the front of the house. The flames racing toward the living room illuminated S-shaped streaks of wetness all around them. The couch. The curtains. The walls. The carpet.

Everything soaked with . . . "Accelerant!" Corbin roared.

In seconds, the entire room was ablaze. Flames devoured the curtains, leaving only pillars of fire licking up the picture window's frame. Accelerant-soaked, the couch roared into a blazing mass. The ceiling above cracked and gave way. Plaster and wood crashed down in a wave of fire and debris over the front door. Embers scattered across the floor.

Their exit choices shrank.

But the fire set to trap them here was nothing compared to what was cooking in the bathroom.

Luna gasped. A circle of fire bloomed around her feet, biting at her ankles. She slapped at the flames with her palms. He spun her around. Shoved her toward the dining room. Darted to the kitchen. Snatched the towel from the dish pile. Back at her side, he beat the flames down, fast and hard, until they died.

"My back! My legs!" Salas shrieked. "Get it off! Get it off!"

Corbin looked up. Saw Blade beating the flames off Salas with his hands. They had to get out of here.

He grabbed a nearby dining chair and hurled it through the window. Glass shattered. "Blade, get Salas out! We're right behind you!"

Blade grabbed Salas's arm and hauled him over his shoulder. They disappeared into the smoke.

He turned to Luna. "Now for—"

The explosion was instantaneous. A deafening roar. A blistering heat. The shock wave lifted him off the floor. He flew backward through the air and slammed into something hard. Pain shot through his shoulder.

Everything went black for a second. He coughed, struggling to clear his vision and the ringing in his ears. His hand touched something smooth and solid. Wood. A table.

The fire. The explosion.

"Luna!"

"Right here," she said from beside him.

He shoved himself up on his hands and knees, biting back the pain in his shoulder. They'd been thrown into the kitchen. The force of the blast must have flipped the table, shielding them from the worst of it.

"You okay?"

"I think so." She was shaky, but at least she was conscious.

Thick smoke filled the air, forcing him to fight for each breath. He pushed the table away and scanned Luna. Soot smudged her face, but he didn't see any other injuries. He hauled her to her feet, his arm tight around her waist.

The dining room ceiling groaned and cracked. A section collapsed in a shower of sparks and burning debris. The window exit was gone.

"The back door!" Luna pointed. "Gordon's out there!"

He could see Officer Gordon through the small window in the back door, smashing the glass with his baton. He was reaching through the broken pane, fumbling with the lock.

A wall of fire surged toward the mudroom, licking at the shelves above the washer and dryer. The heat intensified.

A fireball erupted from the mudroom in a flash of heat and orange light. Corbin yanked Luna down and shielded her body with his own as fiery shrapnel of plastic and wood sprayed across the room.

The back door was open now, but the mudroom was an inferno. No way was he risking that exit.

"The window!" He gestured to the one above the kitchen sink. "Can you climb?"

She nodded and scrambled onto the counter. He pushed the window open.

A tight squeeze, but she managed to wriggle through.

"Luna! Grab my hand!" Blade boomed from below.

A hand reached up, and Luna disappeared into the smoke chasing her out the window.

Corbin boosted himself up. His injured shoulder screamed in protest. Following Luna, he squeezed halfway through the opening and glanced down. The ground seemed miles away.

His shoulder throbbed. Pain radiated down his arm, but he had to get down.

He jumped, landing hard. Legs shaky. He stumbled and collapsed on the weedy lawn. A uniformed officer used a blanket to smother the flames on his back.

Salas was on the sidewalk with Blade and other officers working to get his shoes and vest off. Patches of his pants had burned away. He writhed and moaned.

Corbin couldn't look. He returned his attention to the house. The flames roared with a hungry fury, consuming the structure.

Sirens wailed in the distance, but he didn't think there would be much left by the time the firemen doused the structure. Any evidence of Stryker being held captive here was now lost to the flames.

Luna shrugged out of her tactical vest and lowered herself to the ground. She sat so close beside him that their shoulders touched. Ash and soot smeared her face. She rested her arms on her knees. Smoke wafted from her shoes.

"How's that for a welcome home?"

She coughed a laugh. "Baptism by fire?"

"Literally." They sat watching the house burn. His stomach knotted as he thought about Luna's legs on fire. In that moment, his brain controlled his body without him thinking. Now he hated himself for even letting her be there in the first place. But this was his shot. His one chance to tell her what he'd been holding on to all these years. He just had to work up the courage to say it. "You sure you're okay?"

"I'm a little toasty, but I'll be okay." She nodded at the flaming house. "Someone set a trap for us. Doused everything in lighter fluid."

"The fire moved too hot, too fast. Lighter fluid doesn't do that. This was something else, something highly volatile."

"That's above my pay grade," she said.

He offered a half-hearted smile. They were talking around what had really happened in there. How she'd been paralyzed by the fire and unable to move. He wanted to ask about it, but the sirens made it impossible to hear. And if she told him it was classified, his head might explode.

Emergency vehicles screamed to a stop on the street behind them. They cut the sirens but left the red and blue lights whirring. First responders shouted commands and information, using their training to get the scene under control. Paramedics took over caring for Salas, and he heard Officer Gordon arguing with the paramedic about riding with Salas in the ambulance.

Corbin didn't move to get up. Instead, he watched Luna watching the fire. There was so much he wanted to say but nowhere to start. The mistakes of the past loomed over them like a shadow, but it wasn't time to shine the light there.

Not yet.

Luna turned her head and caught him staring at her. "What?"

Needles stabbed his throat. The pain wasn't from smoke inhalation. "We could've died in there."

She nodded.

"We could've died, and I never would've had the chance . . ." He ran a thumb over her cheek, wiping away a bit of the dirt.

The fact she didn't pull away was a good sign. Something had changed between them, and he had to say the words before the moment evaporated. "I just . . . I need you to know . . . I'm sorry."

Without a word, Luna shoved herself up with her palms and moved past him. Eyes cutting forward, she skirted around him, making sure to keep her distance. The heat of the fire on his face was nothing compared to the fury that radiated from her.

Like a chump, he just sat there. Watched her weave through the crowd of gawking onlookers, shaking her head.

Perfect. He'd taken a risk. Opened up. And Luna had walked away. Again.

Maybe some bridges were simply too damaged to ever be rebuilt.

7

SORRY? HE WAS SORRY? She shook her head as she ordered her Uber because she couldn't believe those three words were supposed to make up for abandoning her all those years ago.

The last time Luna had set foot in Millie Beach she was a teenager with dreams as vast as the ocean. She'd spent her years since vowing never to return. Now she remembered why.

This place was a magnet for regret. A breeding ground for heartache.

Even the crimes here were laced with a desperate, reckless edge. Meth labs booby-trapped to destroy evidence and take out anyone who got too close? That was some twisted logic born of addiction. A maladaptive defense mechanism to protect themselves at all costs—even if it meant taking innocent lives.

A sharp twinge shot through her ankle. She stopped and leaned against a nearby palm tree. Her hand reached to rub the sore spot, but she stopped herself. The denim, charred and stiff, clung to the blistered skin beneath. She gingerly pulled up the leg. A bright red burn, angry and raw, marked her skin.

Great. Just great. Now she had a burn to add to the list of regrets.

Singed hair. Possible smoke inhalation. Ex-boyfriend. And on top of everything else, she'd destroyed her new jeans.

She straightened, biting back a wince. The burn throbbed, a dull ache that radiated up her leg. She'd need to clean it, keep it covered. The last thing she needed was an infection.

Her gaze drifted toward the ambulance. The red and blue lights still flashed. Paramedics bustled around the open back doors. Maybe she should go back. Have the burn dressed. At least a thick gauze pad would keep her jeans from rubbing against the raw skin.

She opened the ride app and canceled the car she'd ordered to drive her back to her rental car at the gym. When she looked up, her eyes landed on a man walking toward her and the chaos behind her. He shuffled along, head down, shoulders hunched, wearing a sweat-stained sleeveless shirt that revealed sun-weathered arms and faded tattoos that continued up his neck. His worn jeans were caked with dirt at the knees, and his once-white tennis shoes had long ago surrendered to the permanent stain of St. Augustine grass. He looked familiar.

Abercorn. He walked through the gawkers held back by a line of police cruisers, their lights flashing, a silent barrier between the burning house and the rest of the world.

Then their eyes met.

He froze, his gaze widening. Then he turned and bolted like a rabbit darting for cover.

"Oh, snap." She bolted after him.

He was fast, rounding the block and weaving through yards. Arms pumping.

"Police!" The word burst from her. Stupid. That was the last thing he needed to hear. He'd run faster now. For sure.

Abercorn headed toward the narrow alleyway between two buildings.

He glanced over his shoulder, eyes wide with panic. He saw her. He stumbled, his foot catching on a loose piece of concrete.

Closer. She was closing in.

He reached the alleyway, a narrow chasm of shadows between two dilapidated buildings. He hesitated, glancing back at her, his eyes darting. Then he scrambled up a chain-link fence, the rusted metal groaning under his weight. He disappeared over the top.

She pushed harder, the pain in her ankle a white-hot fire. Metal scraped against her palms as she pulled herself up. On the other side, she gasped, her lungs burning.

Abercorn was already halfway down the block, sprinting across a busy street, dodging cars that honked their annoyance. She could hear tires squealing, a chorus of angry shouts.

Luna didn't hesitate. She followed him through the traffic, weaving between cars. A truck roared past, its horn blaring, the wind of its passage buffeting her. She could feel the heat of its engine, smell the diesel fumes.

She reached the other side, heart jackhammering. "Stop!"

Abercorn ignored her and scrambled up a dumpster positioned at the rear corner of the U-shaped motel building. He reached the top, hesitated, then jumped, grabbing the railing of the motel's second-story walkway. He dangled precariously for a moment, arms straining, before swinging his legs up and hauling himself onto the walkway.

Luna didn't hesitate. She scaled the dumpster, gagging on the stench of rotting garbage. From this vantage point, she could see Abercorn checking a door handle.

"Luna, what are you doing?" Corbin cut through the adrenaline-fueled haze.

She hadn't even heard him. He must have been chasing her, chasing Abercorn, since the house. "It's Abercorn! I saw him at the fire. He ran."

"Which way did he go?" Corbin hauled himself onto the dumpster beside her.

"Down there." She pointed toward a darkened doorway at the far end of the walkway. "Room 12, I think."

"Stay put. This is police business."

"I didn't chase him this far to watch from the sidelines." Luna launched herself at the railing.

"Luna, wait!"

She sailed through the air, the metal railing a blur. Her fingers grabbed the rusty steel. She swung her legs over, landing on the walkway with a jolt that sent a searing pain through her burned ankle.

Corbin landed on the walkway and pivoted to face her. "You shouldn't be here. You're injured."

"I'm fine. And I'm not staying here." She unsnapped her holster. "Let's go."

His gaze met hers. A flicker of... what? Respect? Admiration? "Just... try not to get yourself killed," he said.

She followed, her leg throbbing with each step. He drew his sidearm and approached the darkened doorway.

"Stay close," he said.

She didn't argue. Her hand brushed against his arm as they moved through the shadows.

They reached the doorway of room 12.

The door stood ajar, a sliver of darkness beyond. The sound of a woman's screams, high-pitched and frantic, spilled out onto the walkway.

Corbin didn't hesitate. He pushed the door open.

A woman, young, her blond hair a tangled mess, cowered in the corner of the room, her hands covering her face. Abercorn scrambled across the room, his back to them, flinging open the sliding glass doors that led to a small balcony. He was already climbing over the railing, his lean body silhouetted against the bright afternoon sky.

"Go around!" Luna shouted, pointing toward the metal staircase at the end of the walkway.

Corbin didn't need to be told twice. He sprinted outside. She heard him crashing down the stairs, the clang of metal echoing through the courtyard.

The air inside the motel was stale, thick with the smell of mildew and cigarette smoke. The sound of a television, a muffled drone, drifted from one of the rooms.

Abercorn was halfway down the balcony railing now, legs dangling, desperation etched on his face. He hesitated for a moment, glancing down at the drop.

"Don't do it, Charles."

He let go. Abercorn hit the sandy ground with a thud, rolled, and scrambled to his feet.

She went over the railing. Didn't climb down. Jumped. The landing sent fire through her ankle, but she lunged at Abercorn anyway, tackling him to the ground.

"What the... hey! I didn't do nothing!" He twisted beneath her.

"Oh yeah? Then why'd you run?" She grabbed a wrist and wrenched it behind his back.

His free elbow jabbed her ribs. Pain shot through her chest, and she lost her grip. He rolled away, scooped up a handful of sand, and flung it at her face.

Sand stung her eyes, scratching at her corneas. Blinking hard, she tried to clear her vision. Through the blur, she saw him scrambling between two parked cars, his skinny frame disappearing into the maze of metal.

She wasn't giving up. She sprinted toward a rusty pickup truck, scrambled onto the hood, and used it as a springboard to launch herself into the air.

She landed on Abercorn's back, driving him face-first into the asphalt. He used her momentum against her, rolling them both until he was on top, her arms trapped beneath his weight.

"Got him!" Corbin's strong hands closed around Abercorn and yanked him to his feet.

For a moment she lay there, chest heaving, sand stinging her eyes. She wiped the grit from her face.

Corbin pulled Abercorn's arms behind his back and clicked the cuffs shut on his wrists. He patted Abercorn down. A brisk, efficient search for hidden weapons.

Luna looked up at Corbin and saw his grim face, his jaw working. He stared down at Abercorn and his eyes blazed with an intensity that both thrilled and terrified her.

She'd never seen this side of him before.

And she wasn't sure what it meant.

"You're under arrest," Corbin growled. He began reading Abercorn his rights. He sounded like he'd done it a million times.

She watched him, her heart still pounding against her ribs. He was different now. The boy she'd known, the one who'd held her hand under the bleachers, the one who'd whispered promises in the darkness of the gym, he was gone. Replaced by this . . . this stranger. This cop.

The required Miranda warning finished, Corbin looked her up and down. His cop eyes cataloged every inch, searching for injuries she probably didn't even know she had. "You okay?"

"I've been worse." She looked away, unable to meet his gaze all of a sudden.

"I need to take him in," he said. "You want to ride with me?"

Ride with him? Spend more time trapped in a car together? She couldn't do it. He may have earned a little respect back there, but he still had a long way to go.

She was robbed of a response by the black SUV that slammed to a halt behind her. The door flew open.

A man in a dark suit hopped out. Tall. Broad shoulders. Silver hair slicked back. Face flushed. "King!" He stormed to Corbin. "You better have a good explanation for defying a direct order!"

Commissioner Jeffery Tinch. Corbin's boss. She'd done her research. His words boomed in a tsunami of anger that crashed into Luna. She took a step back.

Corbin stood stiff. Shoulders squared. "Commissioner. Sir, I—"

"You, you what?" A vein throbbed at the man's temple. "My daughter is missing, and you're out here chasing down some two-bit meth head? And Salas? Burned half to death!" His gaze snapped to Luna, eyes like ice. "And I suppose this is the civilian you brought along and nearly got killed on your unauthorized operation."

Corbin flinched. He still didn't look at her. "Broward County asked FDLE for additional resources and—"

"Don't give me that, Agent!" Tinch's words came like a whip crack. "We both know you're freelancing on this. Playing hero for your old pal Stryker. I get it. He's like family. But my daughter is family too. I gave you a direct order. Carlie is your only priority. Period. I don't care if the Mother Mary herself is missing, you understand?"

"Yes sir. But sir, Stryker is a good man." Corbin stood tall, meeting Tinch's gaze. "He's helped a lot of people, including me. I couldn't just stand by and—"

"I understand your loyalty," Tinch cut him off again. "But right now, your loyalty belongs to this case. To my daughter. You will drop everything else and focus on finding Carlie. Is that clear?"

"Crystal clear, sir." Corbin motioned toward the patrol car where two officers were loading a handcuffed Abercorn. "Can I just wrap things up here? Then I'll be back on Carlie's case, no distractions."

"He can work both, sir." Luna stepped forward, meeting Tinch's gaze. "With my help."

Tinch's eyebrows dropped low. "And why would I allow that? I have no idea who you are or why King would even think of bringing you in on this."

She met his stare, channeling the confidence that had served her well in countless interrogations. "I recently resigned from a federal agency. The details are classified, but I can assure you my background and skills are appropriate."

"You invited a federal agent into this case without talking to me?"

"No, sir." She didn't give Corbin a chance to respond. "I offered my services. I was present during the execution of the search warrant this afternoon. As a consultant."

"A consultant." Tinch jerked his chin up. "And who's paying for this?"

"I'm not charging a fee. I'll work with Blade—" She caught herself. "Detective St. James's task force on the kidnapping case, and I'll help King find your daughter." She held Tinch's gaze. "My former supervisor can vouch for my credentials. If you'll give me your number, I'll have him call you."

Corbin shook his head. "Sir, I don't need—"

"I don't want to hear it. You brought her along in the first place," Tinch said. "Do you have any idea how much trouble you're in right now? You disobeyed a direct order. I could have your badge over this."

"Sir, I know how much this hurts," Luna said. "Believe me, I do. I lost someone too. Someone I'd do anything to find." A daughter she hadn't seen in eighteen years, and now . . . Stryker. "I wouldn't be here if I didn't think I could help. Let me help you bring her home."

Tinch studied her for a long moment. He reached into his pocket and pulled out a business card. He seemed to like the idea of an extra investigator at no cost to his budget.

Luna reached for the card he held between his first two fingers, but he pulled it back and said, "I expect a call in the next hour. Until then, if you so much as breathe on a police cruiser before I clear you, I'll throw you in jail so fast your head will spin. Understand?"

"Yes, sir. I understand how to follow orders. Maybe some of us understand that better than others." She couldn't resist a little dig at Corbin.

Tinch held out the card again. "Good. Then we understand each other."

"Thank you, sir." Corbin said as Luna accepted the business card. "I'll keep an eye on her until I hear from you."

"Don't push it, King." Tinch walked to his vehicle, opened the door, and got in.

Corbin waited until Tinch drove away before he spoke. "What was that all about?"

"What does it look like?" She slid the card into her pocket. "I'm helping you. Unless you'd rather face Tinch's wrath alone?"

He ran a hand through his hair, his expression frustrated. "I don't get you, Luna."

The officer who'd loaded Abercorn into the patrol car approached them. "Taking him to the station. Need a ride?"

"Yes," Corbin said at the same time Luna said, "No."

Corbin frowned. "What?"

"I've got a call to make," she said, already pulling her phone out of her pocket. "Besides, if I so much as breathe on a police car, remember? I'll just walk back to Abercorn's place and catch a ride from there." And maybe have someone look at that burn. She glanced down at her ankle. The denim was stiff and wet. She was guessing it wasn't sweat.

"You sure?" Corbin gestured. "It's not exactly the safest neighborhood."

"Clearly." She laughed. "Yeah, I'm sure."

She turned and walked away, rubbing the burn of sand out of her eyes. She could feel his gaze on her, but she didn't look back. He was trying. She could see that. But it wasn't enough.

She wasn't ready to forgive him. Not yet.

Maybe never.

8

CONSCIOUSNESS CREPT IN SLOW, like waves lapping at the edge of his mind. Stryker clawed his way back to awareness, his mind sluggish and uncooperative. Something was wrong. Very wrong. He tried to move, but his body refused to respond. Limbs heavy. Unresponsive. Why couldn't he move?

Focus. Assess the situation.

He was lying down. That much he could tell. Something hard and cold beneath him. Concrete? The chill seeped into his bones, intensifying the dull ache that permeated his entire body.

His arms. Behind his head. Bound. The bite of rope against his wrists. Expertly tied. No give when he tested them.

Darkness pressed in from all sides. He blinked. Once. Twice. No change. A blindfold? No . . . the air felt open against his face. Just darkness then. Wherever they'd taken him, there was no light.

They. Who were *they*? Shards of memories flurried in his mind. Oh, yes. The Taser. A burst of pain. Blackness.

How long ago? Minutes? Hours? His sense of time was shot.

A metallic taste coated his tongue. Blood. His own? Probably. His nose throbbed, likely bruised. Sand. He tasted sand too. Gritty between his teeth. Near the coast? An abandoned building?

He tried to lift his head. Bad idea. Nausea rolled through him, threatening to empty his stomach. They must have given him some kind of drug, then. Sedative. That would explain the heaviness in his limbs, the sluggishness of his thoughts.

Think. What's the last thing you remember?

The SUV. Dark and nondescript. Rough hands grabbing at him. Dragging him inside. A blur of faces, all unfamiliar. The hypodermic needle. After that, nothing. Until now.

The note. Five words that had turned his world upside down. *They're watching. Don't trust anyone.*

He should have listened. Should have been more careful. This wasn't the way. Captured. Helpless.

No. Not helpless. Never helpless. Never hopeless.

Stryker forced himself to take a deep breath. Then another. Slow. Steady.

Control your breathing. Control your mind.

He had to figure out where he was. And most importantly, how to get out.

Luna. Was she safe?

He'd thought he had more time, had planned to—

A sound. Faint, but there. Stryker held his breath. Strained to hear. A creak. Metal on metal. A door opening?

Footsteps. Slow. Deliberate. Getting closer. His muscles tensed involuntarily, preparing for . . . what? He was bound, drugged. Defenseless.

No. Focus. Gather information. It's all you can do right now.

Light pierced the darkness, a thin sliver that felt like a knife to his eyes. He flinched against the sudden brightness. A silhouette blocked part of the light. Tall. Lean. Male, most likely.

The figure moved closer. Details came into focus. Thin face. Glasses. Neatly combed hair with touches of gray. He looked . . . ordinary. Like someone you'd pass on the street without a second glance. More like an accountant than a kidnapper. He should know this man but couldn't quite place him.

A scraping sound. Something being placed nearby. Metal legs on concrete. A table? His pulse thrummed. What was coming next? *Breathe. Stay calm. Don't show fear.*

"You were warned to stay away." The words came soft. Almost gentle. Paternal. "To mind your own business. I'll never understand why people don't listen." He made a *tsk tsk tsk* sound.

Stryker swallowed, his throat dry and scratchy. Recognition flickered through his foggy mind. The man in black from outside the gym who'd growled at him to back off. The warning had been delivered then. Now came the consequences.

"Why are you doing all this?" He sounded weak. Pathetic. He hated it.

"Well, that's . . . that's a longer story than you and I have time for right now." A smile. Empty. Macabre. "I'm afraid I have other, more pressing matters to which I must attend."

A rustling sound. Something being unrolled. Then the glint of metal caught Stryker's eye.

Scalpels. Forceps. Clamps. Tools meant for healing, about to be used for harm.

He had to stay calm. Had to think.

Don't let him see you break.

"You see, some of us know our purpose." The man picked up a scalpel, testing its edge. He leaned in close. His breath hot. Fetid. "I, for one, choose not to waste valuable time—or resources—when it comes to fulfilling my purpose."

The scalpel traced along Stryker's skin. A feather-light touch that promised pain. He drew back as much as his restraints would allow. "Stop playing games. If you're going to kill me, do it. If not, just tell me why you're keeping me here. Tell me what you plan to do."

At this, the man lifted the scalpel away from Stryker's face. "I already have what I want." He didn't smile, but his eyes gleamed with amusement. "I have your heart."

9

CORBIN STILL DIDN'T GET IT. One minute Luna was walking away, furious with him. The next, she was all but throwing herself at his boss, begging to be part of his case. And now? Now, thanks to her and a top-secret phone call between their bosses, Luna Rosati was his temporary partner. Until further notice. Direct orders from Commissioner Tinch himself.

The sting of Luna's rejection back at the fire was deeper than any burn the flames had left. Okay, so maybe "I'm sorry" wasn't the most eloquent apology. And maybe the timing was off, what with the house still smoldering behind them and paramedics tending to a burned Salas. But at least he'd said it. He should get a little credit for that.

Salas though... Corbin had seen the burns, the blistered skin. Heard the man's screams as they loaded him into the ambo. They'd walked into a trap. Plain and simple. If it hadn't been for God's grace, they'd all be dead. But it didn't change the fact that Salas was lying in a hospital bed, fighting for his life.

The Millie Beach Sheriff's Department interrogation room was small, cramped, and smelled like a mixture of urine and bleach. Corbin's nose wrinkled at the stench. He could feel Luna's presence on the other side of the one-way mirror, watching him. Watching Abercorn.

Charles Abercorn, a scrawny man with more tattoos than teeth, slouched at the table. Handcuffs bound his thin wrists to the metal ring bolted to the table. A sheen of sweat glistened on his shaved head. His bloodshot eyes darted back and forth like a cornered dog. Nervous or high?

Corbin leaned against the mirrored wall with his arms folded. His injured shoulder throbbed, and he shifted, trying to find a more comfortable position.

Blade sat across from Abercorn and tapped his pen on the table. "All right, Charles. Let's start with something simple. Where were you this morning?"

Abercorn's eyes narrowed. "Why? What's it to you?"

Corbin almost rolled his eyes. Why did they have to go through this with every single suspect? "Just answer the question."

"I was at work, all right?"

"Where's this job?" Pushing his drugs on the corner, probably.

"I work landscaping around town."

That surprised Corbin. Most meth addicts were incapable of holding down a job, especially something that involved early hours and physical labor. "What's the name?"

"It's a small crew. Just me and Juan, and our boss Mr. Sánchez."

Blade paused his writing. "Does Mr. Sánchez have a first name?"

"Ernesto. Ernesto Sánchez." Abercorn tried to throw his hands up, but the shackles caught. "Look, you can call him. I'll give you his number."

"What time did you go to work?" Corbin asked.

"Started around six this morning, finished around noon." Abercorn rotated his wrists, and Corbin could see the red lines where the metal bit into his skin. "I left my house at five thirty this morning 'cause I gotta walk. Lost my license a while back."

Corbin glanced at Blade. A quick phone call should confirm that.

Blade pressed on. "And after your morning shift?"

"Mr. Sánchez dropped me off at Waffle House up on the corner. I was walkin' straight home from there. That's when I saw my house on fire!" Abercorn banged his fists on the table as much as he could. "You burned my house down and then you guys arrested me. For nothing!"

"For nothing?" Corbin laughed. "You call cooking meth in your bathtub 'nothing'? You call rigging your house with a trap to start a fire that could've killed four officers 'nothing'? You're lucky we're not charging you with attempted murder."

"Meth? What?" Abercorn yanked his hands toward his lap, but the chain caught again. "No. No way, man. I wasn't cookin' meth. I don't even know how!"

Corbin and Blade exchanged a quick glance. Either this guy was lying, or someone had planned to take care of Abercorn and make it look like a meth lab explosion.

Blade said, "You saw the police cars at your house, and you took off running."

"Innocent people don't run," Corbin said.

Abercorn shifted in his seat. The cuffs rattled. He looked down at the table. "I . . . I panicked, okay? I didn't know what to do."

They let the moment stretch a few more seconds.

Blade tapped his pen on his chin. "Okay, let's talk about those Tasers."

Abercorn's gaze snapped to Blade. "What Tasers?"

"The ones you purchased with a prepaid gift card three weeks ago."

Abercorn swallowed, his Adam's apple bobbing above the collar of his stained T-shirt. "I don't know what you're talking about."

Blade leaned back. Corbin heard the chair creak beneath his weight. "We have the receipts, Charles. We know you bought those Tasers. We know where you bought them. We know when you bought them. Now, why don't you save us all some time and tell us why you needed three Tasers?"

"I told ya," Abercorn said. "I didn't buy no Tasers. You cops are crazy! Burned down my house for nothin'! I'm gonna sue!"

Corbin straightened, pushing away from the mirrored wall. This was going nowhere fast. Time to rattle his cage. "Cut the bull, Abercorn. You're not telling us anything." He thumped Blade on the shoulder. "C'mon, might as well just throw him in lockup and be done with it. Let the Feds take care of this."

Abercorn's eyes widened. He looked from Corbin to Blade. "The Feds? What for?"

"A Taser was used to kidnap someone this morning, Charles. We traced the serial number on one of the AFID dots to you." Blade kept that soothing tone, and Corbin admired his ability to compartmentalize. To navigate anything life or their job threw at him with a calm exterior.

"Let me break it down for you." A wave of stale cigarette smoke and sweat wafted off Abercorn as Corbin walked behind him. "We've got you on conspiracy to commit kidnapping, aggravated assault, unlawful restraint, and use of a weapon during the commission of a felony. That's just for starters."

Blade nodded, picking up the thread. "Don't forget potential charges of false imprisonment, and interfering with a 911 call if the victim tried to use his phone. Oh, and since this happened right outside a restaurant, we could add endangering public safety to the list."

"Plus," Corbin added, "if he was injured in any way during this little stunt, we're looking at aggravated battery charges too. And if he crosses state lines? Now we're in federal territory with interstate kidnapping."

The handcuffs clanked against the ring welded to the center of the table as Abercorn fidgeted. Corbin saw the torn edges of the man's cuticles, the surrounding skin frayed and bleeding where it had been worried away.

Blade tapped his pen on the table again. "All told, you're looking at multiple felonies. We're talking decades in a maximum-security prison, Charles. Decades. And that's if the victim is found alive and well. If something's happened to him . . ."

"Then I guess you'll only have one choice, Charlie boy." Corbin slapped him on the shoulder. "Electrocution or lethal injection."

Abercorn twitched and wiped his cheek on his shoulder. Good. He was sweating now.

Corbin straightened. "So you can keep playing dumb and we'll throw the book at you. Every. Single. Charge. Including manufacturing a controlled substance and reckless endangerment for turning your house into a hazard. And you can wait it out in county for the next few years. Or you can start talking. Tell us what you know, and maybe—just maybe—we can work something out with the DA."

Abercorn's eyes darted between Corbin and Blade, his breath coming in short, rapid bursts. "I . . . I can't."

"Charles, Charles." Blade shook his head and took his time tucking his pen in the inner pocket of his blazer. "We've laid out what you're facing. Now's your chance to help yourself out. What's it gonna be?"

"Fine." Abercorn licked his dry lips. "I didn't use the Tasers, okay? And I don't know nothin' about a kidnapping. I traded 'em."

Blade leaned forward. "Traded them for what, Charles?"

"Drugs. Pills, man." Abercorn dropped his gaze to the table. "I needed a fix, and I was out of cash."

"I'm not buying it," Blade said. "Why buy pills when you have all that meth cooking in your bathroom?"

Abercorn was shaking his head before Blade finished the question. "I told you, man. I wasn't cookin' no meth. I don't touch the stuff. It's oxys I need. Ever since my car wreck, I can't function without 'em."

"So, you're telling me you traded police-grade Tasers for prescription pills?" Blade asked.

"Yeah, my script ran out and—"

"Hold up," Corbin said. "You had money for Tasers but not for pills? I'm no mathematician, but even I know that doesn't add up."

"No, man... You don't..." Abercorn groaned. "All right, all right. Here's what happened. I was hurtin' bad, you know? Needed my pills somethin' fierce. So, I asked around, see if any of my buddies knew where I could score. This friend of mine, he says he knows a guy who needs something done. The guy said he could trade me the pills I needed if I did him a favor. Said he needed some Tasers, but he couldn't buy 'em himself 'cause he'd never pass the background check. So, he offered to front me the cash, I buy the Tasers, and then we make the swap. I get my meds, he gets his Tasers without the paperwork. Seemed like a sweet deal at the time. I swear I didn't know about no kidnapping."

Corbin took a step closer. Abercorn reeked of a man in over his head. "Who's the guy you traded them to? We need a name."

Abercorn's head snapped up. Genuine fear filled his bloodshot eyes. "I can't... he'll kill me if I give him up."

"We can help you," Blade said. "But only if you give us something to work with. Who are these people?"

Abercorn shook his head. Sweat beaded on his forehead. "No, no, you don't get it. This guy... he's connected. He'll find me."

Corbin slammed his hand on the table, making Abercorn jump. "Listen, you little weasel. Right now, the guys who used your Taser are out there, free as birds, while you're sitting here taking the fall. Is that what you want? To go down for a kidnapping you didn't even do?"

"If they find out I talked, I'm dead."

Blade leaned in. "Charles, right now, you're the one facing serious charges. What do you think will happen to a guy like you in prison? The only way out of this is to help us. Give us something we can use."

Abercorn's eyes filled with desperation. He looked from Blade to Corbin, then back again. "I... I don't know, man. I don't know if I can do it." Abercorn was cracking. They were almost there.

Corbin leaned back against the wall, giving him some space. "Think about it, Charles. You help us, we help you."

Abercorn hesitated, his fear warring with the realization of his predicament. He let out a shuddering breath. "Okay . . . okay. I'll tell you. But you gotta promise me, you'll talk to the DA. If I give you the name, I get immunity."

Blade shook his head. "Can't promise that, Charles, but we'll do what we can. You have our word. Now, who did you trade the Tasers to?"

"It was a guy named Marco. Marco DeLuca. He's the one who wanted the Tasers. He's bad news, man. Real bad news."

"Did you physically hand the Tasers to Marco DeLuca?" Corbin asked.

Abercorn nodded, a little too quickly. "Yeah, yeah. Handed 'em right to him."

Corbin wasn't buying it. "All right, Charles. You've done the right thing. We're going to take a little break." He exchanged a look with Blade, who nodded.

"Sit tight." Blade's chair scraped back as he stood. "I'll call the DA and be back in a few minutes."

Abercorn slumped in his seat. "You better," he muttered.

Corbin stepped out of the interrogation room, Blade following close behind. The harsh glare of the hallway lights made him squint after the dimness of the interrogation room. He pushed through the door to the observation room.

Luna waited for them, standing with her arms crossed.

"What did you think?" He glanced back through the one-way mirror.

Abercorn shifted in his seat, pulling at the cuffs that bound his wrists, trying to find a more comfortable position.

"Who's this DeLuca guy?" Luna asked. "What do you know about him?"

"Marco DeLuca." Blade smirked. "That name gets tossed around more than a beach ball at a concert. Every two-bit crook from here to Miami claims he's involved, hoping they'll get credit for his arrest."

"His name comes up for good reason. He's bad news." Corbin had seen the files. The surveillance reports. The confidential informants whispering about a new player, someone moving in on established territory. Someone dangerous. "DeLuca's been on FDLE's radar for months. If he's made a move, this could be bigger than we thought."

"Sounds like we can't ignore it," Luna said.

Blade raised an eyebrow. "You really buying Abercorn's story?"

"Not completely," he admitted. "But we can't afford to ignore any lead. I'll call Major Drugs. They've had DeLuca under surveillance. They should know his every move."

"All right," Blade said. "Keep me in the loop. In the meantime, I'll let Charlie in there stew while I check his alibi for the kidnapping. Then I'll ask him who taught him to decorate his house with an accelerant and rig it to ignite." He paused, then his eyes softened. "How are you two holding up after that fire?"

"Shoulder's a little sore." Corbin flexed his fingers. They ached, the skin tender to the touch. Small burns, red and angry, marked his hands and arms. "And a few singed hairs, I think. Nothing major. You?"

"I'm a little crispy around the edges." Blade grinned and ran a hand over his hair. "Nothing a good conditioner can't fix."

Corbin glanced at Luna. "How about you?"

"No complaints," she said.

Tough as nails, just like he remembered. He noticed the scorched tips of her dark hair, the small cuts on her cheek and arms, barely visible beneath the soot. She was tougher than she looked. Tougher than he was, maybe. "And Salas?" He shifted uncomfortably, the cuts and scrapes on his arms and back protesting the movement.

Blade sighed. "He's got a long recovery ahead of him. Second- and third-degree burns. He's sedated and not allowed visitors because of the risk of infection. It sounds bad. Real bad."

"Does he have family nearby?" Luna asked.

Blade nodded. "Wife and two kids. Just moved here a few months ago. He was so excited to be closer to the beach. Took the kids surfing last weekend, I heard."

"Poor guy," Luna said. "This is going to be tough on them."

"How's your other case going?" Blade asked, shifting the subject. "Any leads on Carlie?"

A familiar tightness settled in Corbin's chest. "Nothing solid yet. Angie and Marge couldn't give me much. But . . ." He glanced at Luna. "Turns out I've got a new partner on the case now. At least for a while." He looked back at Blade. "I'm gonna get her up to speed. See if her fresh eyes can spot something I missed."

Luna remained silent, her expression unreadable, as she continued to observe them. What was she thinking? Was she regretting her decision to help? Or was she already planning her next escape?

"Oh really?" Blade tried to contain a grin. "Well, two heads are better than one, especially on a case like this. I'm glad you've got some help, brother." Blade nodded towards Luna. "Between the two of you, you'll figure it out." He headed out of the observation room and disappeared into the bustling hallway.

Corbin held the door. "Let me make that call to Major Drugs, see what we have on DeLuca. Then we can switch gears." He glanced at Luna and gestured for her to go first. "Time for your crash course on Carlie Tinch."

"I could use a shower and a change of clothes first. Do we have time?" Her gaze drifted to her soot-stained jeans.

He looked down. Fire had charred the denim around her ankles. He saw it then, the white bandage peeking out from the edges of the ruined fabric. "That burn..." He sucked air through his teeth.

She waved a dismissive hand. "It's fine. Just a little scorched. The EMTs gave me some antibiotic ointment. Should do the trick."

"Luna, it looked . . ." Bad. He swallowed the word. He'd seen enough burns in his life to know that one needed more than ointment. "Are you sure?"

"Positive. I've had worse." She met his gaze, a challenge in her eyes.

He nodded. Arguing was pointless. He glanced at his watch. Almost six o'clock. They'd be working late tonight, for sure. He could use something for his aching shoulder. And a shower too. She'd probably appreciate him washing off the grime and sweat. Maybe they could grab a bite to eat. He hadn't eaten all day and bet she hadn't either.

"Okay. Shower first. Then food. My treat." And then they'd talk about that burn again. "Want me to drop you at your hotel?"

"I haven't checked in anywhere yet." She seemed to notice how close she was walking beside him and stepped aside. "My car's still at the gym. Think I can shower there?"

"Yeah, sure." He wanted to suggest she stay with Tori tonight, but he'd already pushed enough. "I'll drop you then meet you at my office. Seven?"

He watched her for any sign of hesitation.

"Perfect."

Maybe this was it. Maybe this case would be the thing that kept her here. Kept her from running. He had a chance now. A chance to make things right. To show her he wasn't the boy who'd walked away all those years ago. He could prove to her, to himself, that he was capable of loyalty. Of commitment. Of love.

If he could keep her from bolting.

As she climbed into his car, he straightened his shoulders. Drew in a deep breath and pushed it out. He should stop focusing on his feelings for Luna and focus on doing his job.

Two cases, both with lives hanging in the balance.

And he was no closer to solving either of them.

10

LUNA SHIFTED HER WEIGHT, favoring her uninjured leg. She rocked back on her heel and launched her fist forward with all the strength she could muster. Her knuckles slammed into the worn leather heavy bag with a thud. The impact vibrated through her bones, but she welcomed the raw, stinging pain as a distraction from the knot of anxiety in her stomach.

An hour. That was all the time she had before she was back at his office, diving into the case, figuring out what she'd gotten herself into with the missing teen, Carlie Tinch. But first, she needed this. Needed to get the rage out.

Another blow, this time a knee that slammed into the bag with the rage of a trapped animal. "Sorry?" She gritted her teeth against the pain that shot up her leg. "He's just . . . sorry?"

A flurry of jabs followed, each one punctuated by a soft grunt. "After all this time, he can't expect 'I'm sorry' to erase everything."

Tori stuck her head around the heavy bag. "He did save your life, mija."

"Saved my life? He did not save my life. We were like, six feet from the front door."

Well, maybe Corbin had saved her life because all she could

remember was staring at the fire. Transfixed. The whole thing a blur of orange and red flames. The only clear image was a pair of strong arms shielding her. Pulling her back, away from the inferno. Arms that belonged to Corbin.

She wasn't about to go there. Too many emotions she wouldn't let surface. Except... anger. Anger, she could handle.

"I didn't need saving." She punched the bag. Softer. "I can take care of myself. Always have." A mantra she repeated to herself all too often.

"Girl, that's all of us. Look around." Tori stretched both arms out.

Luna glanced around the gym at the smattering of youths working out. A young woman, barely a teenager by the looks of it, shadowboxed alone in the corner. Over-the-ear headphones blocked out the world around her. Across the room, a wiry teenager with a mop of brown hair jogged on the treadmill. Two teens wrestled on the center mat, each grappling to pin the other.

She ran her tongue over her teeth. "Reminds me of us."

"See? We're all fighters here, thinking we have to fend for ourselves. Isn't that why this place exists? To teach us not just how to throw a punch but how to truly survive?" Tori set both hands on her hips.

"Yeah, well, some of us had to learn that lesson the hard way. Except Jett, Mr. Perfect Family." The one glaring exception in their ragtag group. The one who'd strolled into the program with a trust fund and a designer gym bag. She was pretty sure it was his father's donations that kept the program running. A far cry from the court-ordered reality the rest of them had faced.

"Yeah, well he's got abandonment issues just the same. Rich or poor. Doesn't change the fact that we all carry scars." Tori's eyes searched Luna's face. "My point is, this gym taught us to fight, yeah, but more importantly, to watch each other's backs. Didn't the Marines teach you that too?"

Tori was right, and that just made it all the more infuriating.

Jett was her friend, and just because he hadn't been sentenced to the program like the rest of them, it didn't mean he hadn't dragged around his own painful baggage. But unlike the rest of them, at least Jett had parents who wanted the best for him, even if they went about it in all the wrong ways. His father's relentless pressure was its own kind of prison.

She swiped a sweaty strand of hair from her face. "Speaking of having backs, shouldn't you be feeding my rage by telling me all the horrible things Corbin's ever said about me?"

"Oh yeah. Right. What a jerk." Tori looked amused. "How dare he apologize to you? Makes me wanna throw a lawn mower to his perfectly chiseled jaw." Tori demonstrated the upward elbow strike on the heavy bag.

"That was almost believable." Luna rolled her eyes and stepped back. She tugged at the Velcro on her gloves with her teeth and peeled them off.

She hadn't realized how much she'd missed this place, these people, until now. The ache in her chest was sharper than any punch she'd thrown at the bag.

"What's the plan?" Tori stuck her hand out, and Luna tossed the gloves to her.

"Now that I've gotten some of my frustrations out, I'm ready to help Corbin." She scooped her sweat-dampened hair behind her ears.

Tori's eyebrows shot up. "Whoa, hold on a minute. Am I getting whiplash here? Help Corbin? After all that . . ." She gestured toward the bag still swaying from Luna's assault.

"The commissioner showed up right after we arrested Abercorn. He was furious with Corbin for working Stryker's case and for letting me serve the warrant with the team. Threatened to take his badge." And she felt responsible. "Corbin's not supposed to be working on any case but this missing girl. I didn't realize."

"Me neither." Tori's brow furrowed. "I figure he's helping Blade because . . . well, you know. Stryker. But we're talking about the commissioner's daughter. Makes sense he'd want the best on it."

The best. Was Corbin really the best? She'd seen glimpses of it. The way he'd reacted in the fire, his quick thinking, his determination to get them out. The strength in his arms as he pulled her through the smoke. She would never have made it out of that house without him. The flames. The heat. The suffocating smoke.

There was a reason behind her deer-in-the-headlights moment. She just wasn't ready to face it.

She looked up, saw Tori watching her, and pressed on. "Anyway, I'm meeting him at his office. I'm going to help with the Carlie Tinch case."

"One minute you're ready to knock his teeth out, and now you're his partner?"

"If Corbin and I want on Stryker's case, we have to play by the commissioner's rules. So, I'm a consultant." She tilted her hands, palms up, like a waitress presenting an invisible tray. "I'd better get a move on. I have a feeling it's going to be a long night getting up to speed on Carlie's case."

"Sounds good, but maybe you want to shower first?" Tori wrinkled her nose. "You ripe, chica."

She had to laugh at that. "Yeah, yeah. I'll hose off before I offend the general public. I'm hitting the showers here then heading to his office."

"Why here?" Tori put a fist on her hip. "Wait, where are you staying? You got a hotel or something?"

She hadn't planned on staying at all. The idea was to find Stryker, get the information she needed, and disappear, all before lunch. "I, uh . . . haven't really figured that out yet. Haven't gotten a hotel or anything."

Tori's face lit up. "Perfect! You're staying with me. No arguments."

"I don't know . . ."

"Come on, it's close to the beach. Not far from Stryker's place. We can hang out, just like old times."

She hesitated. The thought of slipping back into her old life, even temporarily, made her stomach churn. She'd come here for one reason. To find her daughter. Now she was being pulled back into a world she'd left behind years ago.

But as she looked at Tori's hopeful face, she realized that maybe, just maybe, she needed this connection more than she wanted to admit.

"I appreciate that so much, but let me grab a hotel for tonight. I just need a little time to decompress on my own. But I'll definitely take you up on that offer tomorrow, okay?" If she stayed that long.

"All right, all right," Tori said. "I'm holding you to that."

They exchanged cell numbers, and a second later, her phone chimed with Tori's address.

"There's a code to open the front door and another for the alarm." Tori rattled off both codes. "Can you remember, or should I—"

"I'll remember." Especially since the letters of the four-digit code spelled "Luna."

"Now hit the showers 'cuz, girl, you smell like a fire and gym sweat combo." Tori thwacked her on the rear.

"Ow!" Luna laughed. "I'm going."

She grabbed her duffel and made her way to the locker room. The gym wasn't the only thing remodeled. A long mirror stretched across the wall above a wide counter, reflecting the soft, diffused light from the overhead fixtures. Below the mirror, four sinks lined the counter. A few scuff marks marred the walls, and the faucets had a slight tarnish, but it was a space that felt comfortable.

And the best upgrade? Instead of one huge, disgusting communal washroom with that weird brown slime forever growing in the corners, there were private shower rooms. Nothing fancy, though. Single stalls with draw curtains, towel hooks, and porcelain tile changing benches.

The steaming water sluiced over her aching muscles, and Luna let her shoulders slump. What was she even doing here? She was walking a dangerous line, getting close to the people she'd left behind. One lunch with Stryker. That was all it was supposed to be. In and out.

Except... she had missed her friends here. Her family.

All these years, she'd convinced herself that walking away from Millie Beach was the right thing to do. That running was the only way to protect herself. Wasn't that what everyone did when backed into a corner? Her own father had done it. A man whose face she'd never seen, whose voice she'd never heard. He'd disappeared before she was born, leaving her fifteen-year-old mother alone and pregnant.

Her mother's family had turned their backs too. "No daughter of ours," they'd said. So much for unconditional love.

Without support, her mother had been left to figure it out alone. Luna remembered the parade of men who came through their lives. Her mom's desperate attempt to fill the void her father had left. One man after another, each promising to be different. Each leaving another crack in her mother's heart that she'd try to seal with alcohol.

Luna's throat tightened at the memories. Those men with their wandering eyes, their lingering touches when her mother wasn't looking. The nights she'd lock her bedroom door and push her dresser against it, just in case.

By eight, she'd learned to steal. First food when the refrigerator was empty, then whatever she wanted. It wasn't like her mother noticed, lost in her own haze of pills and booze. The day she got caught shoplifting had been both the worst and best day of her life.

The judge had looked at her record, at her home situation, and instead of foster care, offered her Stryker's Warrior program. One last chance. She'd taken it.

Funny how darkly ironic it all was. That despite her promise to never be like her mother, history had repeated itself. Pregnant at sixteen, abandoned by the boy she loved. Except, she'd believed she and Corbin would make it work, that they'd build the family she never had. Instead, they'd all run from the weight of their actions.

But now, back in this place, surrounded by familiar faces and old memories, she felt that familiar itch. The urge to run, to disappear again before anyone could hurt her.

Before she could hurt anyone else.

But first, she had a case to solve. A missing girl to find.

11

AS LUNA SCRUBBED AWAY the sweat and smoke, she couldn't shake the feeling that she'd never be fully grounded, never be at peace, until she learned what happened to the daughter she'd given up.

Which meant she had to find Stryker. He held the key to everything. She'd signed the papers and handed her baby girl to Stryker. Trusted him to find a good home, a family who could give her daughter the life she never had. A life free from the abuse and neglect she'd known as a child.

She'd told herself it was for the best. That it was the only way to protect her baby girl. But the truth was . . . she'd been running. Running from the pain, the guilt, the overwhelming responsibility of motherhood without Corbin by her side. And she'd paid the price, every single day, with a gnawing emptiness that no amount of fieldwork or fabricated identities could fill.

Okay, enough navel gazing. The shower felt great, but had she even washed her hair? She couldn't remember. She did it again, just to be sure. She stepped out of the shower, toweled off, and covered her burn with a fresh bandage. She dressed in simple black jeans and an olive-green linen button down.

At the nearest sink, she opened her cosmetics bag. A few spritzes of surf hair product to enhance her natural curls and a dab of perfume because, man, she still smelled like a campfire. To finish, she swiped on a bit of blush and mascara and told herself it had nothing to do with being with Corbin tonight.

"Nice," someone said behind her.

Luna looked in the mirror at the teen who'd just entered. She was tall, with a swanlike neck and short, spiky hair. All sharp angles that matched the harsh stare. She wore combat boots and jeans with so many rips she was practically wearing none at all.

The teen folded her arms and leaned against the counter. "New transfer?"

Luna capped the mascara tube. "I'm sorry?"

"Clearly you're a cop, but I ain't seen you around here before. Figure you just got a transfer."

No one ever pegged Luna as a cop, and neither did this girl. She obviously just assumed any adult in the gym was law enforcement. The challenge in the girl's sharp gaze said she was exerting power. Showing Luna she wasn't afraid of her, or any authority figure for that matter.

Luna recognized that defiant light. That desperate need to prove she didn't need anyone's help or approval. Because she'd worn that same impenetrable armor herself, all those years ago. Still wore it, if she was honest.

"No. No transfer. Honestly? I can't get out of here fast enough." She dug around in her makeup bag and pulled out an unopened tube of shimmery lip gloss and offered it to the girl. "This looks like your shade. I never wear it. Want it?"

The teen eyed the makeup. Probably weighing the desire to own it against the debt she might owe for taking it. "So, what? You tryna buy me as a narc?"

Luna chuckled. "Not even a little bit, believe me. Here." She rolled the tube across the counter. "I've had it for a while and never even opened it."

After a second of hesitation, she took the tube. "Thanks."

"What's your name?"

"Liv. You?"

"Luna." She rummaged through her bag. Without looking up, she said, "First time I owned makeup of any kind, I was twenty-three." She hadn't planned on wearing eye shadow but found a palette with enough colors to stay talking to Liv. "I told myself I didn't like makeup. Didn't want to wear it. Truth was . . . it was a luxury I couldn't afford." She dabbed a brush into a shimmery cream base layer and took her time brushing it on a lid. "I mean, every penny counts when you're in this place, am I right?"

Liv's eyes snapped to Luna's in the mirror. "No way. You were—"

"A student here. Yeah. One of the first." Luna nudged her makeup bag to Liv. "Take whatever you want. I don't use 90 percent of what's in there. Actually, how about this . . ."

She dug out a few things—mascara, the lip gloss she'd worn today, two hair ties she slipped on her wrist, and that one very special contouring brush, a CIA special issue with a core of hardened steel disguised as soft bristles, because this girl did *not* need a concealed weapon. She slid the bag over to Liv. "All yours."

Liv's mouth fell open. Eyes glued to the designer bag and brain probably calculating how much she could get for it. "How do you know I won't sell it?"

"So sell it." Luna shrugged. "It's yours. What do I care?"

The makeup rattled as Liv dug around with a finger. She pulled out a blue eyeliner pencil. "Why?"

"That color? I know. Someone talked me into it—"

"No, I mean why would you give this to me."

Luna leaned her rear against the counter to face Liv. This was the moment she so often worked to reach with her assets. The moment she earned their trust.

But Liv wasn't an asset. She was a teenager court ordered to live here or go to a juvenile detention center. Same as Luna nearly . . . wow, was it really almost twenty years ago? "Look, I don't know your story, but if you're a student here, I can imagine. I've been where you are. Someone did something nice for me, and I'd like to do the same."

Liv closed the lid and zipped the bag with a delicate touch. "I won't sell it." She scooped it up. Two protective hands held it to her stomach like a mother protecting her unborn baby. "It's the nicest thing I've ever owned. Probably the nicest thing I'll ever own."

"That depends."

"Yeah? On what?"

"Where your focus is."

"My focus is on getting outta here ASAP."

"See, that's the problem. This place will give you everything you need to survive. Out there . . ." She lifted her chin in the general direction of the outside world. "You learn to survive on the streets. In here you learn to survive beyond the streets. You get an education that you won't get out there."

"I get that. But my friends—"

"True friends want what's best for you. They'll wait while you do your thing. If not, they aren't your friends." Luna nudged Liv with a soft elbow. "Meanwhile, follow the rules. Finish high school and read your Bible. Make friends with the LEOs working out here. Stay out of the streets, and most of all . . . stay away from boys."

Liv looked down. Her long lashes hid her eyes. "That's the easy part."

"Why's that?" Luna asked the question she already knew the answer to.

Liv's sharp shoulders hunched forward in a half shrug.

"No, really. Why'd you say that?"

"Guys ain't interested in me. Not like that."

"That's only going to make it harder."

Liv's brow furrowed. "That don't make no sense at all."

"Guys might not be looking at you right now, but one will come along. He'll pay attention to you. Make you feel new things. Secure. Understood. Appreciated. Things you probably missed out on as a kid. Things that will make you do almost anything to not lose that feeling. And you'll be so wrapped up in how you feel, you'll make decisions that could derail your life."

"That what happened to you?"

"I mean . . . yeah. Sorta."

Liv rattled the two-hundred-dollar vanity case. "Don't seem like it messed you up too bad. You're doin' all right."

"Don't mistake the value of this"—she tapped the bag—"for the value of this"—she patted Liv's heart with a flat palm.

Liv bobbed her head once. "I think I know what you're gettin' at."

"And remember that 'guys' aren't the same as men. Men are responsible, trustworthy, loyal. They provide for their families and stick by your side—you know what? I'm lecturing." Speaking about all the things she thought Corbin had been, but then he'd walked away from his responsibility. Dumped her. Like a guy, not a man. "Just . . . stay in line and work the plan. Listen to Stryker. He has your best interests in mind."

Liv released a puff of air. "Seems like the only one he cares about is that one girl who keeps running off. Like, she don't even want to be here, but he keeps chasing after her. Findin' her and draggin' her back."

"What one girl?"

"That girl with the frizzy hair. Can't keep her here."

"Why's that?"

"Oxy. It's got her so wrapped up she can't think about nothin' else. Always popping. Second night here, she got all itchy and slipped out to score."

And Stryker was chasing after her? His rules were pretty strict. You break them, and you're headed back to face the judge. Could this have something to do with why he'd been kidnapped? She wanted to pump Liv for more information, but she had to play it cool. They'd decided not to tell the students that Stryker had been kidnapped. "So what's the deal? Who's this runaway Stryker keeps chasing?"

"How would I know? When I'm not in school, I'm stuck here scrubbing toilets and being forced to do, like, ten thousand sit-ups and push-ups a day."

The response was more bravado. Trying to make it sound like this place meant nothing to her. Luna let it slide. "What's she here for?"

Liv chewed the skin around her thumbnail. "I don't know. Same as all us, I guess."

Shoplifting. Fights. Prostitution. Drugs. "Street life."

"Uh-huh. Like I said, she keeps running off, though. Disappears for a few days, then Stryker walks her back in like nothing happened. Then I wake up in the middle of the night to see her sneaking out, then it's the same thing all over again."

"And Stryker just keeps going after her?"

Liv's head bobbed. "Five, six times already. It's weird cuz he's way stricter with everyone else. But it's like he knows her, you know? Like, knew her for a long time, before all of this."

This was not like Stryker. He'd always said, if they didn't want to be in the program, they could leave. Return to the streets. Or juvie, in most cases.

Why was he so persistent with this one runaway? It had to be more than just the program. Had he known her before? Maybe she'd been through something... something that made him feel especially responsible for—

Luna's heart stopped. For a moment, she was too paralyzed to speak.

Was it possible?

No.

But then... maybe, just maybe.

She had to force herself to slow her breathing. *Keep gathering intel. Find out for sure.* "This girl," she asked. "How old is she?"

"Ain't like I carded her. How should I know?"

Luna almost rolled her eyes at the attitude but refrained. "If you had to guess."

"I dunno." She sucked air through the corner of her mouth until it squeaked. "Sixteen... seventeen? We're taking driver's ed together. She said she was behind because she'd missed so much school."

Or maybe eighteen. The age her biological daughter would be. "Missed school why?"

"Seriously, I'm so not her record keeper." Liv blew out a long breath. "I guess her parents died or something. I don't know! Look, I got my own life to worry about."

She'd annoyed Liv with all the questions about another girl and asking none about her. Luna had to press further, at least a bit. "What's this girl's name?"

"I barely talk to her. It's Tristan or... Treasure... No wait. Trinity. Yeah, that's it."

Trinity.

She rolled the name over and over.

"So this girl... Trinity, you said?"

Liv nodded.

"What's she look like?"

"Dark hair. Dark eyes." She scanned Luna toe to head. "Kinda looks like you, actually."

She clenched her toes together. A trick to avoid showing how fast her heart raced at Liv's words.

Could it be? The one reason she was here...

A teenage girl. And Liv said Trinity looked like her. But if she was Trinity's mother, where was her adoptive family? And why hadn't Stryker told her? Why hadn't he said her biological daughter was in the Warrior program?

All these years, she'd dreamed about the life her child lived without her. Loving parents who threw her elaborate birthday parties. Who tucked her into bed at night and read her stories in a room especially decorated for her. Who drove her to school and kissed her goodbye. Who provided for her so that she had clothes and food and never had to search for her next meal. Who kept her safe and protected.

But maybe . . . maybe she'd been wrong.

12

CORBIN TRACED HIS THUMB around the rim of the whiskey glass and stared into the golden liquid. Answers weren't at the bottom, but he searched there anyway.

His office was a mess. Stacks of files teetered precariously on his desk, evidence photos scattered across the corkboard, and empty coffee cups littered every surface. The only source of light was the desk lamp, casting long shadows across the room, making the space feel even smaller and more cluttered than usual.

This whole day had been a catastrophe. It wouldn't surprise him if he lost his job over it. His boss already had it out for him, and today . . . well, today was nothing but utter disaster.

He picked up the whiskey glass and swirled the liquid. Breathed in the woody scent and set it back down without taking a sip. He wanted the drink with an intensity that burned deep down. But he wouldn't drink it.

Self-control. He still had that.

He also had two people who'd disappeared in their hometown without a trace. His responsibility. Their lives, their families, their futures . . . all depending on him. And he was failing them.

His cell phone vibrated. Blade. "Hey, man."

"I wanted to update you on Abercorn," Blade said. "Got your new partner with you?"

Luna, he meant. "Not yet." The clock on the wall said she was almost fifteen minutes late. Or she'd decided not to come at all. "What's up?"

"Abercorn's alibi checked out. He was at work when Stryker was kidnapped. His boss confirmed they spent the morning on the grass trimmer at the hospital. Surveillance footage proved it. Me and Villanueva went at him hard, every which way, and the dude still swears he hadn't been cooking meth and hadn't rigged his house with the APD."

Anti-personnel device. The booby trap designed to take out anyone who tried to enter the house, with the bonus of destroying evidence. It was kind of genius. The accelerant ignited with a spark from the socket. "You believe him?"

"Jury's still out for me. I doubt he's smart enough to pull it off. I checked his arrests, and not one methamphetamine. Oxy is his drug of choice." Blade sighed. "He swears someone is setting him up to go down for manufacturing and trafficking."

"He's saying someone broke into his house and did this?"

"We're canvasing the neighborhood, pulling doorbell cams, all the usual. We'll see if a witness can corroborate his story. But there's more to bolster his claims," Blade said. "The lab found traces of a unique accelerant in the house. It's serious stuff. I'm texting you now."

"Bury the lead, why don't ya." He studied the chemical breakdown on his screen and exhaled. Diethyl ether. Extremely volatile. Extremely flammable. One spark. That's all it took. If it hadn't been the light switch, static electricity alone could've done it. That house had been a powder keg waiting to blow.

And someone had made sure it did.

"This stuff is serious firepower," he said. "What's it used for?"

Corbin could hear Blade shuffle papers. "Historically it was used as a general anesthetic until the sixties. It's been phased out because safer alternatives exist, but it's still regulated. Now it's primarily used as a solvent in chemistry and pharmaceutical labs and as a fuel additive. DEA keeps tabs on large purchases because it's a key ingredient in methamphetamine production."

"Abercorn's a landscaper, right? How would a guy like that even get his hands on diethyl ether? Don't you need some kind of license?"

"Exactly. Not something you can pick up at your local hardware store or garden center. You need proper credentials and established relationships with chemical suppliers, usually scientific or medical. We checked his background, and there's nothing that would give him legitimate access. Whoever sourced this either has connections or knows someone who does."

"So why would Abercorn torch his own house? It doesn't add up." Corbin hated the uneasy feeling crawling up his spine.

"That's what I'm saying. If he did this, he had help. But more likely, someone else did this to get rid of him."

"But who goes through that much trouble?"

"Someone trying to get rid of the man who bought the Tasers." Blade paused. "Or someone trying to send the police a message."

"What message? Stay away or get barbecued?" He glanced at the clock: 7:21 p.m. Luna still hadn't showed up. Maybe *she* was sending a message. That he was on his own to find Carlie. At least Blade had his back on the kidnapping case. "So, whoever kidnapped Stryker set Abercorn up after he sold them the Tasers?"

"That's our theory. We traced the AFIDs right after the kidnapping and they led us straight to Abercorn's door. If we'd shown up an hour later, he might've tripped that trap and been killed. Hard to question a dead man." Blade hesitated a beat. "Think about it. The timing, the elaborate setup . . . it screams professional job. And professionals don't work for free. Abercorn is scraping by, which means someone else is bankrolling this."

Abercorn was a small-time criminal with a pain pill problem, not a mastermind. Not someone with access to sophisticated chemicals.

Not someone who'd destroy his own property as an elaborate cover-up. This was big. They were dealing with a complicated operation, one with resources and planning that went far beyond what he'd initially thought.

New leads should have his blood pumping. Instead, his chest felt weighted with lead. The image of Luna's face, frozen in terror as flames danced around her legs, flashed before his eyes. He'd put her in danger. Put them all in danger. And now, time was slipping through his fingers.

Maybe Luna's undercover world had followed her back to Millie Beach. Maybe this wasn't just about Stryker. Maybe it was about her too.

"Hey, Corb? Still there?" Blade cut through his spiraling thoughts.

"Yeah. Just thinking." He swirled the glass of whiskey and set it down, watching the liquid tornado dissipate. "I should've taken more time to set up a full operation. Pulled in extra manpower. Pushed for tactical."

"And what? Let Stryker's trail go cold? We worked with the information we had."

Corbin's fingers drummed against his desk. "Maybe. But Luna . . . I shouldn't have let her come. The fire could've killed her."

"Ah, there it is. I was wondering when we'd get to the real issue."

"What's that supposed to mean?"

"Come on. I've known you too long. This isn't just about the case. It's about her."

He opened his mouth to protest, but the words died on his lips. Who was he kidding? Of course it was about Luna. It had always been about Luna.

Unbidden, a memory surfaced. Luna, fifteen and fierce. Her dark hair wild in the summer breeze. They were on the beach. Her laughter rang out, pure and unguarded, as he chased her through the surf. He'd caught her then, pulled her close, their laughter dying as their lips met for the first time. Sweet. Innocent. A promise of forever.

"I loved her, B... I loved her, and I messed it up." He took a slow, measured breath. "She was fire, and I was... well, I was trying not to be gasoline. She challenged me. Pushed me to be better. And for a while... I was."

Blade sighed. "We were kids. Dumb kids. We all made mistakes."

"Yeah, but my mistakes cost us everything. Our relationship, our..." He trailed off, unable to say it. Their child. The one they'd given up, the decision that had torn them apart.

The confession felt like ripping open an old wound. He closed his eyes, afraid of what Pandora's box he'd just opened in front of his friend.

"Have you talked to her? Really talked, I mean?"

Corbin snorted. "Yeah, right. She can barely look at me without wanting to bolt."

"Can you blame her? You both went through something traumatic. And instead of facing it together, you pushed her away."

The truth of Blade's words stung, but he couldn't deny them. He'd been terrified, overwhelmed by the idea of becoming a husband and father. Afraid he'd become just like his own dad one day. So he'd done what he thought was best. Stepped back. Told Luna he loved her but they weren't ready—he wasn't ready to marry her and start a family. He'd thought he was being mature by breaking up with her and agreeing to terminate his parental rights. By keeping his distance during the pregnancy so they wouldn't get attached to a child they wouldn't raise. Back then it seemed responsible even. But all he'd done was drive her away forever.

"I tried to apologize." The words sounded hollow even to his own ears. "After the fire. She just... walked away."

"Look, what I know about women wouldn't fill a thimble, but I do know one apology isn't going to fix years of hurt. You need to give her time. And space."

"But how am I supposed to do that when, thanks to her, we're stuck as partners? When every time I see her, all I want to do is . . ." How could he articulate the mess of emotions Luna stirred in him?

"Is what? Make things right? Or pick up where you left off?" He pictured Blade's penetrating gaze, seeing right through him, as always.

He ran a hand over his face, suddenly feeling every one of his years. "I don't know. I just . . . I don't know."

"Well, figure it out." There was a scratching noise and muffled words like Blade had covered his phone. "I gotta go. Your contact came through with info on DeLuca. I'll catch you up after we talk."

"Thanks." Corbin disconnected and dropped his phone on his desk. He'd almost forgotten about DeLuca, because, if he were honest, he couldn't see anything coming from it. There was ongoing surveillance that clocked the man's every move.

He closed his eyes and pressed his palms to his forehead. A dull pain throbbed in his temples. Tension headache, or mild concussion. Perfect.

The door creaked. His eyes snapped open.

"Corbin?" A gentle rap of a knuckle.

Luna stood in the doorway, one hand on the doorknob. She'd dressed simple, professional. Damp hair curled around her shoulders, a few ends clinging to the fabric of her shirt. He'd never noticed her long eyelashes before. Or the contour of her sunkissed cheekbones. He did know those lips though. The way the upper one had that tiny divot that looked like the M-shaped seagulls he'd drawn as a kid.

He caught himself. Glanced down. Waved her in. "Looks like you found me."

"Sorry I'm late." She pushed the door open and stepped inside. "Paperwork." She gestured to a photo identification card clipped to the small pocket on her shirt. A colored strip on the side signified her clearance as a special consultant. Weapon carry permissions.

"That call from your boss must have been impressive. I've never seen them move that fast."

"You know the federal government. Lightning fast." She pressed her lips together in a tightly coiled smile. "What are you doing?"

"Just . . . trying to make sense of this mess." He busied himself by thumbing through the stacked files, searching for the one full of handwritten notes he'd scratched out during countless interviews. "It won't take long to run you through what I have on Carlie. Truth is . . . it's not much. I could use a fresh perspective."

"I didn't know you drank."

He glanced up to see her eyeing the glass of whiskey still sitting on his desk. "I don't, actually."

"Could've fooled me."

"It's just . . ." He exhaled. "Just something I do. To prove to myself that I don't need it. That I'm in control."

"You only have one?"

"None."

Luna's eyebrow went up. "You pour it and never drink it?"

He nodded.

She took a slow step toward him. "Why do you torture yourself?"

He looked at his drink and worked his jaw. "I'm not—"

"Seems like a waste of money."

"You'd rather I drink it?"

"I'd rather you not be so masochistic." Luna dragged the empty chair around and sat down beside him. "Is this about your father?"

He let his eyes fall to the amber liquid. He could smell the oak. The spice. Feel that pull. The promise of numbing his emotions. "My father was an alcoholic. It ruined him. Ruined our family." He wasn't telling her anything she didn't know. Nothing the whole world didn't know. "He couldn't control himself, but maybe . . . maybe I can."

Once, he thought he could handle it. A drink here, a drink there. No big deal. Until it was. Until the anger he kept in check started slipping through the cracks. The night it all came to a head, he had been drinking. Too much. Too fast. Someone pushed him too far, and his fists were already swinging before he registered the fear in the guy's eyes. That was the moment. The moment he saw his father in himself. The moment he knew he was a breath away from becoming the man he swore he never would.

He blinked, shoving the memory back where it belonged.

"You think you're destined to follow the same path?"

He met her gaze, surprised by the lack of judgment in her eyes. "Don't you?"

She shook her head, her dark hair swaying. "No. I don't."

"You don't know me, Luna. Not anymore. You weren't there. You didn't see..." The shouting, the fights, the smell of whiskey on his own breath.

"I saw enough. I know what it's like to grow up with an alcoholic parent. My mom... she was sick. She needed help. But your dad..." She hesitated. "It was different, wasn't it? He wasn't just sick. He was... cruel."

"He terrorized us. My mom... me... criminals he'd arrested. Everyone." Corbin shifted in his chair, trying to find a position that didn't pull at the burns on his arms, then rested his forearms on his thighs. He took a slow, controlled breath. "I spent my life trying to be the opposite of him. Did everything I could to prove I'm not like him." He laughed. "Even changed my last name. I chose 'King' because of Stryker. The kind of man I wanted to be. Honorable. Trustworthy. Principled but compassionate." Everything his father wasn't. "I just... I don't want to hurt anyone. Not like my father did. I don't want to be him. I have to know I'm in control. No matter what."

She was quiet for a moment, her gaze fixed on his. "You're not him, Corbin. You're not."

He wanted to believe her. He wanted to believe that he could escape the shadow of his father, that he could forge his own path, one that led to redemption, to peace, to love.

"Look..." She leaned closer. "I know you've got this... this thing about your dad. You think you're doomed to repeat his mistakes. But that's not you."

He shook his head. "You don't know. It's in my blood. The anger—"

"I see the good in you. The part of you that wants to help. To protect. The part of you that's nothing like him." Luna's hand rested on his arm. Light but firm. He didn't pull away. He could feel the warmth of her hand through the fabric of his shirt, a warmth that spread through him. "Forgiveness isn't about deserving but about grace. About letting go of the anger, the bitterness, the need for control. You're trying to do it alone, but you can't fight this in your own strength."

"Yes, I can. I can do this."

She shook her head. "You need God, Corbin." A newfound conviction resonated. One he'd never heard from her before. "You need to rely on his strength, not your own. He can help you break free from this. From your father's legacy. From the fear."

He was quiet, absorbing her words. He stared at her hand resting on his arm. She was right. He'd seen it. In Blade's life, in Stryker's life. The power of faith to heal, to redeem, to transform. But he'd always kept God at arm's length. Afraid to surrender, afraid to trust.

Before he could speak, Luna said, "No one should have to testify against their own parent. I'm sorry for everything you went through with your father." Her eyes filled with a compassion he didn't deserve. "I'm sorry I wasn't there for you afterwards."

"I'm the one who should be apologizing. For walking away when you told me you were pregnant. For not being there for you those nine months. For not proposing and being the man you needed me to be. Everything."

He looked at her, really looked at her, for the first time since she'd walked back into his life only hours ago. Seeing her as the woman she'd become, not the one he'd known. "I was selfish. Immature. Scared. Scared of becoming my father, scared of failing you, failing . . ." He swallowed hard. "Her. I thought I was doing the right thing. Protecting you. But I was just . . . running, and . . ." He worked his jaw, fighting the emotions leaping up. "I'm sorry, Luna. So, so sorry."

He braced himself for her to stand and walk out. To reject his apology and tell him some things couldn't be forgiven. But she didn't. Instead, her hand squeezed his arm. "We both made choices. Choices we can't change." She pressed her lips together and looked down. He could tell she was fighting too.

A tear slipped down her cheek, and he caught it with his thumb. He cupped her face, tracing the curve of her cheekbone. Her skin was soft beneath his touch. Warm like the sun on bare skin. She leaned into his palm, her eyes closing.

If only he could close the gap. Hold her. Make sure she was really there. But he held back. The wall. Years of hurt. He was terrified of saying or doing the wrong thing. Afraid she'd bolt again.

She drew back from his touch and opened her eyes. "Wow. I didn't come here to preach at you, but I must say. This was better. So much better than 'I'm sorry' by the curb of a burning house." She gathered the hair around her shoulders and used the movement to put more distance between them.

He stopped himself from reaching for her. She hadn't rejected him. Hadn't walked away. It was a start. Maybe he wasn't as broken as he imagined. Luna had only been back a few hours, and she'd already seen something in him that he hadn't seen in himself. She'd said he was strong. Good.

Nothing like his father.

But one thing was for sure. He had to stop walking on eggshells and do his job.

While he still had one.

13

THE PALE LIGHT OF DAWN seeped through the cheap hotel blinds. How was this her life? She'd spent years running, hiding, building a cover story for herself, never imagining she'd end up back here. Not with Corbin. Not like this. But now, here they were. Partners.

Between the burn on her ankle pulsing with an insistent pain and her thoughts cycling through the image of Stryker being kidnapped, she hadn't slept well. The drab hotel room, the uncomfortable bed, the paper-thin walls amplifying every cough and footstep in the hallway, hadn't helped either. All night she couldn't shake the feeling that she should be doing more. That time was running out. Each passing hour, a grain of sand slipping through the hourglass of Stryker's life.

Fresh from her shower, Luna perched on the edge of the tub and carefully peeled back the dressing on her ankle. The angry red flesh underneath dragged her back to the fire. Corbin's hands on her skin. Smothering the flames. He'd saved her.

A sting shot up her leg as she dabbed antibiotic ointment on the burn, and she hissed through her teeth. She rewrapped the injury with clean gauze and stood, testing her weight. Still painful, but manageable.

Brushing her teeth, she stared at her reflection in the mirror. No longer a CIA operative, but still a phony. How could she tell Corbin that forgiveness wasn't about deserving but about grace all while she clutched her own resentment like a security blanket? The irony. Here she stood, advising him to do exactly what she refused to do herself.

And what about her friends? She'd disappeared without a trace, without explanation. If she expected Harlee and the others to forgive her abandonment, shouldn't she be willing to extend that same grace to Corbin?

Physician, heal thyself.

The logic was simple, the execution impossibly difficult. Maybe it was time to start trying to do things God's way instead of her own.

Her stomach growled. Caffeine. She needed caffeine, but one glance at the crusty hotel coffee maker with its suspicious stains sent her reaching for her keys instead.

She arrived at Corbin's office, greeted by the blessed scent of coffee, and poured herself a cup before settling at Corbin's desk. Last night she'd left him asleep at the conference table, head resting on folded arms. If she were honest, the raw vulnerability in his eyes had shaken her more than she cared to admit.

"Morning," Corbin said. He looked tired, his shoulders stiff beneath his suit jacket, a dark bruise blooming on his cheekbone. The remnants of the fire etched onto his skin.

"Coffee's ready," she said.

"Thanks." He poured himself a cup, wincing slightly as he reached for the sugar.

She studied him, stirring his coffee. He was the same, but different now. Older, obviously. The lines around his eyes, the slight gray at his temples, they suited him. He had a confidence now, an assurance in his movements that hadn't been there before. Even more good-looking than he'd been back then. If that was even possible.

She'd always seen the good in him, even then, when he was lost, angry, fighting his own demons. Yesterday, she'd seen it again. After all she'd put him through, he still cared.

Maybe she should have forgiven him a long time ago.

And what about Trinity?

The girl Stryker wouldn't give up on. The one Liv had said looked so much like her. Who ran from her problems just like Luna had.

Was it possible? Could Trinity be their daughter?

Mercy, the implications made her head spin.

Should she tell Corbin? No, she couldn't. Not until she had more evidence. Not with everything else he was dealing with.

He turned. Caught her staring. "About last night . . ."

"Let's focus. We need to find Carlie. For her sake. For her family's sake. Then, Stryker." She busied herself organizing the files, avoiding his eyes.

"Right. Of course." He shuffled a few file folders and pulled one from the stack. "Did you have a chance to skim this?"

He handed her the file with a photo of Carlie, the pretty blond teenager still wearing braces, attached to the front. Traces of the commissioner were in her eyes, the shape of her face. "She's a beautiful young woman."

"And smart too. Top of her class. But she's been in trouble the last year or two." Corbin rattled off a list that sounded an awful lot like her own teenage transgressions.

Luna opened the file and skimmed Corbin's notes from his interview of Lara Tinch.

"Her home life's a bit of a mess," he continued. "Her mother, Lara, struggles with serious mental health issues. She doesn't leave her room. Heavily medicated. Disconnected." He hesitated, then added, "That's all off the record, by the way. The commissioner wants to keep this whole thing under wraps. Top secret. Can't have a word getting out to his own department, let alone the media."

Luna nodded. The commissioner trusted them. Or maybe he just had no other choice.

"Carlie's under a lot of pressure from her father," Corbin continued. "The commissioner pushes her hard about school, expects perfect grades, extracurricular activities, the whole nine yards." He shook his head. "But he works long hours, travels a lot. She feels neglected. Abandoned. It's no wonder she's acting out."

Kids like that were easy to find. Easy to manipulate. They craved acceptance, belonging. They were desperate for someone to see them, to hear them, even if it meant breaking the rules. She'd been one of those kids once. And it had landed her in a world of trouble. "Classic cry for attention."

"Yeah." He sighed. "I suspect she's been dipping into her mother's medication cabinet, self-medicating. The pills. The escape. It's a dangerous combination."

"It is." Luna's own mother had sought solace in those colorful capsules that promised oblivion. The little bottles. The rattle of pills. That sweet, chemical smell clinging to her mother's clothes. "And I know something about that escape. I lived it. For years, I took care of my mother. I had to be the parent because she couldn't. Growing up like that, it changes you. Not always for the better."

"I know what it was like for you. With your mom. I remember." His hand reached out, hesitated, then settled on the table between them. Close, but not touching.

That tenderness. It had been so long. His hand, so close, so tempting.

No, Corbin's simple gesture shouldn't distract her. Carlie's case. That was where her attention needed to be. Not on Corbin. Not on the past.

She took a long drink of her coffee, then set the mug down. "What about friends? Who's Carlie hanging out with?"

Corbin shuffled a few papers and offered another photo. It looked like a selfie taken by a freckle-faced girl with Carlie braiding the girl's dark hair. Both had their heads tilted and beamed smiles at the camera.

"Carlie's best friend is a girl named Ashley. They'd started hanging out with Ashley's twin brother, Andre, and his friends. They're always loitering around that old liquor store on Palm Street."

"According to your notes, Ashley was the last person to see Carlie before she disappeared, right?"

"That's right."

"Let's go talk to Andre and his friends." She pushed her chair back and stood. "We need to find out what they know."

"Questioning minors without their parents . . ." He shook his head. "It's a gray area, Luna. We need to be careful."

"Careful?" She gave him a look. "We're talking about a missing girl. A girl whose father is breathing down your neck. A girl who might be in serious danger. When was the last time 'careful' got you anywhere?"

Conflict blazed in his eyes. The cop versus the friend. The need to follow the rules versus the urgency of the situation.

"We don't even know if these kids are involved," he said. "We could waste valuable time searching for *them*."

"Or we could be losing valuable leads," she countered. She knew how to push his buttons. How to get under his skin. How to make him forget about the rules and listen to his gut. "Every minute that passes, Carlie drifts farther away."

She watched as he wrestled with the decision, his jaw tightening, his gaze flickering between her and the photo of Carlie on his desk.

"Let's go." She glanced at the whiskey glass still on his desk. Still filled with amber liquid. "Unless you'd rather stay here, staring at your drink."

He got to his feet and grabbed his blazer. "Why do I feel like I'm going to regret this?"

Probably because she was feeling the same way.

14

IT WAS JUST PAST 4:30 in the afternoon, and Corbin had been right—they'd wasted the entire morning searching, ending with Ashley and Andre's house, where the parents had informed them the kids had gone down to one of the beaches to watch a surfing movie being filmed.

At least it was a smooth ride. Luna could get used to the rumble of Corbin's unmarked Charger. The car had power. Presence. Everything her rental lacked. They cruised through the neighborhood toward the beach, a skate park coming into view—a sprawling area with a pump track, scattered skaters, and a dog park nearby.

Things were different than she remembered. The once-charming cottages were replaced by a tangle of rundown houses and overgrown lots. It held a strange stillness. A quiet, almost suffocating calm. As if the neighborhood itself was holding its breath.

She stared at Trinity's profile picture on her phone. Were Trinity's wide brown eyes the same as Corbin's? Did she get her wavy black hair from Luna? Not the lips, though. Those weren't Luna's lips. She'd have killed for lips like that at her age.

"You okay?" Corbin asked.

"Yeah." She locked the screen. "Just . . . processing. It's been a while since I've been back here."

He turned the corner. A series of old, unkempt buildings lined the street. "Yeah, this area's seen better days."

Luna studied his profile, noting the sharp angle of his nose. Trinity had a smaller, delicate nose more like her own.

Ridiculous. She was seeing what she wanted to see. Classic confirmation bias. So desperate to find a connection, she was willing to fabricate one.

Moving on. "I don't think these kids will be happy to see us."

He laughed a dry, humorless sound. "They definitely won't be happy to see me. I'm a cop."

"Can't argue with that." She'd seen the same animosity in the eyes of those she recruited as assets. The anger and fear simmering beneath the surface. Most were taught that cops were the bad guys. Do one thing wrong and they'd haul you off to jail. Often she'd have to agree—even egg the asset on—in order to win trust.

A few seconds ticked by in silence. Corbin's fingers tapped a mindless rhythm on the steering wheel. "So, what did your boss say to get you such high clearance?"

She knew this was coming. "Not sure."

"Right. You're a federal agent, but it's all classified." He did little curved finger air quotes. "How can I trust you as my partner when I don't even know your creds?"

"I'm sorry, Corbin. I'm not at liberty to discuss the details."

"It's fine. Really, I get it." His tone was light, but his eyes were serious when he glanced at her.

She owed him more than that, didn't she? After all, he was helping her find Stryker—and Trinity, even if he didn't know it yet. She couldn't keep pushing him away.

"Okay, fine. Here's the truth. After we . . . after the baby . . ." The words threatened to choke her up. She didn't let them. "After Stryker helped us make that arrangement, I needed to find myself.

I'd flourished in Stryker's program, and I knew I still needed the structure, so I joined the Marines."

The words were easier to say now. They'd been part of her for years. Her secret shame. Her twisted pride. "I worked on my college degree while I was in the service, through correspondence courses and online. And then, I got picked for Marine Intelligence."

"Marine Intelligence?" Corbin's eyebrows shot up. "That couldn't have been easy."

"Tell me about it." Grueling training sessions. Sleepless nights. Training had transformed her. The last time they'd seen each other, she was hiding from the world, afraid of what her future held. Now, she could withstand a lifetime of torture and captivity. "And then . . . then the Agency recruited me."

Corbin jerked his head to look at her. "You're telling me, you're . . . you're . . ."

She held a finger to her lips.

He whistled low. "I'm . . . I'm actually kind of impressed."

"You should be," she said with a small smile.

"So the PTSD . . ." he began, then paused like he thought better of it and tried again. "It's from an operation?"

"That's—"

"Classified," he said.

"I was going to say it's a longer story, but yeah, a classified one."

"I guess that makes sense that you'd sort of disappear." He seemed to relax a fraction. "So you really are here just to see Stryker?"

And to find their daughter. Luna didn't tell him that. Not yet. She couldn't tell him about the possibility that Trinity, the girl Stryker kept trying to save, was their daughter.

She saw the flash of understanding in his eyes, a glimmer of something deeper. She wanted to reach out, to touch him, but her fingers tightened around the strap of her seat belt. "Look, I know you've probably got a million questions, but—"

"I know. And believe me, I get it. After my dad . . . well, let's just say I understand the need to reinvent yourself."

It hadn't even occurred to her that he'd been running from his past as long as she had.

She felt a sudden kinship with him, recognizing the same drive that had pushed her all these years. "Maybe we're not so different."

"Yeah. Maybe."

Corbin pulled his car to a stop across the street from a skate park. The concrete playground had a central bowl surrounded by ramps on one side and several rails and ledges on the other. A high vert ramp dominated the far end.

Beyond the park, the beach was cordoned off. A film crew worked in a swarm of activity, setting up equipment around a makeshift tent. Probably preparing for the moment when the sun dipped toward the horizon. Golden hour. The perfect light.

"This is it." Corbin turned off the ignition and nodded toward a group of teenagers tracing lines across the concrete ramps. "And there they are."

Five teens had congregated at the park. Luna recognized Ashley from the photo. A slim girl with purple-tipped hair standing near the top of the vert ramp, holding her phone out to capture the boys as they launched themselves into the air, one after another.

Another girl sat on the edge of a grind rail about twenty feet away from Ashley, her gaze fixed on her phone. She wore torn jeans and a crop top, her dark hair pulled into a tight ponytail. Behind her, a tall kid paced in front of the graffiti-covered ramp. His oversized basketball shorts and faded band T-shirt hung on his bony body. All limbs and nervous energy. Arms crossed. Eyes darting around. He leaned over and whispered into the girl's ear. She glanced at Corbin's car and got up.

The two disappeared around the corner.

"I think they made us," Corbin said.

"They didn't seem like part of Ashley's group anyway." She opened her door and paused to glance at Corbin. "I'll take the lead on this."

"Whoa, hold on." He started to protest, then paused. "You know what? I'd kind of like to see this."

They got out of the car, and Luna felt the teens' hostile stares. She straightened her spine, channeling the confidence that had served her well in far more dangerous situations, and crossed the street.

As they approached the remaining teens, Luna took stock. Ashley had climbed down from the vert ramp and now stood at its base. Beside her, her twin brother, Andre, watched them approach. Stocky, with the same freckled complexion, he wore designer jeans, a crisp white tee, and a plaid flannel tied around his waist like he'd stepped straight out of a nineties skate video. His skateboard rested against his thigh, but his posture told the real story. Calm. Watchful. The one to keep an eye on. The leader. Or at least he thought he was.

Another skater nailed an ollie off the quarter pipe and landed clean on the ground. He slid to a stop beside the twins, one foot on his board, the other planted for balance. Smaller than the twins, he had shaggy blond hair that fell into his eyes and wore ripped skinny jeans with a hoodie despite the warm weather.

Luna could see these teenagers weren't hardened criminals—not yet. They were scared kids playing at being tough, and that made them unpredictable. Dangerous.

Corbin followed Luna toward Ashley, who pocketed her phone and whispered to Andre. Luna caught a faint whiff of marijuana.

"You boys smell bacon?" Andre asked. "What do you two want? We ain't done nothin.'"

Luna held up her hands, palms out. "We're not here to cause trouble. We just want to talk."

"Talk to this." Andre made a crude gesture with his fist.

Luna didn't flinch. Instead, she smiled and said, "Nice form, but your execution needs work. Here, let me show you." She demonstrated the gesture with exaggerated flair, adding a twist at the end that had the boys laughing despite themselves.

"Where'd you learn that?" Andre asked.

"Oh, you pick up all sorts of things in the Marines." She didn't bother giving them her name.

The skater kid grabbed his board and stood behind his friends. "Don't mind him. He gets nervous around chicks."

"So does my friend here." She cocked her head at Corbin. "You guys got names?"

"Andre," the stocky kid said. "This here's Ashley and that's Jordan."

Ashley wrapped one arm around her middle and chewed the thumbnail of her other hand. She looked at Corbin. "Y'all still looking for Carlie?"

Corbin removed his sunglasses and slid them in his breast pocket. "Yeah, you seen her?"

Ashley shook her head and dropped her hands. "You know, she's supposed to be, like, my best friend. I mean, we were best friends. And then she just, like, totally ghosted me. No calls. No texts. Nothing. She just, like . . . vanished."

"Did she ever talk about leaving town?" Corbin asked.

Ashley shrugged, her gaze dropping to her hands. She picked at a chipped fingernail, a sliver of black polish flaking off. "We, like, talked about moving in together one day. You know, when we're older. Not like, anything serious."

Kids were terrible liars. This girl was practically screaming "I'm hiding something."

Corbin said, "Smart to make plans for your future. Where did you talk about moving to?"

"I don't know. Like LA or New York or something. You know, someplace clutch. Not so lame like here, and not so, like, cliche, like Miami."

Luna caught herself tapping her thigh to tick off every "like" Ashley used.

Ashley continued unprompted. "I would, like, totally move in an instant, but I'm, like, broke. Carlie too. She didn't think it mattered. She wanted to, you know, move to a big city and earn more money, but I told her, like, girl, that's how you end up being trafficked."

Corbin's eyebrows shot up. Luna had to talk to him about telegraphing his emotions. He asked, "You think that's what happened to her?"

Ashley paled and stared at Andre as if the idea that something so awful could happen right here in her hometown had never occurred to her before. "Could . . . could that . . . like, happen?"

Duh, is what Luna wanted to say. What did they think would happen hanging out in a bad neighborhood where gangs fought over territory and merchandise? And they were the merchandise. Instead she said, "It's possible, which is why we're asking you so many questions. We want to make sure she's safe. That's all." She glanced at Andre and Jordan. "What about you guys? You think she's in trouble?"

Andre shrugged. "We thought maybe her dad sent her to that group home."

Corbin's chin lifted a fraction. "What group home?"

"The one with that dude who's always tryin' to preach at us."

"Stryker?" Luna asked. "You guys know him?"

"Yeah," Andre said. "Keeps sayin' we gotta clean up our lives. Go to college, but man, we're good right here."

Corbin glanced at Luna then back to Andre. "Did he want you guys to join the Warrior program too?"

Andre erupted into laughter and nudged Jordan. "Us? Join a team with cops?" He shoved a hand in his pocket. "Ain't no way, man. We hate cops."

"Not all cops are bad," Corbin said.

"Says the cop." Andre cleared his throat and spit a chunk of phlegm onto the concrete beside Corbin. She watched his face redden, but he kept his cool. Andre said, "You're all still on the same team, so the way I see it, you're all bad."

"A cop killed my dad," Jordan muttered.

She looked at Jordan, and her heart ached for the pain in his eyes, but she steered them off the volatile subject. "Know where we can find Stryker?"

Jordan let out a short puff of air. "No. He's probably off on some mission to save the world."

"He's always tryin' to save someone or other," Andre said on a laugh. "We told him to forget about it. It's not worth it. But he don't listen. He's so . . ."

"So . . ." Corbin rolled his hand. "So what?"

"Righteous," Ashley said. "He's, like, one of those 'born again' freaks."

So was Luna, but they didn't need to know that. She let her eyes go wide and played dumb. "What do you mean?"

Andre looked away. "Never mind. It's none of your business."

"Yes, it is," she said. "Stryker's my friend, and Carlie's yours. We're not out here asking questions just to bust your chops. We're trying to help, and a little cooperation would be nice."

"Okay, okay. Don't go all PMS on me." Andre looked at Corbin, probably thinking he'd get a laugh out of the insult. When Corbin crossed his arms, Andre cleared his throat. "Look, the dude knows we're just playin'. Sometimes we be out throwin' bottles and rudes at his place."

"Rudes?" Corbin asked.

"Y'know, talkin' trash. Nothin' crazy, just sayin' we don't like cops. Stuff to get under his skin," Andre said. "He don't get the message, apparently, 'cause bro drops in here one day like we best friends."

Sounded like Stryker. He'd walk into the den of a cartel leader and try to evangelize if given the opportunity.

Corbin asked, "What'd he want?"

"What do you think?" Andre threw his hands up. "He was tryin' to preach, but we be tryin' to skate."

"Yeah, but we got to talkin'. Hung out for a little while," Jordan said. "He gave us some money for food. Then he left."

"Where'd he go? What did you see him do?" Corbin's questions were starting to turn into an interrogation, and she shot him a look.

"We don't know, man. He left. I ain't seen him since." Andre looked to Jordan. "Ain't that right?"

Jordan nodded, and his hair fell into his eyes. He swept it back.

"Besides Stryker preaching at you, what did you talk about?" Luna asked.

Andre's eyes darted toward the street like he was considering a getaway. "He was talkin' about his program where the kids can live there. Sounded all weird to me, man. Then he says we need to leave that girl alone. Not hang out with her anymore."

"Carlie?" Corbin asked.

"No, man, Trinity," Andre said.

"We go to the same school." Ashley didn't look up, continuing to pick at her nail polish. "Or, we used to, I guess."

"I ain't seen her around school for a while," Andre said. "But she hangs with us sometimes."

Luna felt her heart stutter at the name. These kids knew Trinity. Went to school with her. "Did Stryker say why he didn't want you to hang out together?"

"No tellin', lady." Andre shook his head. "Dude is, like, super protective."

Ashley stopped scrutinizing her nails and said, "She's different, you know? Always sick and stuff."

"She's a pillbilly," Jordan added.

Luna wanted to defend Trinity. Maybe it was just the word *pillbilly* she didn't like hearing thrown around. It meant they thought Trinity was struggling. Drowning in a world of pill addiction.

Andre slapped Jordan's shoulder with the back of his hand. "Man, forget her. She's gonna die young, so she may as well live it up while she can. Let her be."

They obviously knew Trinity better than Liv did. "What do you mean, she's going to die young?"

Before Andre could answer, a black Mercedes G-Wagon slid to a stop in the lot.

Andre swore. "It's Steve. He's gonna be peeved."

The door opened, and the man they called Steve stepped out. Thick with muscle and moving with the weight of a tank, he adjusted his linen suit. Mirrored sunglasses hid his eyes, but everything about him screamed danger. The set of his jaw. The tension in his shoulders. Luna could see the rage simmering beneath his stony expression, a slow burn waiting for a spark.

Steve marched over and hiked a thumb. "Find somewhere else to be."

They didn't need to be told twice. The teens made off on their skateboards.

Steve's eyes locked onto her. A predatory smile spread across his face. He put a hand on his waist, drawing back his jacket to reveal his gun. "Now, why don't you two tell me what you think you're doing in my neighborhood?"

Luna could take him, she was sure of it. But what she really wanted was answers. She took a step toward him. "We're looking for our friend, Stryker. Maybe you've heard of him?"

"You're meddling in things that are none of your concern," he said. "I'd advise you to mind your own business."

He stepped forward.

"Don't," Corbin said. "No need for things to get ugly."

They might be past that.

The man's smile widened, revealing teeth that were too white, too perfect. He turned toward Corbin. "Oh, but I think things are about to get very ugly. You see, you're poking your noses where they don't belong. And I can't have that."

Steve took a step closer. His palm touched the butt of his weapon. "Now, here's what's going to happen. You're going to get in your car and you're going to drive away. You're going to forget about Stryker, forget about Carlie, and forget you ever came to this neighborhood." He pointed his finger. "And if I ever see you talking to my friends again, you'll see just how ugly I can be."

This guy was used to pushing people around. Using threats and intimidation to get what he wanted. But he'd made a huge mistake. He'd mentioned Carlie.

They hadn't.

15

ONE WRONG MOVE, and this could go sideways. Fast. The man's cold eyes unsettled Corbin. Calculated. Predatory.

"Oh, this is your neighborhood? I wasn't aware." Corbin kept his tone steady. Years on the force had drilled that into him. Even when his pulse hammered a frantic rhythm. Even when every cell in his body screamed to take the guy down, he held his cool. Unlike his father, he had self-control.

"I don't think you're listening to me, son." Steve's voice rasped like dry leaves skittering across pavement. "Go on and get outta here."

"I don't think so." He moved his gun hand closer to his holster. "Steve, is it?"

Steve's face twisted, and he made a noise that sounded like a growl. His fist slammed into Corbin's chest.

The impact knocked the air from his lungs and sent a starburst of pain exploding in his ribs. He staggered back a step, fighting for balance. The guy hit hard.

Corbin took a defensive stance. Game on.

Steve's right fist was already drawn back, telegraphing his next move. He threw a wild haymaker at Corbin's jaw.

Corbin seized the man's wrist and, instead of blocking the punch, pulled the hand in tighter, throwing Steve off balance. He smacked his palm against Steve's nose, shattering it. Corbin twisted, crushing the man's wrist, feeling the bones grind, hearing Steve's grunt of pain. He spun around the big man's torso, locking him in a standing arm bar.

He hadn't gotten slow in his old age.

"Whoa. Hold on, both of you. This isn't helping anyone." Luna stepped closer.

What was she doing? Couldn't she see how dangerous this was? "I got this, Luna. Stay back."

Steve squirmed, trying to escape the pressure Corbin held on his arm. He could feel the man's pulse hammering against his thumb. "I'm going to let go and you're going to walk back to your car and drive away. Okay?"

Steve swore at Corbin.

"See, that's not smart. What with you in the position you're in, and me in the position I'm in." Corbin arched away, adding pressure on the arm until a strangled cry tore from Steve's throat.

"Okay! Okay!" Steve tapped Corbin's thigh.

Corbin helped himself to the gun tucked in Steve's waistband. "You won't be needing this." He released him with a backward shove.

Steve backed away, cradling his arm. *Good. Let him feel the pain. Maybe next time he'll think twice before pulling a gun.*

Without breaking eye contact with Steve, he released the magazine and let it drop to the ground. He cycled the gun to eject the round from the chamber. His thumb pressed the release button and unseated the slide from the frame. Corbin tossed the parts at Steve's feet. The metallic pieces clattered across the pavement and scattered like dice.

Corbin's chest heaved. Steve's chest too.

"You . . ." Steve's eyes bulged. Thick blood drained from one nostril and pooled above his lip. "You broke my gun!"

His gun? What about his nose?

"Next time, I break your arm." He debated whether to arrest Steve for assault or let him walk. "Get outta here before I change my mind and haul your sorry self to jail."

The man's eyes darted from Corbin to the disassembled weapon at their feet. He kicked the useless frame, and it spun away. "You're making a mistake. A big mistake. You have no idea what you're getting into. You think you can just waltz in here and start asking questions? You think you're untouchable? You're wrong. Dead wrong."

Steve spat at Corbin's feet. A glob of bloody saliva landed with a wet splat near a discarded cigarette butt. "You keep poking around. You'll regret it. Both of you."

The man spun on his heel and stalked toward the SUV. Expensive dress shoes clicked against the pavement. The door slammed. The engine roared, and the tires spit bits of gravel as the SUV sped away. The taillights shrank to pinpricks of red before vanishing around the corner.

Corbin's heart hammered against his ribs. The adrenaline slowly receded, leaving a tremor of unease in its wake. He bent and picked up the disassembled parts of the gun with a glove he pulled from his pocket.

Luna came to stand beside him. The perfume she wore, a light, floral scent, cut through the lingering aroma of gun grease on his hands.

"Wow," she said. "That was . . ."

"Impressive? Terrifying?" He managed a smile.

"A little of both." The afternoon sun cast a halo of light around her head.

He shifted his weight and shuffled the disassembled gun parts in his hands. "You think I should have arrested him?"

Luna tilted her head. "Depends. You looking for a quick arrest or a long game?"

"Long game? Enlighten me." He held up a hand. "On second thought, tell me in the car. I'm melting in this heat."

Luna didn't argue. She fell into step beside him, her silence a weight as heavy as the gun parts in his hands.

The car was an oven. Trapped heat radiated off the leather seats. He cranked the engine, blasted the AC, and grabbed an evidence bag from the glove compartment. The gun parts rattled as he dropped them in. He'd fill out the report later. Right now, he wanted to hear Luna's thoughts.

He glanced at her sitting in the passenger seat as she buckled her seat belt. The way the sunlight caught the auburn highlights in her hair, the subtle curve of her neck as she tilted her head, it was downright distracting.

The AC started to cut through the stifling heat. Good, because it was making him fidgety. He leaned back and rolled his shoulders, trying to shake off the moment. "Okay, lay it on me. What are you thinking?"

"So, you let this . . . this Steve guy walk." She angled to face him. "Although, I'd say he didn't get a complete pass. You did break his nose. And his gun."

"Self-defense."

She shrugged. "Details. My point is, we can tail him. See where he goes, who he talks to. Maybe he leads you to Carlie. Maybe he leads you to Stryker."

A 24/7 surveillance detail? The overtime. The paperwork. It would be a lot, but commissioner Tinch would approve it since it was their best lead at finding his daughter. "There's a lot of maybes. And it'll pull me away from chasing other leads. Questioning Ashley again, for one."

"Fair enough. You don't have time, but maybe someone else does. Hand the gun parts over to the locals. Let them handle Steve for assaulting an officer. They'd probably appreciate the collar."

He saw a flicker of the Luna from this morning. The one who

could compartmentalize, shut down emotion, focus on the mission. Maybe she was right.

But those kids...

They'd been with Stryker, and he had a feeling they were more connected to his disappearance than they let on. He drummed his fingers against the steering wheel. Steve had said, *"You have no idea what you're getting into."* It had his wheels turning.

"Okay, hear me out," he said, splaying all his fingers as if to give himself space to lay it all out. "What if..." Was he really going to suggest this? "What if Jordan and Andre are spotters, identifying vulnerable kids to pull in."

"For what? Runners?"

"Steve is acting like a distributor using these kids for that, but I think it's more than drugs for him. I'd bet my badge on it."

"Carlie," she said softly. "Could explain how she disappeared into thin air."

He nodded, liking the idea more now that he'd said it out loud. But he saw a big problem. "Look, if Carlie is caught up in any sort of trafficking, whether it's drugs or..."—he couldn't bring himself to say the words—"something darker, the commissioner isn't going to want us to move on it until we're rock solid."

Luna leaned back in her seat. "I see your point. But I'm a little light in this area. What exactly are you thinking?"

Corbin chewed the inside of his lip as he considered how to explain. The mere thought of Carlie being involved in something so sinister made his stomach churn. He took a deep breath. "I'm thinking we need to tread carefully. If we're dealing with a trafficking ring, they'll scatter at the first sign of trouble. We can't risk losing Carlie or any other kids involved."

"So, we need to build a solid case." Luna had her eyes fixed on some distant point beyond the windshield. "Gather enough evidence to take down the entire operation in one sweep."

"Yes. No loose ends, no chance for anyone to slip through the cracks." This type of investigation would be difficult, even with

Luna as his partner. "Every minute we spend building that case is another minute Carlie, and who knows how many other vulnerable kids, are out there with these creeps. It's a tightrope walk, and I'm not sure I can keep my balance."

"Who can you trust?"

Besides her, she meant. "Here's what I'm thinking. I'll have Blade put a few guys on Ashley, Andre, and Jordan. Pick them up on something simple. A possession charge. Just something to scare them. With a little pressure, they'll sing. Especially Andre. He's a talker."

"Smart." Luna pressed a knuckle to the corner of her mouth for a moment. "Except I wouldn't waste time with Ashley or Andre right now. I'd go for Jordan."

"Jordan? Why? The kid practically vibrated with hatred for cops. One killed his dad, remember?" She had to be wrong about this.

"Body language. Tone of voice. Microexpressions. He hates cops, sure. But that makes him vulnerable." Luna paused. "Deep down, most people want to do good. They want to be a part of something bigger. Make their world a better place. Jordan's just channeling his anger wrong."

He thought about himself at that age. Reinventing himself. Trying to be the opposite of his own father. He'd needed a cause. A purpose. Something to believe in. Stryker had given him that, but Jordan... "The kid's hatred for cops runs too deep. He won't talk."

"Not to just any cop." Luna's eyes met his. "But he'll talk to you."

To him? No. She was way off. "Why would a cop-hating kid talk to me? I *am* the job, Luna. My whole life is about being a cop."

"He'll talk to you because of your dad."

He clenched his teeth. His father. The man who'd haunted his every step, whose shadow he'd spent a lifetime outrunning.

The knot in his stomach tightened. Everything Corbin was today was the opposite of what his father represented. And now Luna wanted him to use that darkness, that legacy of violence, to get information from a troubled kid? No. He didn't want to bond over his father.

It wouldn't work anyway. He should know. "A kid who hates cops isn't going to open up because of my father."

"When was the last time you saw him, Corbin?"

He hesitated. The image flashed in his mind. His father. Handcuffed. Led away.

A murderer. A monster.

"At his murder trial."

"I get it—" She was cut off by the harsh vibration of his phone in the cup holder.

The Broward County Sheriff's number flashed on the screen. He held up a finger, asking Luna to give him a second, and answered. "King."

The world slowed as he listened to the caller on the other end.

"Okay. Yeah. I got it." He was already shifting the car into drive and pulling out of the parking lot. A hot acid burned his gut. "I'm on my way."

Luna asked, "Everything okay?"

Corbin looked at her then back to the road. "They've found Carlie."

16

LUNA'S BODY JERKED with each bump as Corbin steered the car off the asphalt onto a dirt road bordering the Everglades. Two hours of driving had brought them to this desolate road, barely visible in the fading light. The news of Carlie's death sat like lead in her stomach. Poor girl. Poor Corbin. Her heart ached for him, for the pain etched across his face when he'd received the call.

This was the stark difference between their worlds. Her training was with the living, not the dead. She dealt with abstract threats, faceless enemies, and potential mass destruction. Her job was to prevent catastrophes before they happened. To stop the dominoes from falling. But Corbin? He faced the raw, personal tragedies head-on. Each case, each victim, was a real person with a name, a face, a family left behind. He waded through the aftermath of lives lost.

"Pretty sure this is it," Corbin said, turning onto a gravel driveway.

The car lurched over another bump. A chain-link fence, rusted and topped with barbed wire, enclosed the property. A young officer stood guard at the entrance, blocking the way.

The officer ducked his head to see in the car. "Evening." He checked their credentials, his gaze lingering on Luna's consultant badge, then scribbled their names in a logbook. "Through there, agents. The body's in the woods, past the blue hull, about fifty yards in the woods." He gestured with his flashlight. "Follow the drive as far as you can, then you'll see the cruisers."

"Thanks." Corbin rolled up his window and headed into the sprawling junkyard.

The boat graveyard.

Acres of overgrown weeds and forgotten dreams. Hundreds of boats in various states of decay spread out in every direction. Some, sleek and fiberglass, their lines still hinting at past glory. Others, hulks of rotting wood and peeling paint, sunken into the earth, consumed by the relentless march of time and the humid Florida air.

The driveway meandered around, then disappeared into the maze of boats and overgrown weeds.

They emerged into a clearing, the ground littered with broken masts, tangled fishing nets, and the skeletal remains of long-forgotten vessels. More police cruisers were parked ahead, their lights flashing, along with a couple of ambulances. The doors were open, the beds empty. A group of paramedics stood around, checking their phones and chatting.

She saw the black SUV, its dark windows reflecting the last rays of the setting sun. "Medical Examiner" painted on the side. And in smaller letters beneath it: "Trauma Services."

Corbin parked behind one of the cruisers. "Stick with me."

"Got it." She climbed out, pulling her suit jacket closed, covering the paddle holster clipped to the back of her belt. The sun was beginning to set, but the heat lingered and she questioned the sanity of wearing a suit in the middle of September in Florida. Rules were rules.

Yellow crime scene tape cordoned off a section of the junkyard. She followed Corbin through a narrow path, weeds brushing against her legs, the scent of mildew and decay filling the air. Tick check later. Especially around her ankles and the burn bandage. A group of uniformed police officers stood clustered at the edge of the woods, watching them approach. Recognition dawned in their eyes.

"Hey, King." A burly man with a thick mustache stepped forward. "You the lead on this?"

"Yeah." Corbin gestured to Luna. "This is Agent Rosati."

Agent Rosati. Her heart skipped a beat. He meant the consultant badge, but years of deep cover had ingrained a different kind of meaning to the word *agent* and extreme caution when meeting strangers.

"Special Agent Ron Ayres, at your service." Ayres dipped his head and smiled.

"Nice to meet you." Luna immediately liked the man. He seemed rather unfazed by the situation. Even his wardrobe of a striped, button-up polo under a sports coat, loafers, and a Havana hat matched his casual demeanor.

Corbin swatted the back of his neck. "What've we got here?"

"Nothing pretty. Real messed up back there." Ayres's mustache twitched.

She shifted her gaze to the line of trees where the crime scene tape fluttered in the breeze. A teenage girl. Back there. Carlie Tinch. The pretty blond teenager she'd seen in the photograph. Was Ayres sure it was Carlie?

She asked, "You've seen the crime scene?"

"Yes, ma'am." Ayres blotted his forehead with a handkerchief he'd pulled from his pocket. "Like I said, it ain't pretty."

"Never is." Corbin paused, and no matter the cause of death, she figured this particular victim would be the ugliest case Corbin would ever work. "Who found the body?"

Ayres didn't have a chance to respond.

"Agent King." A woman detached herself from the group of uniformed officers and strode toward them. She wore a crisp white shirt and dark slacks. No tie. No jacket. Her badge hung on a chain around her neck.

Special Agent Jody Miller rushed the introductions and said, "Over here."

They fell into step beside her, listening as she spoke almost rapid-fire. "Witnesses found her a couple hours ago and called it in." Miller gestured to two men sitting on overturned buckets near a hulking sailboat. She checked her notes. "Brock Hepner on the left and Levi Anderson on the right."

To Luna, both men looked like a mix of classic surfer and beach bum. Brock had dark wavy hair and wore faded swim trunks, a dirty tank top, and leather sandals. He had a thick black mustache that she was pretty sure he'd regret when the future Brock saw photos of it.

Levi was taller, with long, curly, sun-bleached blond hair and a few days of beard growth. He held a faded red baseball cap in one hand and a dog leash in the other. A muddy golden retriever lay panting at his feet.

"You the ones who found the body?" Corbin asked.

The men stood up and shifted uncomfortably.

"Yeah," Brock said. "We were just . . . you know, looking around."

"Looking around? Out here?" Corbin glanced over his shoulder.

Brock looked at Levi and said, "Salvaging parts. Looking to see if we could find anything worth selling."

"I had to take a . . . you know . . ." Levi's eyes darted to hers, the ground, then back to Corbin. "Anyway, I went to find a tree. Maizie here followed me cuz I hardly ever have her on a leash. But while I . . . uh . . . did my business, Maizie took off barking. I called and called, but she wouldn't listen. Wouldn't come back. That's not like her." He reached down and patted her side. "She's always so obedient. But she was onto something. I was worried about gators and coyotes so close to the Everglades, so I hollered for Brock to help me track her down."

Brock picked up the story. "We finally found 'er, but she was way in there, digging like crazy. Levi had to put her on the leash to drag her away." He shook his head. "Could smell something awful. Thought she'd found a dead animal or something. That's when I saw it. Something weird. Like a clump of hair. I crouched down to get a closer look. Pushed some dirt away . . . and there was a . . . a . . ." Luna saw his Adam's apple roll. "A human ear."

She turned to look at the woods. The stillness. The silence.

For a moment, the junkyard faded away. Luna was back in that dusty marketplace. Bodies lay strewn across the ground, limbs at unnatural angles. A child's doll, stained crimson, rested in a pool of blood. Lifeless eyes stared back at her. She blinked hard, forcing the images away. This wasn't that war-torn country. She was here, with Corbin, facing a different kind of tragedy.

"You guys did the right thing by calling it in," Corbin said.

"We appreciate your help," she offered. Especially when their reasons for being out here were less than legal. They didn't have to report what they'd found. Could've hauled it out of here and had a wild story to tell their friends.

"You did good too." Corbin crouched and scratched behind Maizie's muddy ears. "Such a good girl." He stood and dusted off his hands. "Mind hanging tight for a while longer? We might have a few more questions. I'll get someone to bring Maizie some water. You guys too."

Luna noticed he'd added the humans last, and she kind of liked that about him.

The men nodded and sat on their buckets. Brock and Levi both petted Maizie and gave her praise. It probably brought them more comfort than it did Maizie. Dogs had a way of doing that for people.

Corbin headed for the wooded area, and Luna followed. He glanced at her sideways. "You sure you're up for this?"

She squared her shoulders and nodded. "I can think of a million other things I'd rather be doing, but yeah."

"Me too," he muttered.

Her gaze swept over the boat graveyard. The sinking sun bathed the junkyard in an amber glow, a fleeting moment of beauty before darkness swallowed the scene. A shiver slithered down her spine, and it wasn't from the humidity.

They walked into the woods, following a narrow path that curved through a tangle of palmetto bushes, towering pines, and strangler figs that wrapped their tendrils around ancient oaks. The humid air was thick with the scent of pine needles and damp earth. And something else. Something sickly sweet. Decay.

The path opened into a small clearing. A blue tarp had been strung between two trees, creating a makeshift tent. Floodlights illuminated the area, casting an eerie glow on the scene. Two officers stood guard, their faces pale and drawn. Hands hooked on their duty belts.

A woman wearing a polo embroidered with the Broward County Medical Examiner's seal, khakis, and blue latex gloves approached them. "Hey, Agent King."

"Dr. Santos." Corbin greeted her with a nod. "This is Agent Luna Rosati. She's consulting on the case."

"A pleasure to meet you, Agent Rosati." The doctor wore her dark hair piled in a loose topknot and very little makeup. There were deep lines at the corners of her eyes, and she had a sharp chin. The woman was thin. Too thin. Luna figured it had something to do with long nights at gruesome crime scenes like these.

"You have a positive ID on Carlie Tinch?" Corbin asked.

"Tentatively." Dr. Santos pulled off her gloves. "She's in early stages of decomposition. The clothing and dental work appear to match. Commissioner Tinch will confirm once we get her back to the lab."

Corbin's shoulders sagged. "You've notified the commissioner?"

Luna remembered the anguish in the father's voice, the desperation in his eyes. He'd wanted to find his daughter, but not like this. She looked beyond Dr. Santos to where two techs in white one-piece suits set up another tent over a shallow grave.

"He wanted to be here. But his wife couldn't handle it." Dr.

Santos wadded her gloves and shoved them into her pocket. "She had a breakdown. They had to sedate her."

"Probably for the best," Corbin said. "No parent should see their child like this. Not even a cop."

Dr. Santos drew in a breath. "And I'm sorry to say, we'll have more parents to console. We've found four graves."

Luna's breath caught. "Four?"

Dr. Santos gave her a grim look. "Yes, and we think there are more."

17

FOUR GRAVES. Four bodies. And more.

Corbin could feel the blood drain from his face. A coldness settled in his gut. He'd been so focused on finding Carlie, on bringing her home safe. From addiction. At worst, trafficking. He'd never considered...

Four families. Four lives shattered. This wasn't just a missing persons case anymore. This was something else. Something monstrous.

The relentless drone of cicadas filled the air, a high-pitched whine that grated on his nerves. He could feel the sweat trickling down his back, the humidity clinging to him like a second skin.

Floodlights, harsh and white, illuminated a section of the woods, casting long, grotesque shadows across the forest floor. Corbin stood with Luna, observing the forensic team as they worked to uncover the remains. To him, their white Tyvek suits made them look ghostly against the dark backdrop of the woods. Blue tarps, strung between the trees, created a series of makeshift tents. Each one marked a grave. The tarps also served another purpose—keeping prying eyes and news cameras at bay.

As if on cue, the distant thrum of helicopter blades cut through the air. He glanced up, though he couldn't see much past the dense canopy of leaves. A news chopper circled overhead, no doubt hoping for a glimpse of the grisly scene below. He was grateful for the tarps now, providing at least some privacy and dignity for the victims.

A massive golden retriever sniffed at the ground, its tail wagging as it moved through the undergrowth. For a moment, Corbin thought it was Maizie, the surfer's dog. But then he noticed the HRD label on the vest. A Human Remains Detection dog. He'd overheard the handler, an older man named Chuck, call the dog Remy.

"Hey, Chuck! Bring Remy this way!" a tech called out from a nearby clearing.

"Come on, Remy," Chuck said. "Find it, boy!"

The dog perked up, its demeanor shifting as it focused intently on the ground near the tech. The dog paused, circled, and sniffed again. Remy lay flat to the ground and whined.

"Good boy." Chuck crouched beside the dog and marked the spot with a small orange flag before giving Remy more praise and affection.

Another grave. How many more?

"We've only uncovered two of the bodies so far," Dr. Santos was saying. Corbin followed her to the second tent with Luna keeping some distance a few steps behind.

"Carlie was the first." Dr. Santos knelt and brushed soil away from the body of Carlie Tinch with a small brush. The young girl's remains lay partially exposed. "We're moving slowly to preserve any evidence."

Corbin felt a knot tighten in his stomach. This was no place for a child, but from the looks of it, she was at least fully clothed. He studied the shallow grave. "Do we have an ID on the second girl?"

"No, that'll be your department. We're calling her Jane One for now. I only recognized Carlie because the commissioner ensured my office checked every Jane Doe that came through for his daughter." Dr. Santos waved them over. "Come closer. I need to show you something that might be difficult to see." She glanced at Luna. "You okay?"

He glanced back at her. Had she ever seen a body like this? "Luna?"

She nodded. "I'm good."

He shuffled around the grave and stood behind Dr. Santos, peering over her shoulder.

Dr. Santos used a gloved finger to lift Carlie's shirt enough to reveal her torso. She clicked on a penlight and shone the beam under the shirt. "See this?"

He moved to see under the shirt and felt his eyes bulge. A Y-shaped incision ran from Carlie's collarbones down to her waist. The edges were neat and precise, held together by a series of small, evenly spaced sutures. He tried to make sense of what he was seeing. This couldn't be right. It had to be a mistake. This looked exactly like . . .

"An autopsy incision," Luna said.

Dr. Santos nodded. "That's what I initially thought too. But look at these suture patterns. There are actually two distinct surgical interventions here."

Corbin leaned in, forcing himself to study the incision. "Two surgeries? How can you tell?"

"See these older scar lines?" Dr. Santos pointed to faint whitish marks partially obscured by newer incisions. "The first procedure appears professional. Precise technique, minimal scarring. But this second procedure . . ." She traced along the fresher incision. "Different suture pattern, less careful. And notice how the tissue is collapsed here and here."

Corbin still wasn't sure what he was looking at.

"The second incision follows the same path as the first," Santos continued. "But see how the chest cavity appears sunken? Something was put in during the first surgery, then everything was taken out during the second. I can't be certain until I get her to the lab, but I suspect multiple organs are missing, not just whatever was the target of the initial procedure."

Beside him, Luna stood. "Organ harvesting?"

"Possibly, or something more... complex," Santos said, lowering Carlie's shirt. The penlight clicked off. "The timing between procedures is unusual. First surgery appears to have healed considerably before the second was performed." Dr. Santos's tone was clinical but not unkind. "And based on the precision of the initial incision versus the second, we're looking at different surgeons."

A wave of nausea rippled in his gut. He'd seen a lot in his years as an agent, but this... this was beyond anything he'd encountered. The idea that someone could do this to a teenager, to any human being, shook him to his core. He found himself silently praying for strength, for wisdom, for any kind of guidance in the face of such evil.

"So, she didn't suffer?" He clung to the one small mercy in this horrific situation.

"It's unlikely she was aware of what was happening," Dr. Santos said.

"What about the other victims?" Luna asked.

"Jane One has the same incisions," Dr. Santos said. "We're still uncovering the other two graves."

"Three," Corbin said.

The medical examiner craned her neck to look up at him.

He pointed to an orange flag. "The HRD might have found another."

Dr. Santos made a sound that sounded like a groan. "I hadn't noticed. It's going to be a long night."

"This is someone's dumping ground," Luna said.

"Again, that's your department." Dr. Santos stood. "But looks to me like you might be dealing with something big."

Understatement of the year. This could be the work of an organ harvesting operation, or a serial killer, though he didn't want to mention the latter. One leak to the media and they'd be overrun.

No matter what they were dealing with, the implications were disturbing. "How long has she been here?"

"Best guess? About two weeks," Santos said, glancing at her notes. "The other victim, Jane One, has been here three to five weeks."

Corbin frowned, recalling the timeline. "Last sighting of Carlie was over a month ago. Could she have been held captive?"

"I'll check her wrists and ankles for ligature marks once we uncover her. If they were running tests or prepping her for surgery, it's possible. The actual procedure to remove organs wouldn't take long—a few hours at most."

Luna interjected, "And if she was a drug user, maybe they needed her clean first."

"Detoxing could take time," Santos agreed. "Days, maybe weeks, depending on her condition."

He turned back to Santos. "Thank you, Doctor. Keep us updated. We need to know everything as soon as you have it."

"I'm calling in some reinforcements, so I should be ready for you tomorrow morning. I'll send a text." Santos knelt and returned to her work.

Corbin watched her for a moment as she slowly brushed dirt from Carlie's arm and paused to photograph the progress.

He exchanged a glance with Luna. "Wondering what you dragged yourself into?"

Luna walked beside him, eyes cast down, following the beam of his flashlight. "I wasn't expecting this."

"Me either." Where had Carlie been for so many weeks, and what had she endured? They had to find whoever was responsible—and stop them before more lives were lost.

Agent Miller met them as they walked out of the woods. "We're about to cut the surfers loose. That okay?"

"I have a few more questions," he said. "You have what you need to find them?"

"Yes, sir," Miller said.

"Good. Hang tight. This won't take long."

They approached the two men pacing near their overturned buckets. Someone had brought the golden retriever a bowl of water. It looked like instead of drinking it, the dog had swum in it.

"I know you're anxious to get going, but I've got just a few more questions," Corbin said. "How did you guys find this place?"

The men exchanged glances. Finally, Levi spoke up. "A friend in Miami owns a boat detailing shop. He told us about it. Said he sometimes comes here to find parts to upsell to his customers."

Basically charge the rich clients the price of a new part but give them the used part. What else did this guy do while he was here? "What's your friend's name?"

"Caleb," Levi replied. "Caleb Morales."

"Thank you," Luna said. "We might need to talk to him. Can you give us his information?"

Levi pulled his phone out and thumbed the screen. Corbin jotted down the phone number and made note of the social media profile and address for the detailing shop.

"Thanks for your help." Corbin gestured to Miller. "Special Agent Miller will escort you off the property. We may have more questions later, so please stay available."

The men nodded, visibly relieved to be leaving the scene. Corbin watched them go, noting the way Brock reached down to pet Maizie. The guys couldn't be too bad. They loved that dog, and they'd risked burglary charges by reporting the body and sticking around. Most criminals would've bolted.

Turning back to Luna, he said, "Let's hope this lead takes us somewhere."

"It's a start. And something tells me we need all the help we can get."

He pointed at the chopper circling. "I don't see how we can

possibly keep this top secret. I'll have to call the commissioner and see where he stands."

Together, they moved away from the makeshift seating area and through the tangled maze of boats and debris. As they approached Agent Ayres, Corbin noted the man's focused expression as he directed officers to document the sprawling scene.

"Ayres," Corbin called out, drawing the agent's attention. "What have you found so far?"

Ayres shook his head. "It's a mess out here. Everything could be trash or could be evidence. We've got officers documenting, but it's slow going."

Corbin glanced around, taking in the discarded items. He didn't envy the job of searching this place. Every boat would be combed over for evidence that this place was more than a graveyard. He decided to start with the obvious. "Any signs of a struggle? Footprints? Anything that stands out?"

"Nothing definitive," Ayres replied, gesturing to the area. "We've marked some potential evidence, but it's hard to tell what's relevant. We're planning to get a drone up in the morning for aerial footage. Maybe that'll give us a clearer picture."

Luna asked, "What about the perimeter? Any signs of recent activity or entry points?"

"We've got officers checking the fence line and any possible escape routes. But so far, nothing obvious." Ayres scratched his cheek. "I've got the local PD canvasing the neighborhood, such as it is. Maybe one of those fancy doorbell cameras caught something."

"Good. Let's make sure we have everything covered. Get me a full sweep of the area and detailed documentation of anything unusual," Corbin said.

"We'll keep at it," Ayres said. "I'll update you as soon as we have something concrete."

Corbin thanked Ayres and turned to Luna. "Let's go talk to Mr. Morales."

As they walked back to his car, he took one last look at the scene. The flashing lights of the police cruisers cast an eerie glow over the rotting boats. What a place to leave victims. Whoever put the bodies here had turned the boat graveyard into a human one.

"The layout of this place," he said, opening his car door. "It's a perfect cover for someone looking to hide bodies. All those boats, the overgrowth . . . it's a labyrinth."

Luna waited until they'd gotten in the car and closed their doors before she replied. "They must know the area well. They'd need to be familiar with the best entry and exit points."

Corbin nodded, starting the engine and pulling away from the crime scene. The car's headlights cut through the darkness, illuminating the twisted path.

He adjusted the air vent, trying to dispel the lingering scent of decay that seemed to have seeped into his clothes. "The drone footage will help us figure out how they're getting in and out."

Luna frowned. "But wouldn't it make more sense to just dump the bodies in the swamp? They'd be harder to find there. Why risk bringing them here and going through all the effort of burying them?"

Corbin nodded, considering her point. "My guess? They were controlling the discovery. If they disposed of the bodies in the Everglades, they could surface at the wrong time."

"You should bring in Tori to study the graves for a pattern. Her expertise as a behavioral analyst and criminal profiler could help. Maybe the killer simply wanted to keep them as trophies. Or someplace he could revisit them."

"Or blackmail," Corbin added. "If it's organ harvesting, they could be holding on to evidence to use against someone. A way to tip the scales if they ever needed to."

That made the most sense. If this was just about disposal, the swamp would've swallowed the evidence whole. But burying them? That meant control. Leverage. Someone in the chain wasn't just making money off stolen organs, they were keeping receipts.

Luna's phone screen lit her face as she swiped. "Oh, great. The media's already reporting this. They've just told the whole world about the bodies."

"That was fast." A little too fast. He gripped the steering wheel tighter. "Let's get Tori on board. If this is a serial offender targeting young girls like Carlie, we need to cross-reference with any similar missing persons cases in the area. Vulnerable teenagers, runaways ... they make easy targets and could be in danger."

His phone rang through the car's infotainment center. He glanced at the center screen where Harlee's name displayed across the top. He tapped the button to answer. "Hey, Har. I've got you on speaker with Luna here."

"Yeah, okay. I need to talk to you." Something in the way she said it cut through the noise in his head. Harlee didn't rattle easy.

"What's wrong?" He tightened his grip on the steering wheel. "What's going on?"

"I saw the news, then Tori filled me in. Is it true? You found Carlie ... and others?"

Tori already knew. Sounded like the Behavioral Investigative Unit had been briefed on the details of the case, the victims, the potential scope. But he wasn't sure why Harlee sounded so upset.

"Harlee, I appreciate your concern, but this isn't really an ATF case. We're not even sure what we're dealing with. Human trafficking. Organ harvesting." Or worse. A killer who murdered for enjoyment.

"Yeah, I know. That's why I'm so worried. Trinity Brown, one of our students." She drew in a breath loud enough for him to hear it. "Corbin ... she's missing."

18

LUNA'S HEART HAMMERED against her ribs. That hint of panic in Harlee's voice meant they were thinking the same thing.

Trinity. Missing. Just like Carlie.

And the other girls.

The ones they'd found in shallow graves.

But Liv had said Trinity ran. Repeatedly. Disappeared until Stryker found her and dragged her back. Liv thought she was still using, and Jordan pretty much confirmed it. So was she running now? Or had someone taken her?

"Harlee, are you sure Trinity is missing?" Luna was still on thin ice with her friend, and throwing doubt hadn't gone over too well last time. "Liv said she runs off sometimes."

Silence hummed through the phone for a beat. "Since when do you talk to Liv?"

Luna shifted. "I met her when I took a shower at the gym yesterday."

Corbin jumped in. "We questioned some teens earlier, and they said they knew Trinity. One called her a pillbilly."

Harlee's sigh rattled the car speakers. "Okay, yeah. Running's her specialty. Oxy's got ahold of her. Started after her heart transplant surgery."

"Heart transplant?" Her mouth went dry. Her daughter, if Trinity really was her daughter, had been close to death. While Luna had been overseas, oblivious, her child's heart had been failing. She'd needed a new one cut into her chest. The thought made Luna's own heart constrict.

"That's serious." She fought to keep her tone neutral when every maternal instinct she'd been suppressing all these years roared to life. She gripped the door handle to steady herself, grateful Corbin was focused on the road. "What happened?"

"Yeah," Harlee said. "From what little I know, she had cardiomyopathy from some virus. Happened before her parents died."

Her parents. Not Luna. Not Corbin. Someone else had been there while their daughter fought for her life. Someone else had held her hand through the terror and pain.

"That's awful, but why didn't Stryker kick her out of the program?" Corbin asked. "He has a zero-tolerance policy for drug use."

Luna stilled herself, waiting for the answer. She'd been asking herself the same thing, and if Harlee even hinted that Trinity might be their daughter, she'd be dropping the biggest bombshell since . . . Her mind flicked to the explosion in Peshawar, but she shut it down and focused on Harlee.

"Honestly? They knew each other before the program," Harlee said. "Stryker was friends with her father, a Miami detective. After her parents were killed by a drunk driver, she bounced around foster care. Started getting into trouble. Stryker felt responsible for her. That's why he's always chasing after her, bringing her back. Not to mention letting her push the boundaries and bend the rules when she's here."

It was true that Stryker had a soft spot for the lost and broken. But this . . . this felt different. Like there was something more.

The thought pulsed through her again. Trinity must be her daughter.

Their daughter.

She glanced at Corbin. Scrutinized his features for microexpressions correlated with an emotional response. Eyes wide. Brow raised. He was hearing this news for the first time.

He asked, "Why's Stryker letting her run wild? She's a bad example for the rest of the kids in the program."

"My guess?" Harlee hesitated. "He feels like her oxy addiction is his fault."

Corbin's and Luna's eyes met, a silent question passing between them.

"Why would he think that?" Corbin asked.

"I sorta overheard them arguing a few weeks back. Trinity was yelling, saying it was his fault she was hooked."

"His fault? How?" She couldn't imagine Stryker ever leading anyone to use drugs. Certainly not a kid.

"I didn't catch the whole conversation," Harlee said. "But apparently he convinced her to have the heart transplant when she didn't want it. She was in a bad place after losing her parents. Had some kind of death wish. The surgery led to the pain meds, and well..."

"Pain meds," Corbin said. "I've seen it a thousand times. People can become addicted in as little as five days."

Five days. That's all it took for those pills to grab hold. No wonder Jordan and the others had called her that name. The thing was, it might not be her fault. "So the heart transplant led to the pain meds?" Luna asked.

"That's what I gather," Harlee said. "I tried to get close to Trinity when she first came to the program. Thought maybe she needed another woman to talk to. But she kept everyone at a distance."

Luna's stomach knotted. The thought of Trinity isolating herself, battling grief and addiction with no support system, broke something inside her. But she couldn't say that. Couldn't reveal how personal this felt.

"I reported her missing to the locals," Harlee said. "She's a minor, and it's been over twenty-four hours."

"Good idea," Corbin said.

She nodded even though Harlee couldn't see her. "I think so too."

Especially if there was someone out there snatching runaways and carving them up for parts. She added, "But you never have to wait twenty-four hours to report a minor."

"That's right," Corbin said. "Don't let local PD tell you otherwise."

"Thanks, you guys. I'll file another report," Harlee said. "I've already talked to the other students, but it wouldn't hurt to nudge the local PD again."

"Any luck finding Steve?" Corbin asked, changing the subject.

"Not yet, but I pulled area footage and I'm running the partial plate I got for the G-Wagon. I'm running biometrics on Mr. Steve. Still searching for a match. And I'm digging into any connections Stryker might have to anyone named Steve. Tell me again why you didn't arrest that guy for assaulting you?"

"Bigger picture." Corbin touched his bruised jaw. "He could lead us to bigger players. I'll file a report and hand his gun over to the locals when I get a chance. Doubt it's registered to him, but as soon as we know his full name, I want to put surveillance on him."

"Fine," Harlee said.

"We have a lead to follow up on, but keep us posted." Corbin disconnected, then looked at her. "I couldn't go into everything with Harlee, but it bugs me that Steve mentioned Carlie by name, even though we didn't."

"Yeah, I caught that," she said.

They'd reached the address of the boat shop the witnesses had given them. Luna pointed out a white metal building with a nautical blue roof. The sign above the entrance read "Morales Marine Services." They pulled into the gravel lot and parked near the entrance.

The place looked deserted. No customers. No cars. Just rows of yachts and sailboats sitting on trailers along the side of the building. Across the street, a nail salon was sandwiched between a surf shop and an upscale thrift boutique.

"Looks like business is good." She got out of the car and followed Corbin to the front door.

A bell jingled as Corbin pushed the door open and held it for her. She stepped inside and stood in front of a small counter and a windowed wall that separated the customer area from the shop. It was surprisingly clean and well-organized. Gleaming boats filled the shop, their hulls polished to a mirrored shine. Tools hung neatly on pegboards along one wall. Four bay doors lined the opposite wall. The scent of wax and cleaning solution hung in the air. This place was the opposite of the boat graveyard.

A man came out of the shop through the glass door, carrying a fishing rod with a microfiber cleaning cloth in one hand. He wore a crisp white polo shirt, khaki shorts, and boat shoes. Sun wrinkles lined his tanned face, and a gold Rolex glinted on his wrist.

"Oops, forgot to put the closed sign out." The man chuckled. "But since you're here, what can I do for you?"

"Caleb Morales?" Corbin flashed his badge. "Agent King, FDLE. This is Agent Rosati. We have a few questions for you."

Well, that wasn't how she'd have gone about it. She cringed. So much for easing him in. Corbin's approach was about as subtle as a SWAT team busting down the door.

Morales's smile faltered. He set the fishing rod down, his gaze flicking between their badges. His smile returned, a bit strained this time. "Sure, officers. What can I do for you?"

"We're investigating a case," Corbin said. "We understand you do some salvaging at the boat graveyard out near the preserve area."

Morales's smile widened. "Salvaging? Now that's an ugly word, Agent. I prefer to think of it as . . . recycling. Giving those old boats a new life." He chuckled.

Corbin's hand twitched. A barely perceptible movement, but

Luna caught it. He didn't like Morales and his nervous laughter any more than she did.

She stepped closer to the counter, her gaze fixed on Morales. "You said you recycle those old boats. What exactly do you do with the parts?"

"Sell them," Morales said, his smile returning. "To other boat owners, repair shops, collectors. There's a big market for vintage parts, Agent. Especially here in Florida."

She'd seen that look before. He was lying. Or at least leaving something out.

"Interesting," Corbin said. "So you've got records? Invoices? Proof of who you've sold to?"

"Of course." Morales gestured toward a computer on his desk. "Everything's computerized now. Perfectly legal. I've got nothing to hide."

Did Morales know what dark things they'd found out there? Was this guy selling more than boat parts?

The door chimed, and a tall, well-dressed man entered the shop. He wore a crisp white linen suit and a Panama hat perched on his silver hair. A gold chain was buried in his protruding chest hair.

"Caleb, mi amigo!" The man pushed past Corbin and clapped Morales on the shoulder. His deep voice held a hint of a Cuban accent. "Thank goodness you're still open. Mi querida Goldie needs a little TLC. And you're the best in the business, Caleb."

"Mr. Fuentes. A pleasure, as always." Morales's smile was strained. "These are from the Florida Department of Law Enforcement."

Fuentes turned and gave Luna a quick up-and-down. "Since when do they make agents as beautiful as this?" He lifted his chin at Corbin. "You're one lucky man to have a partner like this, no?"

"Gracias, señor." Luna couldn't pretend to be shocked over his blatant flirting. The guy had money. Connections. Influence. He'd be used to women throwing themselves at him. At his money, really. She leaned against the counter. "And who might Goldie be?"

Fuentes's eyes crinkled at the corners. "Goldie is my boat. She's a bit of a demanding lady, you know?"

"The *Golden Horizon*," Morales chimed in. "A hundred and ten feet of pure luxury. State-of-the-art everything. You should see the master suite, Agent Rosati. It's bigger than my whole condo."

Probably room for a whole harem in there. "I'll take your word for it."

Fuentes waved a dismissive hand. "Bah, it's just a bachelor pad. A place to entertain a few compadres."

"I'm surprised you can handle servicing a yacht that size here." Corbin gestured to the modest shop.

"We don't do the big jobs here." Morales shook his head. "We have a full-service marina and shipyard down on the water. Anything from routine maintenance to complete refits. We also provide charter crews, and Mr. Fuentes is one of our most valued clients."

"Gracias, amigo, it's why I stopped by. I'm throwing a little party on her this weekend. Nothing too fancy. Just a few friends. But I need a caterer who can handle all my usual requests." He looked at Luna. "Nothing but the best for my guests."

Morales glanced at Corbin, then back to Fuentes. "Well, let's see. Were you comfortable with the caterer who handled your event last time? They specialize in exclusive clientele like you."

Fuentes clapped his hands together. "Perfecto! Yes, set it up. And you'll get my Goldie looking shipshape for the weekend, won't you?" He winked. "No expense spared, of course."

"Of course. Nothing but the best for you, sir," Morales said.

"Perhaps I'll see you aboard on Saturday, florcita?" Fuentes flashed Luna a smile that came across a little more predatory than charming. "I always enjoy the company of a beautiful woman." Fuentes paused at the doorway and grinned. "Enjoy the evening, agents." He tipped his Panama hat and disappeared out the door.

"He seems nice." Luna studied Morales, seeing the beads of sweat forming on his forehead. His hand trembled as he reached for a pen and jotted down a note.

Corbin waved a hand in front of his face. "He wears too much cologne."

Her throat worked as she fought back a laugh. Corbin, jealous? Of a guy like Fuentes, dripping in gold and cologne?

"Back to the boat graveyard." Corbin crossed his arms. "How'd you find out about that place?"

"What's with all the questions about the boat graveyard?" Morales dabbed at his forehead with his shirtsleeve. "Something happen out there?"

Corbin's expression remained neutral. "Just routine inquiries."

"Look, I don't even remember how I heard about the place." Morales gestured vaguely. "It was years ago. A buddy mentioned it."

"A buddy?" Morales was lying again. Luna could tell. The guy was a terrible liar.

"One of my employees, okay?" Morales finally admitted. "He used to work at another shop down the coast. Knew about the place. Said they used to scavenge parts out there."

"And I'm guessing none of you had permission to do that," she said.

"Does it really matter?" Morales spread his hands. "It's a graveyard. Those boats are just rotting away."

Carlie's shallow grave flashed through her mind. The scent of damp earth and decay.

"I'm not really concerned about you stealing boat parts, Mr. Morales." Corbin kept his tone even. "We're looking for people who've been there recently."

Morales hesitated, then shook his head. "Look, if I could tell you, I would. I don't keep tabs on every beach bum who wanders out there."

"Except your surfer friends." Luna raised a brow. She wondered if Corbin noticed the subtle twitch in the corner of Morales's mouth.

"Brock? Yeah, well, he's family." Morales shrugged. "He's trying to start his own little repair service. I threw him a bone. Figured it wouldn't hurt."

Corbin pulled out his phone. "And the employee who told you about it. What's his name?"

Morales told him.

Corbin took his time typing notes into his phone. "We'll be in touch, Mr. Morales." He tucked his phone away.

"Anytime," Morales said, though his smile didn't reach his eyes.

"Dead end for now," Corbin said as they walked to the car. "I've got someone pulling property records. We'll find out who owns the boat graveyard."

She opened the passenger door and paused. Through the shop window, she saw Morales, already on the phone, one hand cupped over the mouthpiece. "Who you think he's calling first? Brock or Fuentes?"

"Or someone else. Someone with a vested interest in keeping the boat graveyard's secrets buried." Corbin settled behind the wheel and started the engine.

"You worried about Fuentes and his special catering request?" She clicked her seat belt and glanced at him.

"I've got enough on my plate right now." Corbin pulled out of the parking lot. "I'll mention it to another agent." He glanced at her. "You hungry? I haven't eaten all day."

Food. The thought of it made her stomach churn. Those images from the boat graveyard, those shallow graves, were seared into her mind. After seeing that, she wasn't sure she'd ever be hungry again. But . . . she hadn't eaten all day either. And her body needed fuel. "Actually, yeah, I could eat."

He navigated the streets, heading toward the coast. "All right, we'll grab some food. But first, I want to take a peek at Morales's other shop."

Always thinking one step ahead. She had to give him that. His instincts were sharp.

Ten minutes later, they pulled up outside a sprawling marina. Dozens of luxury yachts were moored to the docks. Fiberglass hulls gleamed in the moonlight. Lights twinkled on the decks, reflecting their colors on the dark water.

Corbin shut off the engine. "Let's take a look around."

They got out of the car and walked along the pier, the wooden planks creaking beneath their feet. Music drifted from one of the boats, a blend of pulsing bass and sultry vocals. This was a playground for the wealthy, a world of champagne wishes and caviar dreams. A world she'd only ever glimpsed from the shadows.

The darkened windows of the marina office reflected the moon's pale light. A security camera, mounted above the entrance, swiveled. Its red light blinked in the darkness. They walked along the side of the building, a narrow strip of concrete separating the water from the parking lot. Cigarette butts littered the ground near the side entrance.

"What are we looking for?" Luna asked.

"Don't know. Just . . . whatever jumps out." He stopped, both hands on his waist. "Sorry. This is stupid. You're probably exhausted, and no one is here. Let's get out of here. I'll have an officer come down and question the crew in the morning."

What was that? Exasperation? Exhaustion? She knew she felt both. It had been a long day. Missing girls. Kidnapping. Graves. Shady boat dealers. Flirty billionaires. All this and no closer to answers.

"Sure." She followed him as he turned back toward the car.

Corbin was halfway there when Luna stopped. A shadow shifted. Movement. Faint, but she caught it.

Men dressed in black tactical gear. Faces obscured by balaclavas.

"Corbin!" She grabbed his arm and yanked.

The sharp crackle of a Taser. A flash of blue light.

19

A BLUE SPARK ILLUMINATED the darkness for a heartbeat, followed by the hiss of electricity. The Taser probe whizzed past Corbin's ear, missing by a hair. His pulse fluttered in his neck.

Luna's fingers dug into his arm. She'd yanked him back just in time.

No time to breathe. No time to draw his weapon.

Two figures materialized from the shadows, solidifying into men. Masked faces indistinct in the dim light. Intentions crystal clear.

The first attacker was built like a linebacker. The second circled like a predator, a distinct hitch in his step marking his movement. Corbin grabbed for his gun, but the linebacker charged straight at him.

Corbin dodged, but the linebacker whirled and grabbed his head. Nails dug into his scalp. The world tilted as the attacker twisted him off balance. A muscular arm clamped around his neck. Bicep against his throat. He writhed. Fought the pressure.

Corbin clawed at the attacker's arm. He needed space. He needed air.

Hitch stopped circling and drove his knee into Corbin's gut. Precious air burst from his lungs. He tried to double over, but the arm around his neck kept him upright. Black spots pulsed at the edges of his vision. His fingers scrabbled at his holster. The gun was there but unreachable.

"Stop! Or I'll shoot!" Luna's voice sliced through the night.

His vision swam, but he caught a glimpse of her with her Glock aimed in their direction. Stance rock solid. But she wasn't firing. Of course she wasn't. The men were too close, using Corbin's body as a shield.

A third attacker appeared from behind a parked car, moving toward Luna. This one was shorter than the others but moved with liquid precision. How many were there? He strained to see shapes in the gloom and saw Number Three had his arm extended.

"Gun!" Corbin croaked.

A crackle of electricity filled the air.

Corbin's muscles strained against the linebacker's hold. He watched in horror as Luna went rigid. Her body jerked as the Taser's current coursed through her. Her eyes widened, and her mouth opened in a silent scream. She toppled backward, hitting the ground hard. Her gun clattered across the pavement, skittering away into the darkness.

White-hot fury surged, lending him strength he didn't know he possessed. He bucked violently, trying to throw his head back for a headbutt. The linebacker behind him anticipated the move, shifting out of range. Corbin's skull connected with nothing but air, sending a jolt of pain down his neck. Frustration mixed with the anger coursing through his veins.

Fine. Plan B.

He hooked his legs around Hitch, pulling with all his strength. He used his weight to drag them off balance, muscles straining with the effort. They crashed to the ground in a jumble of arms and legs, Corbin sandwiched between the two attackers.

The impact drove what little air he had left from his lungs. For a moment, stars exploded behind his eyes. Rough asphalt scraped against his cheek. The sting barely registered.

Where was Luna? He couldn't see her, couldn't tell if she was okay.

He grappled with the linebacker, managing to lock him into a sleeper hold. His arm trembled, muscles screaming, but he held on. The guy was solid, all muscle and training. He squeezed tighter, praying the man would go down fast.

A hand clawed at his waist. Hitch reaching for Corbin's sidearm.

He swatted frantically with his free hand, trying to maintain the chokehold on the linebacker. It was like fighting an octopus—hands everywhere, grasping, pulling. Salty sweat stung his eyes. Breaths came in ragged gasps.

Metal scraped against leather. His gun.

His heart hammered as he felt the weapon pulled free.

Time slowed. Seconds stretched. Training took over. He wrenched his body, using the linebacker in the sleeper hold as a human shield. Hitch pointed Corbin's own weapon at them, hesitating as his partner struggled in Corbin's grip.

A gunshot erupted, a thunderous blast that seemed to rip the night apart. Corbin felt the shock wave ripple through his body, leaving his ears ringing and his eyes watering. The linebacker in his arms jerked and went limp, suddenly dead weight. The coppery scent of blood filled the air, mixing with the lingering smell of gunpowder.

No time to process. No time to think about the life that had just ended, however justified. Survival. He swept Hitch's legs with every ounce of strength he had left.

Hitch toppled backward. Surprise flashed in the eyes visible behind the balaclava. Corbin's gun discharged twice more and clattered to the asphalt as the attacker fell. Bullets whizzed, pinging off a nearby car. Sparks flew as metal met metal.

Hitch was on the ground, scrambling for the gun.

Corbin beat him to it and shifted the textured grip into his palm. He aimed at Hitch on his back. "Don't move!"

Hitch's hands went up about shoulder height. He grinned, a flash of white teeth visible through the mouth hole in his mask. "You gonna shoot me, Officer?"

Corbin's finger hovered over the trigger. Could he do it? Take a life? What choice did he have? The man was armed, dangerous. But . . . was it the same man who'd taken Stryker?

He couldn't kill him. Not until he had answers. "You're under arrest."

He risked a glance at Luna, heart in his throat. His blood turned to ice to see Number Three searching her prone form for a weapon. Number Three rolled Luna onto her back.

Big mistake.

Her legs coiled, then snapped out with devastating force. Both boots caught the man square in the jaw. The crack of impact echoed across the parking lot. Number Three's head snapped back, eyes rolling up in his skull. He crumpled into a heap like a marionette with cut strings. She'd hit the sweet spot and knocked him clean out.

That was his partner. Tough as nails, even when down.

"Corbin! Watch out!"

He started to turn, but Hitch was already moving. A roll. Swift and smooth. Hitch came up on one knee and jammed his palm upward into Corbin's gun hand.

He dodged just before his own weapon struck him in the face.

Fire bloomed along his side. Corbin hissed, stumbling back. Warm blood seeped through his shirt, sticky against his skin. That's when he noticed the knife.

Already Hitch had his arm back, readying to drive the blade a second time. Corbin dodged.

Hitch came at him again, lunging, but Corbin was ready for it. He shifted his weight, pivoting to the side, and slammed his forearm into Hitch's wrist, deflecting the blade. The knife scraped against his jeans, tearing fabric but not flesh.

Corbin's free hand shot out, fist connecting with Hitch's nose. A satisfying crunch. Blood spurted, splattering against Corbin's shirt. The man flew at Corbin, knocking him back. The ground rushed up to meet him. Pain shot through his shoulder as he hit the asphalt.

Hitch was on him in an instant. Fists flying in a rage-fueled battering. The Glock flew from his grip and landed steps away, just out of reach. They grappled on the hot asphalt. Arms locked. Teeth bared. Hitch's shattered nose was inches above Corbin's, dripping blood.

From the corner of his eye, Corbin sensed movement. A blur of black coming at him.

Luna. She'd somehow gotten to her feet and was moving toward them, silent and swift.

Hitch turned, but Luna's leg was already in motion. Her boot smashed into his ribs. A guttural noise exploded from the man, and he fell sideways.

One fluid motion. Legs pistoning. Core engaged. Corbin pushed off the ground, using his momentum to power himself upright. The cut on his side burned, but he could still move. Could still get them out of this. He reached down and picked up his gun. It clicked into its holster.

He did not want to kill anyone else tonight. He wanted answers.

His hand went to his pocket and closed around the molded grip of his ASP baton. He snapped it open. Twenty-one inches of hardened steel. Ready.

Corbin shifted his stance, falling into a defensive posture. His breath came in short, sharp bursts, each inhale sending a stab of pain through his ribs and side.

The attacker staggered to his feet, clutching his stomach. He glared at Luna. "You little—" He lunged, grabbing Luna by the hair and pulling her into his arms. The knife pressed against her throat.

Corbin froze, his heart a drum in his chest.

Luna's eyes met his. A message there. *Trust me.*

His fist tightened around the baton. Every muscle in his body screamed to attack, but the knife... So close to Luna's carotid. He couldn't risk it.

Luna's gaze flicked down. To Hitch's feet. Then back to Corbin's eyes.

She shifted to her right and slammed both elbows back, connecting with the man's ribs. She twisted, using the momentum to pull away, ducking under his arm. Her leg whipped up in a roundhouse kick to Hitch's temple.

Corbin pivoted on his left foot, driving all his weight forward. The baton struck Hitch's knee. The same knee that had given Hitch his distinctive gait. Solid impact.

Hitch dropped like a stone. A strangled cry ripped from the man's throat. One arm reached out, grasping at the asphalt as if trying to hold onto something solid, something real.

For a moment, Hitch locked eyes with him and Corbin saw the realization dawn. This wasn't going to plan. Whatever that plan was.

Movement made Corbin glance up.

The man Luna had KO'd stirred, pushing himself up on shaky arms. Corbin's heart sank as he watched Number Three's hand close around something on the ground. The streetlight glinted off metal, and he recognized the distinctive shape of a gun.

"Luna, move!" He scrambled for cover behind a parked sedan. A crack.

The rush of air as a round whizzed past.

The shower of glass raining down on his head.

He crouched lower and pressed himself against the cool metal of the vehicle, willing his racing heart to slow. Shards crunched under his feet as he shifted position.

Where was Luna? He couldn't see her. Had she found cover?

Was she hit? He strained his ears, trying to pick up any sound that might give him a clue to either her location or the gunman's.

Another gunshot. The sound jolted him, shattering his focus. Luna. Was she hit? Was she firing? He couldn't tell.

Corbin crouch-walked toward Number Three. In the darkness he saw Hitch on his feet, hobbling away. He melted into the shadows between parked cars. Corbin started to give chase, but a bullet exploded the sideview mirror beside his head. Bits of plastic flew into his face, his hair.

He dropped to his belly and saw Luna flat on her stomach on the other side of the car.

For a moment, they lay there. The only sound was their ragged breathing. The dim orange glow from a nearby parking light spilled across the asphalt between them, just enough for Corbin to make out Luna's face beneath the car. A mix of exhaustion and adrenaline in her eyes.

He pointed to himself, then to Luna.

She nodded.

Using his forearms and the sides of his feet, he combat-crawled, inching his way around the car. The cut on his side burned like fire, but he kept moving. When he reached Luna, he whispered, "You okay?"

"I'll live, but I think he's got my gun." They were close. Close enough to feel her breath mingle with his. "We need to get out of here."

He swallowed. "Yeah, let's give it a minute."

Two minutes passed. Five.

He was about to suggest they make a run for his car when tires screeched in the distance. Corbin drew his gun, wincing at the slight click sound. He crouched and peered through the windows of the Subaru they used as cover.

A dark SUV had pulled up, its engine idling. The driver's door swung open at the same time the rear liftgate opened. Hitch slid out, looking unsteady but determined. Number Three dragged the dead body of the linebacker toward the vehicle.

The two men loaded the body into the cargo space and pressed the power button. Corbin heard a faint warning beep as the gate closed, sealing the dead man inside. Two doors slammed. The SUV rammed into gear and sped to the end of the aisle and turned toward them.

"Let's go." He pulled himself up, stifling a groan.

Keeping their heads low, they sprinted across the parking lot, ducking behind cars for cover. His side burned with every step, but he pushed on. They couldn't afford to slow down. Not when they didn't know if more attackers were lying in wait.

When they reached his car, Corbin opened Luna's door. He watched for movement in the lot while she slipped inside. Once she was safe, he darted to the driver's side, climbed in, and shut the door. He rested his gun on his thigh and wrapped his other arm around his middle to cover the ache in his side.

"I saw them leave the parking lot heading north," Luna said.

"Good. I'll call it in. Just . . . give me a second." He sagged in his seat, the adrenaline draining from his system. Without its numbing effects, the pain in his side flared. He looked down at his hand, surprised to see his fingers slick with blood.

"Luna," he said. "We have a problem."

20

THE HARSH LIGHT PIERCED Stryker's eyelids, dragging him back to consciousness. White. So much white. Different than the oppressive darkness he'd been trapped in before.

The steady beep of monitors filled his ears. Rhythmic.

He was no longer in that nightmarish room.

A hospital. They'd moved him to a hospital.

His mind felt foggy. Thoughts slipped away like smoke. Another sedative. He'd been so fixated on the glint of the scalpel, he'd missed the needle. Amateur mistake. Bound or not, he should have anticipated it. Should have stayed sharp.

Stryker tried to sit up, but his body refused to cooperate. His muscles felt like water. All strength sapped away by whatever drugs they'd pumped into his system. Fatigue weighed on him, threatening to pull him back under.

He tested his arms. Feet. No good.

Restraints bit into his wrists and ankles, holding him firmly in place. Prisoners had more room in their shackles.

But he wasn't on the hard surface from before. A bed. Softer but no less confining.

He glanced down at himself. Someone had covered him with

a thin cotton blanket and folded it at his waist. A white hospital gown with tiny blue polka dots covered his body. His gaze traveled to his arms, noting the tubes and wires snaking from beneath the thin fabric.

Again, he pulled against the restraints. Nothing.

A pinch in his upper arm drew a wince. His eyes followed the tubing up to bags of clear fluid hanging nearby. An IV line, probably. Heart monitor. Pulse oximeter. A thicker tube ran from somewhere beneath the blanket. Catheter, most likely. They were keeping him alive but immobile.

Mirrors lined two walls. One-way windows. They were watching him.

A TV hung in one corner, switched off. Cabinets lined another wall, a sink and counter beneath them. Everything pristine. Sterile.

He tried once more to break free, muscles stretching, straining against the padded cuffs. Nothing. Not even an inch of give.

Maybe he'd miscalculated. Letting them take him. He'd seen their car trailing him. Knew they'd make their move. Figured it was the best play at the time—let them think they'd won. Get inside, gather intel. Evidence. But now? Trapped. Drugged.

He should have found another way.

But deep down, it had been inevitable. They were always going to come for him. He'd just hoped to have more time. Time to warn Luna. To tell her the truth about Trinity. About everything.

The door opened with a soft hiss. The doctor entered. Gone was the nondescript outfit, replaced by a crisp white lab coat over navy slacks and a button-down shirt. An ID badge hung from his pocket, a logo Stryker couldn't quite make out. Not that it mattered. He knew exactly who this was.

His tie. Wow. A riot of clashing colors and bizarre patterns. "Doc, that is quite possibly the ugliest piece of neckwear I've ever seen."

"Good to see you awake." Doc sounded almost cheerful. He tapped at a tablet in his hands, eyes scanning whatever data was displayed there. "You'll be pleased to know you're in excellent health for a man of your age. Quite impressive, really."

He wasn't that old—wait. "How do you know my age?"

Doc looked up, a patronizing smile on his face. "Don't be silly. I have all of my patients' medical histories. It's standard procedure."

"I'm not your patient."

"Now, now. That's no way to talk to the physician who's taking care of you. I am keeping you healthy, after all."

He knew that tone. It was the same saccharine sweet one Tori used when she was in psychiatrist mode.

"Where's Trinity?"

A flicker of . . . something passed across the doctor's face. Annoyance? Concern? It was gone too quickly to read. "Don't worry about Ms. Brown. She's in good hands now."

"She was in good hands before."

Doc's arms formed an X over his tablet as he held it against his chest. "Was she? If that were true, she wouldn't be killing herself with drugs, now would she?"

The accusation hit like a liver strike. Painful. Debilitating. The program had failed her. He'd failed her.

"You know, I just don't understand it." Doc began to pace. "Youngsters like Trinity. They have their whole lives ahead of them. They could be anything. Astronaut. Doctor. Inventor. Artist. Supreme Court justice." He ticked them off on his fingers. "The world is their oyster. And what do they do?" Doc glared at him. "They choose death."

He had a sinking feeling he already knew, but he asked, "What do you mean?"

"They run away from home, chasing after meaningless things. Get lost in promiscuity, alcohol, drugs. Meanwhile, they don't see that they're killing themselves." Doc's words came faster. "STDs. Liver failure. Irreparable damage to their developing brains. And you know what the real tragedy is?"

He continued, not waiting for a response. "While these girls are throwing their lives away, there are others their age suffering through no fault of their own." He stopped at the foot of Stryker's bed, and Stryker had to put his chin to his chest to see him.

"Imagine a girl who dreams of being a surgeon. She's made all the right choices. Made the grades. Volunteered. Saved her money. Gotten into an Ivy League school. And all the while, a disease she didn't ask for, didn't cause, is slowly killing her." Doc punched the last two words. "She doesn't know when she'll die, but she knows she will. It's hopeless. Unless there's a miracle. All the while, girls like Trinity are working overtime to kill themselves... On purpose."

Doc's eyes blazed with outrage. "Can you imagine what that must feel like? To know you would do anything to have a healthy body. A chance to see all your hard work pay off. But then you see a girl your own age simply throwing their perfectly good healthy body away?"

Pieces fell into place. "Is that what you're looking for, Doc? Healthy bodies? Healthy organs?"

Doc wagged his finger at him. "Ah, I knew you were smart. That's why I never should have let you bring Trinity to the clinic. You lack something the others had."

"And what's that?"

"Desperation," Doc said simply. "The desperate need to save your child's life at all costs."

"Even if it means someone else has to die?" He took a moment to push down what he felt rising in his chest. "You're supposed to be helping people here. It's why I talked Trinity into joining the clinical trial."

"I *am* helping people! I saved Trinity's life. Without me, she would've died. I had to bring her back to keep her from destroying herself again." He rounded the bed and jabbed a finger in Stryker's chest. "If you had done your job, none of this would have been necessary."

The accusation stung, but he pushed past it. "What do you mean, you had to bring her back?"

The doctor sighed, running a hand through his hair. "I have to keep my investors happy. They won't keep funding my research if I don't show progress. Not every person survives, but they do live on. And if more people understood how important my work is, then I wouldn't have to take matters into my own hands."

This man didn't see people—he saw resources. Test subjects. And when he'd said he didn't waste resources...

The doctor must have read something in his expression, because a small, satisfied smile played at the corners of his mouth. "Don't worry, Mr. King. Your sacrifice will save lives. Isn't that what you've always wanted? To save lives. To... make a difference?"

Stryker glanced down at the tubes and wires connected to his body. The realization sank in.

He wasn't just a prisoner here.

He was the next experiment.

21

LUNA WAS STARTING to look back fondly on the maelstrom of anguish she'd been in yesterday morning. Back when a coffee date with Stryker was the biggest storm on the horizon. Because this? This was a tempest. A raging hurricane ripping through her meticulously curated life.

How many times could a person cheat death? Two? Three? These last forty-eight hours had been a gauntlet of close calls. The fire. The attackers. She'd stared down men with enough firepower to level a city block with less adrenaline thrumming through her veins than she had now. Probably it was the only thing keeping her on her feet because it was after midnight and she was bone tired.

She stood in the corner, watching as the doctor prepped to stitch the gash on Corbin's side. Despite the fight they'd just endured, a small part of her couldn't help but be impressed. Corbin's talents had shone through tonight, his quick thinking and combat skills saving them both. The way he'd moved. Fluid and precise. It was a reminder of the boy she'd once known, and the man he'd become in her absence.

The thought flitted around her head again. Could Trinity really be their daughter? The timing fit. The resemblance was there. But how could she tell Corbin? And should she now that Trinity had disappeared?

Her eyes focused on Corbin, resting with his hands behind his head, eyes closed. There was a strength in him that she both admired and feared. It was the same strength she'd fallen for all those years ago, and the same strength that had allowed him to confront her when she'd returned. Luna wondered, not for the first time, if she'd made the right choice back then. If the life she'd built for herself was worth the pain of leaving.

"I think we're about ready," the doctor said, rolling the metal tray of instruments closer to Corbin. She'd introduced herself as Dr. Payne, and they'd had a good laugh about the name.

Dr. Payne reached for a fresh pair of gloves. "Okay, Agent King, I'm going to need you to take your shirt off."

Heat crept up Luna's neck. She was already feeling far too connected to Corbin. She didn't need to see him shirtless on top of everything else. "I'll . . . I'll be right back," she mumbled, making a hasty exit. "Just need to make a call."

In the hallway, she leaned against the wall, taking a deep breath. The cool surface grounded her, helping to clear her mind. She pulled out her phone, fingers flying over the screen as she pulled up the social media profile for Trinity Brown.

She scrolled through the few public images, scrutinizing each one. In every photo, Trinity's smile seemed a little more forced, her eyes a little more distant. It was like watching a flower wilt in slow motion. How had no one noticed?

None of the photos or posts she could access mentioned medical issues. She needed more. Needed help. Before she could second-guess herself, she was dialing Harlee's number. The phone rang once, twice, three times. Luna paced the hallway.

"Hello?" Harlee's keyboard clacked in the background.

"It's Luna. Just checking in while Corbin gets stitched up."

"Still can't believe you guys were ambushed like that." The typing paused. "How's he doing, anyway?"

"Good, all things considered. Should be done soon." She hated small talk but liked that Harlee put Corbin before business. "I wanted to ask, have you checked in about?"

A heavy sigh came through the line. "I have, but the local cops didn't seem too eager to look into it. They know she has a history as a runaway."

"Typical." She knew this story all too well. Overworked cops, limited resources, kids falling through the cracks. It was a cycle she'd seen play out too many times, and it never got easier. "Did she take her medications with her? I mean, I assume she needs immunosuppressants or something."

"No, which makes finding her extremely urgent."

Luna's phone slipped from her hand. She tried to snatch it, but it bounced from one hand to the other. Her ankle flew out to break the phone's fall, but it hit the burn spot on her shin before sliding to the floor. Cringing, she snatched it up and put the phone back to her ear.

Harlee was saying, ". . . as a part of a clinical trial at Chiron Bio-Innovation Center."

"Hold up, I think I missed part of that. She had a heart transplant as a part of a clinical trial?"

"That's right. I forget the medical jargon, but the study was to evaluate a new surgical technique on pediatric patients with cardiomyopathy like Trinity's. Stryker helped her get into the program because he knew someone pretty high up," Harlee said. "That was last year, and Stryker had her join the Warrior program after her recovery. That's about all I know."

A nurse approached, informing Luna that the doctor had finished with Corbin. She nodded. "Listen, I'm going to check on Corbin. I'll be in touch."

Luna reentered the room just as Corbin was sliding his shirt back on. She averted her eyes, focusing instead on the bloody instruments and gauze on the nearby tray. The sight made her stomach churn. Not from the blood but because Trinity had needed a heart transplant.

Was it *her* fault? She'd tried to eat healthy and exercise during her pregnancy, but maybe that wasn't enough. Maybe Trinity's heart was more susceptible to the virus because it had been broken by parents who'd abandoned her.

Dr. Payne peeled off her gloves. "The wound isn't serious, but you'll be sore for a few days." She tossed the gloves onto the tray. "You need to take it easy." The doctor looked at Luna and pointed. "You'll help with that, right?"

She glanced at Corbin. Everything in his lopsided smile said he hadn't "taken it easy" for decades and had no plans to start now. "I'll try."

Dr. Payne rattled off care instructions and promised to print them with his discharge papers.

The door swung open, and Blade sauntered in, grinning. "Look at you, tough guy. Showing off your battle scars?"

Corbin rolled his eyes but lifted his shirt to show the white bandage. "How many, Doc?"

"Sixteen," the doctor replied, tossing the bloody gauze into the biohazard bin.

Blade shrugged. "Just a scratch."

"A bleeder, though." Dr. Payne smiled. "It's the bruised ribs that will be the real bugger."

"I'm not worried about that." Corbin waved a hand at his blazer hanging on a hook. "That's the second suit I've ruined."

"Yes, by all means, focus on the things you can easily replace." Dr. Payne shook her head as she headed for the door. "I'll be right back."

Blade pulled up a chair. The earlier levity evaporated. "I really dropped by to make sure you're both okay." He glanced between her and Corbin. "So, any idea who those guys were? The kidnappers?"

"Not sure," she said. "We might have prints on Corbin's gun."

"I turned it over to Officer Pierce, who met us here." Corbin eased his legs off the exam table and let them dangle. "Told her to run the prints through the military and criminal databases. Those guys were too well trained to be regular thugs. They were professionals."

"This, on top of everything else." Blade's expression softened. "I heard about Carlie and the other girls. I'm sorry you'll have to face the commissioner now."

Corbin's jaw tightened. "Yeah, well, he was already threatening my job. I'm preparing for the worst."

"Stay positive. You're not to blame for this," Blade said. "We've got a few deputies out there, and they said this has been going on awhile."

"Dr. Santos texted. We've got five graves so far, but they're still looking. We'll meet her at the morgue in the morning to hear her findings." Corbin looked at Luna for approval, and Luna nodded. She'd be there with him, no doubt about it. "What about you? Where are you with Stryker's case?"

Blade stood and leaned against the counter beside Luna. "DeLuca is a dead end. Literally." He lifted the metal lid off the jar of cotton balls and looked inside. "I got a call earlier to inform me he's dead." The lid clattered back down, and Blade faced them.

Luna's breath caught in her throat. She saw Corbin tense, and his hand unconsciously moved to cradle his injured side. "How?"

"Turns out, he's been in lockup the past three months on a manslaughter charge," Blade said. "Someone shanked him in the shower."

Corbin ran his thumb and forefinger around his mouth. "I knew Abercorn was lying. But who did he sell those Tasers to? If he sold them at all."

Luna started to speak, but the doctor returned then, handing Corbin his discharge papers and a prescription for pain medication and an antibiotic. "I'm serious about taking it easy," she warned.

"Yeah, yeah." As soon as she left, Corbin said, "We need to get back to my office." He tried to stand, sucked air between his clenched teeth, and leaned against the exam table.

"What about taking it easy?" Blade asked.

Corbin shot him a "yeah right" look.

Luna crossed her arms. "What time did you say we're meeting Dr. Santos tomorrow?"

"Six."

She could see the restlessness in his eyes, the need to be doing something, anything, to move the case forward. It was a feeling she knew all too well. The drive to keep pushing, to find answers, even when your body was screaming for rest.

She felt torn. Part of her wanted to dive deeper into Trinity's disappearance, to follow up on the leads or question Abercorn again. But another part recognized their need to recharge if they were going to be effective tomorrow.

"Let me drive you home tonight," she found herself saying.

Blade shot Corbin a look.

Okay, that came out wrong. She tried again. "You shouldn't be behind the wheel with those pain meds."

Corbin looked like he wanted to argue, but exhaustion won out. He nodded.

The case wouldn't be solved in one night, no matter how much they pushed themselves. But tomorrow...

Trinity's face. Those haunted eyes. Luna felt the years of guilt and regret she'd carefully suppressed. She couldn't keep this from Corbin any longer.

He had to know.

22

THE DRIVE TO CORBIN'S HOUSE was quiet, punctuated only by the map program's occasional directions. Luna debated whether to tell him about Trinity. The words hovered on the tip of her tongue, threatening to spill out at any moment. But as she glanced over at his sleeping form, head resting against the window, she decided against it.

Let him rest. He had enough to deal with, including the meeting with the commissioner tomorrow. It could wait. She just hoped she wasn't making another mistake by keeping silent.

At Corbin's house, she parked his car in the garage and helped him out. Her arm went around his waist to guide him inside. He stumbled against her as they walked.

"Sorry." He winced. "I'm so sore."

"It's been a long day." She eased him down on the couch and arranged the pillows behind his back. "Let me get your medication and some water."

"Cups are beside the fridge. There's a filtered water faucet beside the regular one."

She crossed the room to the kitchen where an island with white marble countertops dominated the area. She grabbed a glass from the cabinet, walked to the sink in the island, and filled it with water.

Corbin's place wasn't the sparse bachelor pad she'd expected. His home was warm. Cozy. Travertine tiles stretched across the open living space, softened by strategically placed rugs that tied the room together. The furniture was light, accented with comfortable-looking chairs. Pops of green brought life to the space. Beyond the sliding glass doors, the pool glistened under the moonlight.

What really caught her eye were the plants. They were everywhere. Green, lush, and thriving.

Ferns cascaded from hanging baskets. Succulents lined windowsills. An impressive fiddle leaf fig stood proudly in one corner. Nothing like the sad little apartment where she'd lived in Pakistan. The few plants she'd attempted to keep alive had been little more than twigs in pots.

This... this nurturing, almost domestic, side of him... Corbin was different.

All those late-night study sessions, his brow furrowed in concentration as he pored over textbooks. The whispered promises of a future together, dreams spun sitting on the beach after their early morning run. Stolen kisses between classes, the thrill of young love filling her every waking moment.

This could have been their life together. Their home.

She handed him the water and perched on the ottoman. Pulled the pill bottles from the paper bag and read the tiny labels. Antibiotics. Pain meds.

She twisted the caps off, tapped out the correct doses, then held them out. "Here. Two antibiotics now, then one every twelve hours. And one of these for pain. Only if you need it."

Their fingers brushed, and Luna felt a jolt of electricity that had nothing to do with Tasers or danger. That was ridiculous. She shouldn't be here. Shouldn't be letting those old feelings creep back in. Corbin might have the domesticated life they'd always dreamed of, but it still didn't erase the past. He might have wanted this, but he hadn't wanted it with her.

"What are those?" He pointed to the third bottle.

"Antinausea meds. The painkillers can make you queasy."

"Let's skip those for now." He swallowed the pills, chasing them with the last of the water. "Well, I've met my insurance deductible for the year. All in one day." A weak smile. But at least he was trying to make light of it.

"Rest. The medication will kick in soon." She leaned forward to take the empty glass from him. "Oh, we never ate. Can I make you something before I go?"

"I'm starved. But you don't have to cook. There are some prepped meals in the fridge."

Luna raised an eyebrow but went to investigate. The fridge was impressively well-stocked, unlike her own perpetually bare one. Glass containers with colored lids lined the shelves.

"What are all these?" She pulled out a container, examining the contents. Some kind of chicken dish, it looked like, with roasted vegetables on the side.

"Prepped meals. It's the only way I can eat healthy with my schedule." Corbin gestured with his chin toward the fridge. "Green containers are salads, blue are fish, red are steak, purple is comfort food."

"You even color-coded them?"

He shrugged. "It makes it easier to grab and go. I don't have time to think about what I'm eating when I'm running out the door."

Okay, this was a level of organization that both impressed and intimidated her. It was . . . attractive, in a way she hadn't expected. This glimpse into his life. So organized and put together.

"What'll you have?"

"Purple lid," Corbin requested.

"What's purple?"

"Meatloaf, mashed potatoes, green beans."

Luna grabbed two, deciding to join him. She microwaved their dinner according to his instructions. This new side of Corbin had really thrown her off her game. So domestic. So . . . settled.

They ate side by side on the couch. The food was delicious. Leagues better than the takeout and microwave meals Luna subsisted on. The silence stretched, punctuated by the clinking of forks against glass containers. The tension from the day began to ebb away, replaced by a comfortable familiarity that both soothed and unnerved her.

She'd decided to put talking about the bodies in the boat graveyard off until tomorrow, but sitting here beside him . . . it couldn't wait. She had to tell him her idea.

"While you were getting stitched up, I called Harlee. She told me something about Trinity."

"What about her?" Corbin's gaze snapped to hers as he forked a bite of meatloaf. All traces of drowsiness gone.

"The heart transplant last year was part of a clinical trial at Chiron BioInnovation Center."

Corbin swallowed the lump of food. "A clinical trial?"

"Right." Luna set her container on the coffee table. She couldn't eat another bite. "And those attackers tonight, you said it yourself, they were professionals. So I started thinking—"

"Maybe they're the ones putting those bodies in the—" He stopped. "Carlie. The girls in the graveyard. They were missing their organs. You don't think . . ."

A healthy teen missing her organs. And a sick teenage girl who needed a transplant. "That Trinity could have one of those girls' hearts."

Corbin's container clattered to the coffee table, joining hers. He reached for the bottle of antinausea pills. "Think I might need these after all."

Their daughter. Trinity. The possibility. It was right there. She wanted to tell him. Needed to tell him. But not when this could all be nothing.

"Let's not jump too far ahead. We'll ask Dr. Santos in the morning. See if it's even possible. Medically speaking. Besides, why would traffickers kidnap the commissioner's daughter? They had to know that would bring heat."

"Carlie was a troubled teenager with a history of running away and drug use. She also has a strained relationship with her father, feeling neglected. Vulnerability like that makes her an easy target." Corbin swallowed the pill dry. "And it's possible the kidnappers didn't know Carlie was the commissioner's daughter."

Luna's stomach tightened at his words. The description hit too close to home. Kids like that became easy prey because the world had already trained them to believe they weren't loved. Too soon they became the throwaways. The forgotten ones. And society looked away while monsters circled.

"So they grab vulnerable girls no one will look for right away," she said. "But Carlie threw them a curveball by being connected to someone important."

"That could explain why Carlie went missing weeks ago. Kidnapped. Tested. A positive match. Held captive. Prepped for surgery." He looked up, his gaze meeting hers. "And then..."

"Carlie's heart beating in someone else's chest." And what if Trinity wasn't the only recipient?

His hands went to his forehead, fingers massaging his temples. "How can I ever tell Commissioner Tinch?"

She touched his knee. "One step at a time"

He dropped his hands and nodded. "You're right. And what if Stryker found out what they were doing? Could explain why he was kidnapped."

Was that why Stryker insisted Luna come back to Millie Beach? He wanted her skills to investigate? There was just one problem. "Stryker has a gym full of LEOs. He has connections in every branch of the government—local and federal. There's Tori, Harlee, Blade, Jett... You." She shook her head. "If he knew this was going on—even suspected it—he'd have told someone. Why didn't he?"

Corbin bit his lower lip and fixed his gaze at a point in the distance. His brain had to be processing at warp speed. He looked at her. "He suspects corruption somewhere in the chain of command."

It had crossed her mind a few times, hearing the commissioner so insistent to keep his missing daughter top secret. But if Tinch were involved, his daughter wouldn't be a victim, would she? The next time she saw Commissioner Tinch, she'd study him closer and watch for signs of deception.

"We have a lot to think about, and you've got an early morning." She collected their dishes and carried them to the sink. "Pick me up at Tori's on your way?"

"You sure? It'll be early. Around five thirty."

"I'm used to working on little sleep." She sat on the coffee table across from him. "I'm with you on this, Corbin. Not just for Stryker. For you."

Corbin looked up at her. The pain medication had softened some of the lines around his eyes, but his focus was sharp as ever. "Thank you. I'm glad we're partners. Glad you were there for me today. And honestly . . . it's good to have you back in my life."

She met his gaze. All those years. Gone. She was a teenager again. Awkward. Hopeful.

Corbin reached out, gently sweeping a strand of hair behind her ear. His fingers brushed against her cheek. It was achingly familiar, yet thrillingly new. Good thing she was sitting because her knees would've buckled. Her heart pounded so hard she was sure he could hear it.

Somewhere between the gunshots and the quiet moments, something had shifted. She hadn't meant to feel this way again. Hadn't allowed herself to. But here she was, teetering on the edge. It had been only two days, but she could feel herself starting to fall for him all over again.

She leaned closer. Drawn to him. His hand reached up. Cupped the back of her neck and pulled her closer. The space between them shrank. Her eyes closed. Their breath mingled. Her heart filled with years of longing. Nights spent dreaming.

Their lips almost touched. Oh, how she wanted to close the remaining sliver between them. Erase everything with one... kiss. One moment.

Corbin pulled back. His gaze dropped to his lap. "Luna, I... I can't."

The spell shattered. Reality came crashing back.

All the years, the pain, the distance—it all rushed up, sharp as a blade. Another rejection.

What had she expected? That the scars of the past would vanish in a heartbeat? That he wanted the same life she once dreamed of sharing with him? She'd been a fool to hope things could be different this time.

Luna stood. Her legs wavered beneath her as she fought to hold herself together. She needed to leave. Now. Before the tears burning behind her eyes could fall. Before she said something she'd regret.

She grabbed her blazer from the back of a nearby chair, fumbling with the fabric as she tried to pull it on. Her hands shook. Blast it. She hadn't been this off-kilter in years.

Luna's carefully constructed walls crumbled around her. Years of training, of pushing aside personal feelings for the sake of the mission, vanished in an instant. The living room closed in. Warm lamplight caught on framed artwork and well-tended plants. A life built without her.

She strode toward the door. Just a few more seconds and she'd be out of here. She could lick her wounds in the privacy of a quiet Uber. Find a way to piece herself back together. Become the agent she was supposed to be.

Her fingers grazed the cool metal of the doorknob. Something made her stop.

She turned and looked back. "Good night, Corbin." She surprised herself with the gentleness in her tone. "See you in the morning."

23

CORBIN HAULED HIMSELF UPRIGHT, gritting his teeth as his stitches stretched. The nightstand clock's red digits glared 4:44 a.m. The bathroom tile bit into his bare feet as he stumbled to the sink. A stranger stared back from the mirror, stubble-faced and thumb print bruises under each eye telegraphing how little sleep he'd had.

Luna's face swam before him. Last night, she'd been close enough to kiss. Her breath, warm and inviting. Her eyes, soft in a way he hadn't seen since . . .

Man, he'd wanted to kiss her. To erase the years between them with one touch. But the graveyard had kept flashing behind his eyes—bodies and blood mixing with the haze of painkillers. His head was too fuzzy, his thoughts too fractured to give her the moment she deserved. After everything they'd been through, after all the time and pain, their next first kiss couldn't be some impulsive, hazy blur. She deserved more.

He didn't blame her for bolting.

Cold water shocked his system as he splashed his face.

This time had been different, though. She hadn't bolted without a word. Her walls weren't as high. He could see over them, at least. See through to the pain she hid. Pain he'd caused, yes, but something more. Something deeper. Older. A wound that had festered, hardened. Scars that crisscrossed her soul.

He wanted to shield her, to help her heal. But how could he when every glance, every unspoken word between them carried traces of broken promises and discarded dreams. He ached to show her how deeply he regretted walking away.

But would she ever trust him again?

Rushing through his morning routine, he skipped a proper shave and settled for a quick pass with his electric razor. Time was tight. Picking up Luna from Tori's place and making it to the medical examiner's office before six was nonnegotiable. Being late wasn't an option—not when it might give her another reason to doubt him.

The sun hadn't yet risen when Luna slid into the passenger seat. She held two travel mugs, the scent of fresh coffee filling the car.

"Figured you could use this." She passed him one of the mugs.

"Thanks. You're a lifesaver." Maybe things weren't so bad. If she was bringing him coffee, she couldn't be completely put off by last night's almost-kiss.

Part of him regretted stopping it. If he'd been his old impulsive self, he would've let things go as far as she'd allow. But he wasn't that guy anymore. He had self-control now. Didn't he?

They rode in silence, the familiar streets of Millie Beach passing in a blur. Before long, they pulled into the parking lot of the medical examiner's office.

He drained the last of his coffee and set the mug in the cupholder. "Ready?"

Luna nodded, her expression unreadable.

The automatic doors hissed open, ushering them into the sterile environment of the ME's office. How many times had he walked through these doors to see the aftermath of evil?

A young female assistant, all wide eyes and solemnity, led them down the hallway. Her shoes squeaked against the polished linoleum floor. They passed several closed doors before reaching the office.

"Dr. Santos will be with you shortly." The assistant gestured them inside. She practically bolted as soon as they crossed the threshold.

Mindful of his aching body, Corbin lowered himself into one of the chairs facing Dr. Santos's desk, and Luna settled beside him.

The room was small but tidy. Bookshelves lined one wall, filled with medical texts and journals. The opposite wall held framed diplomas and certifications, displaying the enormous amount of dedication Dr. Santos had in order to earn her expertise. A window behind her desk offered a view of a small courtyard. The green splash of life counteracted the deathly business conducted within these walls.

Before either could speak, the office door swung open. Dr. Amelia Santos strode in. Her white lab coat billowed behind her. She had her dark hair pulled back in its usual neat bun, and her eyes carried no hint of the all-nighter she'd pulled.

"Good morning," Santos said, moving behind her desk. She dropped a stack of folders onto the polished surface with a soft thud and sat in her chair. "The commissioner's arriving any minute, but I've confirmed his daughter's identity." Her businesslike tone was sharp but not unkind.

Corbin leaned forward, bracing his elbows on the arms of the chair. "What have you got for us, Doc?"

Santos opened the top folder, her fingers tracing the lines of text as she gathered her thoughts. The ticking of the wall clock seemed unnaturally loud in the silence, each second moving closer to answers.

"I thought you'd want an update before I show you the bodies." Santos pinned him with serious eyes. "I've finished a preliminary on Carlie Tinch. My suspicions were correct." She paused, her fingers tapping a restless rhythm on the folder. "Her vital organs had been removed. She was otherwise unharmed, except . . ."

Except what? What other indignity had this poor girl suffered?

Santos turned the monitor so they could see. The glossy screen caught the light, and for a moment, Corbin saw his own reflection. Pale, drawn, eyes haunted. He steeled himself and looked at the photo.

Carlie's wrist filled the photo, pale skin marred by ugly, purplish bruises. They formed a cruel bracelet that told a story of struggle and fear.

"Ligature marks?" His words came out rough.

Beside him, Luna's shifting posture was the only indication she'd seen the photo too. How much horror had Luna witnessed in her line of work? How much could any of them take before it broke them?

Dr. Santos pulled up a series of photos, each showing a young woman with the same Y-incision. Corbin's stomach churned as he realized how young they all looked.

"Same preliminary findings for these victims," Santos said. "All healthy girls, prime of their lives. All organs removed, ligature marks on the wrists."

"Could she have died another way?" Corbin's detective's mind searched for alternatives. "Maybe a medical examiner just . . . disposed of the body improperly?"

Even as the words left his mouth, Corbin knew it was a long shot. But he had to ask. Had to search for any explanation that might lessen the horror of what lay before them.

Dr. Santos shook her head. "No, Agent King. What was done to Carlie is fundamentally different from a standard autopsy. We remove organs for examination, yes, but we return them to the body. Here, the organs were removed."

"Which organs are we talking about here?" Corbin dreaded the answer.

"Hearts, lungs, kidneys, liver." Santos ticked them off on her fingers. "The works."

Corbin said, "So you think we're looking at organ harvesting?"

"That's not my department, Agent. I just report what I find. The rest is up to you." Santos leaned back in her chair. "But I will point out that these organs could fetch a price on the black market. Definitely the type harvested for organ trafficking."

The words hung in the air.

Harvested. Like crops. Like Carlie was nothing more than a resource to be used and discarded. The sheer inhumanity of it made his blood boil.

The faces of the victims stared up at him, young lives snuffed out too soon. How many more were out there? How many more families were living in agonizing uncertainty? "Have you identified the other victims?"

"Three out of the five so far." Santos pulled out another file. "Besides Carlie, Sadie Rollins from Panama City Beach and Jennifer Woods from New Port Richey. So far, no two victims are from the same city. All reported missing but assumed runaways."

Luna glanced at Corbin. "These girls go missing in one town and turn up right here in Millie Beach."

This was organized, methodical. How far did it stretch? "Have you reached out to bordering states to see if the other two victims are in their missing persons records?" If the crimes crossed state lines, they could ask the FBI for additional resources.

Santos nodded. "I've got calls in and sent an email with their photos. I also detailed my findings and asked other medical examiners to reach out if they have anyone matching our victimology. So far, nothing's turned up."

"If I may," Luna said. "We know about Carlie, but the girls who have been identified, can you compare how long they were missing before they died?"

Smart question. Why hadn't he thought of that? Corbin watched Santos sift through the files, her lips pressed into a thin line.

"I'm afraid I can't give you a definitive answer at this stage. We've only just received the bodies, and I haven't had the opportunity to perform the autopsies on Miss Rollins or Miss Woods yet." Santos pulled a small calendar out of her desk drawer and flipped through the pages. "What I can tell you is based on when the police reports were filed, it looks like Rollins and Woods were missing between six and eight weeks before they were found, which should help in determining approximate time of death."

Six to eight weeks. Same as Carlie. What had happened during that time? What had these girls endured before their lives were cruelly ended? And how many more were out there right now, waiting to be found?

Corbin's gaze drifted back to the photos on the screen. Young faces, full of promise, now forever silenced. Was this the work of a calculating criminal enterprise or something even darker? A serial killer with a grotesque signature?

The possibilities churned in his gut. Organ harvesting meant multiple players, a network. A serial killer . . . that was a different kind of monster altogether.

And what about Trinity? Was she mixed up in all this somehow?

"We have something we'd like to run by you."

Santos laced her fingers and waited.

"You're familiar with the Warrior program at the Kingdom MMA Gym?"

"Stryker's program, yes." A bit of red rose up her neck to her cheeks. "He and I had coffee together a few times."

Stryker dating? That would be an investigation for another day. "A student in the program has gone missing. She has a history as a runaway, but we learned that she's been the recipient of a heart transplant. Is it possible . . . I mean, can you check to see if she would've been a match to any of these victims?"

Santos blinked a few times, and he could tell she was trying to remain professional. "Yes, that's something I could do, provided you have her medical records. We can start with something basic like blood type." The phone on her desk rang, and Santos said, "Excuse me."

She picked up the phone, spoke a few words, then hung up. "Commissioner Tinch is here. He's waiting outside the lab. If you'll go ahead and meet him, I'll get Carlie ready."

They left her office, and Corbin led Luna to the hallway, where the commissioner paced outside the autopsy room. The man seemed to have aged a decade in the past few hours. His usual commanding presence was gone, replaced by slumped shoulders and red-rimmed eyes. A network of broken blood vessels spiderwebbed across his left cheek.

His heart ached for the man. No one should have to ID their child in a morgue. Though it was better than seeing his daughter's body in the shallow grave. That was an image that would never be erased from Corbin's mind.

"Are you ready, sir?"

The commissioner gave a faint nod.

Corbin pushed open the door. The smell of antiseptic cut right through his exhaustion and jolted him awake. The harsh fluorescent lights of the medical examiner's office cast an eerie glow over the sterile room where steel examination tables and rows of medical instruments lined the walls. Luna kept herself close but out of the way. Giving them space.

Dr. Santos greeted them with a somber nod. Her face wore the mask of professional detachment, but Corbin caught the flicker of sympathy in her eyes as she looked at the commissioner. "I'm so sorry for your loss, Commissioner Tinch."

On the gleaming metal table lay a sheet-covered form. Corbin's throat tightened. He'd seen countless bodies in his career, but this ... this was different. This was personal. This was failure.

Dr. Santos moved to the head of the table. "Are you ready?"

The commissioner inhaled and released a breath. "Yes."

Dr. Santos folded back the sheet, revealing Carlie Tinch's face. A chill snaked down Corbin's spine, and it had nothing to do with the frigid temperature in the room. He heard the commissioner's sharp intake of breath.

Carlie looked peaceful, almost as if she were sleeping. Her blond hair fanned out on the table, framing a face that still held traces of childhood softness. She was just a kid.

"Oh, my sweet girl." The commissioner reached out a trembling hand, stopping just short of touching Carlie's cheek.

Corbin placed a steadying hand on the older man's shoulder, feeling the tremors running through his body. In that moment, he wasn't looking at his boss or the head of the FDLE. He was seeing a father, broken by the loss of his child.

How could God, a loving father, bear to see his children suffer like this?

"I'm so sorry, sir," Corbin said. "I should have—"

The commissioner cut him off with a sharp shake of his head. "Don't. Not now."

Corbin bit back the rest of his inadequate apology. He'd failed, just like his father had failed so many times before. Was this his destiny? To repeat the mistakes of the past, to hurt those he was meant to protect?

"Did they . . ." The Adam's apple bobbed in the commissioner's throat.

"There's no evidence of sexual assault," Dr. Santos said.

The commissioner sagged with relief, and Corbin tightened his grip on the man's shoulder. At least there was that small comfort.

The commissioner's lips wobbled as he stared at his daughter. "Who . . . who could do this?"

"Sir, Dr. Santos has confirmed that Carlie's vital organs have been removed. We might be looking at a sophisticated organ harvesting operation."

Dr. Santos stuck her hands in the pockets of her lab coat. "During my preliminary external examination, I documented Carlie's unusual weight and noticed the sunken appearance of the torso, both consistent with missing internal organs. I confirmed this with an X-ray." Dr. Santos turned to her computer and pulled up a set of images but didn't bother explaining what each one showed. "While the official autopsy will provide more detailed information, these observations were enough for me to determine that Carlie's organs were removed. I wanted to inform you of this as soon as possible, given the implications for your investigation."

"Thank you, Dr. Santos," the commissioner said. "Agent King, a word."

Corbin followed the commissioner into the hallway, bracing himself for the man's anger, his disappointment. But when the older man turned to face him, there was a fire in his eyes that Corbin hadn't seen in weeks.

"I want you to take the lead on this case, King," the commissioner said. "Find out who killed my little girl. Find out who's doing this to these young women."

Corbin blinked, surprised. "Sir, after what happened at Abercorn's house . . . I thought my job was on the line."

"That stunt you pulled, taking a civilian to serve that warrant . . . you nearly got her killed in that fire. Under normal circumstances, I'd have your badge."

Corbin's heart sank, but the commissioner wasn't finished.

"But these aren't normal circumstances. You're the best we've got, King. And right now, I need the best." He placed a hand on Corbin's shoulder, his grip painfully tight. "Find them. Whatever it takes. But do it by the book. We can't afford any mistakes, not with something this big."

Corbin straightened. It was a second chance, one he knew he didn't deserve. But he wouldn't squander it. "Yes, sir. I won't let you down. We'll find who's responsible and—"

"No," the commissioner said, shaking his head. "I don't just want them arrested. I want to see them face-to-face. I want to look into the eyes of the monster who did this to my little girl."

Corbin hesitated, understanding the man's pain but knowing the dangers of such a personal involvement. "Sir, I—"

"This isn't a request, Agent. This is an order. Find them." The commissioner started walking away.

"Yes, sir. But sir?"

The commissioner turned to him, eyebrows raised.

"I can't do this alone."

"What do you mean?"

Corbin took a step closer. "I know you didn't want to bring publicity to Carlie's disappearance, but given what we've uncovered . . . sir, I think we need to form a task force. This is bigger than any one agent can handle."

The commissioner's jaw tightened. He was quiet for a long moment, his eyes distant. "What are you asking?"

"Sir, I'll need the best," Corbin said. "Detectives, forensic experts, maybe even someone from the FBI—"

"No." He stood close to Corbin. Eye to eye. "I'm the commander of the FDLE, the best law enforcement agency in the state. We don't ask for help, we *are* the help. If the agents under my command can't solve this utilizing our vast resources of experts, then those agents shouldn't be working for the FDLE. Am I clear?"

"Yes, sir," Corbin said.

This pride, this insistence on handling it all within the FDLE, wasn't just arrogance. It had to be a man stripped bare by the brutal reality of Carlie's death, clinging to the only semblance of control he could still grasp. He couldn't undo the horror, but he could dictate how they hunted the monsters responsible. It was the only way a man in his position could possibly feel like he wasn't utterly and completely powerless.

"I want to hear from you end of day," Tinch said.

"Yes, sir."

As the commissioner walked away, Corbin leaned against the wall. He closed his eyes. Took a deep breath, then regretted it when his ribs burned.

All he needed was a chance. A chance to make things right. To prove that he wasn't doomed to repeat his father's failures as an officer. The evil they now faced was more horrific than anything he'd encountered before, and he needed experts.

He needed his friends.

If Commissioner Tinch didn't want an interagency task force, he'd have to form one himself. He pushed off the wall, ready to begin the work of assembling his team. Corbin turned back to the morgue doors. Through the small window, he could see Dr. Santos covering Carlie's body with the sheet.

The hairs on the back of his neck stood up, because for a moment, just a fleeting instant, he could have sworn he smelled his father's favorite whiskey. Could almost hear the man's mocking laughter echoing in the sterile hallway.

Corbin shook his head, banishing the phantom. He had work to do. Lives to save. He'd failed Carlie. Failed the other girls. But he wouldn't fail again.

24

LUNA STOLE A GLANCE AT CORBIN as he navigated the early morning traffic, heading to the Kingdom Gym.

Last night's near-kiss replayed in her mind. What had she been thinking? She wasn't thinking, and that was the problem. A moment of weakness, nothing more. Thank goodness Corbin hadn't kissed her. What a disaster that would've been.

She'd carved out a life separate from him and everything in Millie Beach. She couldn't let a moment of misplaced nostalgia undo all that. One kiss, and it all could've come crashing down.

Colleagues. That's what they were now. Nothing more, nothing less. It had to be that way. Lowering her defenses wasn't an option, no matter how her traitorous heart sometimes whispered otherwise. The trust between them had crumbled long ago, and her focus had to be on finding her mentor and her daughter.

Trinity's medical records might hold the answers. If she could just get her hands on them.

She'd exhausted every method searching for the baby she'd given up. Discreet inquiries, classified searches, quiet favors called in from old contacts. Anything louder risked exposure, not just for her but for the daughter she was desperate to find. And yet, she hadn't gone to Stryker first. That part of her life stayed locked away, buried beneath years of regret and choices she couldn't undo. Admitting she was looking meant admitting she regretted giving her daughter up in the first place. And if she never found her? She wasn't sure she could face that either.

But without Stryker, she had nothing—no leads, no answers. Just a hope that had started to feel more like a punishment.

Corbin pulled into a parking spot and cut the engine. He glanced her way. "You good? You seem . . . distant."

Was she? Luna refocused. The case. That was where her energy needed to go.

He waited, one eyebrow raised in question.

"I'm fine. Let's get to work."

She pushed open the door and stepped out, rolling her shoulders to shake off the weight of old choices she couldn't undo.

The automatic doors of the gym hissed open. Thuds of fists against heavy bags and grunts of exertion filled the air. She swept her gaze over the gym floor, taking in the mix of police officers and at-risk youth working side by side even this early. Stryker's vision, still alive and thriving in his absence.

Corbin reached the top of the stairs and glanced back at her. "Coming?"

Yeah, she was coming. But where was she going? Back to a life she'd left behind? Back to the man who'd broken her heart and the friends she'd abandoned? Wow, she was really off her game. Mind spinning in a thousand directions. That was what happened when life got complicated.

He waited, one hand on the railing.

"Coming." She pounded up the stairs.

Corbin held the door to the office open for Luna.

Tori and Harlee stood near a bank of monitors, talking to a man with his back to her. Tall, with broad shoulders that stretched the fabric of his tailored shirt. Dark hair, a touch of wave.

He turned, a smile spreading across his face. A smile that reached his warm, dark eyes, eyes that crinkled at the corners. A neatly trimmed beard emphasized his strong jawline. He had the kind of face that could launch a thousand ships. Or sell a billion dollars' worth of software.

"Luna? Holy smokes, is that really you?"

Jett. Of all of them, he'd always been the most sensitive, the one most likely to understand. To forgive.

"Hey, I thought you couldn't make it." She crossed the room, and he pulled her into a hug.

It felt good. Familiar. Safe. He smelled like sandalwood and success, a far cry from the skinny, nervous kid she'd known. But his hug was the same. A gentle squeeze, a warmth that radiated through her.

"Family emergency." He stepped back, and his eyes searched hers. "I can't believe it's really you. It's been... too long."

"Way too long." She smiled. Not the practiced curve of her lips she'd perfected over the years. This was real.

"Well, sorry I'm late. Had to brief some important people on my updated intelligence-gathering software. You know how it is." He gave Corbin a familiar hug and thump on the back, then gestured to the bank of monitors. "Harlee's been keeping me in the loop, so I'm pretty well caught up."

Harlee snorted. "More like I've been drowning him in data. But he seems to be handling it."

"Speaking of handling it." Tori sat on the corner of Stryker's desk and picked up a rubber band, which she popped against her fingers. "How's things going? Any progress finding Stryker?"

"We have a situation." Corbin walked past Luna. His shoulder gently brushed hers, and she didn't pull away. He eased into a chair. "We ran into some people who definitely don't want us asking questions. This thing is way bigger than we initially thought."

"You talkin' about your ego again?" Blade strode into the room and patted Corbin on the shoulder on his way to greet Jett. They shared a quick handshake that turned into a hug with their hands smashed between their chests.

The gang really was all here.

Except Stryker. It had been too long. Way too long. The clock was ticking.

"So what did I miss?" Blade asked, turning to Corbin.

Corbin cradled his ribs with one arm and laid out their findings. The attacks at the skate park and the marina. The victims. The organ harvesting. Trinity's possible connection. Each detail added another piece to a puzzle she wished they didn't have to solve.

When he'd finished, the room was quiet save for the soft whir of the computer fans. Luna's gaze traveled from face to face, noting the subtle changes in her old friends. Blade's normally relaxed posture had stiffened, his shoulders drawn tight. Tori stretched the rubber band across her fingers. Harlee's eyes had narrowed to slits, her arms crossed and held tight against her body.

Jett cleared his throat. "This is . . . a lot to process."

"Understatement," Harlee muttered.

Blade exhaled, dragging a hand down his face. His eyes, usually warm with humor, had hardened to flints. "This is beyond anything we've dealt with before."

"We need a plan." Harlee's jaw clenched. "How do we shut these lowlifes down?"

Harlee's raw anger mirrored the heat building in Luna's chest. These people had stolen lives, destroyed families. And for what? Profit?

"We form a task force," Corbin said. "Pool our resources, our skills. We treat this like any other high-level operation. Just . . . off the books."

"Off the books? Why?" Blade narrowed his eyes at Corbin.

"Commissioner Tinch is trying to keep a lid on this. He wants these people stopped, but he's tying my hands by refusing interagency help. I think grief is clouding his judgment. Since this seems to be tied to Stryker, I figured you'd all be willing to help."

Silence.

Corbin looked at each of them. "I need your help. All of you."

Luna waited. Like she was watching a play unfold from the back row.

"If you need us, we're there." Blade looked at the others, and they agreed.

"Thanks, I appreciate it. But don't put your jobs on the line. Prioritize your other cases first." Corbin glanced at Luna. She caught the subtle bob of his Adam's apple.

"All right," he said, clapping his hands together. "Jett, we need you to set up a secure database for all our evidence and leads. Something we can all access but that's protected from outside eyes."

Jett nodded, his fingers already flying over the keys. "On it. I've got some ideas for an encrypted system that should do the trick."

"Good. Tori, I want you to start building profiles on our victims. Look for patterns, commonalities. Anything that might help us understand why these particular girls were targeted."

Tori pulled out a notebook and jotted down notes. "All right, I'll need all the information we got on the victims so far."

"You'll have it," Corbin assured her. "Blade, I need you to start reaching out to your contacts in local law enforcement. See if there are any similar cases we might have missed. And Harlee, I need you to dig deeper into Trinity's background. Her friends, her habits, anywhere she might have gone."

Luna found her gaze drawn to Corbin. He was in his element, coordinating the team, piecing together the puzzle. It was a side of him she'd never really seen before, and she couldn't help but feel a twinge of regret for all the years they'd lost.

"What about you two?" Jett asked, looking up from his laptop. "Where do you fit in all this?"

"Our first step needs to be getting Trinity's medical records," she said.

Jett's eyebrows rose. "That could be tricky. Patient confidentiality laws are pretty strict."

"I know, but hear me out." Luna met each of their gazes in turn. Wanting her records wasn't entirely selfish. "If we can prove that Trinity's new heart came from one of the missing girls, we'll have solid evidence the Chiron BioInnovation Center is buying organs on the black market. Probable cause to investigate the clinic. And maybe, just maybe, find Stryker."

Corbin nodded. "She's right. It could be a concrete link between the organ harvesting and a specific recipient."

"Where are her parents?" Blade asked.

"Foster kid," Tori said. "Parents died in a car crash. She started running with the wrong crowd, partying, shoplifting, the usual. Stryker knew her parents and brought her into the program to avoid juvie."

"He saved her, just like he saved us," Luna said.

Harlee snapped her eyes to Luna. "Speak for yourself. I never needed saving."

"Of course not," she said. "My mistake."

Jett gave Harlee a reprimanding look then turned to Corbin. "Don't we have medical records here?"

"Harlee already pulled her file," Tori said. "But it's basic. Name, address, allergies, you know, the stuff the kids fill out on intake."

"We should have a release form around here somewhere . . . yeah. Here it is." Harlee clicked her mouse.

The printer behind Tori beeped and buzzed. She plucked the paper from the tray. "This grants guardianship to Stryker. So legally, he has access to her medical records."

"Which is a problem because he's been kidnapped," Jett said.

Blade took the paper. "She's a missing person with a serious medical condition. Should be enough for a warrant."

"Okay, we'll need her entire medical history, surgical reports, post-op care instructions. Anything we can get from the Chiron BioInnovation Center." Corbin sounded excited now. "Luna and

I will go." Corbin looked at her. "She's proved herself to be rather ... persuasive."

He didn't know the half of it.

"Can I see that?" She gestured to the release, and Blade passed it to her.

Luna leaned against the wall, her arms crossed, trying to project an air of calm she didn't feel. She scanned the form. The usual legal jargon. Stryker's signature. And there, near the bottom, Trinity's full name and date of birth.

May 3.

Her heart sank. A cold knot tightened in her chest. It wasn't her. It couldn't be her. Right year but wrong birthday. Her daughter was born March 5. The date was etched into her like a jagged scar on her soul.

She handed the form back to Blade and forced a stiff smile. "Looks official enough." What a stupid thing to hope for.

But Stryker still needed her. Trinity too. Her mind raced through the information they'd gathered, the connections they'd begun to make.

She said to Blade, "Hold off on the warrant. The killer knows we've found the bodies by now. It's all over the news. We need to take a closer look at that clinic where Trinity had her transplant. If we show up with a warrant, they'll shut everything down, and we'll lose our best lead."

Corbin nodded. "Agreed. But we'll need to be careful. If the clinic is involved in this organ harvesting scheme, they'll be on high alert."

"Then we don't go in as cops." A plan already formed in her mind. "We go in undercover. As potential patients." This was what she was trained for, after all. Creating identities, infiltrating dangerous organizations.

She saw the spark of approval in Corbin's eyes. "That could work. We'll need backstories, medical histories that would make us candidates for their ... services."

"Leave that to me," Jett said. "I'll have everything you need by morning."

Her eyes met each of theirs in turn. Not just old friends anymore. A team. And together, they'd dismantle this operation piece by piece.

Corbin rose with a slight wince and stood behind Harlee. "Where are we on Mr. Steve?"

"Remember I had a partial plate for the G-Wagon? I've tracked down a name. The registered owner of the vehicle is Jed *Steven* Kaplow Jr. Goes by Steve. And interestingly, Kaplow served in the Marines for a few years in a heavy equipment transport unit." Harlee's fingers flew across the keyboard. Her monitor displayed a complex network of lines and data points. "Still searching for any connections Stryker might have to Kaplow."

Corbin nodded to Blade. "How's it going with that kid, Jordan..."

"Metzger. Jordan Metzger," Harlee said, not looking away from her screen.

"Surveilling a minor is tricky," Blade said. "My superiors weren't too keen on it, but they've asked an informant to keep his ear to the ground and let me know if he gets into any trouble."

"Good enough," Corbin said. "Let's get to work. Meet back here tomorrow at six."

Harlee swiveled her chair to look up at Corbin. "Six a.m.? Seriously? I signed up for surveillance, not sleep deprivation."

"Aw, come on, Harlee," Tori said. "You know you love our early morning task force meetings. Besides, think of the coffee we can guzzle."

Early morning meetings? They had a thing for early morning meetings? She didn't get it. It must be an inside joke. One of a thousand inside jokes, a thousand shared moments she'd missed.

"Fine. But I'm bringing donuts," Harlee grumbled. "Lots of donuts."

"Even better." Corbin looked right at Luna and winked. He

stood and walked closer. He leaned in. Put his lips close to her ear. "How would you feel about being my wife?"

Heat crept up her neck. Her skin tingled where his breath grazed her ear. She refocused. This was a job. An assignment. A necessary deception. Nothing more.

Okay, maybe a little more. The thought was quickly banished.

"I thought you'd never ask." A smile tugged at the corner of her lips.

"I'll tell Jett to set up our cover story that way."

"What are you two whispering about?" Blade asked.

Corbin straightened. "Just discussing getting married."

Harlee's eyebrows shot up. Tori coughed to cover a laugh.

"We're going undercover." Luna shot him a look. "As a married couple."

Jett, ever the pragmatist, only asked, "Which one of you needs the new heart?"

"Luna will need the heart. She's the undercover federal agent," Corbin said.

"Actually, it would be better if Corbin needed the transplant," Luna countered. "He's already injured."

Corbin's lips quirked up. "Fine, pick on the guy who got stabbed." His expression sobered. "Tinch still has us partnered up. We'll hit up the South Beach Pediatric Center where the Warrior kids get their physicals."

"Won't you need a warrant?" Tori asked.

"I'd rather us fly under the radar. For now we'll use the release form. They might not hand over everything, but if we can at least snag Trinity's blood type, Dr. Santos can cross-reference with our victims. See if any match up as potential donors."

Luna nodded. "After that, we scope out Chiron. Keep our eyes peeled for anything out of place." Like a group of professional kidnappers dragging victims inside.

"Solid plan." Corbin glanced at his watch. "We should get going."

A long shot, sure. But maybe the BioInnovation Center held answers. The key to finding Stryker. Finding Trinity.

Not her daughter. Another girl, though. One in danger. This time, Luna wouldn't stand idle. She had backup now. A team. People she trusted. And Corbin.

She was right where she needed to be. Not running. For once.

25

THE COMMISSIONER would have his badge if he knew Corbin had formed an unofficial interagency task force. His job was hanging by a thread as it was. Pursuing this could snap that thread entirely. Trinity was out there somewhere, her heart possibly the key to unraveling this whole organ harvesting ring.

Risk his badge or risk more lives? Some choices made themselves.

After everything they'd been through, he could trust his friends. And Luna. Working with her lit something inside him he thought long dead. It felt . . . right. Like he was finally where he was supposed to be.

Commissioner Tinch didn't need to worry about how they caught his daughter's murderer so long as Corbin did it.

Even if it meant losing his job.

Corbin pulled into the doctor's office parking lot and cut the engine. "Did you bring the release form?"

"Right here." Luna handed him the folded paper.

"Let's hope this is good enough," he said, scanning the document. His eyes caught on a detail that made his heart stutter. "Wow," he murmured.

Luna tilted her head. "What is it?"

"Trinity's birthday." His throat tightened a fraction. "It's the same as . . ." He swallowed. "The same day our daughter was born." The baby girl they'd given up all those years ago.

"I think you're mistaken. It says Trinity was born on May 3. Our daughter was March 5."

Corbin shook his head, pointing to the date on the paper. "No, look. It says right here—3/5. That's March 5th."

Luna snatched the paper back, her eyes widening as she stared at the numbers. A long moment passed before she spoke. "Oh. I . . . I read the date wrong." Her voice seemed quiet. Small. "I guess between the military, the Agency, and living overseas for so long, I'm used to putting the day before the month."

Something shifted. A shadow crossed her face.

"Luna? What's wrong?"

She folded the paper quickly, tucking it away. "Nothing. We should hurry."

She was shutting him out. Again. Bolting, but in a different way. He wanted to press further, but Luna was already opening her door, stepping out into the parking lot.

He got out of the car. Headed for the doctor's office.

March 5th. The day he'd held their baby girl for the first and last time. The nurse had written it neatly on a card for the bassinet, her hand steady while his world had fallen apart. Luna had been silent then, tears streaming down her face. He hadn't known what to say. What could he say? They hadn't talked in months and now the weight of their choices felt too heavy for words.

She must be thinking about it too. That date. That moment.

This time, he would talk to her about it. But bringing it up now wouldn't help either of them. Later, when they were trapped in a car for hours on a stakeout with nothing to distract them and no way to escape the conversation.

The glass doors of the South Beach Pediatric Center slid open, and a rush of cool air washed over him. The place reeked of antiseptic and anxiety. Corbin hated doctors' offices. And hospitals. The smell always brought back memories he'd rather forget.

The waiting area was packed. A married couple leaned forward, watching their daughter color outside the lines of a unicorn picture. A kid, maybe five, coughed into his Spiderman mask as his mother rubbed his back with a weary hand. A thin woman in a business suit bounced her legs and thumbed her phone screen, occasionally glancing at the sleeping infant nestled in one of those car seat and stroller combos.

Luna walked past, making a beeline for the receptionist's desk. "Ready?"

Game face. It was a look he'd seen a thousand times before. On suspects, on witnesses, on victims. But seeing it on Luna . . . it sent a thrill through him. She was in her element.

"Sure." Get this over with, and the quicker, the better.

The plan was to let Luna use her powers of persuasion to get as much information as they could. *If* they could.

A woman sat behind the desk, her gaze fixed on a computer screen. A nameplate identified her as Sharon Rodriguez. She snapped her gum every few seconds and tapped her acrylics on the keyboard. The pink nails were studded with rhinestones and shaped like tiny two-inch daggers.

"Can I help you?" The gum snapped again.

"We're hoping you can." Luna's smile dripped with honey. "How are you today? I love those nails, by the way. Where did you have them done?"

Sharon fluttered her fingers to give them a better look. A tiny silver jewel dangled from the tip of her pinky. "My daughter has a shop over on Fifth. She's the best in town. Probably in the state."

"No!" Luna gasped. "Fabulique? On Fifth and Sunshine?"

Sharon's smile grew wide, showing the dot of fluorescent-green gum clenched in her molars. "You've heard of it?"

Luna leaned on the counter and flashed a grin. The kind he imagined had charmed diplomats and disarmed terrorists. "Okay

"... that place is amazing," she said. "I had the absolute best mani-pedi there two weeks ago."

She had? He inspected Luna's nails. Short and soft pink with white tips. What did they call that? French? Boy, he really had nothing to contribute to this conversation.

"Did you happen to meet Kelly?" Sharon asked.

"Yes, she's the one I saw!"

He'd never seen Luna this animated. Well, not since their early days. That one night when they'd lain on a beach blanket in the middle of the night to watch the meteor shower. They'd ended up talking. Joking. Teasing. He'd given her a nickname that had her belly laughing. A secret between just them. And there wasn't a moment that night when they weren't touching.

"Okay, no way that's your daughter," Luna was saying. "You do not look old enough to have a grown daughter."

"That's so sweet of you to say." Sharon blushed and straightened the stack of file folders on her desk.

"It's true. Kelly was so kind. So talented. And a businesswoman? Wow, you've done a wonderful job raising her."

"Oh, honey, she gets all her talent from her daddy. But I'll tell her you said that. She'll love it."

"You know..." Luna leaned in. "I've been meaning to bring my friend here. He's never had a mani-pedi, can you believe it?"

"No ... way." Corbin started to shake his head, but Luna's foot connected with his shin. A sharp, pointed jab.

"No way would I miss it." He forced a smile.

"Well, tell you what," Sharon said. "You bring him in, mention my name, and Kelly will give you both a discount."

"You got it." Luna winked. He couldn't believe it. Actually winked. "We'll be there next week for sure."

"Well, enough jabberjawing," Sharon said. "What doctor are you here to see?"

Luna jumped in. "Actually, we were hoping to have a quick chat with Amanda, in billing? It's about a ... family matter."

Sharon pursed her lips. Those daggerlike nails tapped a nervous rhythm against the desk. "Well, I'm not really supposed to let people back there without an appointment..." She glanced at Corbin, then back at Luna. "But you seem like nice folks. Let me give her a call."

Sharon made the call and then pointed down a hallway. "Last door on the right. She's a sweetheart."

Luna fell into step beside him. The transformation was instant. Gone was the bubbly, charming woman who'd just sweet-talked their way past the receptionist. Her smile vanished. Her shoulders squared, her gaze distant, guarded.

He'd almost forgotten how quickly she could shift, how easily she could compartmentalize, build walls around herself. It had thrown him off balance. That bubbly personality wasn't an act, he knew that. But it was a side of her she chose to conceal until she needed it. A tool to get what she wanted. And it had worked. She'd charmed Sharon into doing something she clearly wasn't supposed to do.

Something he never could have pulled off.

They reached the last door on the right. A neat, handwritten nameplate was taped to the open door. Amanda Dunn. He tapped his knuckles against the frame before he stuck his head in.

The office was an efficient mess. Stacks of files lined one side of an L-shaped desk. A computer monitor dominated the other. Ceiling-high file cabinets lined three walls, each drawer meticulously labeled with color-coded tabs. He wouldn't be able to function in this kind of organized chaos.

The woman standing behind the desk fanned herself with a file folder. She was in her late forties, he guessed. Short, with blond hair dyed a shocking pink on top. One side of her head was shaved, the pink hair sculpted into a wave. A rhinestone glittered in her nose piercing. Thick black glasses framed intelligent blue eyes. A small fan oscillated on her desk.

"Come in, come in! Hot flashes all day long. I swear, I'm melting. And the AC in this building is a joke." Amanda gestured to the stacks of files on her desk. "Heaven forbid I take *one* vacation day to give Mom a ride to the VA in Coco. Dermatologist appointment." She stopped fanning and planted a fist on her hip. "Do you know how hard it is to get appointments there? Months! And of course, it had to be the week I was supposed to reorganize the entire billing system. So now . . ." She waved a hand. "Chaos. But anyway, what can I do for you?"

"I'm Special Agent King with the FDLE, and this is my partner, Agent Rosati. It's about a patient." He tried to channel Luna's charm, the easy smile that could melt glaciers. "Trinity Brown. We're concerned family friends. And, well, has anyone told you that you look amazing today?" He stumbled, the words tangled in his mouth. He was failing miserably.

Amanda raised an eyebrow. The corner of her lip twitched. "Family friends, huh? That's what the last two said. And the ones before that." She plopped down in her chair and leaned back, eyes magnified behind her thick glasses. "You law enforcement boys really need to work on your cover stories if you want medical records without a warrant."

He felt heat creep up his neck. Busted. "Okay, you got me. We're investigating a missing person case. We need to access Trinity Brown's medical records."

"No can do, Agent King. Not without a warrant," Amanda said, shaking her head. "I'm the gatekeeper of these records. Patient confidentiality is sacred to me. I take my job very seriously."

"Believe me, I understand." He was so not good at this. Not like Luna. "I wouldn't ask if it wasn't important. Trinity's a juvenile. She's in the Warrior program—"

"Oh, that program's amazing!" Amanda exclaimed, her eyes lighting up. "A few years back . . . three . . . maybe four. Wait, has it really been five years? Anyway, my friend's sister's nephew was in trouble with the law, facing serious jail time. But then he got into that Warrior program, and it turned his whole life around. He's got a job now, a wife . . . it's a miracle, really. He had this awful rash on his back, the poor kid, and—"

"Yeah, that same program turned my life around." For someone so worried about confidentiality, she was sharing details about a complete stranger pretty easily.

But fine, if flattery wouldn't work, maybe honesty would. "That's why I'm so worried about Trinity. She's been ditching the program, hasn't been seen in days. And we just learned she has some serious medical problems. I just . . . I need to make sure she's okay."

"Oh, that's so sad," Amanda said. "It breaks my heart to see those kids struggling. We get teenagers here all the time. Even little ones. It's just not right. But . . ." Her face hardened. "My hands are tied. I can't give you anything without a warrant or a parent or guardian's consent."

While Corbin spoke, Luna stood quietly beside him. She'd picked up a framed photo from Amanda's desk and studied it. A young girl with a bright smile, holding a dog with floppy ears.

"Actually, the program has legal guardianship of Trinity," Corbin said, hoping this would be the magic phrase.

"Oh, well that's different." Amanda's eyes brightened. "Let me see the paperwork."

Luna unfolded the document Harlee had printed, the crisp paper crackling in the quiet office. She slid it across the desk.

Amanda scanned the document, her brow furrowing. "Hmmm . . . this names a Stryker King as the guardian. Any relation?"

Stryker King. His father figure. The man who'd saved him from becoming a statistic, from following in his own father's footsteps. The man who was like a father to him in every way that mattered. They shared a last name, yes, but only because Corbin had changed his because he couldn't bear to carry the weight of his biological father's name, the name that reeked of violence and betrayal, for the rest of his life.

He could lie. Say yes, just to get another shot at the file. But he couldn't do that. He'd rather wait for Jett and Harlee to find something. "No. We're not related."

"Too bad," Amanda said. "I could probably make an exception for a close relative. You know, father, brother, sister, mother..."

Luna returned the framed photo to Amanda's desk. Pushed one corner with a finger to straighten the position. She clasped her hands behind her back.

This was a dead end. A waste of time. "Well, thank you anyway. We really appreciate—"

"I'm her biological mother," Luna said.

Corbin was shocked into stillness.

Luna was... Trinity's mother? How... what...

March 5th. The date.

He tried to speak but couldn't. Words wouldn't form.

And he was pretty sure his mouth hung open.

26

WHAT HAD SHE DONE? She needed to get out of there. Out of the stifling office. Away from Corbin. Away from the past mistake that hung heavy between them like the suffocating air that blasted her as the clinic doors slid open.

The Florida sun beat its relentless assault. Heat radiated off the asphalt. She could feel Corbin's gaze on her back, the weight of his unspoken questions pressing down on her.

How could she explain? How could she tell him that Trinity, the girl they'd been searching for, the girl Stryker risked his life for, might be their daughter? The daughter they'd given up. The daughter she'd spent years trying to find.

Her hand went to her stomach, the familiar ache returning. A physical pain, a constant reminder of the choice she'd made. The choice they'd made. The choice that had shattered her dreams. Her future.

She reached Corbin's car and yanked the door handle. Her fingers trembled, her hand slick with sweat. She just wanted to go somewhere. Alone.

"Luna, what was that?" He was beside her now. "What was that all about?"

"Does it matter? I didn't get the file, did I? Now unlock the car. It's baking out here."

The click of the remote signaled respite. A place to gather her thoughts. Corbin opened the passenger door for her. She slid into the seat, the leather warm against her skin.

Without a word, he got in, started the engine, and put his forehead on the steering wheel. She could see his hands gripping the leather, knuckles white. The muscles in his jaw bunched. He was holding it together. Barely.

She waited, listening to the grind of his molars as he fought for control. She knew that sound. The desperate struggle to rein in the anger before it exploded. It made sense now. Why he'd tempt himself with the very thing that drove his father into madness. Control the temptation. Control the anger. Experience told her it didn't work that way.

But this was her fault. She'd pushed him. Pushed them both, revealing the truth about Trinity like that. It had been a reckless move, a desperate attempt to find answers. But now . . . now she had to face the consequences.

She wanted to reach out, to touch his arm, to offer comfort, to reassure him. But her hand remained frozen on her lap. She'd let him speak first.

Finally, he lifted his head. Released his grip, his brown eyes shadowed with pain.

"Is it true?" His eyes searched her face. "Is Trinity your—our daughter?"

Her breath caught. How could she answer that? She didn't know for sure. Not yet.

"Trinity is a lost girl who needs our help. I started to suspect . . . well . . ." She met his gaze. Kept her expression carefully neutral. "The truth is, I just don't know. Not yet."

He shook his head, brow pinched. "Luna, why didn't you tell me?"

She sighed, leaning back against the headrest. "I guess I was afraid."

"Afraid of what?"

"Of being wrong. Of being right. Of... of stirring up all the pain and regret we buried." She let her gaze drop to her hands. "It's not just about me. It's about you. I didn't want to put you through that—not when I don't even have answers yet. I'm sorry, Corbin. I should have told you as soon as I suspected."

He was quiet for a long moment, his gaze fixed on some point over her shoulder.

When he finally spoke, he said, "I understand. I do. But Luna, we're partners now. We can't keep things from each other. Not if we want to solve this case."

"You're right." She nodded, feeling the truth of his words settle in her chest. "No more secrets."

Corbin's expression softened, and for a moment, she saw a glimpse of the boy she'd fallen in love with all those years ago. "Okay. So, partners?"

He held out his hand, and Luna took it, feeling the warmth of his skin against hers. "Partners," she agreed.

As they shook hands, Luna sensed a shift in the air between them. A clearing of old hurts, a tentative step toward... something. Trust, maybe. Or forgiveness. Whatever it was, she knew it was necessary. For the case, for Stryker, for all the lives hanging in the balance.

He released her hand and brushed her hair from her forehead. Cleared his throat. "So, is Trinity our daughter? Is that why Stryker gave her so many chances?"

If only she knew for certain. Had a DNA test, or at least Stryker to tell her. "According to her intake form, the birth date is a match."

Corbin's phone buzzed in the cup holder. He glanced at the

screen, and his eyes closed for a beat before he answered. "Commissioner."

She listened to his side of the conversation, piecing together the fragments. "Yes, sir ... I understand ... Yes ... It's important ... We're on it, sir."

Corbin winced, holding the phone away from his ear for a second. "Yes, sir. Rosati and I have a lead. Yes, sir. Following up now. Got it."

He disconnected the call and turned to her. "That was a call to, quote, 'Light a fire under us.' As if we didn't already have one." He flashed a lopsided grin. "You ready for a stakeout?"

Corbin didn't wait for an answer. He backed out of the parking space and pulled out into traffic. He turned onto Ocean Drive, the road winding along the coast. Beyond the car windows, the waves surged and pounded against the shore, a relentless, chaotic force that mirrored her own roiling inner state.

No more secrets. She'd promised him that, hadn't she? But some secrets were buried deeper than others. Secrets she wasn't sure she could ever reveal. Classified secrets.

He pulled into a secluded spot overlooking the research facility, parking the car beneath the shade of a sprawling banyan tree. The engine purred, then fell silent. The automatic shutoff kept the AC running, at least until they drained the battery.

The Chiron BioInnovation Center stood on a bluff overlooking the Atlantic, a gleaming white fortress of glass and steel. It looked more like a luxury resort than a medical facility. Palm trees swayed in the ocean breeze, their fronds casting long shadows across the manicured lawns. A fountain, its water cascading in a series of graceful arcs, gurgled softly in the center of a courtyard. The facility straddled not only the ocean but the edges of Millie Beach.

Beneath the surface of beauty and tranquility, a darkness lurked.

Not taking his eyes off the building, Corbin said, "You think this is where they're holding Stryker?"

"Maybe." She shifted in her seat to settle in.

He turned to her, and his eyes lingered on her hands. "I noticed your manicure back at the clinic. Very... professional."

She cringed. Busted.

"I also noticed you told the receptionist you'd had them done two weeks ago. Here. Locally."

Honesty. It was time. Or was it? She'd spent a lifetime hiding behind masks, becoming someone she wasn't. Revealing the truth, even a sliver of it, seemed dangerous. Like stripping naked in a crowded room.

"What I'm about to tell you is off-the-charts top secret." She had her eyes on the employee entrance of the research facility but glanced at Corbin as she spoke. "I'm cleared to tell close family a redacted story, and right now, I guess you're the closest thing I have to family."

He turned to her fully now. "You can trust me, Luna. I promise. We're partners, remember?"

She took his hand and nodded. Where to begin?

Peshawar. The market. The vibrant colors of the stalls, the scent of spices, the press of bodies, the sudden blinding flash, the deafening roar, the acrid smell of smoke, the screams, the blood, the dust settling on a scene of unimaginable horror.

A child's lifeless eyes staring up at her, a silent accusation.

"I had an asset get killed." The words came out a whisper. "I don't know how, or why, but she'd been compromised. Forced into wearing a suicide vest." She stared at the research center, eyes almost unfocused. Seeing but not.

"Analysts back at CIA headquarters had sent a cable saying all checks were complete and I was clear to proceed with the meeting. I traced my escape routes, watched for tails. Did everything by the book. Except..."

The narrow alley filled with tables of fruits, vegetables, and sacks of spices. The scent of cumin and curry wafting through the air. Children sitting on the side of the road with cupped hands held up.

"My eyes locked onto a street kid begging for money or food."

Luna shook her head at the memory. "A girl with dark hair and eyes that mirrored mine. I remember feeling struck. A piece of my past, one I'd tried so hard to keep buried, shot to the surface. I was back here. Holding a tiny life in my arms. Seeing the girl with such a striking resemblance reminded me that somewhere in the world a child I'd brought into being was thriving. A child I'd relinquished for a chance at a better future."

She risked a glance at Corbin.

He squeezed her hand. "A sacrifice made with love but one that left an indelible mark on your heart. Mine too."

"I couldn't afford involuntary emotional leakage, so I walked to my meeting across the street. I sat with my asset on a wooden bench and sipped tea. I didn't want to look at the beggar girl, but my eyes involuntarily drifted in her direction. So I used it. Used it to get closer to my asset. To make her more comfortable.

"It's a technique we call 'You Me, Same Same.' The more my asset saw herself in me, the faster and stronger we would bond." It sounded so evil when she said it out loud now.

"You did the same thing to the receptionist, right? Bonded over manicures?"

She bobbed her head. "Yeah, like that. So I told the asset that the street kid reminded me of myself. I told her I grew up like her and I wanted to make the world a better place. So children like her could have food and a safe place to live."

"Did it work?"

"Yes . . . and no." She pushed out a long breath and got lost in the past.

A man across the street pointed a camera in her direction. Red flags went up. Probably, there was nothing to worry about. Just a tourist photographing the clock tower.

Then why did adrenaline race through her veins at the sight of him?

She should get up and walk away, but she needed more time with Aisha. They'd come this far, and all she needed was the name.

She sipped her tea and watched the tourist out of her periphery. "Do you remember the painting we were discussing?"

Aisha stared into her tea and gave a short nod.

They couldn't very well sit and talk about bombings and terrorists in public, so Luna spoke in code. "What day will the painting be in the museum?"

"I don't know the exact day, but within three days of Muharram."

The Islamic New Year. This year it would fall in early July, only a few months away. "What's the name of the artist?"

Aisha's head hung low, eyes transfixed on the cup. Her hands trembled. Luna flicked a glance in the direction of the tourist. She didn't see him.

"This is bigger than one . . . artist. There are many." *Aisha turned to look at Luna.* "One man controls the paintings, the museums, the artists. Everything."

A cold sweat broke out on Luna's neck. "Who is it, Aisha?"

Aisha shook her head. Tears slid down her cheeks. "I'm sorry. So sorry."

Aisha lifted the hem of her tunic a fraction.

Enough that Luna saw the wires.

"It was a bomb." She forced herself to breathe, to stay in the present. "A suicide bomber. Right in the middle of the marketplace in Peshawar. I barely escaped with my life. My asset. A beggar girl. So many others. They weren't so lucky." She cleared her throat, forcing the words out. "Shrapnel embedded in my thigh."

He didn't speak, but his silence was enough. It had been so long since someone had simply listened. Truly listened. Without judgment, without expectation.

"They brought me back to the States to recover." She kept her tone of practiced detachment. "They wanted me to lay low while they figured out if my cover had been compromised. Said I needed to reconnect with my real identity." A humorless laugh escaped her lips. "Except I didn't even know who that was anymore. And all I could think about was . . ."

"Our daughter," he said.

"I wanted to know if she was okay. Maybe . . . maybe she'd want to meet me now that she's eighteen. I searched for her using the channels I had, but nothing. Then finally worked up the courage to call Stryker. To ask him to help me find her. He said he would, but only if I met him in person."

"So you came back to Millie Beach."

"Covertly, at first." She looked at him then, meeting his gaze. "I needed to do some . . . recon."

"The manicure?" he asked.

"Okay, maybe a little self-care was in order." She released Corbin's hand and splayed her fingers, inspecting. Those perfectly polished nails felt like a betrayal. A symbol of the secret life she'd used to keep herself away from her friends.

She curled her fingers into fists and held them in her lap. "I only stayed for one day. Then I had to go back to DC for a senate hearing on the incident. By the time I got through that ordeal, I'd decided. I'd risk meeting Stryker."

She paused. It hadn't felt like a conscious decision but more like a driving force pushing her to come home. For what? To witness his kidnapping?

"Luna, I'm so sorry. For everything. For Peshawar. For our child. For . . ." He dropped his eyes. "Leaving you to deal with it all alone."

She wanted to tell him it was okay. Wanted to brush it aside, to pretend it didn't matter anymore. But the truth was, it did matter. It always had.

"It wasn't all your fault. We both made choices. Choices we can't take back."

The silent understanding in his eyes was almost enough to make her forget the years of hurt, the distance, the walls she'd built around her heart.

Almost.

"So, what now?" He looked at her, his gaze searching, hopeful. "Where do we go from here?"

"We have a case to solve."

He reached for her as if to hold her, but he sucked air between his teeth. "Ouch. Can't lean that way."

She studied him now. His face was pale, a sheen of sweat on his forehead. "Are you okay?"

He leaned back in his seat, his hand going to his side. "I don't know, Luna. I'm feeling a little run down."

She put her wrist to his forehead. Warm. "Did you take your antibiotics?"

He shook his head. "Forgot."

Her concern overrode her desire to finish the stakeout. Corbin could call in another unit to sit here all day. "Come on, hero. We need to get you home. You need some real rest. We can't afford you getting an infection. We have plans tomorrow."

"Tomorrow," he repeated. "We go in undercover."

27

CORBIN EASED HIS CAR to a stop in front of Tori's house. What was he doing here at this absurd hour? Luna would probably murder him for showing up unannounced. If she was even awake. But the moment he'd opened his eyes that morning, he knew he couldn't wait another second to talk to her. To explain. The truth had been eating away at him for far too long, and he had to clear the air between them before they risked their lives going undercover.

He killed the engine and sat there staring at the front door. This was stupid. Reckless, even. They had a high-stakes undercover operation to prepare for, and here he was, ready to dredge up ancient history.

But if he didn't tell her now, would he ever?

He climbed out of the car, biting back a groan as his stitches pulled. The salt-tinged air filled his lungs. He approached Tori's front door, his feet feeling heavier with each step. Before he could knock, it swung open.

Luna stood there, dressed in running shorts and a lightweight jacket, her hair pulled back in a ponytail. His heart skipped a beat. Even now, after everything, she still took his breath away.

Her face paled, and her hand flew to her chest. "Is it . . . Stryker? Is he—"

"No, no, it's not about Stryker. We don't have an update on him yet."

"You scared me half to death." She dropped her hands and stepped onto the porch, closing the door behind her. "Although, I don't know if I should be relieved or not."

He couldn't blame her. In their line of work, no news wasn't necessarily good news. "Sorry, didn't mean to worry you."

A gentle breeze caught Luna's hair and blew strands across her forehead. She scraped them back and tucked them behind her ears. "So, what are you doing here so early?"

"Couldn't sleep." A half-truth. His restless night had little to do with insomnia and everything to do with the woman standing before him, but the pathetic excuse was all he could muster. "What about you? What are you doing outside at this hour?"

Luna's dark eyes searched his face, and he fought the urge to look away. What did she see when she looked at him? The boy who'd abandoned her? Or the man he was trying to become?

"I was about to go for a run on the beach. Want to join me?"

Run? His body screamed in protest at the mere thought. Not just the stitches and his sore ribs. When was the last time he'd slept more than a few hours? But the idea of spending time with Luna . . . "I'm pretty beat, but if you don't mind walking . . ."

"I was teasing about the run," Luna said. "Probably you shouldn't run with stitches in your side."

"I don't think I could if I tried." He followed her down the steps.

"How about a nice slow walk?"

"That I can do," he said. "Let me throw my shirt in the car."

While she waited, he unbuttoned his dress shirt and tossed it in the front seat. The white cotton T-shirt he wore underneath wasn't fashionable, but it was comfortable.

They set off down the dark street. The sound of ocean waves roared, even from blocks away. Corbin kept a careful distance between them as they walked side by side. He wanted to close that gap, to reach out and touch her, to make sure she was really here. But he held back.

How should he begin? What should he say? He was terrified of saying the wrong thing, but he wanted to be honest. The way she'd been yesterday.

Just as he opened his mouth to speak, Luna broke the silence. "I'm sorry about the commissioner. The way he's treating you, it's not right."

Carlie. The teen's face flashed in his mind, her bright smile now forever dimmed. "I can see it from his side. His only child was murdered, and I didn't stop it."

"It's the awful part of your job. You can't blame yourself. He shouldn't either."

Couldn't he? He was supposed to find her. He'd failed. And that wasn't even the worst of it.

He kicked a rock, and it skittered across the asphalt into the grass. "I'm worried I might lose my job over this. I was already on thin ice, and then the incident with the fire . . . I shouldn't have let you come."

"I didn't give you much choice, now did I?" She turned her head toward him. "If you hadn't agreed, I would've been there before you had a warrant. And then . . ." She looked away. "Then, I don't know what would've happened."

He thought about how she'd stood there, surrounded by flames, unwilling—or unable—to move. "I think I understand why the fire affected you the way it did. The explosion?"

"I froze. When I saw the flames. I just . . . I couldn't move. And you . . ." She trailed off, shaking her head.

"Luna, I—"

"No, let me finish." She cut him off. "You saved me. Again. Just like you did all those years ago when Stryker first brought me to the program."

Back then Luna, barely fifteen, was all hostility and distrust.

Somehow he'd been the one to break through her walls, to show her that not everyone was out to hurt her.

"I didn't save you," he said. "You saved yourself. I just... helped a little."

Luna didn't respond.

There was something else, something she wasn't telling him. A lot, actually. He could see it in the way she avoided his gaze, in the tension in her shoulders. He let the silence linger.

"I froze in there." She glanced at him, then back down. "That's the first time it's ever happened to me."

He wanted to reach out. Pull her close. Tell her it was okay. But he held back.

They reached the beach and paused at the end of the wooden path to take off their shoes and socks. Corbin rolled up the cuffs of his pants and they left their shoes on the boardwalk. Luna bent and picked up a seashell. Wiped the sand off the ridges and tucked it in her pocket.

The sand was cool and soft beneath his bare feet as they made their way to the water's edge. The ocean stretched out before them, an inky expanse broken only by the white foam of breaking waves.

To the east, the first hints of light were beginning to peek over the horizon. Sunrise was still an hour away, but already the night was losing its grip. In an hour, the sun would rise, painting the world in gold and pink, and they'd have to prepare for the day. To go undercover. Yeah, he should have tried for more sleep, but walking beside Luna, he couldn't bring himself to regret it.

This was exactly where he wanted to be.

"So, what's really on your mind?" The sound of the waves nearly drowned out her words, and he drifted closer.

They continued down the beach, the waves lapping at their feet. Corbin became acutely aware of Luna's presence beside him. The way the predawn light softened her features. The slight brush of her arm against his as they navigated a piece of driftwood. His skin tingled where they'd made contact, and he found himself wanting to close that gap again, but he resisted.

This was it. No more running. "I owe you an explanation. About why I left. Why I couldn't . . . why I thought I couldn't be a father."

Luna's expression remained neutral, but Corbin caught the slight tightening around her eyes. A glimpse of the pain he'd caused her, still raw after all these years.

"I'm listening."

He licked his dry lips, tasting salt on his tongue. Where to start? How to explain something he barely understood himself?

"It's about Damien Sullivan. My father."

Luna glanced at him, a flicker of understanding in her eyes. Of course she remembered. She'd been there for the fallout, after all.

"I know you saw the news reports," he said. "The trial. But there was so much more I never told you. So much I couldn't face back then."

They walked in silence for a few steps. A seagull cried overhead, its mournful call echoing the ache in his heart. He'd never said these words out loud before.

"He didn't just drink. He beat my mom. Beat me. For years. And I just took it." The words felt like broken glass in his mouth. "I didn't protect my mom, and I grew up thinking how my father acted is what it meant to be a man. To be a cop. He planted evidence, beat confessions out of suspects. And the day they finally fired him . . ."

Luna's hand brushed against his, a fleeting touch that nearly broke him. He pressed on, the words tumbling out now that the dam had burst.

"When they fired him, when he killed those officers . . . I was relieved. Can you believe that? My own father goes on a rampage, gets arrested, and all I felt was relief that it was finally over."

He picked up a piece of driftwood and threw it, sending it skittering across the sand. Childish, maybe, but it helped release some of the tension coiled inside him.

"I changed my name because I couldn't bear to be associated with him anymore. I wanted to be like Stryker, to be good. But when you told me you were pregnant..." He swallowed hard, shame burning in his chest. "All I could think was that I'd end up just like him. I was already drinking, Luna. Already struggling with my anger. What if I snapped one day? What if I hurt you or our baby?"

He forced himself to meet her gaze, to face the hurt he'd caused. "I thought I was protecting you both by breaking it off and signing my paternal rights away. But, if I'm being honest with myself, I was just a coward. A coward running away from my fears instead of facing them."

They'd stopped walking now and were facing each other as the sun began to peek over the horizon. Luna's face was bathed in golden light, her eyes shimmering with unshed tears. Corbin's chest tightened. He'd put those tears there, years ago and now.

"So you ran," she said.

Corbin nodded, shame burning in his chest. "I didn't want to hurt you. But that's exactly what I did, just in a different way."

Luna was quiet for a long moment, her gaze fixed on the ocean. She caught a stray strand of hair and scraped it behind her ear.

Corbin held his breath, waiting for her response. Would she understand? Could she ever forgive him?

"You're not the only one who ran, Corbin." She turned to him, her eyes soft. "We were both so young. Scared and unprepared. We made mistakes."

"I've spent all these years trying to be nothing like him." The admission burned in his throat. "Changing my name, working with Stryker, joining FDLE. But sometimes I wonder if it's enough. If I can ever truly escape his shadow."

Luna reached out, her hands slipping around his shoulders. The warmth from her touch chased away the frost of old wounds.

"You're not your father, Corbin," she said firmly. "The man I've seen these past few days? He's brave, compassionate, dedicated to justice. That's who you are."

Her words washed over him, a balm to wounds he'd carried for so long. But doubt still gnawed at him, a persistent whispering that he didn't deserve her kindness. "How can you be so sure?"

"Because I see you," Luna said simply. "The good and the bad. While we'll always face the consequences of our choices, I'm learning that trusting in Christ gives us forgiveness for our past and the chance to walk a new path."

Could it really be that simple? That the grace he'd denied himself for years was being offered so freely?

"I don't deserve your forgiveness."

"Maybe not," Luna said, a small smile playing at her lips. "But you have it anyway. That's what grace is all about, isn't it?"

The mention of grace caught him off guard. How long had it been since he'd thought about faith, about the God that Stryker was always talking about? He'd turned his back on all of that, convinced he was beyond redemption.

"I'm not sure I know much about grace," he admitted.

"Then maybe it's time we both learned."

Corbin's heart raced as he gazed into Luna's eyes. She was even more beautiful now. How was that possible? He found himself drawn to the subtle lines at the corners of her eyes. What stories could those lines tell? What had she been through in all these years apart? What made her build so many walls? And how could he break them down?

Luna's hands slid from his shoulders to the back of his neck. Her touch conveyed a tenderness that took his breath away. The rising sun bathed them in a warm, golden light, as if God himself was conspiring to create this perfect moment.

She hesitated for a heartbeat, searching his face. Then, with a soft exhale, she closed the distance between them.

Their lips met in a kiss that spoke of forgiveness, of lost time, of a love that had never truly died. Corbin's arms encircled her waist, not out of passion but out of a deep-seated need to be close, to reconnect with the other half of his soul.

When they finally parted, Corbin rested his forehead against

Luna's. The world around them seemed to fade away, leaving only the two of them, basking in the light of a new day and the promise of a fresh start.

Even after all these years, even with all the pain and unanswered questions between them, she still had this effect on him. "I've missed you," Corbin whispered.

Luna's fingers traced the line of his jaw. "I've missed you too," she murmured. "More than I realized."

As they stood there, wrapped in each other's arms with the sunrise painting the sky in vibrant hues, a sense of peace washed over him. For the first time in years, hope bloomed in his chest. Maybe, just maybe, there was a chance for redemption after all. For both of them.

28

LUNA PULLED INTO A PARKING SPOT at the Kingdom Gym and cut the engine. Now that she was here, she wished she hadn't eaten breakfast. What lay ahead wasn't sitting well with her.

This wasn't her first undercover operation. Far from it. But it was the first time she'd be going in with Corbin. With someone who knew her.

Or at least, had known her once upon a time.

She forced a deep exhale, willing her heartbeat to slow. "You've got this, Luna. Just another mission. Just another cover."

But it wasn't just another cover, was it? This time, it was personal. This time, it was about finding Trinity. About uncovering the truth behind Stryker's disappearance. About facing a past she'd spent years running from.

Jett's sleek Tesla pulled up beside her, and he lifted four fingers off the steering wheel in a wave.

She stepped out of her car at the same time Jett did. "Morning. You're here early."

Jett's smile was wan, the exhaustion evident in the lines etched around his warm, brown eyes. Dark circles underscored a sleepless night. "Lots to do. You ready for this?"

Ready? Was she ever truly ready? She squared her shoulders. "As I'll ever be."

They went inside. The gym, usually alive with the sounds of exertion and the sharp tang of sweat, was subdued this early. Still, a few people pounded away at the heavy bags and others ran an endless path on the treadmills. The thud-thud-thud and whirring had a rhythmic comfort.

Blade emerged from the office, a stack of folders tucked under one arm. "Conference room, five minutes." A taut professionalism replaced his usual easygoing demeanor.

Luna nodded, making her way to the small kitchenette. She needed coffee. Lots of it. Black and strong, just the way she liked it. Just the way she liked everything in her life. Controlled. Predictable. No fuss.

As she waited for the pot to brew, her mind wandered to Corbin. How would he handle this? He was a good agent, no doubt. But undercover work... it was a different beast entirely. One slip, one tell, and the whole operation could come crashing down around them. And he had a weakness. Her.

"Penny for your thoughts?"

Luna jumped, sloshing her freshly poured coffee on the counter. Tori stood in the doorway, thumbs tucked in the back pockets of her jeans, her gaze assessing.

"Just... preparing." She forced a smile, hoping it didn't look as strained as it felt.

Tori's gaze softened. "Ay, mija, it's okay to be nervous, you know. This ain't no ordinary day at the office."

"I know. It's just..." She wasn't nervous. Not really. Fictional characters, inventing a life, faking her appearance—that's who she was. It wasn't Corbin. But she couldn't say that. "There's so much riding on this, Tor. If we mess this up..."

"Hey, we've got you." Tori's hand on her arm was warm. Firm. "All of us. We're in this together, a'right?"

That was the problem. Luna was taking a huge risk relying on her friends for this covert operation. She used to have an entire network of analysts, tech specialists, and field operatives at her disposal. Even so, she'd been responsible for people dying. And that was the true source of her unease.

Rather than insult her friends with those forebodings, she patted Tori's shoulder and said, "Thanks, girl."

They filed into the conference room, a small, windowless space that reeked of stale coffee. The others were already there, seated at the oval table. Harlee sat in a high-back leather chair and swiveled herself an inch to the right, then an inch to the left. Blade paced back and forth, his hands tucked in his pockets, jingling coins or maybe keys.

She sat beside Corbin at the far end of the table. A few hairs curled slightly at his forehead. He wore a crisp white shirt, the sleeves rolled up to his elbows, revealing the familiar lines of muscle, the strength that had always drawn her to him. Even after all these years, all the pain, all the distance . . . he still had that effect on her.

Jett cleared his throat. "All right, let's get started. We've got a lot to cover and not much time." He tapped a few keys on his laptop, the screen illuminating his face with a colorful glow.

A series of images flashed on the TV mounted behind him. "I've created comprehensive cover identities for both of you," he said, nodding to Luna and Corbin. "Meet Alexander and Lorelai Sinclair, power couple extraordinaire."

Luna's heart skipped a beat at the name. Lorelai. She'd used that name on a mission in Prague years ago. The familiarity of it sent an icy ripple through her chest, but she kept her expression neutral. No need to complicate things further.

She studied the images, impressed by the level of detail. Bank statements, social media profiles, even a wedding photo that looked eerily real. Not that she'd wear that dress—not the point. How had Jett managed all this in such a short time? Maybe their cloak-and-dagger lifestyles weren't so different after all.

"Alexander." Jett's attention locked onto Corbin. "You're a thirty-five-year-old tech mogul. You made your fortune in blockchain technology and have since branched out into philanthropy. Your net worth is estimated at around $500 million."

"Nice." Corbin nodded. "And the medical condition?"

"Hypertrophic cardiomyopathy. You'll refer to it as HCM. It's a condition where the heart muscle becomes abnormally thick, making it harder for the heart to pump blood. You were diagnosed two years ago, and your condition has been deteriorating rapidly over the past six months."

The gravity of their cover story hit her anew. They weren't just playing dress-up. They were stepping into the shoes of people facing a life-or-death situation.

"Now, let's go over the symptoms you'll need to portray," Jett said, switching the slide. "The primary symptoms of HCM include shortness of breath, especially during physical activity. You'll need to appear winded after minimal exertion. Chest pain is another common symptom, particularly during exercise. You might occasionally wince or press a hand to your chest."

Corbin nodded, jotting down notes. "What else?"

"Fatigue is a big one," Jett said. "You should appear tired most of the time, like simple tasks are exhausting. Palpitations are also common. You might occasionally put a hand to your throat as if you're feeling your pulse racing." Jett demonstrated. "In severe cases, which is what we're portraying, there's a risk of fainting or even sudden cardiac arrest."

Luna watched as Corbin absorbed the information, already seeing him start to embody the role. His posture changed. A slight slump to his shoulders made it appear as if he carried an invisible weight.

"Lorelai, you're a former model turned philanthropist. You've been married to Alexander for seven years, and you're desperately searching for a way to save his life. You've exhausted all conventional treatment options, which is why you're turning to the Chiron Bio-Innovation Center."

She could work with this. The desperation of a wife facing the loss of her husband... it wasn't so different from her own desperation to find her daughter and her mentor.

"What about security measures?" she asked. "Extraction plans?"

Blade stepped forward. "We've set up a series of fail-safes. You'll both be fitted with covert communication devices. State-of-the-art, undetectable by standard security scans. Harlee?"

Harlee produced a small case, opening it to reveal what looked like flesh-colored erasers. "These babies are top of the line," she said. "They'll allow you to maintain constant contact with us without raising suspicion."

Luna examined the devices, impressed. Almost as covert as earpieces she'd used in her days with the Agency. "Drawbacks?"

"They operate via Bluetooth connected to your cell phone, same as what the Secret Service use."

"So as long as we have cell coverage, we're good to go," Corbin said.

Blade nodded. "We've also set up a series of code words. If either of you feel that your cover is compromised or that you're in immediate danger, use the phrase 'clear skies ahead.' That'll trigger an immediate extraction."

"And how exactly will that extraction work?" Corbin asked, voicing the question on Luna's mind.

"I'll be leading a team on standby at all times," Blade explained. "Two blocks from Chiron, there's an abandoned warehouse. We've set it up as our command center. The judge is ready to sign off on our warrant, but he needs something to tie Chiron to the trafficking victims or proof of illegal activities inside the facility. Once you have something concrete, we'll have probable cause to get the warrant. Tori?"

Tori stood up, spreading a map across the table. "I've mapped out multiple escape routes," she said, her finger tracing lines across the paper. "We've accounted for various scenarios. On foot, by car, even a helicopter extraction if things get really dicey."

Luna studied the map, memorizing the routes. It was good. Thorough. But would it be enough?

"What about inside the facility?" she asked. "Do we have any intel on the layout?"

Jett shook his head. "Limited. We've got blueprints from when the building was first constructed, but we have to assume they've made modifications. You'll need to gather that intel once you're inside."

Luna nodded, her mind already cataloging potential choke points and security measures they might encounter.

"Now," Jett said, his tone shifting, "let's talk about your backstory. You'll need to know each other inside and out. Any inconsistencies could raise red flags."

For the next hour, they drilled. Favorite foods, how they met, vacation spots, family history. Every detail of Alexander and Lorelai Sinclair's lives was scrutinized and memorized.

As they wrapped up the briefing, Corbin pulled Luna aside. "Can we talk for a second?"

Luna nodded, following him into the hall. "What's up?"

Corbin ran a hand through his hair, a gesture so familiar it made Luna's heart ache. "I'm worried about the commissioner. If he finds out about this task force..."

Luna's brow furrowed. "You think he'd shut us down?"

"Worse. I'll lose my job. Everything I've worked for..." Corbin trailed off, his expression pained.

Before Luna could respond, Blade appeared at their side. "I couldn't help overhearing. You don't need to worry about Tinch. This isn't the FDLE's task force. It's mine. As far as anyone's concerned, this is all part of the kidnapping case that started when Stryker disappeared. You're just assisting me."

Corbin's shoulders sagged with relief. "You're sure?"

"I've got you covered, brother." Blade tossed a light punch at Corbin's arm. "Now, let's get you two ready to play house."

As Blade walked away, Luna found herself alone with Corbin,

the space between them diminishing. Without thinking, she leaned in, her lips brushing his in a soft, stolen kiss.

Corbin melted into the kiss, his hand coming up to cup her cheek. For a heartbeat, the world fell away. There was no mission, no danger. Just them.

And Tori.

Standing behind Corbin, arms crossed and a smirk tugging at her lips.

Luna pulled back. Heart galloping. "Sorry," she murmured. "We were just . . . practicing our cover."

Tori's smile widened. "Maybe you should practice some more."

Luna opened her mouth to respond, but Tori cut in, louder this time. "All right, lovebirds. Time for your makeover. Corbin, you're with Harlee. Luna's with me."

Luna's cheeks burned with the sudden rush of heat, but Tori just winked. "Don't mind me," Tori said. "Just keeping your cover story believable."

Luna followed Tori to a small changing room, where Tori unzipped a garment bag to reveal a stunning designer jumpsuit. "Lorelai Sinclair wouldn't be caught dead in anything less than Gucci."

Neither would Lorelai Russel from her mission in Prague.

She slipped into the jumpsuit, luxuriating in the cool silk gliding over her skin, adding layers to the character she was about to become. The fabric clung perfectly to her frame, and it had pockets. Perfect.

Tori worked her magic with makeup, contouring Luna's face to accentuate her cheekbones, adding a touch of sadness to her eyes. "You're worried about your husband," Tori coached. "Let that show in your expression."

Luna focused on the weight of those words, allowing the character of Lorelai Sinclair to settle over her like a second skin. She let herself imagine the fear, the helplessness of watching someone you love slowly fade away. When she opened her eyes and looked in the mirror, the reflection staring back was almost unrecognizable.

She stepped out of the changing room and stopped short. Corbin stood there looking... broken. His confident posture had melted, and his skin looked pale and drawn. Harlee's expert hand had drained the life from his features, leaving behind someone who looked... fragile. Vulnerable.

Their eyes met. Her lungs forgot how to work. This was the man she was supposedly desperate to save—Alexander Sinclair. But all she could see was Corbin, stripped of everything that made him untouchable.

Corbin's gaze swept over her, the surprise and admiration in his eyes unmistakable. He took a step closer. "You look incredible. But Tori forgot something... something very important." Before she could respond, he revealed a massive diamond wedding ring. Gently, he slid it onto her finger, his touch lingering as he held her hand a moment longer.

Her eyes dropped to his hand, where a matching wedding band glinted on his finger. The weight of the ring on her finger felt too real, too significant.

Their eyes met again, and for that brief second, Luna saw not just Corbin but the life they could have had. She nearly lost herself in the thought.

"You ready for this?" Corbin's question pulled her back to the present.

Luna nodded and slipped her arm through his. The solid warmth of him beneath the expensive suit grounded her. For a fleeting moment, she let herself imagine this was real—that they were truly married, truly facing this crisis together.

But no. *Focus, Luna. This is a mission. Nothing more.*

They made their way to the parking lot, where a sleek black Bentley awaited them. Jett handed over the keys. "Remember, you're not just rich. You're obscenely wealthy. Act like it."

Luna slid into the driver's seat, the buttery leather cool against her skin. The scent of the car's luxurious interior wrapped around her, grounding her in the role she was about to play. As Corbin settled into the passenger seat beside her, his movements were slow and deliberate. As she guided the sleek black Bentley out of the parking lot, Luna sensed that something had shifted between them. That somehow, in stepping into these new identities, they'd opened a door that wouldn't easily close again.

"Comms check," Harlee said in her earpiece. "You reading me?"

"Loud and clear," Luna said, grateful for the distraction.

"Remember, I've got a team on standby." Blade came through next. "Anything goes sideways, we're there in minutes."

Luna nodded, even though she knew Blade couldn't see her. "We've got the extraction phrase memorized."

The Chiron BioInnovation Center loomed ahead, a shining monolith of glass and steel. Luna's heart rate picked up. This was it. No more rehearsals, no more briefings. It was time to step into the lion's den.

She parked, then turned to Corbin. "Ready, Mr. Sinclair?"

He met her gaze. "Absolutely, Mrs. Sinclair."

They stepped out of the car, and Luna rushed to Corbin's side to support him as he feigned weakness. As they approached the entrance, the mission settled over her like a cloak.

Find Trinity. Save Stryker. Uncover the truth. Find justice for Carlie and the other victims.

With a deep breath, she pushed open the door, stepping into the cool, antiseptic interior of the Chiron BioInnovation Center. As they entered the lobby, Corbin stumbled slightly, his hand going to his chest. Luna's arm tightened around him instinctively, her eyes widening with practiced concern.

"Darling, are you all right?" she asked just loud enough for the receptionist to overhear.

Corbin nodded, his breathing labored. "Just . . . need a moment," he gasped.

Luna guided him to a nearby chair. Was this part of the act, or was Corbin genuinely struggling? She knelt beside him, taking his hand in hers.

"Deep breaths, love," she murmured, falling easily into the role of doting wife. "That's it. Nice and slow."

The receptionist approached, her face a mask of professional concern. "Is everything all right? Should I call for assistance?"

Luna looked up, allowing a flicker of fear to cross her face. "No, thank you. This happens sometimes. It's why we're here, actually. We have an appointment with Dr. Forest."

The receptionist's eyes softened with sympathy. "Of course. Let me check you in. Names, please?"

"Alexander and Lorelai Sinclair," Luna replied.

As the receptionist tapped away at her computer, Luna turned back to Corbin. He met her gaze. So far, so good.

"Mr. and Mrs. Sinclair?" Luna looked up to see a young woman in a lab coat approaching. "I'm Dr. Sheridan. I'll be assisting Dr. Forest today. If you'll follow me?"

Luna helped Corbin to his feet, noting how he leaned heavily on her, his breathing still slightly labored.

As they followed Dr. Sheridan down a long, sterile hallway, Luna couldn't shake the feeling that they were walking into the belly of the beast.

29

CORBIN SETTLED into the plush leather chair, his hand absently rubbing his chest. It wasn't a total phantom ache. The stitches in his side no longer hurt, but they itched like fire, and his ribs still zinged with pain if he took a deep breath.

Unlike the white walls and harsh fluorescent lighting they'd just navigated, this room was swathed in warmth. Wood paneling. Soft, recessed lighting. A carefully constructed illusion of comfort. Yet he couldn't relax. The hairs on the back of his neck prickled, a sixth sense whispering that someone—or something—was watching their every move.

Dr. Sheridan's smile was all perfect teeth and practiced charm. "Mr. and Mrs. Sinclair, Dr. Forest will be with you shortly. Can I get you anything while you wait? Water? Coffee?"

"Water would be lovely, thank you," Luna replied with a hint of transatlantic elegance. Lorelai Sinclair, brought to life. He was struck by how effortlessly Luna could slip into a role, how easily she could become someone else.

When Dr. Sheridan left the room, he leaned close to Luna and let his lips brush against her ear. "Nice touch with the accent. Very posh."

Luna's lips quirked in a half smile. "Well, darling, one must keep up appearances."

The door opened, and Dr. Sheridan returned. "Mr. and Mrs. Sinclair, this is Summer Reeves, one of our brightest interns. She'll be observing today's consultation, if that's all right with you."

The young woman handed them each a water. "Here you are."

Summer was no more than eighteen or nineteen with a shock of auburn hair pulled back into a tidy ponytail. She wore a crisp white lab coat and a name badge clipped to the lapel. The lab coat was slightly oversized, adding a touch of youthful awkwardness to her otherwise professional appearance.

Corbin's eyes met Luna's for a fraction of a second. This wasn't part of the plan, but they'd have to roll with it.

"Of course," he said. "Always good to see young people interested in medicine."

Summer stepped forward, her green eyes bright with intelligence. "It's a pleasure to meet you both. I hope you don't mind my presence. This internship is a crucial part of my college application process."

There was something about her that tugged at Corbin's heart. A familiar spark in those eyes, that reminded him of... Carlie? He'd been staring at her photo for weeks, he felt like he practically knew her.

"Not at all," Luna said. "It's admirable that you're pursuing such a challenging field."

Summer beamed, her whole face lighting up. "Thank you, Mrs. Sinclair. To be honest, I'm somewhat of a computer nerd. But I've always been drawn to medicine, so why not blend the two. I especially love cardiology. The heart is such a fascinating organ, don't you think?"

Before he could respond, Dr. Forest came in a flurry and plopped behind the desk. "Mr. and Mrs. Sinclair, I apologize for keeping you waiting."

"No need to apologize." Corbin took shallow breaths for effect. "We appreciate you... seeing us on such... short notice."

Dr. Forest's eyes narrowed as he assessed Corbin. "Yes, well, your case sounded quite urgent. Please, tell me what brings you to our facility."

Corbin launched into the backstory they'd carefully crafted. "It started about two years ago. Shortness of breath, fatigue, chest pain. At first, I thought it was just stress from work, but it kept getting worse. Especially the last six months."

Luna reached over, taking his hand in hers. The gesture was meant to sell their cover, but Corbin couldn't help noticing how perfectly their fingers intertwined.

"We've seen multiple specialists," Luna added. "They all say the same thing. Alex needs a new heart, and soon. But the waiting list..." She looked at him, eyes glistening with unshed tears.

Oh, she was good.

Dr. Forest leaned forward and laced his fingers together. "I understand your frustration, Mrs. Sinclair. The organ donation system is far from perfect. That's why we're working on alternative solutions here at the Center."

"Alternative solutions?" Corbin prompted, his curiosity genuine.

Dr. Forest smiled, a hint of pride in his eyes. "We're at the forefront of bioengineering technology. Our goal is to create fully functional, lab-grown organs that are compatible with any recipient."

"It's truly revolutionary work," Summer chimed in. "Dr. Forest has dedicated his life to this mission."

"Indeed." Dr. Forest nodded. "It's a personal mission of mine. My daughter, Elizabeth, received a heart transplant when she was just a child. The process was... harrowing, to say the least. I vowed then to find a better way."

There was conviction in Dr. Forest's voice, but also something else. A hardness that set Corbin on edge.

"That's admirable," Luna said. "But surely, creating organs from scratch must be incredibly complex. How close are you to achieving this goal?"

Dr. Forest's smile tightened. "Closer than you might think, Mrs. Sinclair. We've made significant strides in recent months. In fact, we're on the verge of a major breakthrough."

Corbin turned his attention to the young intern. "And what made you choose this particular internship, Summer? It must be quite competitive."

"Well, to be honest, nepotism." A faint blush colored Summer's cheeks. "My parents' connection to the Center. They've been helping fund Dr. Forest's research."

"Oh, lovely." Luna placed her hands neatly in her lap. "Your parents must be quite philanthropic."

Summer's expression clouded. "Yes, ma'am."

Dr. Forest cleared his throat. "Now, Mr. and Mrs. Sinclair, shall we discuss your options?"

As Dr. Forest launched into an explanation of their groundbreaking technology, Corbin found himself drowning in medical jargon.

"... and with our proprietary bioprinting technology, we're able to create custom organ scaffolds that are then seeded with the patient's own cells," Dr. Forest was saying. "This drastically reduces the risk of rejection."

"It sounds almost too good to be true," Corbin said.

Dr. Forest's smile didn't quite reach his eyes. "I assure you, Mr. Sinclair, our results speak for themselves. Perhaps you'd like a tour of our facilities? Seeing is believing, after all."

Luna squeezed Corbin's hand. This was their chance.

"We'd love that," Luna said. "Wouldn't we, darling?"

Corbin nodded, plastering on an eager smile. "Absolutely."

"Good job," Blade said in his ear. "Find something we can work with."

As they stood to follow Dr. Forest out of the room, Summer fell into step beside them. "I hope you don't mind if I tag along," she said. "I never get tired of seeing the labs."

"Not at all," Corbin replied, studying the young woman's profile. "So, Summer, what are your plans after this internship? Medical school, I assume?"

Summer's face lit up. "Well, undergrad at Harvard. I've graduated high school early, and thanks to my dual credit classes, I have my associate's degree already. I'm starting college in January. My goal is to become a surgeon, but..." Her expression faltered. "My parents aren't thrilled about it. They'd rather I follow in their footsteps."

"And what do your parents do?" Luna prodded.

"Mostly, they invest in businesses," Summer said.

Dr. Forest led them through a series of high-tech laboratories. Corbin tried to take in every detail, noting the layout, the security measures, the comings and goings of staff. But his attention kept drifting back to Summer and their conversation. She was intelligent and compassionate and had a presence that resonated deeply with him. What could his life have been like if he'd had her passion, drive, and resources at that age?

"And here," Dr. Forest announced, pausing before a set of heavy double doors, "is where the real magic happens. Our bioprinting lab."

He swiped his badge, and the doors slid open with a soft hiss. The lab beyond was a marvel of modern technology. Banks of computers lined the walls, their screens displaying complex 3D models of human organs. In the center of the room stood several futuristic-looking machines. The bioprinters, Corbin assumed.

"This is incredible," Luna breathed, her eyes wide with genuine amazement.

Dr. Forest beamed with pride. "These printers are capable of creating intricate organ scaffolds down to the cellular level. We then seed them with stem cells harvested from the patient, allowing the organ to grow and develop naturally."

As Dr. Forest launched into a more detailed explanation, Corbin noticed Summer hanging back, a shadowed expression on her face. He sidled up to her. "Everything all right?"

Summer startled slightly, then forced a smile. "Oh yes. It's just . . . sometimes I wonder about the ethics of all this," she whispered.

His pulse quickened. "What do you mean?"

"Ask him how quickly you can get an organ," Summer said, keeping her voice low.

Corbin nodded. "This all sounds incredible, Doctor. But how soon could I receive one of these bioprinted organs?"

"Mr. Sinclair, I'm afraid I can't offer you a fully bioprinted organ just yet. We're close, but not quite there in terms of full functionality and long-term viability."

Luna squeezed Corbin's hand, her eyes reflecting disappointment.

"However," Dr. Forest continued, "what we can do is begin the process of building your custom organ scaffold. This way, if a traditional transplant doesn't become available in time, you'll have another option waiting in the wings. It's not a guarantee, but it could be a lifeline."

Corbin nodded, processing the information. Then, with a glance at Luna, he asked, "Is there any way to . . . to move up on the donor list? Money is not an issue for us."

Dr. Forest's eyebrows raised. A fleeting look passed over his face before he schooled his features. "Mr. Sinclair, while I appreciate your situation, I'm afraid the transplant list is not something that can be circumvented with money. It's based on medical need and compatibility."

He paused, then added, "However, there are sometimes . . . alternative channels that can be explored for patients in dire circumstances. We could discuss those options in more detail at a later time."

Before Corbin could respond, Dr. Sheridan appeared at the lab entrance. "Dr. Forest, you're needed urgently in OR 3."

Dr. Forest's expression tightened. "I see. Mr. and Mrs. Sinclair, I apologize, but I'm afraid I'll have to cut our tour short. A rather delicate procedure requires my attention."

"Of course," Luna said. "We understand completely." As they turned to leave, Luna veered slightly, grazing Dr. Sheridan in a fleeting collision. Her fingers moved. There, then gone. Too fast for untrained eyes. She offered the doctor a quick, apologetic smile.

Corbin caught the faintest nod. Done.

"Summer," Dr. Forest said, his tone clipped, "please show our guests back to the lobby and reschedule our consultation."

With that, he swept out of the room, Dr. Sheridan on his heels.

They followed Summer down the hall. When they approached the consultation room, Corbin said, "Actually, would it be possible to use the restroom before we leave? All this excitement has my heart racing."

Summer nodded sympathetically. "Of course. There's one just down the hall, around the corner. I'll show you."

As they walked, Corbin noticed Luna's hand straying to her pocket, where he knew she'd stashed Dr. Sheridan's pilfered badge.

"Here we are," Summer said, gesturing to the restroom. "We'll wait for you back at the consultation room."

"Thank you, Summer," Luna said. "You've been so helpful. I might as well take advantage of the ladies' while we're here."

"Sure." Summer looked between them. "You can find your way back to the room?"

"We sure can," Corbin said.

As soon as they were out of Summer's sight, Luna pressed Dr. Sheridan's badge into Corbin's hand. "I saw a restricted access door near the bioprinting lab," she whispered.

Corbin nodded. This was it. Their chance to uncover the truth behind the Center's operations.

Two minutes later, they were at the unmarked door Luna had spotted. Corbin swiped the badge, holding his breath. Nothing happened.

"That's odd," Luna murmured. "It should work everywhere, shouldn't it?"

Footsteps approached. They ducked around a corner just as a man wearing scrubs came into view, swiping his own badge at the door. This time, it opened with a soft beep.

Corbin's hand shot out, catching the door a split second before it latched shut. He and Luna exchanged a look, both knowing this might be their only chance. He peeked around the door and waited until the man disappeared around a corner. With a nod to Luna, they slipped inside.

The corridor beyond was dimly lit and eerily quiet. They crept forward, Corbin's every sense on high alert. As they rounded a corner, his breath caught in his throat.

Before them stretched a vast laboratory, easily twice the size of the one they'd toured upstairs. But it wasn't the size that shocked him. It was what he saw inside.

Rows upon rows of cylindrical tanks lined the room, each filled with a pale, pinkish fluid. And floating within each tank was an organ. Hearts. Lungs. Blobs he thought might be livers. All in various stages of development.

"Oh my goodness," Luna whispered. "Corbin, look."

He followed her gaze to a bank of smaller tanks near the back of the lab. Inside each one, unmistakably, was a human fetus.

His stomach churned. This wasn't just about organ transplants. This was—

A noise from behind made them both freeze. Footsteps, growing closer. They ducked behind a row of equipment.

"I'm telling you," a voice drifted to them, "we can't keep this up. Someone's going to catch on."

"Calm down," came Dr. Forest's clipped reply. "Everything is under control. The ends justify the means, remember that."

"But the girls—"

"Are necessary sacrifices for the greater good. Now pull yourself together. We have work to do."

Corbin felt sick. The missing girls, the organ harvesting. It all clicked into place. Dr. Forest used live humans in his experiments.

As the footsteps faded, he turned to Luna. The horror in her eyes mirrored his own.

"Blade, did you catch that?" Corbin whispered then listened to his comms. "Blade, do you read?"

Nothing.

Luna showed him her phone. "No service. Comms don't work."

"Wait, we need evidence." He used his phone to snap photos of the facility.

She put her hand on his arm. "This doesn't matter. We don't know if it's illegal to perform this type of research. We need something more concrete. We need to find Stryker and Trinity if she's here. We have to find them before Forest..."

He didn't need her to finish that sentence because he'd been thinking it too. "Okay, let's go."

They retraced their steps as quickly and quietly as possible. Corbin opened the door and an alarm blared to life.

"Intruder alert," a computerized voice announced. "Security breach in Sector 7."

"Run!" Corbin hissed, grabbing Luna's hand.

30

THEY'D TRIGGERED THE ALARM—a shrill, piercing sound that ricocheted off the sterile walls, drilling into Luna's skull. Cameras. Had to be. She'd scanned the corners and ceilings for obvious surveillance, but somewhere she'd missed something. These people were too smart for standard setups.

Corbin, his hand pressed against his side, followed close behind. "Hidden cameras?"

"You read my mind. This way." She shoved open a heavy metal door marked "AUTHORIZED PERSONNEL ONLY."

They stumbled into a narrow corridor. Red emergency lights cast long, distorted shadows, painting the walls in a grotesque dance of light and darkness.

Summer stood at the end of the hallway, her eyes wide, her body blocking their escape route. She rushed to them. "Mr. Sinclair? Mrs. Sinclair? I've been looking everywhere for you. What's going on?"

Luna's heart thundered as she made a split-second decision that went against every instinct honed over years of covert operations.

"Summer, we're not who we said we are and he's not sick." Breaking cover was unthinkable, a cardinal sin in her line of work. Yet here she was, shattering the very foundation of her training. "We're the police, and we believe a teenager named Trinity Brown and an older man named Stryker King are being held here somewhere."

She waited, eyes locked onto Summer's face, searching for any hint of betrayal. Luna had faced torture without breaking, endured countless dangerous situations without flinching. But this moment, this vulnerability, terrified her more than any of that.

Summer's expression flickered through a range of emotions. Shock, confusion, and then something Luna couldn't quite place. Was it fear? Resignation?

Summer pulled a small, white device from her pocket and pressed a series of buttons on something that looked to Luna like a toy. "Give me a sec. I'm shutting down the alarm panel."

The shrill wail of the alarm faltered, then died, replaced by a blessed silence.

"There." Summer pocketed the device. "That should buy us some time, but it won't last long." Her eyes darted to the corridor behind them. "Follow me."

Luna's legs moved before her mind caught up, chasing Summer's retreating form down the sterile corridor. "What was that little thing you used?"

"Flipper Zero. It can clone key cards, disable alarms, mess with access controls. Basically, a hacker's multitool. I got suspicious a while back, wanted a way to poke around, so I ordered one. With the right programming, I'm able to open doors my security badge doesn't." She shot Luna a quick grin. "Handy, right?"

Luna's pulse hammered. "I'll take handy over dead. Keep going."

Summer glanced back. "What's wrong with him? I thought he was faking the heart condition."

"It's a long story," Corbin said. "One that involves some very bad people who don't like us very much."

"Well, if they catch you here, they won't kill you," Summer said. "At least, not right away."

"What do you mean?" Luna asked.

"I've overheard Dr. Forest talking." Summer's eyes darted to the ceiling, as if searching for the invisible eyes watching them. "He says he doesn't waste resources."

Resources. Organs. Not people. Not lives. Just . . . resources.

The rhythmic slap of their shoes against polished floors seemed to echo Luna's frantic pulse as they rounded a corner. Another corridor stretched before them. This place was a seemingly endless tunnel of white walls and fluorescent lights. A shadow flickered at the far end of the hallway.

"Someone's coming." Summer pushed Luna and Corbin into a nearby alcove, concealing them in the shadows.

A security guard's boxy frame filled the hallway.

"Corn nuts," Summer whispered. "He's searching for whoever set off the alarm."

They were trapped. Nowhere to run. Nowhere to hide.

Luna stepped forward. She had to do something. She had to create a distraction. "Sir? I'm so sorry. The alarm is my fault."

The guard turned, his gaze narrowing. "Who are you?"

"I'm Mrs. Sinclair. We're here for my husband's consultation." She gestured to Corbin, who was still pale faced, clutching his chest. "We were just leaving, and I think I accidentally tripped the alarm."

The guard studied them for a moment.

"It was my fault," Luna forced a nervous laugh. "I'm so clumsy. I bumped into a door, and . . ." She trailed off, letting the implication hang.

"Yeah, my wife's a bit of a klutz." Corbin managed a weak smile.

The guard grunted, his gaze flicking between them. He punched a code into the keypad. The red light above the panel blinked green. "All right, folks. False alarm. But try to be more careful, okay?"

He turned and continued down the corridor, his footsteps fading into the distance.

Summer emerged from the alcove, her eyes wide. "That was close. Too close. We need to get out of here."

They reached a stairwell, the air growing colder, damper, the sterile scent of the upper floors replaced by a musty odor of disuse. Summer led them down a flight of stairs. Her small frame navigated the stairwell with the agility of a seasoned operative.

She swiped a security badge at the next door. A green light flashed above the keypad. They hurried through, entering another long corridor. White walls. Linoleum floors. The relentless buzz of fluorescent lights overhead. The same sterile, impersonal atmosphere that pervaded every inch of this place.

"How does your badge work on all these doors?" Corbin asked.

"Like I said, I've been getting suspicious about what's going on around here," she explained as they hurried through. "So I've been carrying my Flipper to work every day. When Dr. Forest wasn't looking, I cloned his badge onto the device and used it to reprogram mine. I've been poking around."

"I don't get it," Corbin said. "That little device can do all that?"

Summer nodded. "It hacks radio protocols, Wi-Fi networks, and . . . oh, access control systems like the ones on these doors."

"Impressive." Luna admired the girl's audacity. She'd always had a soft spot for those who dared to defy authority.

Summer swiped her badge at the next two doors. They entered a wing that felt different, quieter. A place where secrets were kept.

"This section has always been highly restricted, and I saw that some patients were brought down here to these rooms for treatments no one discussed," Summer said. "If Trinity is anywhere in the facility, she would be here."

They reached a room at the end of the corridor. The door was ajar, a sliver of light spilling out. Luna's heart pounded against her ribs. *My daughter. In there.*

She stepped forward. Pushed the door open.

Trinity lay in a hospital bed, her wrists and ankles restrained, her gaze fixed on the television playing reruns of a TV show Luna watched back when it was originally broadcast. The familiar theme song was a jarring juxtaposition against the sterile white walls and the scent of antiseptic.

"Who are you? What are you doing here?" Trinity's eyes widened. Luna saw a flicker of fear.

She was beautiful. Dark, wavy hair, just like Luna's. Corbin's eyes, warm and expressive. A small, delicate nose, just like Luna's.

But something was missing. That instant, overwhelming connection, the rush of maternal love. She hadn't felt it. Not the tidal wave she'd imagined. But maybe it didn't always come like that. Maybe some connections didn't crash. They gathered.

"Don't be afraid. We're here to help you." Luna moved toward the bed, her gaze lingering on Trinity's face, searching for a glimmer of recognition, a spark of connection.

"How did you get in here?" Trinity's voice trembled. "Are you with . . . them?"

"We're not with anyone but you." Corbin began unbuckling the leather restraints on Trinity's wrists. "We're getting you out of here."

Summer worked to remove the ankle restraints.

Trinity sat up. Swayed.

"Easy, there." Luna steadied her by the shoulders. "Have you been drugged?"

"They didn't give me anything," she said. "Not this time. Dr. Forest said he was keeping me here to . . . to keep me clean. He was mad that I . . . I have an addiction. Pills. It started after my heart transplant."

"I know." Luna stroked Trinity's hair. "You've been through a lot."

Summer stepped forward, holding a tablet Luna hadn't seen before. "Let me check your records. See if they gave you anything."

Corbin asked, "How'd you get into that thing?"

"It's a long story." Summer smiled. "One involving some minor computer skills."

"You hacked into their system?" Trinity was clearly impressed.

"Let's just say I have a way with computers." Summer glanced at Luna. "You guys aren't the only ones with hidden talents."

Corbin looked over Summer's shoulder. "What's it say?"

"She had a transplant, all right," Summer said. "But it's not what we thought."

Luna felt a chill. "What do you mean?"

"The heart." Summer's wide eyes met Luna's, then she looked at Trinity. "The heart they gave you... it's bioprinted."

They stared at Trinity. A bioprinted heart. Not a human heart. Trinity's face paled. "What? What does that mean?"

"It means..." Luna struggled to find the words. The truth, so cold, so unreal. "It means they didn't give you a human heart from a donor. They gave you a... a man-made one. Grown in a lab." Probably this one.

"But... but that's not possible. They told me it was a real heart. From someone who died in an accident. They told me I'd be okay." Trinity's words frayed like a girl unraveling one thread at a time.

"Hey, let's try to stay calm." Luna reached for Trinity's hand. It was cold, clammy. Fragile, like it might break under her touch. Her chest tightened as she fought the urge to pull her hand away and shield her own heart. But she couldn't. Not when her daughter needed her most.

"You're going to be okay. We're getting you out of here." The words felt too small, too insufficient for the magnitude of this moment.

"No!" Trinity shook her head, her eyes wide with terror. "I don't want a fake heart. What if it stops working? What if I die?"

Wet trails marked Trinity's face as she cried. Her body trembled like a leaf caught in a storm. Luna's breath hitched as she pulled her close, wrapping her arms around the girl she'd lost so long ago. She wasn't just holding a scared, trembling teen. She was holding the baby she'd kissed goodbye, the little girl she'd dreamed of a thousand nights, now alive in her arms.

"You have to stay calm, Trinity," Luna said. She gently rocked her as if soothing a child, stroking her hair. "Getting upset won't be good for you in this condition." She'd almost said "your heart" but caught herself. Trinity was frightened enough without her adding to it.

Summer handed the tablet to Corbin and moved beside Trinity. "You've been doing great all this time. Most likely you don't feel good because you're going through withdrawals. I think you'll be fine once you get your strength back."

Corbin stood silently beside her with his gaze fixed on the tablet. Luna nudged him, and he turned the screen toward her.

"Her blood type," he whispered. "It's AB negative."

AB negative. Luna was O positive. Corbin was O negative.

They couldn't be Trinity's parents.

The realization hit her like a crushing blow. After so many questions, so many false starts, she finally had the answer.

The girl in her arms wasn't her daughter. Not biologically. But she'd risked her life for Trinity, and she would do it again and again if that's what it took to keep her safe. Blood didn't make her family. Choice did.

Trinity was sobbing, near hysterics. They couldn't sneak her out like this.

"It's okay," Luna whispered. "You're safe now."

"No, I'm not." Trinity pulled back. "I can't trust anyone. Not after what they did to me."

"You can trust us. We're friends of Stryker," Luna said. "We were in the Warrior program too."

"He's the reason we came to find you." Corbin added.

"You really know Stryker?" A flicker of hope flashed in Trinity's eyes. "Where is he? Is he okay?"

"We're going to find him," Luna said. "I promise."

"But first, we need to get you out of here." Corbin handed the tablet to Summer and moved toward the door. "Give me a minute to find a cell signal and I'll call for backup."

"I'm... I'm... scared." Trinity sniffled. The tears began to subside. "I don't think I should leave. My... heart."

Luna said, "We're going to get you the medical care you need."

She eyed Corbin as he came closer. He shook his head and dropped his phone into his pocket. Still no signal. They couldn't stay here and wait to be discovered. They had to get Trinity out. Not only could her heart provide evidence of every sinister thing happening here, but she wasn't sure if it was even viable.

"Okay, Trin," Luna said. "We're going to all leave together. We have some medical experts on standby, and they need to look at your heart."

Trinity shook her head. "I feel weak. What if I can't make it? How do I know I can trust you?"

"You can trust them." Summer dabbed Trinity's tears with a tissue she'd plucked from a box. "They're Alex and Lorelai Sinclair and they're with the police."

"Actually, that's our cover names," Luna said. "I'm Luna Rosati, and that's Special Agent Corbin King."

Summer's eyes darted between Luna and Corbin. "Luna and . . . and Corbin?" Her voice dropped to a near whisper. "You guys . . . you're . . . you're my parents."

31

THEY WERE KEEPING HIM alert now. But he couldn't move his legs.

Stryker tried to shift. Flex his toes. Nothing.

A heavy numbness pressed down. A leaden weight that started at his chest and extended to his feet.

Paralyzed.

Just breathe. Stay calm.

Nothing else had changed. Crisp hospital sheets against his skin. A gentle rise and fall of his chest with each breath. He could see the sterile white walls of the room. Medical equipment. One-way mirrors mocked his helplessness.

Relentless beeping of the monitors. An insidious reminder of his precarious existence.

But he couldn't move his legs. He couldn't feel them.

The injection. The sharp prick in his back. A zing down his spine ten times worse than jamming his funny bone.

A burning sensation spreading through his veins.

The doctor's cold, clinical tone. "This will make things easier for you, Mr. King."

Easier for him, maybe. But for Stryker, it was a living nightmare.

How long? How long would this paralysis last? Was it temporary? Or had they done something irreversible? Something that would leave him trapped in this prison of his own body forever?

He tried to call out, to ask for help, but only managed a strangled gasp. They'd taken his voice too.

He was a living, breathing specimen, trapped in a cage of flesh and bone.

A soft hiss. The door opening.

He blinked. Waited. A sliver of hope flickered. Maybe Luna. Maybe Corbin. Maybe someone had come to rescue him.

Not Luna. Not Corbin.

Dr. Forest. The man who held his life in his hands. The man who saw him as nothing more than a resource. A means to an end.

And someone else.

A woman. A young woman. Face pale. Lips pale. Bloodless. Drawn. Skin . . . translucent. Blue veins winding like a road map of fragility.

Wheelchair. Her chest rising and falling. Her breathing shallow. Labored.

"Stryker, this is Dr. Elizabeth Forest." Dr. Forest stopped the wheelchair beside the bed.

The bed whirred. Rose to a forty-five-degree angle. He could see the woman more clearly now. She looked older than he'd thought. Forty perhaps. Her eyes a dull blue, shadowed with fatigue. Like she'd seen too much.

"Elizabeth is my daughter," Forest said.

"It's a pleasure to meet you, Mr. King." Elizabeth lifted a hand but let it fall back to her lap. "I've heard so much about you." She sounded strong despite her frail appearance.

He licked his cracked lips. Fought the lingering nausea. "All . . . good . . . things . . . I hope."

"The best," she said.

Dr. Forest said, "Elizabeth's a brilliant young doctor. A pioneer in her field." He glanced at his daughter. "She's the one who developed the bioprinting process. The one who's going to change the world."

Elizabeth's gaze dropped to her lap. "It's not just me, Dad. It's a team effort."

"Nonsense, darling." Forest patted her hand. "You're the brains behind it all. The genius who saw the potential when everyone else dismissed it as science fiction."

He turned to Stryker, his eyes hard. Intense. "You see, Mr. King, we're not monsters. We're visionaries. We're trying to save lives. To solve a crisis that's plaguing humanity."

"Crisis?" Stryker's brow furrowed. "What crisis?"

"The organ shortage," Elizabeth said. "It's a global epidemic, Mr. King. Millions of people are dying every year, waiting for a transplant. The demand far outweighs the supply. Did you know that in the United States alone, over a hundred thousand people are on the organ transplant waiting list? And every day, seventeen people die waiting for a lifesaving organ. That's seventeen people who could have been saved if we had the technology to create new organs."

"Living donors... are... are an option." The words felt weak. Inadequate in the face of her passion.

"Kidneys and livers, but it's not enough." Forest cut him off. "And even when there are living donors, it's a risky procedure. You're asking a healthy person to undergo major surgery, to potentially sacrifice their own health, for someone they might not even know."

Elizabeth said, "It's never going to be enough. What about hearts? People can't die fast enough to save everyone who needs a heart."

"So, you're justifying your actions?" He'd found his voice. Planned to use it. "You're justifying kidnapping innocent people, harvesting their organs? Just because they made mistakes, because they struggled with addiction, you decided their lives were expendable? That their bodies were just... resources?"

"It's not like that, Mr. King." Elizabeth leaned forward in her chair. "We're not targeting just anyone. We're focusing on those who are already lost. Those who are throwing their lives away. Those who, in a sense, have already chosen death."

"They're still human beings." He shifted. The restraints bit into his wrists, but they weren't paralyzed like his legs. "Those people deserve a chance." He studied Elizabeth's face, searching for a flicker of doubt, a hint of compassion in those cool blue eyes. He saw none. "You're playing God, deciding who lives. Who dies."

Elizabeth's fingers tightened on the arms of her wheelchair. She rolled forward an inch and thrust her chin forward. "Someone has to. He doesn't seem to care much anymore."

"He?"

"God," Elizabeth said in a breath of disdain. "He lets innocents suffer. Lets children die. Where's the justice in that?"

Elizabeth's pain was real. Her desperation was justified in her mind. But she was wrong. So wrong.

But Stryker sensed there was still good in her. He had to reach her.

"You see kids like Carlie. Like Trinity." Stryker swallowed the bile rising in the back of his throat and continued. "You see their mistakes, their struggles, and you think they're beyond saving. Lost causes." He paused. "You know the story Jesus told. About the shepherd leaving the ninety-nine to find the one lost sheep. That's what we do, Elizabeth. That's what we're called to do. Even one lost sheep is worth finding. Worth bringing back to the flock."

She shook her head.

"You're brilliant, Elizabeth. You're capable of amazing things." Stryker glanced at Forest, then spoke, his tone low, just loud enough for Elizabeth to hear. "Don't waste your talent on this. Don't let your father drag you down with him."

"He's not dragging me down," Elizabeth said. "This was my idea, Mr. King. My vision." She rolled her chair closer. "I went to Yale with a man named Everett Reeves. He understood. He saw the potential. He helped me secure the funding, the resources, the ... connections we needed to make this happen."

Reeves.

Summer's adoptive parents.

He'd placed Luna and Corbin's baby girl in the arms of Patricia Reeves, her husband Everett looking over her shoulder.

"It's about saving lives, Mr. King," Elizabeth said. "Don't you see? My father ... he's trying to save me. He's trying to save us all."

Forest placed a hand on his daughter's shoulder, leaning close to Stryker's ear. "And your sacrifice is a small price to pay for the greater good."

32

CORBIN STARED AT SUMMER, his thoughts skidding out of control. Parents? Summer's parents. No, it couldn't be. Impossible. Yet, as he scrutinized the young woman standing before him, that spark of recognition the first time Summer walked into the room slapped him in the face.

He'd dismissed it then, telling himself he was seeing Carlie. But no, it wasn't Carlie's features he'd seen. It was Luna's.

Not Luna now, not the hardened agent. This was seventeen-year-old Luna, all fire and defiance. The girl who'd stolen his heart all those years ago.

Eighteen years. A lifetime. And the girl was staring right at him. His daughter.

He dragged in a slow, deliberate breath. The sterile white walls of the room seemed to waver, the steady beeping of the heart monitor blurring into the background noise. He gripped the metal foot-rail of the hospital bed.

Think. Process. Don't let emotion take over. Years on the force had drilled that into him. Except . . . this wasn't a crime scene. This was . . . family.

Luna's hand found his, fingers intertwining. He didn't pull away.

He needed her warmth, that familiar touch, to anchor him. Her eyes, wide and disbelieving, met his. She looked at Summer, her expression a mirror to what was going on inside him.

Luna pulled Summer close. He followed, his arms circling both of them, a tangle of limbs and a lifetime of what-ifs compressed into a single, awkward embrace.

He released Summer and asked, "How? How do you know?" Corbin's voice betrayed him there at the end.

"Stryker told me," Summer said. "I've been an intern here for over a year. My parents, Everett and Patricia Reeves, they donate so much money to the clinic that Dr. Forest couldn't exactly say no when they insisted I work here."

"And that's how you know Stryker?" Luna asked.

"He and Trinity came in for appointments all the time after I started. We sort of became friends. He said he knew my parents, and I told him I'd found out I wasn't biologically their daughter when I studied genetics. I mean, it's not that hard to figure out when your blood types don't add up."

Corbin glanced at Luna, and she suppressed a small smile.

Summer's eyes darted to Trinity in the hospital bed. "Anyway, I'd see them at least once a month, sometimes more. Trinity always complained about being here so much."

"Every single time," Trinity confirmed, a weak smile crossing her pale face.

"So Stryker just randomly told you we're your biological parents?" Corbin shook his head. "That doesn't make sense."

"No, it wasn't random. I started noticing things weren't right here, you know? Restricted areas I couldn't access, charts for patients who didn't exist. Men in black who'd come and go through secured entrances." Summer glanced toward the door. "At first I thought it might be insurance fraud or money laundering or something. But then I realized Dr. Forest was performing all these heart transplants with no paper trail."

"Did you tell anyone? Call the police?" Luna asked.

"I went to Stryker. I knew he used to be a cop and he runs that Kingdom MMA Gym where he trains law enforcement. I figured he'd know what to do." Summer fidgeted with the tissue in her hands. "He promised to look into it."

"That's when things got weird," Trinity interjected. "He started acting all paranoid."

"I've been worried about him ever since I saw him at the grocery store a few weeks ago. I was going to say hello and I wanted to see how Trinity was doing, but there was this man watching him. I recognized him from here. He followed Stryker to his car, and I thought that was weird."

"What did you do?" Corbin pressed.

"The man got into a dark SUV and followed Stryker out of the parking lot. I hurried to my car and followed them. Not closely. I didn't want them to see me, but I ended up losing them at a light," Summer said. "I waited until Stryker's car was back at the gym, then I . . . I left him a note under his windshield."

"This note?" Luna pulled out her phone and showed them the photo she'd taken of the note.

They're watching. Don't trust anyone.

Summer said, "Yeah, that's it."

Corbin asked Luna, "When did you see the note?"

"I dropped by Stryker's after I left you at the diner. He'd offered to let me stay with him, so I didn't see the harm in poking around. I found it tucked in his Bible."

"The day before I left the note, he pulled me aside here at the clinic." Her gaze moved between Luna and Corbin. "Said he'd discovered something while investigating. He was planning to expose it all, but first he needed to tell me something important. That he'd known my parents for a long time and known how hard they'd tried to conceive their own child." Summer exhaled and continued. "He said he'd been the one to place me with my parents. And their connection to the research center, well, he thought they might be involved in something illegal. I just remember he mentioned the Nexus Initiative."

Luna's eyes widened. "Did he say why he decided to tell you then? After all this time?"

"He said..." Summer hesitated. "He said if anything happened to him, I needed to know the truth. That my biological parents were good people who might be the only ones who could stop what was happening here."

Corbin felt a chill. It was all connected. The kidnapping, Chiron, the girls in the graveyard, Trinity. The bioengineered transplant had most likely saved her life, but it could also end it. Paternal protectiveness roared up inside of him.

His eyes slid to her in the hospital bed. She looked pale, her breathing shallow. Her hand pressed into her chest. Her symptoms mirrored the ones he'd been faking. "You okay?"

"My heart," Trinity said in a strained whisper. "It's... it's racing."

He exchanged a look with Luna. This wasn't good. They had to get Trinity out of here. To a real doctor in a real hospital. "I think we're going to need that chopper after all."

"The sooner the better," Luna said.

"Blade, do you copy? We need immediate extraction. Clear skies ahead." He covered his earpiece with his hand, listening.

Silence.

"Blade? Do you copy?" He checked his phone again. "No connection. What about you?"

Luna shook her head. "Nothing. The comms aren't working down here."

"We're too deep underground," Summer said. "No cell signal. No radio frequencies. They might even have jammers as a security precaution."

"Then how do we get out of here?" His frustration simmered, threatening to boil over.

"Everything down here runs on a private mesh network," Summer explained, her fingers flying over the tablet. "It's designed to be completely isolated from the outside world. I can't get access with this either." She flipped the tablet, showing Corbin the red error message flashing on the display.

"We're trapped," Trinity said.

"Not yet," Summer said. "I know a way out. But we have to hurry."

"Stryker?" Luna asked, her gaze fixed on Summer. "Is he here?"

"I... I'm not sure," Summer said. "But if he's been kidnapped ... like you said ... then ... yeah. He's probably here."

"We can't leave him." Trinity started to cry again. "I won't go without him."

Corbin inhaled, trying to steady himself. A shot at rescuing Stryker. That was something. But escaping this facility without backup and two teenage girls who needed him? It felt impossible.

"We won't leave him," Corbin said. "Summer, if he's here, where would he be?"

"I overheard Dr. Forest arguing with one of the guards. They were talking about moving someone, a man, somewhere more secure." Summer pulled up a map of the facility on her tablet. "I think they might hold him in this area." She pointed to a section on the lower level. "There's a network of access tunnels down there, probably to move patients discreetly, stuff like that. I've seen those electric carts around that wing. Why else would they need them unless they're transporting people who can't make it on their own."

"Someone who's been drugged or restrained," Corbin said.

"I might need one of those carts myself. I'm already exhausted," Trinity said, rubbing her chest. Her body shuddered with another wave of chills.

Luna moved to Trinity's side and placed a hand on her shoulder. "We'll get you out of here. And we'll get you the help you need to get through this, whatever it is."

He knew this was a gamble, relying on a teenager to navigate them through a high-security facility. But they were out of options. He turned to Luna. "We need to figure out what to do about collecting evidence. We need proof. Something to show the world what's going on here. Something to shut them down."

"Isn't finding Stryker and Trinity held here enough?"

"That's second-degree kidnapping," he said. "These guys would be out in less than ten years."

"What about one of those... hearts?" Luna gestured toward the door. "One of the bioprinted ones."

"Or Trinity?" Summer looked up from her tablet. "She's evidence, isn't she?"

"I never gave anyone permission to do this to me. To... to Frankenstein me like this." Trinity's breaths were rapid. Shallow. "He cut me open. Took out my heart. Put in this... this fake one."

Corbin's chest tightened. He couldn't imagine the terror, the violation. "Yes, but that's medical malpractice. We need more. Something more concrete. More incriminating. Something that proves Carlie and the other victims were here when they had their organs harvested."

"There's the data vault," Summer said. "But I'm not sure where it is. I've never seen it."

"Think, Summer. Where would they put it if they wanted to keep it safe? Cloud storage? Something we can hack?" Harlee and Jett could figure it out, he was sure of it.

"No, not the cloud. Too risky." Summer's brow furrowed, her lips moving silently as she processed the information. "Besides off-site, the safest place would be... down here. Somewhere secure. Hidden." Her gaze darted around the room, then settled on Corbin. "There's a room two floors down. It's filled with computer equipment. Servers and networking. I've only peeked inside."

Corbin nodded. The data vault. It had to be there. "If I could get inside, I could find a way to download the patient list, the financial records. All the evidence we need to expose the whole operation."

"I've got a flash drive," Summer offered.

He turned to Luna. "I'll go after the data vault. You guys find Stryker."

"What?" Luna's eyes widened. "No. We need to stick together. It's too dangerous to split up."

"We don't have a choice. We need proof Carlie and the others were here. For their families. We can't risk them moving or deleting the evidence." He met her gaze. "You help Trinity and focus on finding Stryker. Summer can guide you. Once you're clear, radio for backup. Medical support. The works. I'll meet you at the rendezvous point."

"Corbin, no." Luna shook her head. "Don't leave me again."

He could hear fear in her voice for the first time since... since she'd been in the hospital. With Summer. Their daughter. There was conflict in Luna's eyes. He felt it too. That pull between his paternal instincts, the need to protect all three of them, and the need to do his job. Solve this case.

"It's not like that." He reached for her hand, his fingers intertwining with hers. "The Commissioner needs closure. You saw the anger and despair in his eyes."

She nodded.

He continued, "And... what about the others? There could be more out there, with these... these hearts or other organs, not knowing."

"Come on, Trin." Summer's gaze softened as she turned to her. "Let's get you out of that gown and into some real clothes. You'll feel better, I promise."

As Summer led Trinity into the bathroom, Luna turned back to Corbin. "I thought we were in this together. Partners?"

"We are." He pulled her close, his arms encircling her waist, the warmth of her body a comfort against his aching ribs. "This isn't the same, Luna. I love you. Always have. Always will." He tilted her chin, his lips brushing against hers. "And I just found my daughter. I'm not going to make the same mistakes again. Not this time. I promise."

She yielded to his kiss. Soft, hesitant at first, then responding with a fierceness that made his head spin. The taste of her, familiar and intoxicating, a reminder of all they'd lost, all they could still have.

They broke apart, the girls' chatter in the bathroom a reminder of the danger that still lurked.

"What about the data vault?" Luna asked. "How are you going to get in?"

"I'll figure it out." He stroked her cheek, his thumb tracing the curve of her jaw. "And then I'll be right behind you."

The bathroom door opened, and Summer emerged, her arm around Trinity, who was dressed in a pair of leggings and a sweatshirt, her face pale but determined.

"Okay, here's the deal." Summer pointed to a spot on her tablet's map of the facility. "If the data vault is where I think it is, then it's on the sub-level, two floors down. You'll need a key card or maybe a six-digit code to get in."

"And how do we get those?" Corbin asked.

"We improvise." Summer's lips curved in a smile as she handed him the tiny Flipper device and explained how to use it. "Keep pressing this button until the unit finds the frequency and the door unlocks. I've managed to disable the alarm so you won't trip it again," she said. "But it won't last. Maybe ten minutes, tops."

Corbin looked at Luna. He knew, without a doubt, that she could handle this. She was the strongest woman he knew.

He kissed her, a quick, hard press of his lips against hers. "Be careful."

"Always am." She smiled, a flash of her old fire.

"Let's go, Trinity." Luna placed a hand on the girl's shoulder, her gaze meeting Corbin's. "We'll find Stryker and get you home."

He watched Luna lead Trinity into the hall, Summer following close behind. He didn't want to let them out of his sight, but he knew he had to trust them. He had to trust himself.

Summer ran back. "Wait! I almost forgot." She reached into her pocket and pulled out a small flash drive. "Here. Take this." She pressed it into his palm. "It's loaded with a program that'll clone any hard drive. It'll take three minutes."

"Three minutes," he repeated, his mind calculating the odds, the risks.

"You'll be careful, right?" She looked up at him, eyes searching his, as if trying to gauge whether she could trust him. "I just met you, and I don't want to lose you. I want to get to know my . . . my father."

He swallowed the lump in his throat. *Father.* The word sounded foreign but right. He forced a calmness he didn't feel, trying to calm the rush of emotions.

"I'm not going anywhere, Summer. Not without you." He guided her chin up, his gaze meeting hers as he did. "I don't know what happens next, but I'm here. To help you. To make sure you're safe. And maybe . . . maybe we'll have time to get to know each other."

Her eyes flickered with something. Hope, fear, or both. Then she was gone, running down the corridor.

The flash drive was cool against his palm for a fleeting moment before he shoved it into his pocket and took off in the opposite direction.

The clock was ticking.

Ten minutes before the alarm would be tripped.

Three minutes to clone the hard drive.

33

LUNA HURRIED DOWN the corridor, each step a reminder of Trinity's fragile heart, the borrowed time ticking away with every beat. Summer led the way, clutching the tablet as she navigated the labyrinthine corridors.

Summer. Her daughter. The daughter she had yearned for all those years. The missing piece, found in the most unexpected way. Now she was leading them toward freedom. It was almost too much to comprehend.

And Trinity—who somehow felt like her daughter too, no matter what her DNA said—was teetering on the edge of collapse. The withdrawals too much for her young body.

And a bioengineered time bomb ticking away in her chest.

She lagged behind, pale and shaky, her hand pressed to her chest with each labored breath.

"Trinity, are you okay?" Luna reached out, touching the girl's arm, needing the reassurance of that physical connection.

"I'm perfect. Just . . . detoxing. Let's find our friend." Trinity squeezed Luna's hand with a surprisingly strong grip. "He needs us."

They rounded a corner. Summer glanced over her shoulder. "This is the access corridor to the secure wing. It should be just a few more doors down."

A metal door blocked the end of the hallway. Summer swiped a key card on the pad, and Luna heard a beep. The red LEDs above the keypad blinked erratically before turning a reassuring green. A section of the wall hissed, sliding to the side to reveal a narrow opening that led into a dimly lit tunnel.

"It's a service corridor." Summer motioned them through.

The air inside was cold, damp. The stench of bleach and something... metallic... made her stomach churn.

Ahead, two electric carts, their white paint chipped and scratched, sat side by side. Summer gave one of them a little kick. "Just what we need."

"Oh, thank goodness." Trinity practically collapsed into the passenger seat.

Summer slid behind the steering wheel and looked at Luna. "Ready?"

Luna took the empty seat, the cushioned vinyl giving way with a swish of air. "Let's do this."

Summer keyed the ignition. Nothing happened.

"You sure this thing works?" Luna asked.

Summer pressed the pedal, and the cart lurched forward, whirring to life. "Just like a golf cart." She took it slow at first, then picked up speed.

The walls of the tunnel were bare concrete, stained with damp patches that gleamed in the cart's headlight beams. Luna had her head on a swivel, scanning every shadow.

"It's like that movie," Summer said. "The one with the girl who gets hunted in that abandoned hospital?"

"Quiet," Luna whispered. The darkness pressed in, amplifying her every sense. Every drip of water from the pipes overhead, every rustle in the darkness, sounded like a footstep, a whisper, a threat.

They rounded a bend, the tunnel opening into a wider space.

Ahead, a set of double doors. A keypad glowed beside the right door.

Summer eased the cart to a stop. "End of the line."

"Stay close," Luna said, "but behind me. I'll open the door and make sure it's safe."

"Here." Summer handed Luna the key card. "We should have access anywhere Dr. Forest does."

Luna swiped the key card through the slot, her hand hovering over the door handle. The lock disengaged with a soft click. She pushed the doors open, revealing another sterile white corridor, this one lined with closed doors.

Empty. No guards. No cameras that she could see, but that didn't mean they weren't there.

Luna's heart pounded. They were close now. So close. She just hoped they hadn't come too late.

She motioned for Summer and Trinity to follow, her eyes darting around the corridor, scanning for threats.

"Where are we?" Trinity whispered, her hand resting on Summer's arm.

"I think this is the patient observation area." Summer pointed toward a glass-enclosed nurses' station, its counter a jumble of charts, syringes, and half-empty coffee cups. The high stools were empty. The silence ominous.

Trinity's hand went to her chest, her breath catching. "This . . . this is familiar."

Luna's stomach clenched. She knew exactly what Trinity meant. This was the dark, sterile room where she'd been held captive, subjected to Dr. Forest's experiments.

They crept down the hallway. One-way mirrors allowed her a quick glance inside each patient room. Empty. Empty. Empty.

Luna paused at the last room. This one felt different. Inside, the bed was unmade, the sheets a tangled mess, as if someone had just been pulled away. Hospital restraints—heavy-duty leather straps—lay on the unmade bed.

"This must be where he was," Luna said. "We're too late. He's gone."

Trinity's shoulders slumped, defeat mirrored in her pale face.

Summer gripped the tablet tighter, her gaze flickering back down the hallway, the hope draining from her eyes. "Where would they have taken him?"

Luna pressed her lips together, fighting to contain the despair that threatened to engulf her. "I don't know."

She checked her phone. Still no connection. No hope of backup.

They rounded the nurses' station, their steps silent on the tile floor. Luna snatched up the phone on the desk. *Please work.* She pressed it to her ear. A dial tone, a faint, reassuring hum. Finally something going right. She punched in Blade's number. Waited.

A rapid, insistent busy signal blasted in her ear. Her thumb pressed the disconnect button. She released it, tried 911.

Same thing.

"Try nine," Summer said. "Get an outside line."

She added it to Blade's number and 911. Neither worked.

"How about zero," Trinity suggested.

Luna punched the key and felt her eyebrows raise when she heard, "Chiron BioInnovation Center. How may I direct your call?"

She hadn't thought this far ahead. Asking for help might only send them trouble. She took a deep breath, pitching her voice low, a gruff, masculine growl. "There's a bomb in the building. You've got three minutes to evacuate. Then it goes boom. You tell the cops that it's all clear skies ahead."

She slammed the phone back on its cradle and glanced up at the wide eyes staring back at her.

"Why'd you do that!" Trinity shook her head. "You're going to cause a panic."

"Our friends are waiting outside," Luna said. "Ready to extract. Once they see everyone running out, they'll understand and send help."

The alarm blared through the hallway, the shrill sound drilling into her skull.

Trinity flinched, her hand instinctively flying to her chest. "What is that?"

"Shhh . . ." Summer's gaze darted down the hall. "Someone's coming."

"This way." Luna grabbed their hands and pulled them toward a nearby doorway.

They stumbled into a small, darkened room. A storage room of some kind. The heavy steel door clicked shut behind them, sealing them inside. Luna pressed her back against the cool metal.

She held a finger to her lips. Quiet.

They crouched in the darkness, barely daring to breathe, listening to the heavy footsteps approaching, the murmur of voices growing louder.

"Clear!" one of the guards called out.

"Check the south rooms," another voice ordered.

The voices faded, moving on to search another part of the facility.

Luna released a breath. But Trinity's hand tightened on her arm. "What is this place?" she whispered.

It took a moment for Luna's eyes to adjust to the dim light. A yellow safety cabinet stood against the far wall, its door ajar. She peered inside. White plastic jugs lined the shelf, each marked with red-and-white hazmat stickers. The bold black lettering on the bottles read "Diethyl Ether."

Shelves lined the walls, stainless steel and sterile, each one filled with containers. Glass containers of various sizes, labeled with dates and alphanumeric codes. And within each one, floating in a pale, pinkish liquid, were organs.

The proximity to the human tissue made bile rise in the back of her throat.

"Oh my goodness . . ." Summer shrank back, hand flying to her mouth. She bumped a metal tray, sending it clattering to the floor.

The sound, amplified in the silence, echoed through the room.
From the hallway, a voice. "Did you hear something?"
Luna's hand instinctively went to her holster, her fingers closing around empty air.
They were trapped. And unarmed.

34

A TRIO OF GUNSHOTS pinged off the server rack inches from beside Corbin's head, showering him with sparks and metal shards. He dropped to a crouch, heart hammering against his ribs.

Sweat beaded on his forehead. Stupid. He'd taken too long finding this room. Now he was pinned down with no clear exit.

He peered around the corner of the server rack. A man in black stood at the far end of the aisle, gun raised. No mask. Just cold, determined eyes.

As the man advanced, Corbin caught the subtle hitch in his gait. The marina. The guy he'd kneecapped.

Corbin's hand went to his pocket, fingers closing around the ASP baton. His only weapon against a gun. Great odds.

The flash drive felt like it was burning a hole in his other pocket. He had to get that data. Lives depended on it.

Three minutes. That was all he needed.

Three minutes to clone the hard drive and potentially bring down this entire operation. Mr. Hitch-in-his-step included.

He scanned the room. Rows upon rows of server racks stretched before him, a maze of blinking lights and humming machinery. Tangles of multicolored cables snaked across the floor and climbed the walls like technicolor vines. The low, persistent hum of cooling systems working overtime filled the air, a constant drone that set his teeth on edge.

There. A terminal, half-hidden behind a mess of wires. To reach it, he'd have to cross open ground. Exposed. Vulnerable.

Two more firecracker pops. He flinched as sparks erupted from the rack above him, raining down hot pinpricks on his skin. Too close. Far too close.

Corbin sprinted, keeping low. Pain lanced through his side where the stitches pulled. He gritted his teeth, pushing through it.

The terminal loomed closer. Ten feet. Five feet. Almost there.

A shout of rage echoed behind him. Hitch had spotted him and squeezed off three rapid bursts.

Corbin dove the last few feet, sliding across the smooth floor. His shoulder slammed into the base of the terminal, sending a jolt of pain through his body. But he'd made it.

He fished the flash drive from his pocket. His fingers shook as he plugged it in. It didn't fit. He flipped it over and tried again. Still no good. What in the world? He looked at the USB slot, looked at the drive. Yeah, he had it right, so why wouldn't it—this time it slid home.

The screen flickered to life. A prompt appeared. *Run Secure-Dump_v2.7?*

He clicked it. A progress bar appeared.

1%.

Footsteps. Slow. Deliberate. Getting closer. Hitch was taking his time, savoring the hunt.

5%.

Corbin's eyes darted between the painfully slow progress bar and the aisle where he knew Hitch was advancing. He pulled out the ASP baton. He might have to turn Mr. Hitch into Mr. Gimp.

10%.

"Come out, come out," Hitch called. His voice was eerily calm. "We can end this quickly. Or not. Your choice."

15%.

His mind raced, processing options, discarding plans as quickly as they formed. He couldn't stay here. He was a sitting duck, trapped between the terminal and the approaching threat.

20%.

He had to move. Create a distraction. Buy himself more time.

25%.

Corbin unclipped his belt, sliding it free. Careful not to make a sound, he looped it around the nearest cable bundle.

30%.

The footsteps stopped. Corbin held his breath, every muscle tense.

"I know you're here. I can smell your fear. It's . . . intoxicating."

35%.

Corbin closed his eyes, steadying himself. Now or never.

In one fluid motion, he yanked hard on the belt. Cables snapped free. For a heartbeat, nothing happened. Then, sparks erupted as live wires made contact.

The gunman cursed, momentarily distracted by the sudden light show.

Seizing his chance, Corbin burst from his hiding spot. The ASP baton extended with a satisfying click, becoming a solid rod of hard metal. He swung with all his might, aiming for the wrist.

A satisfying crack echoed through the room as metal met bone. The impact reverberated up Corbin's arm.

The gun clattered to the floor, skittering away across the smooth surface.

Hitch recovered quickly. With a roar, he barreled into Corbin's waist, tackling him. Something tore. Stitches maybe.

They went down hard. Corbin's back slammed against the cold floor, driving the air from his lungs. Stars exploded behind his eyes as his head connected with the ground.

Hitch was on top of him. His hands pressed into Corbin's throat, thick fingers digging into soft flesh. He gasped, struggling to draw breath. The baton. Where was the baton?

45%.

The number flashed in Corbin's peripheral vision, a cruel reminder of how much time he still needed.

With a surge of desperate strength, he jabbed Hitch in the solar plexus, driving the wind out of him. Maybe breaking a rib or two. Hitch coughed out a hunk of air.

The pressure on Corbin's throat eased.

He didn't waste the opportunity. He bucked his hips, throwing the larger man off balance. They rolled, grappling for dominance. Corbin's ribs screamed in protest as they slammed against a server rack.

50%.

Hitch was strong, but Corbin had desperation and years of training with Stryker on his side. He fought dirty, using every trick he'd ever learned.

Corbin chopped him in the throat, nailing his windpipe. Hitch gagged, his grip loosening. Corbin followed up with a knee to the kidney, feeling a grim satisfaction as the gunman's eyes bulged with pain.

55%.

Corbin pressed his advantage, driving the man back toward the sparking cables.

60%.

Hitch's eyes widened as he realized the danger. With a snarl, he lunged for Corbin, catching him off guard. His shoulder connected with Corbin's chest. They hit the ground hard, Corbin on the bottom this time.

65%.

The impact sent shock waves of pain through his body. His vision swam. The taste of copper filled his mouth—he'd bitten his tongue in the fall.

70%.

Hitch's hands closed around Corbin's throat, squeezing with renewed vigor. Corbin clawed at the man's arms, trying to break his grip, but it was like trying to bend steel.

Spots danced at the edges of his vision. His lungs burned, screaming for air.

75%.

Corbin's fingers scrabbled for purchase, searching desperately for something, anything to use as a weapon. His hand brushed against something solid. The ASP baton.

80%.

With the last reserves of his strength, Corbin's fingers closed around the baton. He tightened his grip, summoning every ounce of power he had left.

He swung. The baton connected with the side of the man's head with a thwack. Hitch's eyes rolled back, his grip on Corbin's throat slack.

85%.

Corbin gasped, sucking in precious molecules of oxygen. His throat felt raw, each breath a painful rasp.

90%.

The gunman staggered to his feet, swaying like a drunk. Blood trickled from a gash on his temple where the baton had struck. His eyes were unfocused, dazed.

He took an unsteady step back.

Right into the exposed wires.

95%.

Hitch's body went rigid. Muscles locking in place. A horrible, guttural sound escaped his lips as electricity coursed through him. The smell of burning flesh filled the air.

Corbin turned away, unable to watch. His stomach roiled, threatening to expel its meager contents.

98%.

The horrible sound cut off abruptly. There was a thud as the gunman's body hit the floor, smoke rising from his twitching form.

100%.

The terminal beeped, the sound jarringly cheerful in the aftermath of violence.

Download complete.

Corbin crawled to the terminal and yanked the flash drive free. Panting, he tucked it securely in his pocket, patting it to reassure himself it was really there.

The hilt of Hitch's gun stuck out from the tangle of cables beside the terminal. He crawled to it and picked it up. Checked the rounds.

Half a load. Good. Plenty of rounds.

But it wouldn't ride in his waistband, not without his belt. He'd just have to carry it.

He stood. Pain shot through his side, but his legs held.

He turned, his gaze falling on the gunman's body. The man's eyes stared sightlessly at the ceiling, his face frozen in a rictus of pain and surprise.

A wave of nausea washed over Corbin. He hadn't meant for this to happen. It was self-defense, yes, but the brutality of it shook him to his core.

But there was no time for regret or self-recrimination.

Corbin stumbled toward the exit, his legs unsteady beneath him. Every step sent shock waves of pain through his battered body. His throat throbbed where the gunman's fingers had dug in, and he could already feel bruises forming. Blood soaked through his shirt, but not as bad as before. He'd be fine.

A tremor ran through the building.

The floor beneath his feet shuddered, and a distant boom echoed through the corridors. An explosion.

He yanked the door open, nearly falling into the hallway beyond.

Emergency lights pulsed an angry red, casting eerie shadows that danced along the walls. A siren wailed. No smoke. Not yet.

Corbin sprinted down the hall, heading for the service tunnel.

35

THE GROUND SHUDDERED beneath Luna's feet, a tremor that pulsed through her bones. The shelves rattled. Jars clinked together. The distant boom of the explosion rolled through the building like thunder.

Luna couldn't move. Couldn't breathe. The market. The beggar girl. Aisha's lifeless eyes.

What if it was the lab? Or the vault. What if Corbin was trapped? She could almost feel the heat of the explosion, smell the smoke, hear the echoing boom that reverberated through her.

"What was that?" The voice of one of the guards was closer now.

"Sounded like a blast ball or stun grenade. We'd better check it out." Footsteps retreated, growing fainter. "C'mon!"

Stun grenade. Not a deadly explosive. Just a distraction.

Luna waited, counting her heartbeats until she was sure the guards were gone. She did a four-count breathing exercise. When her hands were steady again, she said, "Okay, I think it's clear."

"Are you sure they're gone?" Trinity whispered. She clutched the edge of a shelf for support.

"Only one way to find out." Luna eased the storage room door open and peered out. The hallway was empty.

Summer put her hand on Luna's arm. "Was that . . . a bomb?"

She shook her head. "No. Special ops tactical diversion. Big noise, bright flash. It's meant to stun and distract."

"Worked for us," Trinity said.

"We have law enforcement outside waiting for our signal," Luna said. "That's probably them making a move."

Trinity's eyes widened. "So that was your people?"

"Maybe. Or Corbin creating a distraction," Luna said. "Either way, we're safe."

"Yeah, but what about Corbin?" Summer asked. "What if that was meant for him?"

"He knows what he's doing." How many times had she told herself that in the field when operations went sideways? But this wasn't just any partner. This was Corbin.

"What do we do?" Summer asked.

"We stick to the plan. If that was Corbin buying us time, we can't waste it," she said. "Help might be on the way, but Stryker might not have time. I say we keep moving."

She studied the girls' faces. Summer gave a determined nod. Trinity, pale but resolute, did the same.

"Okay, we can't go back the way we came. The guards went that direction."

Summer nodded. "Let's keep moving forward."

A door at the end of the hall caught Luna's attention. Unlike the others, it had a small window. "This way."

She approached with caution and peered through the window. It was a surgical scrub room. They slipped inside. The room was small, almost claustrophobic.

Stainless steel dominated. Long sinks lined one wall, each one equipped with a gooseneck faucet and foot pedals. Dispensers for soap and hand sanitizer were mounted above, their chrome surfaces gleaming under the harsh fluorescent lights overhead.

Luna's gaze scanned the room. "Let's find a way out of here."

She moved to the opposite wall where a door, clad in stainless steel, had a small, rectangular window of reinforced glass set at eye level. The edges were sealed with a thick, black rubber gasket. A red light, small and pulsing, glowed above the frame.

Through another window, she could see into an operating theater.

"Stryker," she breathed.

Stryker lay on the table, tubes and wires snaking from his body. His eyes were closed, a breathing tube down his throat. A woman in a specialized wheelchair that gave her height was pulling on surgical gloves. Beside her, Dr. Forest was being helped into a surgical gown by Dr. Sheridan.

Her blood ran cold as she saw the array of surgical instruments.

They were about to operate on Stryker.

Without thinking, she burst through the door, Summer and Trinity right behind her.

"Stop!" Luna shouted, her voice echoing in the sterile room. "Don't touch him!"

Everyone froze. Dr. Forest's eyes widened in shock, then narrowed.

"What are you doing?" Dr. Sheridan hissed. "This is a sterile environment!"

But Luna wasn't listening. Her eyes were locked on Stryker's still form, on the machines. She started for the operating table.

Dr. Forest snatched up a scalpel. His surprise morphed into a cold smile. "Ah, ah, ah. I wouldn't do that if I were you." His gaze shifted to Summer and Trinity and back to Luna.

She took a step forward, hands raised. "Get away from him. Now."

Luna felt Summer and Trinity move closer, flanking her. She straightened, drawing strength from their presence.

"It's over, Forest," Luna said. "Whatever you're planning, it stops now."

The woman in the wheelchair turned, her eyes locking onto Luna's with an intensity that sent a chill down her spine.

Dr. Forest's smile didn't waver. "Oh, I don't think so," he said. "In fact, I'd say things are just getting interesting."

Luna took another step forward, but before she could act, the doors behind them burst open. Two men rushed in, grabbing Summer and Trinity. One wrapped his arm around Summer's neck, while the other pressed a gun to Trinity's temple. Dr. Forest's enforcers.

"No!" Luna cried.

Dr. Forest's smile widened as he pressed the scalpel against Stryker's throat. "I wouldn't move if I were you."

Luna froze, torn between the girls and her mentor. Her mind raced, seeking a way out of this nightmare.

Dr. Forest's eyes gleamed with a manic light. "Since we're all here, why don't I explain why we're doing this? It's time you understood. Then maybe you'll agree that everything we're doing here serves a greater purpose."

He glanced at the woman in the wheelchair. "This is my daughter, Elizabeth. She's a brilliant surgeon, but she's dying. We've tried everything, including two transplants, but her new heart is failing, just like the others. Stryker"—he spat the name—"has interfered with all our hard work. Because of him sticking his nose in my business, Elizabeth might never get the heart she needs to survive."

Luna's brow furrowed. "Why not just print one for Elizabeth? Isn't that what your research is about?"

Elizabeth spoke up, her voice soft but determined. "We've tried. But our trials haven't worked yet. The bioprinted hearts . . . they fail."

Dr. Forest nodded. "It's all a part of the clinical trial, you see. We remove the healthy heart and give the patient their bioprinted heart. The healthy heart goes to someone in need. Someone who won't waste the new life we gave them. Then we study the bioprinted heart in our patient."

Luna narrowed her eyes. "The victim you mean."

Elizabeth ignored her. "It works at first. The hearts beat just fine. The patients recover and gain strength. But then, like clockwork, four or five weeks later, their bodies reject the heart."

"But we don't just let them die," Dr. Forest added. "That would be cruel. I take them into surgery and remove the bioprinted heart, along with all the healthy organs."

Summer's eyes widened in understanding. "Because you don't waste resources, right?"

Dr. Forest beamed at her. "Exactly, my dear. You're very bright."

"What about me?" Trinity asked. "You gave me a bioprinted heart a year ago."

"You're the special one," Dr. Forest said. "The only one whose heart hasn't failed yet."

"So why did you kidnap her?" Luna spat the question.

"Because she was wasting it!" A dark shadow passed over Dr. Forest's features. He stared at Trinity. "You were destroying what I created. Killing yourself with drugs. You were wasting the precious life I gave you. If it hadn't been for me, you would have died a long time ago waiting for a donor."

Trinity paled, her hand flew to her chest.

Luna felt sick. The enormity of what they'd done, the lives they'd destroyed, all in the name of saving one person. It was overwhelming.

She had to keep them talking, had to find a way out of this.

Trinity's face suddenly contorted in pain. She clutched at her chest, her breathing becoming labored. "I . . . I can't . . ." Her legs buckled and she sagged against the enforcer who had been holding the gun to her temple, nearly dragging him down with her.

"Trinity!" Luna cried, lurching forward, only to be stopped by the enforcer's gun.

Elizabeth's eyes widened in alarm. "Dad, do something now!"

Dr. Forest's calm demeanor shattered. He dropped the scalpel and rushed to Trinity's side, barking orders. "Get her on the table! We need to stabilize her immediately!"

The enforcer holding Trinity scooped her up and laid her on an empty surgical table.

"We can't lose her. She's our only successful case." Dr. Forest pressed his fingers to Trinity's neck, checking her pulse.

"Dad, please! We need her." Elizabeth wheeled herself closer. "We have to study why her heart lasted so long!"

"Sheridan!" Dr. Forest's hands flew over Trinity's body, attaching monitors. "We need the stabilizing agent! Now!"

Dr. Sheridan nodded. "I'll get it from the lab." She rushed out of the room.

Trinity's body lay limp on the table.

Luna saw an opening. She spun and drove her elbow hard into the temple of the enforcer holding Summer.

Summer slammed her heel down on the man's instep. He gasped and released her, stumbling back with his right foot dangling at an awkward angle behind him. He hobbled a step, then another, left leg working overtime to stay upright.

Luna shifted her weight. She turned her hips, brought her foot knee-high, and pistoned her heel down and forward. It cracked against his shin. The leg, bearing the guard's full weight, collapsed with a pop. "My leg! You broke my leg!"

Pain ripped through her scalp. The second enforcer had grabbed a fistful of her hair and yanked her back. He shoved the barrel of his gun into her spine.

Rage snapped loose.

She twisted away from the gun and jabbed her fingers into his eyes. He roared, stumbling away. Her knee shot up into his groin. He folded and sank to the floor, gasping.

Luna scooped up the gun he'd dropped.

"Summer, run!" Luna shouted, already moving toward Trinity.

Summer darted for the scalpel on the floor where Dr. Forest had dropped it. Dr. Forest slammed into her from behind. His arm locked around her waist. He yanked her tight against his chest. The scalpel, now in his hand, pressed against Summer's throat.

"That's quite enough," Forest snarled, positioning himself between Luna and Trinity. "One more step, and I'll open her throat. And as for Trinity..." His eyes flickered to the table. "Well, without immediate treatment, I'm afraid she doesn't have long."

Luna froze. Her heart pounded. She'd taken down the enforcers, but at what cost? Now both the girls were in immediate danger.

"What do you want?" The gun trembled in her hand.

Dr. Forest's lips curled into a cold smile. "What I want is your cooperation. You're going to help us escape this facility. And we'll be taking Stryker's... resources... with us."

Luna's stomach turned at his implication. "You're insane."

"Perhaps," Forest conceded. "But I'm also the only one who can save Trinity's life right now. So what will it be? Will you help us? Or will you watch both of them die?"

The beeping of Stryker's heart monitor punctuated the silence. She didn't have a shot. How long had it been since they'd gone dark? Reinforcements had to be close. They had to know things had gone sideways. So where was the cavalry?

Summer squirmed in Forest's grip, but the blade was too close. Trinity wasn't moving. Her life could be slipping away.

They were out of options.

She raised her hands with the gun hanging from one finger.

The door to the operating room burst open with a resounding crash.

Corbin leaned heavily against the doorframe, his shirt soaked through with blood. His face was pale, but he held a gun aimed at Dr. Forest—a weapon he shouldn't even be able to hold with the way his fingers shook. Yet there he was, still standing, still fighting.

"Let them go."

Forest staggered back a few steps, dragging Summer with him. A rivulet of blood bloomed at her throat.

Luna curled her fingers around the gun and brought it up. The first enforcer—the one with the shattered leg—had dragged himself to the wall and collapsed there, motionless. Maybe unconscious. Maybe just praying no one touched his leg again.

She kept her aim steady, eyes flicking between Forest and the other one. The guard she'd nailed in the groin had made it to his feet, listing to one side but still breathing. Still dangerous.

"How nice of you to join our little party," Forest said to Corbin. "But I'm afraid you're outnumbered here."

With a few shaky steps, Corbin moved behind Elizabeth's wheelchair, the muzzle of his gun trained between her shoulder blades. "Let them go or your daughter gets to experience what it's like to be on the other side of your twisted experiments."

Elizabeth gasped. "Dad . . ."

Dr. Forest's face contorted. "You wouldn't dare!"

"Try me," Corbin snarled. "I've seen what you've done. The lives you've destroyed. Don't think for a second I won't do whatever it takes to stop you."

"You're bluffing," Dr. Forest said, but his voice had lost its edge.

Corbin's eyes narrowed. "Want to bet Elizabeth's life on that?"

"Fine. You win."

Dr. Forest shoved Summer into Corbin, and he caught her, taking his gun off Elizabeth.

In that moment of distraction, Elizabeth wheeled herself to Stryker's side, grabbed a needle from a nearby tray, and plunged it into his IV. Her thumb pushed its contents into the line.

Stryker's medical machines went haywire.

Luna rushed to Stryker's side, heart thundering in her ears. The machines surrounding him screeched and beeped in frantic discord.

Summer was there, eyes wide as she scanned the monitors.

Luna whirled to face Elizabeth. "What did you give him?"

The woman's lips curled into a cold smile. She remained silent, her eyes fixed on Stryker's convulsing form.

A commotion erupted from behind. Dr. Forest and the enforcer bolted for the door, but their escape was cut off.

"Broward County Sheriff's Department! Freeze!" Blade's voice boomed through the chaos.

The room filled with the sound of boots on tile as Blade and his tactical team burst in, Harlee right behind them.

In a matter of seconds, Forest and the enforcer were cuffed, arms wrenched behind their backs. One agent kept a gun trained on the man with the shattered leg while another checked for a pulse.

"Luna!" Harlee rushed to her side. "Are you okay?"

She nodded, her attention already back on Stryker. "We need medical help here! Now!"

Summer's voice was tight. "It's a combination of barbiturates and . . . something else. It's creating a complex overdose. We need to stabilize him immediately or the brain edema could—"

"There's a medevac chopper waiting," Blade interrupted. "Priority is getting any patients out of here."

As the medical team swarmed around Stryker, Luna's eyes darted to Trinity. She was stirring, eyes fluttering open.

"Luna?" Trinity's voice was weak but present.

She rushed over, taking Trinity's hand in hers. "I'm here, sweetheart. You're going to be okay."

EMTs assessed Trinity with Summer hovering nearby.

Blade approached Luna, worry lines creasing his forehead. "We had to use flash bangs and concussive blasts to fight off some black ops guys trying to destroy evidence. What we found in the lab . . ." He shook his head.

"The EMT says Trinity's vitals are good," Summer interjected. "Even her heart. Probably she just passed out, but they want to take her to the hospital for a full workup."

Luna nodded, her gaze meeting Corbin's across the room. Though his movements were slow, he reached her side and took her hand.

"We're going with her." Corbin's voice left no room for argument.

As they prepared to move Trinity to a stretcher, Corbin reached into his pocket, pulling out a flash drive. He pressed it into Blade's hand.

"Everything you need is on here," Corbin said. "All the evidence. Make sure it gets to the right people."

Blade pocketed the drive. "We'll take care of it. You take care of them."

As they wheeled Trinity out, Luna felt a wave of exhaustion wash over her. But beneath it all, a spark of hope flickered. They'd made it. Against all odds, they'd survived.

And now, finally, they could start to heal.

36

THE STEADY BEEP of the heart monitor punctuated the heavy silence in the hospital room. Luna stood at the foot of Stryker's bed, fingers intertwined with those around her. She felt Corbin's strong grip on one side, Tori's reassuring touch on the other. Blade, Harlee, and Jett completed the circle, their heads bowed, eyes closed in reverent silence.

Luna held her voice soft but filled it with conviction. "And we thank you, Lord, for the healing that is already taking place in Stryker's body as he rests. We trust in your perfect timing and your infinite wisdom. Thank you for bringing us all together, for protecting us, and for giving us hope. In Jesus's name, amen."

As the last word fell from her lips, a wave of peace washed over Luna. It wasn't just Stryker's unwavering faith that filled the room now. It was her own rekindled belief, strengthened by the trials they'd all faced together.

She opened her eyes, looking at the faces around her—the team that had become her family. Each one bore the marks of their pasts but also the light of hope and the strength of their bond.

Stryker lay still, his chest rising and falling in a steady rhythm. Tubes and wires seemed to sprout from every inch of his body.

His face, usually so animated and full of life, was slack and pale. But she could feel the healing energy in the room. An almost tangible force born of love, faith, and the power of prayer. For the first time, she allowed herself to believe that Stryker would truly be okay.

"I remember when I first met Stryker." Harlee's fingers stroked his hair. "He looked at me like I was the most precious thing in the world."

A sad smile tugged at Tori's lips. "He never stopped looking at you that way, carnalita."

"Even when I was at my worst," Blade said, "he never gave up on me."

Stryker had never given up on anyone, had he? Not on Trinity, not on any of them. He'd been the one constant in their traumatic worlds. The steady rock they could all lean on. And now . . .

The door opened with a soft click, and the doctor stepped in. Luna straightened, her body tensing as if preparing for a fight.

"Hello, I'm Dr. Shannon, the attending neurologist for Mr. King. I understand you all are his family?" The doctor, her soft brown hair pulled back in a ponytail, her round eyes kind and concerned, glanced from one person to the next. She wore a white lab coat over dark blue scrubs, her name badge clipped to the pocket.

"Pleasure to meet you, Doctor," Jett said. "What can you tell us about his condition?"

"Mr. King remains critical. The edema is still a major concern. We've induced a coma to give his brain a chance to heal, but I must warn you—even if he wakes up, there may be long-term effects we can't predict at this stage."

Luna heard the words, understood their meaning, but they felt distant, as if they were being spoken about someone else. Not Stryker. Not the man who had risked everything to save Trinity, who had stood by them all, through thick and thin.

As Dr. Shannon continued to explain the intricacies of Stryker's condition, Luna felt a familiar weight settle in her chest. Guilt. If she hadn't triggered those events at the research center, if she had been faster, smarter, better . . .

She blinked hard, forcing back the tears that threatened to spill. This wasn't about her. This was about Stryker, about the price he'd paid for their freedom. The cost of Dr. Forest's twisted ambitions.

The doctor left, and the room once again fell into a heavy silence. Luna felt suffocated by it, by the grief and fear that hung in the air like a tangible thing. She closed her eyes and offered another silent prayer for Stryker's healing. The peace she'd felt earlier that morning seemed harder to grasp now, but she reached for it anyway.

"He wouldn't want us to lose hope," Corbin said, his gaze sweeping over the group. "Stryker's faith was always his strength. And you were right before, Luna. We need to have faith and trust God now, not just ourselves."

Faith. The word resonated differently now than it had just days ago. Her own rekindled faith had given her strength through this nightmare, even if it still felt fragile at times.

Corbin was right—Stryker wouldn't want them to give up hope. And neither would God. She was learning, step by uncertain step, to trust him again after all this time.

Corbin wrapped an arm around her. For a moment, they just stood there, watching Stryker breathe.

"I know what you're thinking," Corbin said. "This isn't your fault."

Her quiet laugh was sharp and bitter. "Isn't it? If I hadn't—"

"If you hadn't what? Tried to find our daughter?" Corbin faced her now. "Luna, you did the best thing. You brought down a corrupt organization. Saved Trinity and Stryker. You found our daughter."

Our daughter. Summer. The child they had given up all those years ago was now back in their lives, carrying the weight of her own guilt and confusion.

    Luna glanced at the faces of her friends gathered around Stryker. There was no judgment there, no accusation. Just understanding and . . . Corbin. Watching her like she was the only person in the room.

37

CORBIN SHIFTED in the leather chair in the commissioner's office, wincing at the streak of pain shooting through his body. A little over a month later, and his injuries still nagged at him. Luna sat close, her presence grounding him in a way nothing else could. Her hand brushed his, a reassurance of support after everything they'd been through. Everything they'd overcome.

The past several weeks had turned his world inside out, leaving him adrift in a sea of change, but Tinch's office remained exactly the same. Actually, something was different. The air felt lighter, tinged with a weariness that seemed to emanate from Commissioner Tinch himself. Gone was the fiery determination that had driven Tinch to push so hard for answers about Carlie. In its place sat a man worn down by grief and the weight of his position. Corbin recognized the look. He'd seen it in his own eyes often enough.

"Agent King," Tinch began, his voice lacking its usual bite, "you've been cleared of any wrongdoing in the deaths of Jed Steven Kaplow and Jason Cossic."

Kaplow, aka Steve, who attacked him at the skate park and who later was shot with Corbin's own service weapon at the marina when he'd used his body as a shield. Cossic, the man he'd called

Hitch, electrocuted in the data vault. The memory of that night flashed through his mind, vivid and visceral.

He nodded, not trusting his voice. The deaths may have been justified, may have saved their lives, but that didn't make them any easier to bear.

"We've also confirmed that Kaplow and his men were behind the arson at Abercorn's house," Tinch added. "Abercorn's plea agreement revealed he'd sold the Tasers directly to Kaplow. Forensics matched the accelerant used in the fire to some found at Chiron. It was a direct attempt to eliminate a potential witness."

Tinch continued, outlining the official findings, but Corbin's mind drifted. To Summer, the daughter he'd held once in the hospital, only to never see again until their shocking reunion. To Trinity, the girl who'd stumbled into their lives and found a place in their hearts. To Luna, the woman who'd brought it all crashing down around him and somehow built something beautiful from the rubble.

If she hadn't come home...

A lump lodged in his throat. Where would he be if she hadn't? Still chasing ghosts and trying to prove he wasn't his father? Still trying to control everything and afraid to let anyone close?

"King? You with us?"

Blade's voice snapped him back to the present. He sat in the chair beside Corbin with his brow furrowed. Corbin cleared his throat. "Yeah, sorry. Just... processing."

Tinch leaned back, his eyes narrowing as he measured Corbin from across the desk, but he pressed on. "As I was saying, the scope of this thing is bigger than we initially thought. The Nexus Initiative has its tentacles in everything—politics, finance, research. It's not going to be easy to take down."

"But we will," Blade added, his jaw set. "The FBI's given me clearance to join the task force. We're going to follow every lead, no matter how high up the organ harvesting and illegal research goes."

"I expect you to keep me informed every step of the way, St.

James. I know you've got this under control, but don't forget—this isn't just another case for me. My daughter was one of their victims."

His voice cracked on the last word, and for a moment, the stoic commissioner looked painfully human.

Blade nodded. "You have my word."

Corbin understood the tension Tinch carried. He wanted to be out there too, chasing these monsters down and dragging them into the light. But as a material witness, he didn't have that option. Not anymore. The US Marshals had made that clear when they'd turned his home into a safe house. They'd been assigned to protect him, Luna, Trinity, and Summer—a safeguard against the powerful people who'd orchestrated this nightmare and were desperate to cover their tracks.

It grated, being forced to sit on the sidelines. But the flicker in Tinch's eye as he said the word *victims* hit home. Corbin had other priorities now. Two girls who needed him and a woman he couldn't lose again.

"What about Everett and Patricia Reeves?" Luna asked.

Tinch sighed, the lines around his eyes deepening. "The Reeves are singing like canaries, trying to save their own skin. But their information is limited. They were more concerned with the profit than the details."

"And what about Dr. Forest?" Corbin wanted to know how he'd pay for his crimes.

"We've hit a wall with him. He's not talking. Claims he was just following orders, trying to save lives," Blade said.

"And his daughter?" Corbin asked, thinking of Elizabeth Forest and her failing heart.

"Also tight-lipped," Blade said. "But the feds are impressed with her work. Might let her continue from prison. They're thinking she can still help with research for other legitimate medical projects."

Corbin's mind flashed to Trinity, to the unnatural heart beating in her chest. A miracle of science, or a ticking time bomb? They still didn't know. "She doesn't deserve it after what they did." To Trinity and to Stryker, who was still in a coma.

"Which brings me to the boat graveyard," Tinch said. "We've identified more victims, going back years. This thing... it's been going on longer than we thought."

Corbin's stomach churned. How many lives had been lost? How many families torn apart? And they'd never even known.

"But we're finding others," Blade added. "Thanks to the data you pulled from the vault, we're locating patients the police thought to be runaways. Some of them... some of them are in the boat graveyard."

"How many?"

"Dozens," Blade said.

He felt Luna's hand slip into his, a gentle squeeze of support. His heart swelled.

"We did manage to trace some of Chiron's financial transactions." Blade pulled out a series of documents, spreading them across the desk. Bank statements, property records, offshore account details. Corbin's eyes widened as he took in the figures.

"This is... a lot of money," he said.

Blade nodded. "More than we initially thought. And it's not just the Reeves. We're seeing similar patterns with other high-level members of the Nexus Initiative. They've got accounts all over the world, shell companies, the works."

Luna leaned in, her eyes scanning the documents. "This is organized crime on a massive scale."

"Exactly," Blade agreed. "We're talking human trafficking, money laundering, probably weapons deals too. The Nexus Initiative? We've just hit the tip of the iceberg."

They'd known it was big, but this... this was beyond anything they'd imagined.

"What's the news with the survivor?" Tinch glanced at the paper on his desk. "Trinity Brown."

"Honestly? We're not sure yet," Corbin said. "The doctors want to run more tests, to understand why Trinity's body hasn't rejected the bioprinted heart when so many others did. But..."

"But that would mean more poking and prodding," Luna said. "More time in hospitals. She's having a hard time with that."

"We'll talk to the doctors, see what they recommend," Corbin said. "But any decisions about further testing or treatment are hers to make. We'll be there to support her."

Commissioner Tinch released a long breath. "You know, I was tough on you, King, but I'm glad to know I put my trust in the right place. You did amazing work. Both of you. In fact, I was hoping... Agent Rosati, how would you feel about joining our team? Officially?"

Luna stiffened beside him. Corbin held his breath, torn between hope and understanding. He knew how valuable she'd be to the department, how much good she could do. But he also knew the toll her work had taken on her.

"I appreciate the offer, Commissioner," Luna said. "But my resignation from the CIA isn't final. It's a bureaucratic process, trying to leave the Agency. I'll think about it though. Thank you."

The rest of the meeting passed in a blur. More details, more plans, more promises to stay in touch. But his mind was already elsewhere. On the house that was slowly becoming a home. On the girls waiting for him there.

As they left the office, he turned to Blade. "Working with the FBI, huh? It's an incredible opportunity. Great way to get your foot in the door."

"Hey, don't think you're getting rid of me that easy. We've still got work to do." Blade clapped him on the shoulder.

Corbin smiled. "Wouldn't have it any other way, brother."

Blade glanced down the hall where Luna paced with her phone to her ear. "You know, I heard those boys, Andre and Jordan, got picked up for possession. I was thinking of talking to the DA about inviting them down to the gym. Maybe Tori and I can get through to them. Show them another way."

Luna had wanted him to talk to Jordan, but they hadn't had time. Everything had unraveled too fast. "Definitely talk to Andre, but Jordan? He's not gonna set foot in a gym full of LEOs. That kid's still carrying a lifetime of hate for cops. Let me chat with him. See if I can soften him up first."

"Good idea." Blade folded his arms. "Kaplow's gone, but there's always another guy waiting to take his place. Someone who'll use those kids, chew them up, and spit them out. Stryker didn't let that happen to us." Blade's voice was quieter now. "He saw something in us worth saving. He made sure we saw it too."

"Stryker took a chance on us," he said. "Someone has to do the same for them."

Grudges were heavy things. He'd been carrying his own for so long he barely noticed it anymore. But seeing these kids, their hearts calcified by pain and betrayal, made him wonder what his own heart looked like from the inside. How much space had bitterness taken up? How many opportunities for healing had slipped by because he couldn't let go?

Maybe Jordan could learn to forgive.

And maybe so could he.

"You know," Corbin said, "the hardest part isn't forgiving someone else. It's admitting you need that forgiveness too." He stared at his hands, surprised by his own words.

Blade was quiet for a moment, then asked, "You gonna visit your old man anytime soon?"

Corbin dragged a hand through his hair, glancing toward Luna. She leaned her back on the wall, still on the phone. He exhaled. "I'm thinking about it."

Blade didn't press. He just nodded once, like he understood.

Maybe he did.

Luna's hand rested on his thigh as they drove home. "I feel bad ... kicking you out of your own place," she said. "You sure you don't want me to stay with Tori?"

"It's fine." He brushed his thumb over her hand. "Blade's been a great roommate. Though I swear, that guy's going through my prepped meals like he's never eaten a home-cooked meal in his life."

Luna's lips twitched in a small smile. "Well, at least someone's getting use out of your cooking. I'm pretty useless in the kitchen."

"We're keeping everyone safe, which is what matters." His eyes flicked to her, his expression softening. "And we're doing the right thing." This time he wanted to do it God's way.

The US Marshals nodded as they entered through the garage, their presence a reminder of the danger still lurking. Powerful people with more money than conviction and desperate to save their skin. They definitely had a target on their backs. But even that couldn't dampen the warmth that filled him as he stepped inside.

The house was alive in a way it had never been before. Soft music drifted from the kitchen, mingling with the sound of laughter. The smell of something baking filled the air.

"Hey, Dad." Trinity's voice rang out, followed by the sound of footsteps thundering down the hall.

Dad. The word still sent a thrill through him, even if it felt strange to hear. Just a few days ago, she'd started calling him that—and Luna "Mom"—as if the titles had always belonged to them.

Trinity barreled into him, and Corbin caught her in a hug. Her strength surprised him. Only weeks ago, she'd been so frail he wouldn't have imagined her sprinting down a hallway, much less slamming into him full force. The new heart was still a question mark, but her recovery felt nothing short of miraculous.

He held her close, marveling at how quickly she'd wormed her way into his heart. "Hey, kiddo," he said, pressing a kiss to the top of her head. "What have you been up to?"

"Summer's teaching me how to bake," Trinity said. "We're making cookies. Real ones, not that health food junk you keep in the pantry."

Corbin laughed, a deep belly laugh that chased away the last of the day's shadows. "Is that so?"

Summer ducked her head out of the kitchen, a streak of flour on her cheek. She looked uncertain, still finding her place in this new dynamic. "I hope that's okay. We, um, we wanted to surprise you."

"It's more than okay. This is your home." He held out an arm, inviting her into the embrace. After a moment's hesitation, she joined them.

Luna wrapped her arms around all of them, completing the circle.

The timer on the oven dinged, and Summer hurried to pull out a tray of golden-brown cookies. The smell of chocolate and vanilla filled the air. Trinity bounced on her toes, eager to taste their creation.

"Careful, they're hot," Summer warned, but Trinity was already reaching for one.

"Ow!" she yelped, dropping the cookie back onto the tray. "Why didn't you tell me they were hot?"

Summer rolled her eyes, but there was affection in her voice. "I literally just did, dummy."

"Hey, no name-calling," Corbin said automatically, then paused. When had he become this person? This . . . *dad*?

Luna caught his eye, a knowing smile on her face. She understood. This was unfamiliar territory for both of them, but somehow, it felt right.

As they settled around the kitchen island, cookies cooling on a rack and glasses of milk poured, Corbin took a moment to really look at his family.

Trinity, all energy and sass, her eyes bright with mischief. The scar on her chest, a reminder of all she'd been through, was barely visible beneath the collar of her shirt. But her smile was wide and genuine. Not the angry, scared girl they'd first met.

Summer, more reserved but with a quiet strength that reminded Corbin so much of Luna. She was still finding her footing, still learning to trust that this was real, that she belonged. But there was a softness in her eyes now, a tentative hope.

And Luna. Wow, Luna. She caught him staring and raised an

eyebrow, a silent question. He just shook his head, overwhelmed by the love that washed over him.

"So," Trinity said. "When do I get to go back to school? Because as much as I love being stuck in this house with you lovebirds, I'm getting antsy."

Corbin chuckled. "Soon, I hope. The marshals are working on a security plan. We want to make sure it's safe before we send you."

"What about me?" Summer looked down and picked at the cookie in her hand. "I was supposed to go to college after my internship, but my parents ... I mean, the Reeves, they were going to pay for it. I don't know what I'm supposed to do now."

Summer's whole life had been turned upside down. Her adoptive parents, the only family she'd ever known, were facing serious charges. They'd cut off all communication, scapegoating Summer for their arrests. The future the young woman had worked so hard for was suddenly uncertain.

"Whatever you want," Luna said, reaching out to take Summer's hand. "You're not alone in this, sweetheart. We'll figure it out together."

Summer nodded, blinking back tears. "I just ... I don't know who I am anymore. Everything I thought I knew about myself, about my life ... it was all a lie."

Corbin's heart ached for her. He knew that feeling all too well. "Not everything," he said. "The person you are, the kindness and strength you've shown ... that's all you. Your parents didn't give you that. God did."

"He's right," Trinity chimed in, her mouth full of cookie. She swallowed and continued. "You're pretty cool, for an old person."

"Old?" Summer laughed, the tension breaking. "We're the exact same age!"

"Yeah, but I'm finishing high school and you're going to college, which makes you ancient."

Summer rolled her eyes and tossed a chunk of cookie at Trinity. As the girls bickered playfully, he felt Luna's hand slide over his back. He turned to her, seeing his own emotions mirrored in her eyes. Joy, love, a touch of fear. This was all so new, so fragile. But also so incredibly right.

"We're really doing this, huh?" he murmured, low enough that only she could hear.

She smiled, that soft, secret smile that had always been just for him. "Looks like it. You ready for this, Agent King?"

He thought about the man he'd been just a few weeks ago. Alone, driven by a need to prove himself, always looking over his shoulder for the ghost of his father. That man would have run from this, from the messy, complicated beauty of family.

But he wasn't that man anymore.

"More than ready." And he sealed the promise with a kiss.

The moment was broken by twin sounds of disgust from the girls.

"Ugh, get a room." Trinity groaned.

"Seriously," Summer agreed. "There are children present."

Corbin laughed, pulling Luna closer. This was his family. Messy and complicated and absolutely perfect.

"Our children," he said, the words sending a thrill through him. "God help us all."

38

LUNA STOOD ALONE in the kitchen of the safe house—Corbin's house—folding laundry, of all things. The domesticity of the task felt strange, almost surreal after everything they'd been through. But there was comfort in it too.

The sound of laughter drifted in through the open window, and Luna glanced out to see Summer and Trinity by the pool. They were splashing each other, their faces alight with joy and mischief. For a moment, Luna could almost forget the darkness that had brought them all together, could almost believe that this was just a normal family on a normal fall evening.

Her phone buzzed. Deputy Chief Langston's name flashed on the screen. Calling from his personal number, not the Agency. She answered with a curt, "Hello."

"Rosati." Langston's voice was all business. "I'm surprised you haven't accepted the new mission in Malaysia yet. It's perfect for you."

"I'm retired, remember?"

"You're still on that? I've got the contract paperwork right here.

C'mon... this is your chance for a fresh start. No ties, no baggage. Just how you like it. Think of it like starting all over."

"Starting over?" she repeated. "I think that's exactly what I'm doing."

"You're really doing this?"

Her gaze drifted back to the window, to the girls sitting on the edge of the pool in the fading sunlight. "I'm really doing this."

He sighed. "I'll cancel the reinvestigation to renew your clearances." The call clicked off.

She slid her phone on the counter. No ties? Langston couldn't have been more wrong. The ties that bound her now—to Summer, to Trinity, to Corbin—were stronger than any she'd ever known.

"Everything okay?"

Luna turned to find Corbin leaning against the doorframe, his eyes soft with concern. She nodded. "Yeah, I think it is."

He moved to stand beside her, his gaze following hers to the pool where the girls were now engaged in what looked like a heated splash war. "They're good together."

"They are," Luna agreed. She hesitated for a moment before adding, "That was Langston."

Corbin raised an eyebrow. "And?"

Luna shook her head. "I'm not an operative anymore, Corbin. That chapter of my life is over. I have . . . other priorities now."

Corbin looked at her with an intensity that made her heart race, like he was trying to memorize every detail of her face. Slowly, deliberately, he reached into his pocket and pulled out a small box.

"Luna," he said. "Can we share forever?"

He opened the box to reveal a ring—not the massive diamond she'd once dreamed of but a simple band that she recognized immediately. It was the promise ring he'd given her when they were just kids, full of dreams and hope for the future. The ring she'd left with the adoption papers for him to sign.

Tears blurred Luna's vision as Corbin slid the band onto her finger. The ring wasn't just a symbol of what they'd been but of everything they were about to become. The past, the pain, all of it led here, to this moment. "It's . . . beautiful," she managed, her throat tight with emotion.

Corbin pulled her close, his arms strong around her. "I owe you a bigger one," he murmured against her hair. "And after that, maybe a bigger house. A bigger car. To hold a bigger family."

Luna looked up at him, her heart so full she thought it might burst.

This was it, she realized. This was what she'd been searching for all along. Not the thrill of the mission or the satisfaction of a job well done, but this—a family, a home, a love that could weather any storm.

The road ahead wouldn't be easy. There were still challenges to face, wounds to heal, a world to change.

But they would face it together. As a family.

And that, Luna realized, was all she'd ever really wanted.

Epilogue

Six Months Later

The woman in the mirror was a stranger. Gone were the sharp edges and guarded eyes of a CIA operative. In their place, someone softer gazed back. Someone open. Someone who'd found her way home.

Luna's fingers traced the intricate lace of her wedding dress. The delicate fabric caught on calluses earned from years of fieldwork, a reminder of the life she'd left behind. Stryker's beach house, once foreign territory, now felt like a sanctuary. A place of new beginnings.

"Mom?" Summer's voice, still new and wonderful, pulled her from her reverie. "We're all done."

She turned. Her daughters stood before her, a vision that made her heart swell. Summer's auburn waves cascaded over an emerald dress that brought out flecks of gold in her green eyes. Trinity, resplendent in soft lavender, had swept her dark hair into an elegant updo.

"You both look beautiful," she said.

Trinity guided her to the full-length mirror. "Come on, you have to see yourself."

Her breath caught. The simple white dress hugged her curves before flowing out gently. Her dark curls, with their hints of auburn, were swept up, a few tendrils framing her face. She looked ... happy. Truly, radiantly happy.

"You're gorgeous," Summer breathed, her eyes shining.

She blinked rapidly, willing herself not to cry.

Trinity dabbed at the corner of her own eye. "If you ruin that makeup, we'll have to start all over."

"We'd better get going." Summer glanced at her watch. "Dad's waiting, and I think he might spontaneously combust if he has to wait much longer."

As the girls hurried out, she allowed herself a moment of reflection. Not even a year ago, she'd returned to Millie Beach searching for one daughter. Now, through some miracle, she had two. The prodigal daughter, returned to the fold. And not just returned but restored twofold.

She'd been frozen for so long, guilt and fear an impenetrable barrier around her heart. Now, as she stood here on the brink of a new life, that ice had melted away. In its place, a warmth she'd almost forgotten she could feel.

She swiped at her eyes, careful not to smudge her mascara. No more tears. It was time to move forward.

She scooped up her bouquet of soft-pink tulips and made her way outside. The warm sand shocked her bare feet, grounding her in the moment.

White chairs lined a path in the sand, leading to a simple arch draped in flowing fabric. Pink tulips, matching her bouquet, adorned the arch and chairs. The late afternoon sun bathed everything in a warm, golden light, as if nature itself was celebrating with them.

And there, at the end of the aisle, stood Corbin.

Her heart thundered as she began her walk. The sand shifted beneath her feet with each step. Waves lapped gently at the shore, their rhythm steady and soothing. A cellist played rich, resonant tones that blended with the natural symphony around them.

With each step, she felt the weight of her past falling away. The deception, the covers, the constant fear and doubt. None of it mattered anymore.

Here, now, she was simply Luna. A woman in love, walking toward her future.

Corbin's eyes never left her face as she approached. The love and awe she saw there made her knees weak. How had God blessed her with so much? To not only find her way back to him but to build this beautiful family together?

Their vows were simple, honest. Promises to love, support, and cherish. To face whatever came their way as partners, equals. When they kissed, Luna poured every ounce of love and gratitude into it.

"I now pronounce you Mr. and Mrs. King," the officiant announced.

A thrill ran through her at her new name. A name chosen, not assigned. A name that represented family, love, belonging.

The reception, held under a white tent on the beach, was everything she had never allowed herself to dream of. Soft lights twinkled overhead, casting a warm glow over the gathering. The cellist continued to play, his music a gentle backdrop to the joyous conversations around them.

Corbin leaned in close. "How are you feeling, Mrs. King?"

She savored the words, the newness of them. "Happy," she replied. "Impossibly, wonderfully happy."

Yet, even in this moment of joy, there was a twinge of sadness. She glanced at the empty chair they'd left for Stryker. "I just wish he could be here."

Corbin squeezed her hand. "We'll celebrate again when he wakes up. You know how stubborn he is. He won't stay down for long."

She nodded, clinging to that hope. Stryker had survived so much. Surely he could survive this too.

The cellist took a break, and Trinity and Summer commandeered the music system, identical mischievous grins on their faces.

Trinity grabbed the microphone. "Time for the father-daughter dance!"

Her heart swelled as she watched Corbin dance with both girls, his face alight with joy. He twirled them, laughed with them, treasuring each moment. This was what they'd fought for, what they'd risked everything to protect.

Tori and Harlee joined her at the table, and Luna marveled at how far they'd all come. From scared, angry teenagers to this—a family forged through love and shared experiences.

Tori gestured to the celebration around them. "Did you ever imagine you'd end up here?"

She shook her head. "Never. But I wouldn't change it for anything."

They chatted about the ongoing investigations, the loose ends they were still tying up. But tonight wasn't about work. Tonight was about new beginnings and second chances.

The yacht cut through the turquoise waters between Miami and Dry Tortugas National Park, a private sanctuary where the Gulf of Mexico met the Caribbean. For their honeymoon, Corbin had chartered the luxury yacht, *Ohana Rising*, complete with a personal chef and crew. A floating refuge where they could disappear from the world, from everything that had chased them.

As night fell, they stood on the deck, watching the sun sink into the sea. Corbin's arms wrapped around her, solid and sure. An anchor after years of drifting. Her body melded into his, feeling the steady rhythm of his heartbeat against her back.

"I still can't quite believe how much our lives have changed," Corbin said. "Do you ever regret leaving the CIA?"

Regret?

Summer's laughter drifted through her mind. Trinity's bright smile. Their makeshift family they'd stitched together from the shattered pieces of their past.

She shook her head. "Not for a second. This is what's real. Us. Our family. It's what I've been searching for all along, I just didn't know it." She turned, facing him. "I'm looking forward to this new normal. Together. And I'll keep helping out at the gym as long as Stryker's in the hospital. Recruiting assets and turning them to the good side will still be my job. Just with better hours and a lot less danger," she added with a smile.

They ate dinner on the deck and talked about Summer in college and Trinity not far behind, both proud and a little wistful.

A seagull carved lazy arcs across the amber-streaked sky. "I'm glad they're going together," Luna said. "And that Trinity's heart is stronger than ever. She can finally live the life she deserves."

Corbin was quiet for a moment, thoughtful. "You know, I've been thinking about how lonely it might be without them. What do you think about extending our family? Doing it right this time. The pregnancy, the diapers, the late-night feedings—all of it."

Luna's world tilted. Another child? An opportunity to experience all the moments they'd missed with Summer and with each other. She looked into Corbin's eyes and knew her answer.

"Whatever comes next," she said, "I'm all in. As long as we're together."

"Always," Corbin promised, and she knew it was true.

Whatever challenges lay ahead, they would face them side by side.

They kissed as the last light bled from the sky like watercolor. This wasn't an ending, it was a beginning written in grace and love. In possibility.

The start of their greatest adventure yet.

And for the first time in her life, Luna was ready to surrender to the journey.

Three Weeks Later

Corbin's knuckles whitened as he gripped the steering wheel, the leather creaking under the pressure. The car idled in the parking lot, its gentle rumble much like the turmoil churning inside him. He'd been sitting here for fifteen minutes, willing himself to move, to take that first step.

The imposing structure loomed before him. A fortress of concrete and steel that seemed to suck the very warmth from the air. Corbin's eyes traced the razor wire atop the fences, glinting wickedly in the harsh Florida sun. This place was designed to keep people in, but right now, it felt like it was keeping him out.

He glanced at his watch. If he didn't move soon, he'd be too late. The thought almost made him laugh. Late for what? A family reunion?

With a deep breath that did little to calm his racing heart, Corbin killed the engine. The sudden silence felt oppressive, broken only by the faint jangle of keys as he pocketed them. He could still drive away. Pretend this whole thing had never happened. Go back to Luna, to the daughters he was just getting to know.

But he couldn't. Not really. Because as much as he hated to admit it, the man waiting inside held answers. Answers they desperately needed.

Corbin stepped out of the car. Straightened his tie. His badge felt heavy in his breast pocket. A reminder of everything he'd worked for.

The walk to the entrance seemed to stretch for miles, and each step brought a fresh wave of memories. His father's rages. The smell of whiskey on his breath. The sound of his mother's muffled sobs. Corbin's stomach churned, threatening to expel the meager breakfast he'd managed to choke down that morning.

At the main gate, a bored-looking guard glanced at his credentials before buzzing him through. The heavy metal door clanged shut behind him with a finality that made Corbin's skin crawl. He was in. No turning back now.

Another guard, this one more alert, approached. "Agent King? I'm Officer Hammond. I'll be escorting you today."

Corbin nodded, forcing his face into a neutral expression. "Thanks. I'm here to see Damien Sullivan."

Hammond's eyebrows rose slightly, but he didn't comment. Instead, he gestured to a nearby locker. "First things first, we'll need to secure your weapon. Can't have any firearms inside, even for law enforcement."

Corbin unholstered his gun and locked it away. The absence of his sidearm left him feeling off-balance, like he was missing a limb.

They moved through the checkpoint and through a series of mantraps. Each buzz and clang of the doors rattled his nerves. The farther they went, the more oppressive the atmosphere became. The walls seemed to close in, and the air grew thicker with each step.

"So, what brings an FDLE agent out here to see Sullivan?" Hammond asked as they walked. "Must be something big."

Corbin's jaw tightened. "Just following up on a few things." He couldn't explain that he was here to see his father. The man who had nearly destroyed his life.

Hammond nodded, clearly sensing Corbin's reluctance to elaborate. "Well, you should know, Sullivan has been a model prisoner. No incidents in over a decade."

A model prisoner. Wasn't that sort of an oxymoron for a man like his father? As if that could erase everything that had come before. The beatings. The terror. The lives destroyed.

They reached the last door, heavy and solid. Hammond paused, his hand on the handle. "All right, Agent King. Here's the deal. You'll have thirty minutes. We'll have cameras on you, monitoring from the observation room. If Sullivan tries anything, just give the signal, and we'll shut it down. But I have to warn you, our response time is fifty-two seconds."

Corbin nodded, not trusting himself to speak. Fifty-two seconds was a lifetime in an attack.

"Remember," Hammond added, his voice low, "no matter what he says, no matter what history you two might have, he's a con. Don't let your guard down."

If only Hammond knew how impossible that would be. Corbin's guard had been up for twenty years, a wall built brick by painful brick.

The door swung open, and Corbin stepped inside. The room was small, dominated by a metal table bolted to the floor. And there, seated on the other side...

His father.

The years had not been kind to the man. The once-imposing figure had grown soft, a paunch straining against the faded prison jumpsuit. A deep scar the size of Corbin's thumb rested in the hollow of his throat. The color reminded him of a cold steak. His hair, once a sandy blond like Corbin's own, had faded to a dull gray. But the eyes. The eyes were the same. Dark and intense, boring into Corbin with painful familiarity.

The smell hit him next. A pungent mix of stale sweat and institutional soap that made his nose twitch. This was what twenty years in prison smelled like.

"Well, well," his father drawled. "Look who finally decided to pay his old man a visit."

Corbin's throat went dry. He forced himself to move, to take the seat across from the man who had dominated his nightmares for so long. The metal chair was cold and hard beneath him.

"Hello, Dad." The words tasted like ash in his mouth.

His father leaned back, the chains of his shackles clinking. "Twenty years, and that's all you've got to say? I'm hurt, son."

The familiar mocking tone set his teeth on edge. He clenched his jaw, reminding himself why he was here. "How have you been?"

Damien shrugged. "Oh, you know. Three squares. Roof over my head. Can't complain." His eyes narrowed. "But I doubt you came all this way for small talk. Why are you really here, Corbin?"

"I got married." Corbin's hand went to his wedding ring, twisting the smooth metal. "And I'm a father now."

"Well, congratulations," he said. "Doesn't explain why you're here, though."

Corbin met his father's gaze, steeling himself. "I had to come. I had to see the man who almost took all of that away from me."

Damien's face hardened. "And how exactly am I to blame for your life choices? If I recall, you were a father before you were a husband."

Years of pent-up anger bubbled to the surface. "You want to know how? Your drinking, your abuse. The way you beat Mom, beat me. The anger, the rage you passed down to me like some twisted inheritance. It nearly ruined me."

He leaned forward, his words coming faster now. "And then there's the small matter of your rampage. Murdering those cops. Do you have any idea what that did to me? To my career? To every relationship I've ever had? To be the son of a cop killer?"

Nights spent cowering in his room, listening to the crash of bottles and his mother's begging. The shame of showing up to school with bruises he couldn't explain. The whispers that followed him through the police academy, the sidelong glances from fellow officers who wondered if he'd turn out just like his old man.

Damien's face remained impassive, but he could see the tension in his jaw. "So you came here to what? Yell at me? Make me feel guilty?"

Corbin took a deep breath, forcing himself to calm down. This wasn't why he'd come. Not really.

"No," he said. "I came to tell you about the forgiveness and redemption I've found through Jesus. The healing that's taken place in my life."

A harsh laugh erupted from Damien's throat. "Jesus? You came all this way to preach at me?"

"I'm not preaching," he said, even as he recognized the defensive tone in his voice. "I'm telling you about the change in my life. How I have peace. Joy." He paused. Gave himself room to let the right words come. "I've forgiven you, Dad," Corbin said. "For everything."

The words hung in the air between them. He watched his father's face, searching for any sign of emotion. But Damien's expression remained carefully neutral, a mask honed by years behind bars.

"I've left a Bible for you with the guards. I wondered if you'd want to read it yourself, and we can talk about it. When I come visit." He swallowed. The words were out there now. The offer. The reconciliation.

Silence stretched. Corbin could hear his pulse thundering in his ears. Part of him wanted his father's anger and wrath. Then at least he'd have an excuse to walk away. But the other part, the bigger part of him, wanted this relationship more than anything else.

Finally, Damien spoke. "Why? Why would you do that? Why leave your fancy house and wife to come preach forgiveness to a washed-up old con?"

"Because." Corbin smiled. A small, joyful thing. "The Shepherd will always leave his flock of ninety-nine to go find the one lost sheep."

He stood, ready to leave. He'd said what he came to say, laid bare the wounds of the past and the hope for the future. It was more than he'd ever expected to share with this man who had loomed like a shadow in his nightmares.

"Wait." Damien's voice stopped him.

Corbin turned back, surprised to see a flicker of vulnerability in his father's eyes.

"That gym you used to go to," Damien said, shifting in his seat. "The one where all the cops work out. You still go there?"

Corbin nodded, uncertain where this was going.

"That girl, the one who used to go there too. Victoria Crew. You still know her?"

She hated being called Victoria, but he wasn't about to offer any details about her to a prisoner. Not even one who shared his blood. "Yeah," he said cautiously. "We're still friends."

Damien's eyes shone with an intensity that made Corbin's skin crawl. "I want her to come visit me."

"What? Why?" The words burst out before Corbin could stop them. His mind raced, trying to connect the dots between his father and Tori.

Damien leaned back. "I was a bad cop, Corbin. Did things I shouldn't have. But I also saw things. Ugly things. The worst of humanity." He paused, his gaze distant. "I was there that night. The night the Crew family was murdered."

Corbin's blood ran cold. The Crew murders. One of the most brutal cases in Millie Beach history. He'd heard whispers about the cold case throughout his career, but the details had always been closely guarded. And now, here was his father, claiming to have been there?

"I was the responding officer. I saw the blood. The bodies." Damien cleared his throat. "I was the one who found her. A scared little thing hiding in her parents' closet that night."

Corbin's throat felt tight. He could picture it all too easily. A young Tori, terrified and alone. Hiding from the gruesome scene unfolding on the other side of the door.

"She won't want to come here," he managed. "She won't want to talk about that night." She never talked about that night.

"I think she will, son." A bitter smile pulled at Damien's lips. "She'll come. Because I know who murdered her family."

Letter to the Reader

Dear Reader,

Thank you for joining me on this journey through Girl Lost, *Luna and Corbin's story. As you may have noticed, this story is about more than just suspense and romance—it's about the scars we carry from our past, and how with God's grace those scars can be redeemed to help others.*

Luna's and Corbin's struggles were deeply personal for me to write. Like Luna, I grew up in the shadow of addiction. My mother's battle with substance abuse often left me feeling lost and burdened with responsibilities far beyond my years, and ultimately left me in foster care. It took me a long time to understand that God was using those experiences to shape me into someone who could walk alongside others in their pain. Luna and Corbin's story reflects that truth—how brokenness can draw people closer and how healing often comes in unexpected ways.

This novel also explores the fascinating and sometimes troubling advances in medical technology. The idea of 3D printing organs is no longer just science fiction. Researchers are already creating groundbreaking innovations, like 3D-printed earlobes for burn victims or lab-grown meat, which could revolutionize how we address food and organ shortages and other medical challenges. While these advancements hold great promise, they also raise important ethical questions about how far we should go and at what cost. Yet one thing remains certain: People will go to incredible lengths—both good and bad—for the ones they love.

As you close this book, I hope you'll think about who might need its message of hope and redemption. Is it a friend walking through their own valley? A family member searching for healing? Maybe even your book club or church library. A book's journey doesn't end when you finish it; its life grows when you share it. And please leave a review letting others know how you enjoyed it.

If you'd like to stay connected and hear about the next book in *The King Legacy* series—or just be encouraged through stories of redemption—please subscribe to my newsletter at KateAngelo.com. You'll be the first to know about new releases, exciting updates, and exclusive content. You can also find me on Facebook, Instagram, and X—I'd love to hear what you thought of Luna and Corbin's story!

Thank you for letting these characters into your life. I hope their journey left you with a renewed sense of God's grace and the healing power of love.

Blessings,
Kate Angelo

READ ON FOR A SNEAK PEEK
AT THE NEXT BOOK IN

THE
KING LEGACY
SERIES

AVAILABLE SEPTEMBER 2026

1

THE COLD EDGE OF A BLADE kissed Tori Crew's throat, drawing a hot rivulet of blood that began its slow descent down her neck.

"Don't move." The whisper brushed against her ear. A voice threaded with malice that made her stomach turn.

Her pulse hammered against the knife pressed to her carotid, but she remained motionless in the pre-dawn darkness. At 4:30 a.m., the parking lot at the Kingdom MMA Gym was quiet.

No witnesses, no help.

The fighter in her knew exactly what to do. Elbow to solar plexus, heel to instep, grab the wrist and twist. Three seconds and he'd be on the ground. But he had the blade pressed just right. She couldn't make a move without him slicing through a major artery. One wrong angle, and she'd bleed out before she hit the pavement.

She slowed her breathing. Took stock. Learn first, strike when the odds shift.

"You're bleeding," he breathed. "Such a... pretty shade of red against your skin."

She forced herself to think. Catalog details. Male. Approximately six feet tall based on the angle of the knife. Maybe 5'10".

Right-handed. Gloves. No detectable accent. No alcohol on his breath. Not impulsive. Calculated. Educated.

"Who are you?" She worked to keep talking despite the tremor threatening to overtake her body.

"I'm the one who watches. Your... shadow. A part of you." His hot breath against her neck made her skin crawl. "You've been busy this week. Two new cases, six trips to the gym, and you changed your coffee order to vanilla instead of caramel." His fingers trailed across her collarbone, following the thin gold chain of her necklace. "I like that perfume on you. Jasmine, right?"

Her stalker. The one who'd been leaving notes on her car. The one who'd been calling and hanging up. The one the police couldn't catch because the "nonthreatening harassment" apparently didn't meet the threshold for a credible threat.

He'd been watching everything.

Her stomach twisted, not with fear—she could handle fear—but with fury. "You think that makes you powerful? It makes you pathetic."

The knife pressed deeper. Not enough to do serious damage but enough to elicit another drop of blood. His finger caught the droplet sliding down her neck, then traced it back up to the wound. "Beautiful. Your blood is even prettier than I imagined."

"What do you want?" She analyzed his posture, the tension in his arm, the way he held the knife.

"To show you that I can take you anytime I want." His laugh was soft, almost tender. "This is just the beginning, Dr. Crew. I'm not done toying with you yet."

Fight instinct coiled through her muscles, but her mind overrode it. Information. Get information. Every criminal had a pattern, a motivation. Understanding him meant catching him. And catching him meant ending this nightmare.

"Why me?" she asked, trying to get a glimpse of his face in her peripheral vision, but he remained carefully positioned behind her.

"Because you think you understand the darkness," he said. "But you don't. Not like I do."

A pair of headlights cut through the blackness, illuminating the street where they stood outside the gym. The harsh white light temporarily blinded her. The pressure on her throat vanished.

She spun, fist cocked for a power jab at his face, but only struck air. He'd peeled away and ran along the wall, black clothing blending into the darkness as he vanished into the alley beyond.

The car screeched to a halt beside her. The driver's door flew open, and Detective Blade St. James erupted from his unmarked Charger, a hand on his holstered weapon. "Tori! You okay? Someone bothering you?"

Her fingers went to her throat and came away sticky with blood. She stared at the crimson smear, a savage anger building inside her chest. He'd touched her. Cut her. And vanished like smoke.

Blade's eyes widened at her blood-slick fingertips. His jaw clenched, a muscle twitching along the sharp line of his cheekbone. "You're bleeding."

The same thing the stalker had said.

"It's just a scratch," she said, suddenly aware of how her heart was racing. Adrenaline flooded her system now that the immediate danger had passed.

He pulled out his phone. "We need to call this in. Get you to a hospital."

"No." She caught his wrist. "I'm fine. I said it's just a scratch." Not the first time Blade had rushed to her rescue. But five-foot-three didn't make her helpless, despite what every man seemed to believe. She could take care of herself. Friends or not, his knight-in-shining-armor routine still grated sometimes.

"What happened? Who was that?"

"My stalker." She pressed her fingers harder against the cut to stem the bleeding.

"Stalker? What stalker? Since when do you have a stalker?"

"Three weeks, give or take." She saw a red droplet on the back of her other hand. He'd said he like the color of her blood. "He's been watching me, following me."

"And you didn't think to mention this?"

"I filed a report, but you know stalker cases." She lifted her eyebrows. "Nothing they can do."

"Nothing they can do? Tori, he had a knife to your throat. That's attempted murder."

"It's not that simple."

"It is that simple. We file a report, dust for prints, canvass witnesses—"

"There are no witnesses at four thirty in the morning." She swept her arm toward the deserted street. Empty parking lot. Silent alleyways. "And he wore gloves, so no prints. This isn't some amateur, Blade."

"All the more reason to report it. This guy's been watching you for weeks, and now he's crossed the line to physical assault. He's escalating."

His eyes lost their hard edge. The brush of his finger beneath her chin sent an unwelcome jolt through her. Half comfort, half irritation. He tilted her face to examine the cut. "This needs medical attention."

"It's superficial. I have a first aid kit in my bag. I'll clean it up in the car." She stepped back from his touch, needing space to think. "Don't make that face at me, Blade. I'm a big girl."

"You are the most stubborn—" Blade caught himself, taking a step back. He looked at the alley like he expected the stalker to lunge at her again. Some of his resolve seemed to slip. "Fine. But we're not done talking about this."

Something in the way he said it sent a different kind of shiver through her. She'd known Blade practically her whole life, ever since the court ordered them into the Warrior program at the Kingdom MMA Gym as teenagers. Back then, he'd been a bit much with all that restless energy and impulsive chatter. But even then, she'd respected him. He never backed down from a fight, never let anyone mess with her. He'd always been the one standing between her and the next punch like the big brother she never had.

Lately, she caught herself turning to him more than she meant to. Confiding things. Trusting him in a way that felt... different. And when he wasn't around, she noticed.

Worse, when he was around, she noticed things she shouldn't. The way his forearms flexed when he rolled his sleeves. The cleft in his chin. The way his eyes softened when he smiled.

Not that he was smiling now.

He flicked a hand at his ride. "Get in the car. I'll check the area."

"He's gone," she said, but Blade was already moving, his flashlight sweeping across the shadowy spaces between the buildings where her attacker had disappeared.

She watched him work, checking every shadow like he expected the guy to pop out swinging. But he was long gone by now. Too smart to stick around.

She slid into the passenger seat and shut the door with more force than she meant to and pulled down the visor mirror. An amber light illuminated the cut at her throat and she lifted her chin to examine the wound. It was small, barely a scratch, but it had bled enough to leave a thin crimson line down to her collarbone, staining the collar of her cream blouse.

Tori couldn't generate enough saliva to swallow. If Blade had been even a minute later, she might be dead. Instead of pulling up to pick her up, he could've found her bleeding out in that alley.

"Gracias, Jesús," she muttered, digging through her bag for the travel first aid kit she always carried. A habit from her foster care days. Always be prepared, always have what you need to take care of yourself.

The driver's door opened. Blade got in, jaw tight, eyes scanning before settling on her.

"Nothing. No footprints, no evidence. The guy's a ghost."

"Not a ghost," she said, pressing the antiseptic wipe to her neck.

"Just careful. Methodical. He's been watching me, learning my patterns."

"And you didn't think to vary your routine?" His tone snapped harder than she expected. "Basic security protocol, Tori. You of all people should know better."

The criticism stung, mostly because he was right. She'd been careless, overconfident. She'd told herself she could handle it, that she wasn't afraid. But that was before she felt the cold steel against her skin. Before she heard him whispering threats in her ear.

"I know. I screwed up."

Something in her tone must have registered with Blade, because his expression softened. He reached across the console, his hand hovering near her arm before he pulled it back, seemingly thinking better of it.

"We'll catch him," he said. "I promise you that."

She nodded, trying to ignore the flutter in her stomach at his intensity. "Let's focus on today. We have a four-hour drive to Union Correctional, and Warden Mills won't wait if we're late."

Blade didn't start the car immediately. Instead, he turned in his seat to face her fully, studying her with those penetrating dark eyes that always seemed to see more than she wanted them to.

"Are you sure you're up for this? We can reschedule. Corbin's father isn't going anywhere."

"I'm fine," Tori insisted, despite the tremor in her hands that she couldn't quite control. "It's just adrenaline."

"Tori—"

"I said I'm fine," she repeated, sharper than she intended. She softened, switching to Spanish, her fallback language when emotions ran high. "Estoy bien, de verdad. I need to work."

Blade didn't look convinced, but he nodded anyway. "Okay. But if you change your mind—"

"I won't," Tori said, tucking the bloodied wipe into a small plastic bag and sealing it. Evidence. Just in case. "Now drive, Detective, before the morning traffic turns our four-hour trip into six."

He started the engine, casting one last concerned glance her way before pulling away from the curb. The streetlights cast alternating pools of light and shadow across his features, highlighting the firm line of his jaw, the furrow between his brows.

She turned to look out the window, watching as the Kingdom MMA Gym receded in the side mirror. Somewhere in those shadows, her stalker was watching. Waiting. Planning his next move.

She pressed her fingers to the wound on her neck, feeling the sting of it. A reminder that she was dealing with someone dangerous. Someone who had gotten close enough to hurt her. Someone who had promised he wasn't done.

"You know what he said to me?" she said suddenly, breaking the silence in the car.

Blade glanced over. "What?"

"He said I think I understand the darkness, but I don't." She turned to meet his gaze. "But he's wrong. I understand darkness better than most. I grew up in it."

"So, what are you thinking? Profile?"

She nodded, grateful for the shift to professional territory. "Male, late twenties to early thirties. Intelligent. Meticulous. Comfortable with weapons. Possibly military or law enforcement background."

"That narrows it down to about half the men in Florida," Blade muttered.

"He's also narcissistic, with delusions of grandeur," she continued, ignoring his comment. "He sees this as a game between us. He's not just stalking me, he's testing me."

"Testing you for what?"

She stared at the road ahead. The sun began to peek over the horizon, casting long shadows across the asphalt. "That's what I need to figure out."

They drove in silence for several minutes. Tension hung between them, thick enough to cut with a knife. Okay, maybe a poor choice of metaphor.

"So," Blade finally said, "you want to tell me what really happened back there? Because I know you. You're a third-degree black belt. You teach self-defense classes. There's no way this guy got the drop on you unless you let him."

The car suddenly felt ten degrees warmer. "What are you saying?"

"I'm saying you weren't fighting back. Not really." His eyes flicked to her, then back to the road. "Why?"

For a moment, she considered deflecting, making a joke, changing the subject. But this was Blade. He deserved honesty.

"I needed to understand him," she admitted. "I needed to hear him speak, feel his presence, gauge his confidence."

"You risked your life for a psychological assessment?"

"I took a calculated risk." She shifted in her seat to face him. "And now I know things about him I didn't before. Things the police can't ignore."

Blade shot her a look that was half concern, half grudging amusement. "You really are something else, you know that?"

"So I've been told." She leaned back in her seat, trying to ignore the phantom sensation of cold steel against her skin and the whispered promise of more to come.

"Should I be worried about you?" The corners of Blade's eyes crinkled in that way that always betrayed his words, no matter how casual he tried to sound.

A tiny part of her warmed at his genuine concern, even as she wished he'd stop treating her like a china doll.

The stalker had mentioned darkness. A darkness she supposedly didn't understand. How wrong he was. Foster homes. Violence. Survival. She understood darkness intimately. She'd been born into it, raised in it, fought her way out of it. But she'd never let it consume her.

"I'm one of the good guys, remember?" Her smile reached her eyes this time. "Now quit driving like a Florida snowbird. We've got a killer to see, and it would be rude to keep him waiting."

Blade shook his head. Admiration and exasperation battled

across his features. "One of these days, Dr. Crew, your curiosity is going to get you killed."

"Maybe." She smiled. "But not today. Today, the only thing that matters is what Damien Sullivan knows about my parents' murder. And not even a knife-wielding stalker will keep me from hearing what he has to say."

Kate Angelo is the *Publishers Weekly* bestselling author of *Hunting the Witness*, Selah Award winner of *Deadly Holiday Hijack*, and Amazon Top 100 Bestseller of *Driving Force*. Kate works alongside her husband championing stronger marriages and families. Her journey from foster care to bestselling author fuels her fast-paced romantic suspense, where flawed characters discover hope and healing through life's fiercest trials and relationships. When she's not putting fictional people through the wringer, she's out creating real-life happily-ever-afters at conferences and events nationwide. Learn more about Kate at KateAngelo.com.

Sign Up for Kate's Newsletter

Keep up to date with Kate's latest news on book releases and events by signing up for her email list at the website below.

KateAngelo.com

FOLLOW KATE ON SOCIAL MEDIA

Kate Angelo Author   @KateAngeloAuthor   @TheKateAngelo

Be the first to hear about new books from Revell!

Stay up to date with our authors and books by signing up for our newsletters at

RevellBooks.com/SignUp

FOLLOW US ON SOCIAL MEDIA

@RevellFiction

A Note from the Publisher

Dear Reader,

Thank you for selecting a Revell novel! We're so happy to be part of your reading life through this work. Our mission here at Revell is to publish stories that reach the heart. Through friendship, romance, suspense, or a travel back in time, we bring stories that will entertain, inspire, and encourage you. We believe in the power of stories to change our lives and are grateful for the privilege of sharing these stories with you.

We believe in building lasting relationships with readers, and we'd love to get to know you better. If you have any feedback, questions, or just want to chat about your experience reading this book, please email us directly at publisher@revellbooks.com. Your insights are incredibly important to us, and it would be our pleasure to hear how we can better serve you.

We look forward to hearing from you and having the chance to enhance your experience with Revell Books.

The Publishing Team at Revell Books
A Division of Baker Publishing Group
publisher@revellbooks.com

Revell